MAGIC TRIUMPHS

MAGIC TRIUMPHS

Ilona Andrews

ACE
New York

ACE

Published by Berkley

An imprint of Penguin Random House LLC

375 Hudson Street, New York, New York 10014

Library of Congress Cataloging-in-Publication Data

Names: Andrews, Ilona, author.

Title: Magic triumphs / Ilona Andrews.

Description: New York : Ace, [2018] | Series: Kate Daniels ; 10

Identifiers: LCCN 2018014421 | ISBN 9780425270714 (hardcover) | ISBN 9780698136823 (ebook)

Subjects: LCSH: Daniels, Kate (Fictitious character)—Fiction. | Shapeshifting—Fiction. | Magic—Fiction. | BISAC: FICTION / Fantasy / Urban Life. | FICTION / Romance / Paranormal. | FICTION / Action & Adventure. | GSAFD: Fantasy fiction.

Classification: LCC PS3601.N5526625 M355 2018 | DDC 813/.6—dc23

LC record available at https://lccn.loc.gov/2018014421

First Edition: August 2018

Printed in the United States of America

3   5   7   9   10   8   6   4   2

Cover illustration by Juliana Kolesova

Book design by Tiffany Estreicher

To the readers

ACKNOWLEDGMENTS

First and foremost, we need to thank our editor, Anne Sowards, who has guided us, corrected us, and, most importantly, encouraged us to be better with each book. Her professionalism and her friendship have been invaluable. Without Anne, we would still be buried in the slush pile.

Next, we want to use this opportunity to recognize our agent Nancy Yost and the A team at NYLA: Sarah, Natanya, Amy. They are honestly the best in the biz. Lastly, we want to acknowledge our beta readers; you guys catch stuff that we never see, and you make the books better.

This book, the culmination of this story line, is dedicated to our fans, the ones who have been with us since the beginning, the ones who took a chance and stuck with us as we told Kate and Curran's story as well as we could. You know who you are, and we can never thank you enough. Without your support and enthusiasm, the series would have probably ended with *Magic Strikes*. We are so grateful to you. If you've never read us before, and this is your first Kate book, thank you for buying it, but please put it down and find a copy of *Magic Bites*. It's not our favorite, and we would probably rewrite it if we could, but we all have to start somewhere, and it's always better to begin at the beginning.

PROLOGUE

THE PAIN SPREAD from my hips into my whole body, pulling my bones apart. I gritted my teeth. It twisted me until I thought I would break and then let go. I slumped back into the water.

Andrea dabbed my face with a cool rag. "Almost there."

Curran squeezed my hand. I squeezed back.

Above us the ceiling of the cavern reflected the shiny water patterns. Pretty . . .

"Stay with us," Doolittle told me.

I could just close my eyes for a minute. Just for one minute. I was so tired.

"Does it always take this long?" my aunt snapped.

"Sometimes," Evdokia said, her hand on my stomach.

"It never took that long for me."

"Each woman is different," Andrea told her.

A contraction gripped me. It felt like my bones split open. It passed and I slumped back down.

"It's been sixteen hours," my aunt snarled. "She's exhausted and hurting. Do something. Give her some of those pills your civilization likes so much."

"She can't have any pills," Evdokia said, her voice calm. "It's too late. The baby is coming."

"Give her the pills or I'll kill you, witch."

"If you give her anything, it will hurt the baby," Andrea said.

The baby. I snapped out of the fog and back to reality. We were in the witch forest, inside the cavern with the magic spring. I could feel the Covens working outside. They had sheathed the cavern in a blanket of impenetrable magic. As long as it held, my father wouldn't find us. At least that was the idea. Around me the water of the magic spring splashed. I lay in the smooth hollow of the stone, my head raised, my feet facing the pool of water. Evdokia stood between my legs, up to her hips in the water. Doolittle waited on my right. There were too many people here.

Another spasm gripped me. The pain tore at me.

"Push," Doolittle said. "Push. Just like that, good . . . Good."

"You've got this," Curran told me. "Come on, baby."

I gripped his hand and pushed. A blinding pulse of agony shot through me and then suddenly it was easier.

"One more," Doolittle said.

"Push," Evdokia urged. "You can do it."

"Push. One more."

There was no more to be had, but somehow I found some, pushed again, and suddenly my body felt so light. The pain spread through me, hot and almost comforting. I blinked.

"Congratulations!" Evdokia raised something out of the water and I saw my son. He was red and wrinkled, with a shock of dark hair, and he was the most beautiful thing I had ever seen. He took a deep breath and screamed.

Curran grinned at me. "You did it, baby."

My aunt glided into the water, a translucent shadow. Evdokia cut the cord and held my son up to her, and Erra took him, holding him up by the pure magic coursing through her ghostly arms. A pulse of power shot through her and into the baby. For a second, my son glowed.

"The blood bred true." Pride vibrated in Erra's voice. "Behold the Prince of Shinar and know he is perfect!"

Magic burst above us. I felt it even through the barrier, aimed at the witches' shield like a needle. My father was coming.

My aunt broke apart into a cloud of pure glowing magic. The cloud swirled around my son. He floated in the cocoon of Erra's magic, shielded by her essence.

The needle of my father's magic smashed into the witches' barrier. For a torturous fraction of a second it held, but the needle burrowed, pushing harder and harder. A moment and he would be through.

He would not get our son.

Power tore out of me in a focused torrent of pain. I sank every ounce of my strength into it. My power met the invading magic. The water of the pool rose in long strands and hung suspended in the air above the dry lake bed.

Words of power slid from my lips. *"Not today. Not ever."*

We struggled, the magic vibrating between us, the currents of power coursing and twisting as if alive.

The needle pushed, the weight of Roland's full power behind it.

I screamed and there was no pain in my voice, only rage. Magic flooded into me, the land giving me the reserve I needed, and I sent it against the intruding power.

The needle shattered.

The water collapsed back into the cavern's lake.

I slumped back. My father had failed.

I was done. I was so done.

Curran jumped into the water. Erra released our son, and Curran caught him. My aunt re-formed. Something passed between her and Curran, an odd look, but I was too tired to care.

Curran laid our baby on my chest. I hugged him to me. He was so tiny. So tiny. A life Curran and I had made together.

Curran wrapped his hands around me, lifting both of us to him.

"Name the child," Erra said.

"Conlan Dilmun Lennart," I said. The first name belonged to Curran's father. The second came from Erra. It was the name of an ancient kingdom, and she said it would protect him.

Conlan Dilmun Lennart squirmed on my chest and cried. There was no better sound in the world.

Thirteen months later

A THUD JERKED me awake. I was up and moving, my sword in my hand, before my brain processed that I was now standing.

I paused, Sarrat raised.

A thin sliver of watery, predawn light broke through the gap between the curtains. The magic was up. On my left, in the little nursery Curran had sectioned off from our bedroom, Conlan stood in his crib, wide-awake.

The room was empty except for me and my son.

Thud-thud-thud.

Someone pounded on my front door. The clock on the wall told me it was ten till seven. We kept shapeshifters' hours, late to bed, late to rise. Everyone I knew was aware of that.

"Uh-oh!" Conlan said.

Uh-oh is right. "Wait for me," I whispered. "Mommy has to take care of something."

I ran out of the bedroom, moving fast and quiet, and shut the door behind me.

Thud-thud-thud.

Hold your horses, I'm coming. And then you'll have some explaining to do.

It took me two seconds to clear the long staircase leading from the third floor to the reinforced front door. I grabbed the lever, slid it sideways, and lowered the metal flap covering the small window. Teddy Jo's brown eyes stared back at me.

"What the hell are you doing here? Do you know what time it is?"

"Open the door, Kate," Teddy Jo breathed. "It's an emergency."

It was always an emergency. My whole life was one long chain of emergencies. I unbarred the door and pulled it open. He charged in past me. His hair stuck out from his head, windblown. His face was bloodless and his eyes wild. He'd flown here at top speed.

A sinking feeling tugged at my stomach. Teddy Jo was Thanatos, the Greek angel of death. Freaking him out took a lot of doing. I thought it had been too quiet lately.

I shut the door and locked it.

"I need help," he said.

"Is anybody in danger right now?"

"They're dead. They're all dead."

Whatever was happening had already happened.

"I need you to come and see this."

"Can you explain what it is?"

"No." He grabbed my hand. "I need you to come right now."

I looked at his hand on mine. He let go.

I walked into the kitchen, took a pitcher of iced tea out of the fridge, and poured him a tall glass. "Drink this and try to calm down. I'm going to get dressed and find a babysitter for Conlan, and then we'll go."

He took the glass. The tea trembled.

I ran upstairs, opened the door, and nearly collided with my son. Conlan grinned at me. He had my dark hair and Curran's gray eyes. He also had Curran's sense of humor, which was driving me crazy. Conlan started walking early, at ten months, which was typical of shapeshifter children, and now he was running at full speed. His favorite games included running away from me, hiding under various pieces of furniture, and knocking stuff off of horizontal surfaces. Bonus points if the object broke.

"Mommy has to go work." I pulled off the long T-shirt I used as a night-gown and grabbed a sports bra.

"Baddaadada!"

"Mm-hm. I'd sure like to know where your dada is. Off on one of his expeditions."

"Dada?" Conlan perked up.

"Not yet," I told him, reaching for my jeans. "He should be coming back tomorrow or the day after."

Conlan stomped around. Besides early walking and some seriously dis-turbing climbing ability, he showed no signs of being a shapeshifter. He didn't change shape at birth, and he hadn't shifted yet. By thirteen months, he should've been turning into a little baby lion on a regular basis. Doo-little had found Lyc-V in Conlan's blood, present in large quantities, but the virus lay dormant. We always understood it was a possibility, because my blood ate the Immortuus pathogen and Lyc-V for breakfast and asked for seconds. But I knew Curran had hoped our son would be a shapeshifter. So did Doolittle. For a while the Pack's medmage kept trying different strate-gies to bring the beast out. He would still be trying except I'd pulled the plug on that.

About six months ago, Curran and I visited the Keep and left Conlan with Doolittle for about twenty minutes. When we came back, I found Conlan crying on the floor with three shapeshifters in warrior form growl-ing at him, while Doolittle looked on. I'd kicked one out through the win-dow and broke another's arm before Curran restrained me. Doolittle assured me that our son wasn't in any danger, and I informed him that he was done torturing our baby for his amusement. I might have underscored my point by holding Conlan to me with one hand and shaking Sarrat, cov-ered in my blood, with the other. Apparently, my eyes had glowed, and the Pack's Keep had trembled. It was collectively decided that further tests were not necessary.

I still took Conlan to Doolittle for his scheduled appointments and when he fell or sneezed or did any of the other baby things that made me fear for his life. But I watched everyone like a hawk the whole time.

I buckled my belt on, slid Sarrat into the sheath on my back, and pulled my hair back into a ponytail. "Let's go see if your aunt will watch you for a few hours."

I scooped him up and went downstairs.

Teddy Jo was pacing in our entryway like a caged tiger. I grabbed the keys to our Jeep and went out the door.

"I'll fly you," he said.

"No." I marched across the street to George and Eduardo's house. I would have to buy George a cake for all the babysitting she'd been doing lately.

"Kate!"

"You said nobody is in immediate danger. If you fly me, I will dangle thousands of feet above the ground in a playground swing carried by a hysterical angel of death."

"I'm not hysterical."

"Fine. Extremely agitated angel of death. You can fly overhead and lead the way."

"Flying will be faster."

I knocked on George's door. "Do you want my help or not?"

He made a frustrated noise and stalked off.

The door swung open and George appeared, her dark brown curls floating around her head like a halo.

"I'm so sorry," I started.

She opened her arms and took Conlan from me. "Who is my favorite nephew?"

"He is your only nephew." After Curran's family died, Mahon and Martha, the alphas of Clan Heavy, raised him as their own. George was their daughter and Curran's sister.

"Details." George scooped him to her with her good arm. Her bad arm was a stump that stopped about an inch above the elbow. The stump was four inches longer than it used to be. Doolittle estimated that it would completely regenerate in another three years. George never let the arm thing slow her down. She smooched Conlan on his forehead. He wrinkled his nose and sneezed.

"Again, so sorry. It's an emergency."

She waved. "Go, go . . ."

I turned right and headed toward Derek's house.

"Now what?" Teddy Jo growled.

"I'm getting backup." I had a feeling I would need it.

I STEERED THE Jeep down an overgrown road.

"He looks like someone shoved a wasp nest up his ass," Derek observed.

Above us and ahead Teddy Jo flew, erratically veering back and forth. His wings were made of midnight, so black they swallowed the light. Normally his flight was an awesome sight to behold. Today he flew like he was trying to avoid invisible arrows.

"Something's got him really agitated."

Derek grimaced and adjusted the knife on his hip. During his time with the Pack, he'd always worn gray sweats, but since he had formally separated from Atlanta's shapeshifters, he'd adjusted to city life. Jeans, dark T-shirts, and work boots became his uniform. His once-beautiful face would never be the same and he worked hard on maintaining a perpetually grumpy, stoic, lone-wolf persona, but the old Derek was coming out more and more. Occasionally he would say something, and everyone would laugh.

I wasn't in a laughing mood now. Anything that got Thanatos agitated was bad. I'd known him for almost ten years now. He'd lost his cool a few times, like when he punched a black volhv straight in the face over his sword being stolen. But this was on a different level entirely. This was frantic.

"I don't like it," Derek stated, his tone flat.

"Do you think the universe cares?"

"No, but I still don't like it. Did he say where we're going?"

"Serenbe." I steered around a pothole.

"Never heard of it."

"It's a small settlement southwest of Atlanta. It used to be a pretentious wealthy neighborhood and called itself an 'urban village.'"

Derek blinked at me. "What the hell is an urban village?"

"It's a cute architecturally planned subdivision in some picturesque woods for people with too much money. The type who would build a million-dollar house, refer to it as a 'cottage,' stroll outside to be one with nature, and then drive half a mile to buy a ten-dollar cup of special coffee."

Derek rolled his eyes.

"In the last couple of decades, all the rich people moved back into the city for safety, and now there's a farming community there. Mostly the houses sit on five acres or so, and it's all gardens and orchards. It's nice. We went there for the peach festival in June."

"Without me."

I gave him my hard look. "You were invited. As I recall, you had 'something to take care of' and decided to do that instead."

"It must've been important."

"Have you thought about investing in a cape? As much time as you spend running around the city righting wrongs, it would come in handy."

"Not a cape guy."

The Jeep rolled over the waves made in the pavement by thick roots, probably from one of the tall oaks flanking the road. Before the Shift, this trip would've taken us roughly half an hour. Now we were almost two hours into it. We drove down I-85, which with all the traffic and problems took us about ninety minutes, and were now weaving our way west on South Fulton Parkway.

"He's landing," Derek announced.

"Oh goody."

Ahead, Teddy Jo swooped down. For a moment he hung silhouetted against the bright sky, his black wings open wide, his feet only a few yards above the road, a dark angel born in a time when people left blood as an offering to buy their dearly departed safe passage to the afterlife.

"Show-off," Derek murmured.

"Green doesn't look good on you."

Teddy Jo lowered himself onto the road. His wings folded and vanished into a puff of black smoke.

"Do you know what he is when he's flying?" Derek asked.

"No, enlighten me."

Derek smiled. It was a very small smile, baring only an edge of a fang. "He's a nice big target. You can shoot him right out of the sky. Where is he going to hide? He's six feet tall and has a wingspan the size of a small airplane." Derek chuckled quietly.

You could take the wolf out of the woods, but he would always be a wolf.

I parked by Teddy Jo and opened the door. A blast of sound from the enchanted water engine assaulted my ears.

"Leave it running," Teddy Jo screamed over the noise.

I grabbed my backpack and stepped out of the Jeep. Derek exited on the other side, moving with fluid grace. We took a right onto a side road and followed Teddy Jo, leaving the snarling Jeep behind.

The trees overshadowed the road. Normally the woods were quiet, but this was the summer of the seventeen-year cicada brood. Every seventeen years, the cicadas emerged in massive numbers and sang. The chorus was so loud, it screened all normal forest noises, distorting birdsong and squirrel chittering into odd alarming sounds.

A hastily erected sign by the side of the road announced, STAY OUT BY ORDER OF THE FULTON COUNTY SHERIFF.

Underneath was written, COY PARKER, YOU CROSS THIS LINE AGAIN, I'LL SHOOT YOU MYSELF. SHERIFF WATKINS.

"Who's Coy Parker?"

"Local daredevil kid. I had a chat with him. He didn't see anything."

Something about the way Teddy Jo said that told me Coy Parker wasn't about to poke his nose into this mess again.

"Why didn't they post guards?" Derek asked.

"They're stretched too thin," Teddy Jo said. "They've got five people for the whole county. And there isn't much to guard."

"What's all this about?" I asked.

"You'll see," Teddy Jo said.

The road curved to the right and brought us to a long street. Driveways peeled away from the road, each leading to a house on about a five-acre lot. Tall fences flanked the houses, some wood, some metal, topped with razor wire. Here and there a wrought iron fence allowed for a glimpse of a garden. With transportation chains disrupted by the Shift, a lot of people turned to gardening. Small farms like this sprang up all around Atlanta, sometimes in the city, but more often just on the outskirts.

It was quiet. Too quiet. This time of day, there should have been normal life noises: kids screaming and laughing, dogs barking, enchanted water engines growling. The whole street was steeped in silence, except for the horny cicadas singing up a storm. It was creepy.

Derek inhaled and crouched low to the ground.

"What is it?" I asked.

His upper lip trembled. "I don't know."

"Pick a house," Teddy Jo said, his face devoid of all expression.

I turned down the nearest driveway. Derek took off down the street at what for him was an easy run and for most people would've been an impossible sprint. A wolf could smell its prey from almost two miles away. A shapeshifter during its lifetime cataloged thousands of scent signatures. If Derek wanted to track something, I wouldn't stand in his way.

I scrutinized the house. Bars on the windows. Solid walls. A good post-Shift home: secure, defensible, no-nonsense. A narrow crack separated the edge of the solid blue door from the doorframe. Unlocked. I pushed it with my fingertips, and the door swung open on well-oiled hinges. The stench of rotting food wrapped around me. I stepped inside. Teddy Jo followed.

The house had an open floor plan, with the kitchen off to the left and a living room space to the right. On the far left, behind the kitchen and the island, a table stood with the remnants of someone's breakfast on it. I moved closer. A glass bottle of maple syrup and plates with what might have been waffles covered with fuzz.

No proverbial signs of struggle. No blood, no bullet holes, no claw marks. Just an empty house. A street of empty houses. My stomach sank.

"Are all the rest like this?"

Teddy Jo nodded. He stayed at the entrance to the room, as if not wanting to enter the space. There was something disturbing about it, as if the air itself were solid and still. This was a dead house. I didn't know how I knew it, but I felt it. Its people had died, and the heart of the home had died with them.

"How many?"

"The whole subdivision. Fifty houses. Two hundred and three people. Families."

Damn.

What could do this? Had something compelled them to abandon their breakfast and simply walk out? A number of creatures could put humans under their control, most of them water-based. A Brazilian encantado could probably enchant an entire family. A strong human mage with a focus in telepathy might be able to keep four people under and make them obey his commands. Let's say someone walked these people out of their house. Then what?

Outside I took a deep breath. Derek sauntered over.

"How are you involved in this?" I asked.

"I was called," Teddy Jo said.

Ah. A Greek family had prayed to him, probably offered a sacrifice. In the old days it would've been a slave. Now it had probably been a deer or a cow.

"I drank the blood," he said.

A pact had been made. He'd accepted their offering, and that obligated him to do something in return.

"What did they want?"

His voice was hollow. "They asked if their son was dead. He was supposed to get married on Saturday. He and his fiancée didn't show. They became worried and came to check on them on Sunday. They found this. The family called the sheriffs. They are coming today to process the scene. That's why we had to get here before they did."

"What about their son?" Derek asked.

"Alek Katsaros is dead," Teddy Jo said. "But I can't return his remains to his family."

"Why?" This was what he did. If a human of his faith or of Greek descent died, Thanatos would know exactly where his body fell.

"I'll explain on the way."

"Before we go," Derek said, "there's something I need you to see."

I followed him to the back. A furry brown body lay behind the wrought iron fence. A shaft thrust out of the dead dog's eye.

"Almost everyone had dogs," Derek said. "They're all like that. One shot, one kill."

Shooting with a bow and arrow was an acquired skill that required a lot of practice. Shooting a dog with an arrow through the eye from a distance large enough that the dog didn't freak out at the sight or scent of a stranger was just about impossible. It would have to be a one-of-a-kind virtuoso shot. Andrea, my best friend, could do it, but I didn't know of anyone else who could.

I went back inside and let myself into the backyard. Neat rows of strawberry bushes with the last berries of the season dark red, past the point of picking. A little wooden wagon with a doll inside. My heart squeezed itself into a tight, painful ball. There used to be young children here.

Derek hopped the six-foot fence—razor wire and all—like it was nothing and landed next to me. His gaze snagged on the doll. A pale-yellow fire rolled over his eyes.

I crouched by the dog, a big shaggy mutt with a lab's goofy face. Flies buzzed around the body, swarming on the blood seeping through the wound and the shaft in his left orbit.

It was an arrow, not a crossbow bolt, with a wooden shaft and fletched with pale-gray feathers. Old school. Arrows weren't bullets. Their trajectory was a lot more arched. The arrow would rise a few inches, then fall, and considering the dog's reaction time, the shooter had to be around . . . thirty-five yards away. Give or take.

I turned. Behind me a large oak spread its branches just outside the fence.

Derek followed my gaze, took a running start across the garden, jumped, and bounced into the oak branches. He came back a moment later.

"Human," he said. "And something else."

"What?"

"I don't know."

The hair on his arms was standing up. Whatever it was, it didn't smell right.

"What kind of scent is it?"

He shook his head. "The wrong kind of scent. Never smelled it before."

Not good.

I glanced at Teddy Jo. "Do you have more to show me?"

"Follow me."

We left the subdivision behind and got back to the Jeep. Teddy Jo got into the passenger seat. "Keep going down the parkway."

I did.

The archers killed the dogs first. That was the most likely scenario. Unless they just hated dogs for some odd reason, it was done to keep the animals from barking. That put a hole into my mind-control theory. A creature or a human with the ability to subdue the will of others probably wouldn't have bothered with dogs.

A kitsune might've made sense in an odd way. People disagreed on whether kitsune were actual magic animals, fox-spirits, or shapeshifters, but everyone agreed kitsune were trouble. They originated in Japan, and the older they got, the stronger their powers grew. They could weave illusions and influence dreams, and they hated dogs. But kitsune were physically foxes, with that unmistakable scent even in human form.

"Did you smell any foxes?" I asked.

"No," Derek said.

Scratch that theory.

Ahead a road cut through a low hill to the right, ending in the parkway.

"Turn here," Teddy Jo said.

I made the turn. The Jeep rolled over the old road, careening over the bumps. Ahead a huge building squatted, pale and windowless. A hole gaped in the roof.

"What's this?" I asked.

"Old Walmart distribution center."

Derek jerked his door open and leaped out of the Jeep. I slammed on the brakes. He bent over the side of the road and retched.

"Are you okay?" I yelled.

"Stench," he ground out, and retched again.

I shut off the Jeep. The sudden quiet was deafening. I didn't smell anything out of the ordinary.

Quiet. Where the hell were the cicadas?

Derek came back to the Jeep. I tossed him a rag to wipe his mouth.

"This way." Teddy Jo started up the road toward the warehouse.

We caught up with him. He pulled a small tub of VapoRub from his pocket and held it out to me.

"You'll need it."

I smeared some under my nose and gave it back. Teddy Jo offered it to Derek, who shook his head.

About twenty feet from the warehouse, the reek washed over me: oily, nasty, tinged with sulfur, the stench of something rotting and awful. It cut through the VapoRub like the ointment wasn't even there. I almost clamped my hand over my mouth.

"Fuck." Derek stopped to dry heave.

Teddy Jo's face was made of stone.

We kept going. The stench was impossible now. Every breath I took was like inhaling poison.

We rounded the building. A glossy puddle spread in front of us, large enough to be a pond. Translucent, grayish beige, it flooded the entire back parking lot. Some sort of liquid . . . No, not liquid. Jellied like a layer of agar, and where the sun hit it just right, making it glow slightly, chunks of something solid darkened it.

I knelt by it.

What the hell was I looking at? Something long and stringy . . .

It hit me.

I spun around and ran. I made it five yards before the vomit tore out of me. At least I got far enough away to not contaminate the scene. I retched everything out and then dry heaved for another minute or two. Finally, the spasms died.

I turned. From this point I could still see it, a clump within the solid gel. Human scalp, the brown hair braided and tied with a pink scrunchie. The kind a child might wear.

The thin mask that made Teddy Jo human tore. Wings burst out of his shoulders, and when he opened his mouth, I glimpsed fangs. His voice made me want to curl into a ball. It was suffused with old magic and filled with raw, terrible grief.

"Somewhere in there is Alek Katsaros and Lisa Winley. His future wife. I can feel him, but he's spread through the whole of it. I cannot bring him back to his family. He is lost. They are all lost in this mass grave."

"I'm so sorry."

He turned to me, his eyes completely black. "I can tell the cause of death at a glance. It is who I am. But I do not understand this. What is this?"

Derek's face was terrible. "Is this vomit? Did something eat them all and regurgitate?"

I had a sick feeling I knew exactly what it was. I walked along the perimeter of the puddle. It looked about two feet deep at its center, settled into a pothole in the uneven parking lot that had sunk in due to rain and neglect. It took me four tries to circle the puddle, mostly because I had to stop and dry heave. I peered at the clumps of hair and loose gobs of flesh.

I'd witnessed plenty of violence and gore, but this was on another level. This was very high on the list of things I wished I had never seen. My chest hurt just from looking at it. I swallowed bile.

"What are you looking for?" Thanatos asked me in his arcane voice.

"It's what I'm not finding. Bones."

He stared at the gel. A muscle in his face jerked. He opened his mouth and screamed. It was not any sound a human could make, a cutting shriek, part eagle, part dying horse, part nothing I had ever heard.

Derek spun to me, a question on his face.

"It's not the vomit of some monster," I told him. "Someone boiled them."

Derek recoiled.

I could barely speak. "They boiled them until their flesh fell off, extracted the bones, then dumped the broth here. And whatever they put into that liquid is either magic or poison. There are no flies and no maggots. There are no insects around it, period. I don't hear a single cicada. All of those people and their children are in that."

Derek squeezed his hands into fists. A ragged snarl tore out of him. "Who? Why?"

"That's what we'll have to find out." And when I found them, they would wish they had been boiled instead.

I DROVE BACK to the subdivision. The phone in the first house worked, and I dialed Biohazard's number with Luther's extension from memory. I could've just reported the whole thing to the front desk, but this was bad enough that I had to cut through the red tape.

The phone rang. And rang. And rang.

Come on, Luther.

The line clicked. "What?" Luther's irritated voice said.

"It's me."

"Whatever it is, Unclean One, I don't have time for it. I have important wizarding to do—"

"Someone boiled two hundred people and dumped the liquid and their remains near Serenbe at a Walmart distribution center."

Silence.

"Did you say 'boiled'?"

"I did."

Luther swore.

"The mass grave is unsecured and magically potent. There are no bugs in it, Luther. No insect activity anywhere for approximately a quarter mile.

I've got a basic chalk ward around it now, and Teddy Jo's watching it. The sheriff's department is coming today to process the scene, so if you want to get here before them, you have to hurry. It's off South Fulton Parkway heading west. I'll mark the turnoff for you."

"I'm on my way. Do not leave that grave site, Kate. You do whatever you have to do to keep anything from spawning in there."

"Don't worry. I'll sit on it."

I hung up and dialed home. No answer. Figured. Curran was still out.

I called George. Conlan was down for a nap. He had eaten some cereal and successfully run away from her twice.

I hung up and dug through the kitchen of the dead house for salt. A big bag waited for me in the pantry. I carried it outside to the Jeep just in time to see Derek hefting four forty-pound bags like they weighed nothing.

"Where did you get this?"

"Found a communal hunters' shed," he said. "They must've used this for a deer salt lick. There is more."

"We'll need it."

We headed toward the shed.

"Talk to me about scent trails," I asked.

"Human," he said. "But there's something else with it. A screwed-up scent. When you smell a loup, it smells wrong. Toxic. You know there will be no talking. Either you kill it or it will kill you. These things stink like that. Loup but no loup."

"Corrupted?" I guessed.

"Yeah. That's a good word for it. They took the people out to the mouth of the subdivision."

I waited but he didn't say anything else.

"And then?"

"The scent stops," he said. "It reappears by the puddle."

"Stops like they teleported?"

"Pretty much."

I'd run up against teleportation a couple of times. Teleporting a single human being took a staggering amount of power. The first time, a gathering of very powerful volhvs, Russian pagan priests, had done one, but it had taken a sacrifice to do it. The second time had been a djinn. Djinn were elder beings, extremely powerful and very rare. There simply wasn't enough magic in the world to support the continuous existence of one. That particular djinn had been imprisoned inside a jewel. It was a sophisticated prison that sustained him between magic waves, when technology was at its highest. Even so, he'd required a human with a significant reservoir of magic whom he'd possessed in order to do his tricks, and then he'd hidden in Unicorn Lane, where some magic flowed even during the tech, for his final act.

How the hell did whoever this was disappear two hundred people?

I really didn't want to deal with another djinn. I'd had a stroke, well, several small strokes simultaneously, and almost died the last time.

I turned to Derek. "Could you tell from the scents if all of the people disappeared at the same time?"

"Yes, and they did."

"Two hundred people and whatever herded them," I thought out loud. "Teleportation is right out. Too much magic. It has to be a pocket reality."

Derek glanced at me.

"Remember during the last flare when Bran appeared? He spent most of his time in the mist outside of our reality."

"I remember the rakshasas and their flying palace in a magical jungle."

Of course he did. After what they'd done to his face, he would never forget them. "This is probably similar. Someone came out, grabbed a bunch of people, and took them somewhere." Which would imply the presence of an elder power, which meant we were all screwed.

The elder powers—gods, djinn, dragons, the great, the powerful, the legendary—required too much magic to exist in our reality. They did exist somewhere, in the mists, in other realms or dimensions, loosely connected to us. Nobody quite knew how it all worked. Nobody knew what would happen if one of them manifested and was caught by a tech wave. Conventional wisdom said they would cease to exist, which was why the only time we saw any elder beings was during a flare, a magic tsunami that came every seven years. During the flare, the magic stayed for at least three days, sometimes longer.

This area wasn't particularly saturated with magic. If we were dealing with an elder power, this one had balls. Normally, my knee-jerk response was to blame every odd, powerfully magical thing on my father, but it didn't feel like him. I hadn't sensed any familiar magic, and there was nothing elegant or refined about dumping the remains like that in some forgotten parking lot. My father's magic shocked you with beauty before it killed you.

"It took two hundred people to its lair to boil them?" Derek asked. "Why?"

"I don't know."

"Did they want the bones?"

"I don't know. I'm not sure if the bones were incidental to this. There are worse interpretations."

Derek stopped and looked at me.

"They may have boiled them slowly while they were alive to torture them," I said.

He turned to the shed.

"The world is a fucked-up place," I told him. "That's why I'm glad I have Conlan."

He gave me a sharp look.

"The world needs more good people in it, and my son will be a good person."

IT TOOK OVER two hours before the loud snarling of enchanted car engines announced Biohazard's arrival. Two SUVs fought their way up the road, growling and spitting. Behind them a heavy armored truck brought in a cistern. Behind that came two more SUVs. The vehicles spat out people and containers of orange safety suits. They took one whiff of the air rising from the puddle fifty yards behind us and got masks on.

Luther strode toward us. Stocky and dark-haired, he was wearing boots, a pair of stained shorts, and a T-shirt that said KNIGHT IN THE STREETS, WIZARD IN THE SHEETS.

"I like the T-shirt," I told him. "Very professional."

He didn't rise to the bait. He just stared at the jellied mass grave. We'd made a basic salt circle around it. The pavement was too broken for the chalk lines.

"I'll need a statement," he said. "From the werewolf and Thanatos, too. Where is he?"

I nodded. Teddy Jo had taken a spot on top of the warehouse roof, looking down at the grave. Black smoke curled from him, swirling around his body. If he'd had the power, he would've plucked the remains of a young couple from that grave and resurrected them. But he didn't. None of us did. Only gods brought people back from the dead, and the results were usually mixed, to put it kindly.

"He's grieving," I told Luther. "One of his people is in that. He can't shepherd his soul to the afterlife. To do that, he would have to perform rites over the body, and there is no way to separate it. He can't bring the body back to the family. He is very angry, so I would be gentle in my questioning."

Luther nodded.

I told him about the scent trail disappearing. The more I talked, the deeper his frown grew.

"An elder power?" he asked.

"I hope not."

He stared at the grave again. "Whole families, even the children?"

"I think so."

"Why?"

I wished I knew why. "The bones are missing."

He grimaced. "The highest concentration of magic is in human bones. That's why ghouls chew on them. Do we know for sure that they extracted the bones and kept them?"

"No, but statistically there should've been at least some bones in there. A skull, a femur, something. I only saw soft tissue."

He sighed and for a moment he seemed older, his eyes haunted. "I'll let you know after we excavate and go through it."

We stood for a long moment, united by outrage and grief. We would both dig into that, he from his end and I from mine. Eventually we would find the one responsible. But it would do nothing for the families whose remains lay in the parking lot, dumped like garbage.

Finally, Luther nodded and went to get into his orange suit while I went to give my statement.

HELL WAS BEING stuck behind a teamster convoy driving across Magnolia Bridge. Normally I would've turned off onto the side street, but Magnolia was one of those new bridges that spanned the rubble of collapsed over-passes and fallen buildings and was the fastest way back to the office, and my head was still full of boiled people. By the time I realized what was happening, it was too late.

It cost us a solid half hour, and when we pulled up to Cutting Edge, the afternoon was in full swing. Derek got out, unlocked our parking lot chain, and I drove into my spot and parked.

The street was relatively quiet today, the heat having chased off most of the customers normally frequenting Bill Horn's tinker shop and Nicole's car repair place. Only Mr. Tucker lingered. Time and age had whittled his once broad-shouldered and probably muscular body to a thin, slightly frail frame. It had also stolen most of his hair, so he kept it so short, it looked like white fuzz floating over his dark-brown scalp. But the years hadn't destroyed his spirit. He walked our street twice in the morning and at least once in the afternoon, carrying a large placard. The placard said, ATTENTION! THE END OF THE WORLD IS HERE! OPEN YOUR EYES!

As I climbed out of the Jeep, Mr. Tucker delivered the same message at the top of his voice, just as he'd done countless times before. But, being Southern, Mr. Tucker also believed in politeness.

"Repent! The end is here! How you folks doing today?"

"Can't complain," I lied. "Would you like some iced tea? It's hot out."

Mr. Tucker raised a metal canteen at me. "Got some tea at Bill's. Thank you. I'll see you around."

"Okay, Mr. Tucker."

A car went by slowly, obviously looking for something. Mr. Tucker lunged toward it, shaking his placard. "Repent! Open your eyes! You're living in the Apocalypse!"

I sighed, unlocked the side door, and went inside. Derek followed me, grimacing. "He's going to get hit by a car one day."

"And when he does, we'll take him to the hospital."

Mr. Tucker was right. We were living in the Apocalypse. Slowly, with each magic wave, a little more of the old technological world died, and the new world and its powers and monsters grew a little stronger. Being one of the monsters, I supposed I shouldn't complain.

We needed to clear our caseload. Serenbe had to take precedence. I checked the large chalkboard hanging on the wall. Three cases active: a ghoul in Oakland Cemetery, a mysterious "critter" with shiny eyes scaring the students at the Art Institute and eating expensive paint, and a report of an abnormally large glowing wolf in a suburb off Dunwoody Road. Derek approached the board and wiped the wolf off.

"Got it last night."

"What was it?"

"Desandra."

I blinked at him. "The alpha of Clan Wolf?"

Derek nodded.

"What is she doing in Dunwoody Heights?"

"She tried to enroll her boys in gymnastics class in the city, and one of the other parents threw a giant fit, so they asked her to leave. She's been rolling in glow-in-the-dark powder and menacing that woman's house for the last three nights."

"Did you explain to her that intimidation isn't in the Pack's best interests?"

"I did. She told me that she would've gotten away with it if it weren't for me, a meddling kid."

I stoically kept a straight face. "Good job on closing the case."

"Sure."

"So where did you put the Scooby Snacks?"

"Hilarious," he said dryly.

I pondered the board. A year ago, I would've tossed the paint case at Ascanio and forgotten about it. But Ascanio was scarce lately. He barely came in anymore. The last couple of times I had to call him instead of him bugging me for jobs nonstop. School had taken up a lot of his time, but he'd graduated last year.

He was still nominally on the books. I picked up the phone and dialed the Bouda House.

Miranda answered with a breathy "Hello."

"It's me."

The sexy breathiness vanished. "Oh, hi, Kate."

"Is the evil spawn around?"

"He's helping Raphael with something."

That was the answer I'd gotten the last time I'd called, too. "Okay. Would you let him know that I have a job if he's interested?"

"Sure."

I was Ascanio's employer, but Raphael and Andrea were his alphas, and Clan Bouda valued loyalty to the clan above all else. Raphael trumped me. "On second thought, never mind. We'll handle it."

"Okay," Miranda said.

I hung up. With Ascanio MIA and Julie off with Curran on his hunting adventure, we were down to just me and Derek.

"You want me to take it?" he asked.

"No, I need you for Serenbe. We'll have to pass it on to the Guild." I hated passing gigs to the Guild. I promised to do the job when I took it, and I took pride in making sure we got it done. Now I would have to explain to the clients that we were too busy. It was bad business and it made me feel lousy. But sometimes I had no choice.

I dialed Barabas at the Guild. I could've gone to the Clerk, but since Barabas was the head admin, it would be faster. Besides, the mercs walked into dangerous situations all the time. They needed to know about Serenbe. The more people who knew, the better our chances of figuring this out were.

He picked up on the first ring. "Yes?"

"I have to send you two gigs. One is a nuisance job, but the ghoul extraction will need someone good on it."

"Is your father invading?"

"No, but something bad happened." I brought him up to date on Serenbe. "Whoever did this got away clean. I have a feeling it won't be a onetime thing."

There was a long tense silence.

"Are you okay?" I asked.

"I am. I'm trying to think of a way to notify the mercs that also won't cause a panic."

"If you figure that out, call me back." I could use some pointers in the notifying etiquette department.

"I will. We'll take care of the gigs."

"Thanks."

I hung up, pulled the two files on the ghoul and the paint eater, and put them on my desk. I'd pass them on to Barabas when I got home today. Being neighbors had its advantages.

"You really think this will happen again?" Derek asked.

"Yes."

"Why?"

I leaned against the table. "They killed the dogs, got two hundred people out, and made them disappear. Nobody escaped. None of the attackers died, or at least we didn't find any of their bodies or large pools of their blood. Nothing went wrong. They had no screwups. You don't get that good at controlling large numbers of people unless you practice."

"You think they've done it before."

"I know they've done it before, and more than once. If they've done it more than once, it's likely they need a continuous supply of humans for something, so they'll do it again. I need to be there to stop them. This city is not going to be their hunting ground if I can help it. So, you and I are going to call the Pack, the People, the Order, and every other person in charge we know and notify them that this happened." Biohazard would be sending its own notifications, but I wanted to put the net out as wide as I could.

Derek moved to his desk. "Dibs on the Pack."

"Knock yourself out."

. . .

"Kate?" Derek's face blocked my view.

I rubbed my forehead. "Yes?"

"Food?" he asked.

Food? I hadn't eaten at all today. "Food would be amazing."

He nodded and went out the door.

In the past two hours, I'd talked to the three county sheriff's offices where people knew me: Douglas, Gwinnett, and Milton. Beau Clayton, the Milton County sheriff, and I went way back. He didn't like hearing about the disappeared people.

I called the Order and asked to speak to Nick Feldman and was told by Maxine, the Order's telepathic secretary, that he was in the city but out at the moment, so I had to leave a message with her. I kept it short.

If the Order knew anything, they wouldn't share it with me, and they didn't trust my information. In the eight months I'd been back at work, we'd had to cooperate on a few cases, and every time working with Nick Feldman, the current knight-protector, was like pulling teeth. My mother breaking up his parents' marriage was bad enough, but Nick also spent some time undercover in Hugh d'Ambray's inner circle, and he got to see firsthand how my father operated. He hated our whole family with the passion of a thousand suns and had made it his life's mission to make sure we didn't exist.

Derek had taken the city's law enforcement, the Pack, and some of the street contacts he'd been building. Between us, we'd pretty much covered it. Only the People were left.

I dialed the number.

"You've reached the Casino Help Desk," a young man said into the phone. "This is Noah. How can we make your day wonderful?"

That would take a miracle. "Put me through to Ghastek or Rowena, please."

"May I ask who is calling?"

"Kate."

"Are they expecting your call?"

Great. I'd gotten a new apprentice or journeyman. "No."

"I'm going to need a last name, ma'am."

"Lennart."

"One moment, please."

There was a beep and Noah spoke to somebody. "Hey, there's a Kate Lennart calling for the Fearless Leader. She's not on the list."

Apparently, Noah hadn't mastered putting people on hold.

"Kate who?" another male voice asked.

"Kate Lennart?"

"You idiot, that's the In-Shinar!"

"What?" Noah squeaked.

"You put the In-Shinar on hold, you dumbass! Ghastek's going to hang you by your balls."

Ugh.

"What do I do?" Panic spiked in Noah's voice.

You could connect me to Ghastek. If I said something now, it would only freak them out more.

There was some random beeping. I had a vision of Noah frantically pawing at the phone, smacking keys at random like a toddler. A disconnect signal beeped in my ear.

The last time I attended the induction of candidates to the ranks of journeymen, Ghastek introduced me as "Behold, the Immortal One, the In-Shinar, the Blood Blade of Atlanta." I spent the whole ceremony trying to kill him with my brain. When I chewed him out afterward, he asked who I would rather risk my life for, the Blood Blade of Atlanta or Kate Lennart, small business owner. I should've told him to stuff it. I had only myself to blame.

I put down the phone and counted to five in my head. That should give them enough time to get their crap together.

I redialed.

"Help Desk," Noah croaked.

"It's me again. Calling for Ghastek."

"Yes, lady ma'am, um, In-Shinar, um, Your Majesty."

I waited. Nothing happened.

"Noah?"

"Yes?" he said in a desperate near-whisper. He sounded close to death.

"Transfer the call, please."

He made a small strangled noise, the line clicked, and Rowena's smooth voice answered. "Hello, Kate. How is Conlan?"

Telling her that one of her journeymen just called me "lady ma'am" would be counterproductive. "He's fine."

"When will you bring him by?"

Rowena came from the same village as my mother. They shared a similar magical talent, although my mother's had been much stronger. The talent came with a price. Women who possessed it had a hard time getting pregnant and an even harder time carrying a child to term. I was an exception; perhaps it had to do with Roland's genes, but Curran and I had had no trouble conceiving. Rowena never had children of her own, but she desperately wanted some. She once told me that while my father was alive, the world wasn't safe enough for her children. Instead she lavished all of her maternal affection on my son.

"As soon as I can. I have some bad news."

"Is it your father?" A hint of alarm undercut her words.

"No. At least, I don't think so."

I explained Serenbe.

"That's horrible," Rowena finally said.

Not much shocked a Master of the Dead. Not much shocked me either. By now I'd told this story about seven or eight times. You'd think repetition would file the sharp edge off it, but no, every time was as disturbing as the last.

"We'll call down to Biohazard and try to get some samples for analysis," Rowena said.

"That would be amazing."

I said good-bye and hung up before she had a chance to ask me if Conlan had developed any magical powers. Everybody wanted my son to be something more. He was perfect the way he was.

Someone rapped their knuckles on my door.

"Come in," I called.

The door swung open and Raphael walked in, carrying a dark-green bottle. He wore a dark-gray suit.

"Beware the boudas," I said. "Especially when they bear gifts."

He smiled. "Can I come in?"

"Please." I pointed to my client chair. "Sit down."

He did. His black hair fell on his shoulders in a soft wave. Usually when people used words like "smoldering" to describe a man, I just laughed. However, for Raphael that word felt entirely appropriate. There was something about him, something in his dark-blue eyes, in the way he carried himself with a hint of feral shapeshifter cutting through the polish, that made women think of sex. Luckily, I was immune.

"What's in the bottle?"

He pushed it across the desk to me. The handwritten label with a cute orange-yellow apple read, B's BEST CIDER.

I whistled. "Now I know it's bad."

When Curran and I got married, Clan Bear provided several barrels of honey ale for the wedding. The ale was a roaring success. Raphael realized that the bouda clan house sat in the middle of an apple orchard and sensed a business opportunity. B's Cider hit the market a year ago, and like all things Raphael touched, it turned to gold.

He leaned back in the chair, one long leg over another. Life with Andrea was good to Raphael. He looked clean-cut. His suit fit him so well, it had to be tailored.

"Let me guess, your tailor is holding your latest outfit hostage and you want me to liberate it."

"If I asked you to do that, everything would be covered in blood and my suit would be ruined. No, I'd ask my wife. She'd shoot him between the eyes from a hundred yards away."

That she would.

"I came to talk about the boy," he said. "I brought the cider, because it isn't an easy conversation."

Oh.

"I've come to ask you to let him go."

I thought as much. "Why isn't Ascanio here to speak for himself?"

"Because you took him in when nobody would have him. Aunt B sent him to you because he was impossible to handle, and she knew that sooner or later he would do the wrong thing or say the wrong thing, and someone would rip out his throat. You gave him a job, a place he belonged, you trained him, and you trusted him. You turned him into someone who is now an asset to the clan. He understands all of this. He's loyal to you."

He paused. I waited for him to continue.

"But he also wants things."

"What things?"

"We can start with money. He can earn money here, but he wants more. He wants wealth."

He and I both knew that Ascanio wouldn't get wealth working for me. Cutting Edge paid the bills, but it wouldn't make anyone rich. I had no interest in expanding. I liked that we were small.

"Also, he wants acceptance, responsibility, and power. He wants to climb the clan's power hierarchy. At his core, he's a bouda, and he needs other boudas to acknowledge how good he is."

"Okay."

"Both of these are means to an end." Raphael leaned forward. "What he really wants is . . ."

"Security," I told him. "I taught him for almost four years, Raphael. He grew up without a male role model in a hellish place, so when he went to the clan, he fixated on you. He wants to be you. A respected, successful, dangerous alpha. I figured all this out a long time ago."

"He's been working for me for the last six months," Raphael said.

"Aha."

Raphael chewed on his lip. "There is no point in trying to be diplomatic, so I'm just going to come out and say it. Male nineteen-year-old boudas think with their balls. Andrea and I spend half of our time fighting to keep them out of Jim's rock-hauling camp."

Like Curran, Jim constantly improved the Keep, adding on towers, walls, and escape tunnels. A good portion of those improvements were built by boudas between ages twelve and twenty-five performing the Pack's version of community service for various infractions. The boudas couldn't seem to stay out of trouble, and Jim always welcomed free labor.

"Ascanio is different from his peers," Raphael said. "He thinks with his head, and he's strategic in his decisions. When we sent him down to Kentucky, he ran into h . . ." Raphael paused. ". . . into trouble. He handled it. Better than I did."

"I have no doubt he did."

"We need him, and he needs us. And I realize that my mother dumped him on you, and you spent four years stabilizing, teaching, and hammering him into what he is today, and now that he's useful, we want him back and it's unfair. I'm sorry. I owe you. Our entire clan owes you."

"You don't owe me anything. I did it for him, not for you."

"But you did it and someone has to appreciate it. I'm here to say that we acknowledge it and we won't forget. If you leave it up to him, he will never walk away from you. He can't. His sense of loyalty won't let him. But he won't be happy here. He wants recognition and acceptance from the Pack. Like it or not, you're not just anyone, Kate. You are the In-Shinar. The longer you keep him with you, the harder it will be for him to be seen as separate from you."

He just had to throw it in my face. I sighed. "Do you see any chains around here, Raphael?"

"No." His smile was sad.

"Okay then. He isn't an indentured servant. He's free to do as he wants. I'll take him off the payroll as of today. He is welcome to come back anytime, but I will stop calling."

"Thank you," he said.

"It's not about you. He should do whatever makes him happy."

Raphael nodded again. He looked miserable.

I let him off the hook. "How is Baby B doing?"

He grinned. "A wolf boy tried to steal her toy at the picnic last week. She chased him down, took the toy away, and beat him bloody with it."

"You must be so proud."

"Oh, I am."

"I'll see you around, Raphael."

"You will, Kate."

He left.

Well, that was that. I felt oddly hollow. No more funny one-liners. No more tortured Latin. No more off-color jokes. It had been moving to this moment for a while, but it still made me feel empty.

Derek walked into the office. "What did Raphael want?"

I shook my head. "Nothing important."

Derek eyed the bottle of cider and pulled two small paper bags out of a larger paper bag. The delicious aroma of Mexican spices filled the air. Chicken soft tacos. My favorite. The closest Mexican place was about two miles off. He'd gone to get them for me.

I got up, got two glasses, opened the cider, and poured some for us. He landed in the client chair and bit into his taco. I chewed mine. Mmm, delicious.

"I'm going to go back to Serenbe tomorrow," he said. "I want to do a wider search. See if I can pick up a trail."

"Okay," I said.

We chewed some more.

"Do you ever want wealth?" I asked.

Derek paused his chewing. "No."

"I mean, do you ever want more money?"

He gave me a one-shouldered shrug. "My bills are paid. Got enough for food, got enough for tools of the trade, can buy Christmas presents. What else would I need?"

I nodded. We drank our cider and ate our tacos, and it was nice.

3

TWO BIG GRAY eyes regarded me from a round face, lit up by the morning light filtering through the kitchen window. Conlan pushed the oatmeal away. "No."

"Yes."

"Huny."

I crossed my arms. "Did Grandma give you honey muffins yesterday?"

His eyes lit up. "Gama!"

"Grandma isn't here."

My son made nom-nom noises.

When I was pregnant, I tried to avoid doing dangerous things, which left me with a lot of time on my hands. I'd spent it reading baby books. Those books made it crystal clear that giving honey to your baby before he was a year old made you a terrible mother. The moment a spoon of honey would touch his lips, the words "Awful Mother" would appear on your forehead, forever branding you as a parenting failure. I had explained this to Mahon and Martha. They listened, nodded, and agreed, and then proceeded to ignore me. They'd been giving him honey and various honey-infused sweets since he was able to hold them in his tiny hands and then lied to my face about it. Werebear parents-in-law came with their own challenges.

"You're not getting honey. You will eat oatmeal."

"No." He pushed the cereal away.

"Okay. Then you'll go hungry."

"Huny!"

In baby terms, my son was developing at the speed of light. At thirteen months, most babies had a vocabulary of three or four words. Mama, dada, bye-bye, uh-oh. The experts called this phase passive language acquisition. My sweet dumpling was making tiny sentences and arguing with me about honey. At this point, I wasn't sure if I was proud or frustrated. Probably both.

"I have to do a lot of work today," I told him. "And neither your grandparents nor your aunt can watch you, because they have clan business. So, you're stuck with me."

"Huny." Conlan sniffled.

"I don't negotiate with terrorists. Oatmeal or nothing."

I put some oatmeal into my own bowl from the pot, added salt and butter, and spooned it into my mouth. "Mmm. I'm going to eat all this and be nice and full."

Conlan watched the spoon travel to my mouth. One. Two . . . Three . . .

He pulled the bowl to him and dug in with his spoon. Hunger won again. My son wasn't a shapeshifter, but he certainly ate like one.

I licked my spoon. Today was going to be a busy day.

The phone rang. I picked it up. "Hello."

"Hey, Kate," Luther said.

He didn't call me a heathen or a troglodyte. Things were bad. "How did it go?"

"You were right. They extracted the bones."

My mind took a moment to digest it. "What kept the bugs away?"

"We don't know yet. The substance is magically inert, but not devoid of magic. It registers blue on the m-scan, but I can't tell you if it's due to human remains or the nature of the solution itself. Is your sensate around?"

"No." Julie was still off with Curran. I wished they were home.

"A pity."

"Did you find any inhuman blood in any of the houses?"

"We found hair," Luther said. "Coarse, reddish brown, short. In one of the houses, someone tore a chunk of it out of their attacker."

"DNA?"

"We are running it now."

"Is it hair or fur?"

"Good question. It has an amorphous medulla, consistent with human hair, and a coronal cuticle, which can occasionally be found in humans but typically indicates a rodent, a bat for example. Human head hair continues to grow until we cut it. This hair exhibits synchronized growth, meaning at some point it stopped growing, like fur. It wasn't cut. But it also exhibits a club root, which is typical to humans. It is inconsistent with shapeshifter hair in some respects and consistent in others."

"Are you trying to tell me this is a human-bat hybrid?"

"Don't be ridiculous." Frustration spiked his voice. "I'm trying to tell you that I spent twenty-four hours digging in a jellied mass grave and then analyzing what I found, and I have nothing to show for it."

"That's not true. You have a sample for comparison."

"I'll let you know if I find anything else."

"Thanks."

"And, Kate? If you run across this again, I want to know about it the moment it happens."

"That might be a little difficult, Luther. Last I checked, telepathy wasn't among my talents—"

He hung up.

"Someone's pissy," I told Conlan.

Conlan didn't look impressed.

I dialed Nick's direct number. Usually I went through the proper channels, meaning Maxine, but he hadn't called me back, and Biohazard wouldn't notify them. The Order's legal status as a law enforcement agency had always been murky; however, after the Wilmington Massacre, the knights were firmly outside the law. Some kids at UNC in Wilmington took a fun new drug that turned them into monsters. It also robbed them of their intelligence, because their monstrous rampage consisted of running around their dorm and growling at passersby. The Order was called in, and instead of securing the scene and waiting, the knights made an executive decision to go in and slaughter everyone they found. Midway through the slaughter, the magic wave ended, and the kids turned back into humans. The Order didn't stop. When the blood stopped spraying, twelve young people were dead. At the trial, the knight-protector of the Wilmington chapter testified that he didn't care if they returned to human form or not. In his opinion, they stopped being human when they took the drug. The national fallout was catastrophic.

Some states still recognized the Order's semi-law-enforcement position, but Georgia wasn't one of them. All cooperation between law enforcement agencies and the Order had ceased as of last year. I didn't care for the Order's methods or for Nick calling me and my baby abominations every chance he got, but the Order had accumulated decades' worth of magic knowledge. If my going to Nick would help prevent another Serenbe, it would be worth it.

The message I'd left yesterday was short. It had only two words: "Call me." He knew I wouldn't come to him unless it was an emergency. Since he hadn't called me back, I felt the need to make this one slightly longer.

That done, I sat Conlan down and got his fire truck out of storage. The truck was a gift from Jim and Dali for his first birthday. Large enough for a small child to sit in and climb on, it had a tiny enchanted water engine, which powered lights and a ladder during magic waves. It must've cost them an arm and a leg. Conlan adored the truck. He showed no interest in riding in it, but he liked to climb on the roof, which usually took him a solid minute and multiple tries. Once he ascended, he would wave his arms and make strange noises. Sometimes he fell asleep on top of it. Like his dad, my son enjoyed being in high places.

Conlan began his epic journey, and I pulled files on mass disappearances, landed on the floor close enough to catch him if he decided to swan-dive, and tried to review what little was known about people vanishing.

Of all the recorded mass disappearances, the Roanoke colony was the most famous, but there were others. Easter Island, whose inhabitants had melted into thin air, leaving behind only statues. Ancient Puebloans, who were once called Anasazi, meaning "ancient enemies." The village of Hoer Verde in Brazil. That one was especially creepy. The theories said that the

Easter Islanders might have starved to death and Roanoke's colonists might have died of plague, but everyone was pretty sure something really bad had happened at Hoer Verde. Six hundred Brazilians vanished without a trace in 1923, leaving behind a gun that had been fired and a note that read, *There is no salvation.*

All those were pre-Shift. Post-Shift, disappearances increased in frequency but were usually eventually solved. Typically something had eaten the people or some magic disease had nuked everyone and burned itself out. One case listed mysterious blue lights floating in the air, which caused the population of a small town to strip naked and run off into the woods after them. They were eventually found by local sheriffs, confused and embarrassed. The worst injuries suffered amounted to scratches and severe cases of poison ivy exposure.

There was nothing in any of the files about boiled people or jellied mass graves.

The phone rang. I grabbed it, watching Conlan trying to scoot backward on the truck's roof.

"Hello, Kate," Maxine said.

That ass. Couldn't call himself. Made his secretary do it. That was a new low, even for Nick. "Hi, Maxine. How is my nemesis?"

"We need your help."

"I'm sorry, what?"

"We need your help," she repeated.

Conlan got to his feet and made a tiny hop on top of the truck, achieving a lift of about an inch. I walked closer to the truck.

"What can I do for you?"

"We've received a group from Wolf Trap."

Wolf Trap, Virginia, housed the Order's national headquarters.

"I believe they are here to remove Nikolas Feldman from his position as knight-protector."

What? Nick was the first decent knight-protector that office had had in the last ten years. His predecessor managed to get the entire chapter killed.

"Why?"

"Nikolas has been rather vocal in his criticism of the Order. It has caused problems." There was an awful, vulnerable edge to Maxine's voice. In my time with the Order, she'd been unflappable. No matter what happened, Maxine handled it with her trademark efficiency.

"Within the chapter?"

"No, the knights of the chapter are devoted to him. In the past, we have become a refuge for . . ."

"Problem cases," I finished for her. Atlanta always was the dumping ground for troublesome knights.

"Yes. Nikolas has a unique talent when it comes to helping people find their niche. He makes sure that they become useful. Most of them owe their lives to him in more than one way."

The Order encouraged loyalty to the local knight-protectors, and the Atlanta chapter was no exception. In the few times I'd seen Nick interact with his knights, the relationships seemed to be based on mutual respect. They did what he told them to do, and they didn't question him in my presence.

"The Order would have to have a reason for removing him," I thought out loud. "One can't just pull a knight-protector out of his chapter. Is performance down?"

"No. Our ratio of completed petitions is at an all-time high."

"Then what's the problem?"

"He has been direct in expressing his frustration with their noninvolvement in the claiming of Atlanta and the general situation with your father."

Oh great. I could imagine the reports filed with Wolf Trap. *Are you aware that an abomination named Kate Lennart has claimed the city of Atlanta? Why are you not doing anything about the claiming of Atlanta? Are you planning on doing something about this matter in the near future? Could we have a time frame in which this issue might be resolved?* When something got under his skin, Nick was un-shut-up-able, and the Order at large desperately wanted to ignore my existence. They didn't have the power to do anything about me. I was pretty sure they hoped I would just somehow go away, and here was Nick, shining a big searchlight on the problem they were pretending to not see.

"They don't believe he possesses the diplomatic flexibility necessary for the post," Maxine said.

"How do you know that?"

"I scanned their minds."

Whoa. For Maxine, that was a massive breach of ethics.

"I had no choice," Maxine said quietly. "I've given twenty-five years to the Order. I've felt an entire chapter die one by one. I can't do this again."

She sounded at the end of her rope. "Let me guess, they are going to remove him because he isn't diplomatic enough to work with me?"

"Yes." Anxiety vibrated in Maxine's voice. "He was invited to a lunch. He went armed. Before he left, he had a particular mind-set. You must understand, this chapter is all he has."

Oh, I understood perfectly. Nick would go down swinging. They didn't summon him to Wolf Trap, because he wouldn't go, and they didn't want to do this within the chapter's walls, in front of the other knights, where he was at his strongest.

"You must understand, when I said that the knights are devoted to him, I meant that they are deeply committed to his goals."

If Nick went down, the chapter would revolt. They'd picked a hell of a time for this.

Conlan balanced on the edge of the truck.

If I didn't handle this right now, the chapter would collapse on itself. Nick would likely die, and that was the last thing I wanted.

"Where is this lunch?"

"At the Amber Badger."

It would take me twenty minutes. It would take him at least thirty to get there from the chapter. These knights from Wolf Trap really wanted to put some distance between him and his people.

"When did he leave?"

"About five minutes ago."

"I'm on it. Keep everyone calm, please."

I hung up and lunged forward just as Conlan jumped off the truck. He landed in my arms and giggled. My son, the daredevil. It's good that I have a short reaction time.

I hugged him and smooched his forehead. "Let's go get dressed. We've got to save Uncle Nick Stupidhead from himself."

· · ·

I WALKED INTO the Amber Badger carrying Conlan. He hadn't wanted to put on clothes. I'd successfully wrestled him into a T-shirt and a pair of shorts, but it took me ten minutes longer than planned to get to the restaurant. Here's hoping I wasn't too late.

The hostess smiled at me. "Can I help you?"

"I'm looking for a party of the Order's knights. Armed, scary, probably scowling."

"This way."

The inside of the Amber Badger resembled a medieval tavern, with stone walls, scrubbed wooden floors, pendants on the walls, and sturdy wooden tables. It was half-empty, and I had no trouble spotting Nick and three knights at a table near the far wall. Nick's face had that detached cold look he got just before his sword came out of its sheath. The other three, two men, one dark-skinned in his forties, one white and slightly younger, and a Hispanic woman about my age, held themselves with the ease of seasoned fighters. Not relaxed but not tense either. A half-full platter of pretzels with cheese and beer sauce rested on the table. Oh good, they were still on appetizers. They wouldn't fire him until the main course.

I marched straight to the table.

Nick raised his head and saw me. His eyes widened.

I came to a stop by the table. "Knight-protector."

"Yes?"

The three other knights stared at me.

"Can I steal a moment of your time?"

Nick appeared to waver.

Say yes. Say yes, you moron. I am trying to demonstrate rapport here.

"Sure," he said.

"Oh good. Let me grab a chair." I handed Conlan to Nick.

He took the baby and held him very carefully. Perhaps he was worried Conlan would explode.

"Can this wait?" the female knight asked.

"No," Nick told her.

"Baddaa!" Conlan told him.

Nick picked up a pretzel and offered it to my son. Conlan grabbed it and stuck it in his mouth. I pulled up a chair and sat down.

"What is it?" Nick asked.

"Am I interrupting something important?"

"Yes."

"Good. If you returned my phone calls, I wouldn't have to hunt you down all over the city. A bit of professionalism, Nick. That's all I'm asking."

He leaned forward. "Oh, professionalism."

"Mm-hm."

"I'm supposed to offer a professional response to 'Call me, you stubborn dickhead.'"

"Nick! Earmuffs."

Nick clamped his hands over Conlan's ears. "Sorry."

"You *are* a dickhead. You know I wouldn't call unless it was urgent." At least I knew he checked his messages.

Conlan squirmed.

"What is this about?" Nick growled.

"Someone cleared out Serenbe. They went through, shot all of the dogs with sniper precision, rounded up approximately two hundred people, boiled them to extract the bones, and dumped the remains by the old Walmart distribution center."

The table suddenly went quiet. Nick dropped his hands from Conlan's ears. "When?"

"The disappearance was discovered last Sunday. I found out yesterday, when we found the mass grave."

"Who's on it?"

"Biohazard and Teddy Jo. One of his faithful died and is now in that sludge."

"Is it Roland?"

I shook my head. "It didn't feel like him."

Conlan must've decided that Nick needed cheering up, because he took his soggy pretzel out of his mouth and tried to feed it to the knight-protector. Nick gently guided the pretzel away from his lips.

"It was done with skill and precision. No survivors. Almost no evidence."

"You think there will be a repeat performance."

"It's a safe bet."

"Okay," he said. "Who's got it at Biohazard?"

"Luther. I called it in."

"Something of this magnitude, he'll bring in the GBI. He'll probably go to Garcia. She owes me a favor. I'll call her, see if they'll bring us in on it."

"It would help." I took Conlan from him. "Say bye to Uncle Stupidhead." Conlan waved his hand. "Bye-bye."

"Bye-bye!" Nick waved back.

I got up to leave. "Thank you for letting me interrupt your important lunch. You're not planning on taking off somewhere with your friends, are you?"

"No," Nick said, his face made of stone.

"Good, because the city needs you, and you don't have a costume, so sending bat signals with floodlights is right out."

I offered everyone a big smile. There. All professional.

"Mrs. Lennart," the dark-skinned knight said. "I'm Knight-abettor Norwood. I would like to visit you at a later date."

I glanced at Nick. "Who are the Holy Trinity?"

"They're from out of town," he said.

I shrugged. "You're welcome to come by. Nick knows where to find me."

"You seem ordinary," the female knight said.

"Good."

"I could kill you right now," she stated.

I rolled my eyes, turned, and walked out.

I DROVE BY Cutting Edge to check my messages. When I pulled into the parking lot, a courier was sitting on my doorstep. She was about twelve, short, Latina, and armed with a shotgun. She stuffed a big yellow envelope with a Biohazard stamp in the corner into my hands, had me sign the receipt, and took off on her bicycle without a word. The envelope contained several typed pages with the analysis and brief write-up of the scene at Serenbe and a twelve-page list of names, one per line. The dead.

I glanced through the report. They m-scanned the houses in Serenbe. Blue across the board.

I brought Conlan in, checked my messages, which were nonexistent, grabbed the case file Derek and I had put together yesterday, loaded Conlan back into the car seat, took my paperwork with me, and drove home. I could just as well work from the house, and at least at home I had toys and a familiar environment to back me up.

Two point five seconds after being put into the car seat, my son started screaming. We didn't even make it out of the parking lot. I got out and checked the car seat for hidden dangers. The seat was fine. Conlan was also fine, despite all of the squirming and pulling on the car seat belt. I offered him a sippy cup with juice, and he threw it on the floor.

"Oh no, is it tantrum time?"

It was definitely tantrum time, complete with wailing and real tears. I kissed him on the forehead. "I love you. We have to go home. I can't hold you right now, but you're safe."

Conlan shrieked. I got back into the driver's seat and headed home. I couldn't really complain. Conlan rarely cried, but once in a while he pitched a fit, usually because he was tired and didn't want to fall asleep. He was a baby and babies threw tantrums, because life was hard and not fair and their wishes were rarely taken into account.

The real question was, how long would it take him to figure out how to unbuckle himself? That day was coming, and then we would be in real trouble.

I missed Curran. I wanted him to come home. This whole thing was deeply disturbing, and it felt like a part of me had gone missing. I wanted him back, and I wanted us to all be together.

About fifteen minutes into the drive, Conlan gave up singing the sad song of his people and fell asleep.

The Serenbe nightmare bothered me. Two hundred people, families, children . . . That wasn't just murder; it was an atrocity. I would've liked to think only something inhuman was capable of it, but the entire history of humanity proved me otherwise. All of the magic scans pointed to human magic. Was it some sort of massive human sacrifice? If it was, what the hell were they summoning with it?

Whatever it was, I would find it and kill it. And then I would find the ones responsible and make them regret not dying with it.

It took me roughly thirty minutes to get to our subdivision. Our house sat in the middle of a short, curved street tucked into the crook of the forest, which my husband bought and named the Five Hundred Acre Wood. Originally it was the beginning of a new sprawling neighborhood, but the woods proved too aggressive. The development barely got off the ground before it was cut short. Then we moved in, which made all but two human families find quieter accommodations. Now our street was mostly people who had separated with us from the Pack. The other two streets were settled by shapeshifters who, for work reasons, decided to live in Atlanta. Even when Curran tried to distance himself, the Pack still found him one way or another.

I didn't complain. The place was a fortress without walls, and if I sneezed the wrong way, about forty spree killers armed with fangs, claws, and nasty dispositions would come running. Even so, I'd sunk so much power into the perimeter wards that the entire College of Mages would have a tough time breaking through. I had this recurring nightmare of my father teleporting in and stealing my son.

The driveway before our house was empty. Curran was still gone. *Come on, honey. Time to come home.*

I tucked the file and the envelope under my arm and picked up Conlan. He was still sleepy and draped himself over my shoulder, all warm and limp. I unlocked the door, walked inside, and dropped the file off on the table.

"Here we are," I murmured to Conlan, hugging him to me gently. "We're home. We're going to go upstairs and take a nice nap."

Conlan jerked in my arms.

"What is it?"

My son yanked his head back, staring at the door, his eyes wide and terrified.

The doorbell rang.

Conlan made a low rough noise. Alarm shot down my spine. Babies didn't make those noises.

"It's oka—"

My son rammed his forehead into my mouth. I tasted blood. He threw his entire weight back, tore out of my arms, landed on his feet, and ran for the stairs.

What the bloody hell? I dashed after him in time to see his feet disappear into our bedroom on the third floor. He'd cleared the entire staircase in about a second. The lock clicked shut. Our bedroom door had a custom door handle that locked when closed. You had to push a switch on top of it to open it, something Conlan hadn't yet figured out.

Okay. Door first, son later. I wiped my mouth with the back of my hand, pulled Sarrat out, and slid the small viewing window open.

Grass, a maple tree, and driveway. No fire-spitting monsters. No vicious killers. The tech was up.

I listened.

Quiet.

Yeah, there was probably a terrestrial man-eating octopus crouching on the wall just above the door waiting to pounce.

It'd been a long time since we'd had fried calamari. Technically, calamari was squid and not octopus, but as long as I fried it, who cared about the details?

I didn't have time to mess around. I needed to get this sorted and figure out why my son was freaking out. I swung the door open. The front lawn was empty. A wooden box waited in front of the door. About two feet long, a foot wide, and maybe eight inches deep. Plain untreated wood, probably pine. Two metal hinges on the left side.

Someone had waited until I came home, then dropped it off on my doorstep. They were in our neighborhood, watching our house, and I didn't notice when I came home, because I was a moron. I'd gotten comfortable in the past eighteen months. *Sloppy*, Voron's voice said from my memories. *Yeah, I know.*

I stepped outside, carefully padded past the box, and jogged to the end of the driveway. The street was deserted in both directions. I didn't feel anyone watching me. Whoever had delivered it had come and gone. Didn't bother to stick around to see if I got it.

I turned back. The box looked perfectly harmless. Right, and as soon as I touched it, it would sprout whirring metal blades and carve me to pieces.

I crouched and poked the box with Sarrat. The box didn't seem impressed. Poke. Poke-poke. Shove.

Nothing.

Fine. I slid the tip of my blade between the lid and the box and flipped it open. A thick layer of ash filled the box. On it lay a knife and a red rose. And that wasn't freaky. Not at all.

The knife was about twenty inches overall, with a fourteen-inch blade, sharpened all the way on the left and to a half point on the right side. Plain wooden handle, no guard. Simple, efficient, brutal. Reminded me of a skean, an Irish battle knife.

The rose was burgundy red, the color of merlot. Or blood. Long thorns. I sheathed my saber and picked up the box. It smelled faintly of fire. Not sulfur or smoke, but that particular heated scent when the wood got very hot just before it was about to burst into flames. There was something else, too. The hint of a darker and sharper odor I couldn't quite place.

I took the flower out, picked up the knife, and shifted the ash with the blade. Nothing hidden in the ashes.

Was this some sort of threat?

Whatever it was, it seemed inert enough for the time being. I'd have to deal with it after I found my son.

I went into the garage, got a plastic bin, put the knife and the rose back into the box, placed the box into the bin, and carried it to the shed in the back. The shed served as my depository of weird crap I didn't want to have lying around the house. I set the plastic bin in a salt circle on the floor, locked the shed, ran back inside, washed my hands, and bounded up the stairs two steps at a time.

It was quiet. Way too quiet for comfort.

I unlocked the door, stepped inside, and locked it behind me. From my vantage point, I could see through the arched entrance to the small nursery area Curran had sectioned off from our room. Conlan's crib was empty, his blanket hanging halfway over the wooden rail. The bathroom door on my left remained shut, secured by a small latch bar only an adult could reach. That was the only way to keep Conlan out of the bathroom. He kept trying to eat soap and then cried when he realized it didn't taste delicious.

The only good hiding place was under the bed. Curran liked to sleep high, and our bed was a massive beast that rose a full eighteen inches off the floor, not counting the box spring and mattress. Plenty of space.

"Conlan?" I called. "Where is my boy?"

Silence.

I moved forward on my toes. Curran and I played hide-and-seek with him all the time. Usually one of us would grab him and hide while the other one counted. Conlan was ridiculously easy to find, because he cracked up when you got close. To stay quiet wasn't in his nature.

A step toward the bed. "Where is Conlan?" I sank right into the rhythm of the game. "Is he in the corner? No, he isn't."

Another step.

"Is he in his crib? No, he isn't."

Another step. "Is he under the bed?"

A clawed paw shot out from under the bed and swiped at my leg. I jumped a foot in the air and three feet back.

It couldn't be.

I dropped down on the floor. A pair of glowing gray eyes stared at me from under the bed. Gold light rolled over them, the telltale shapeshifter fire. I'd seen that gold glow just five days ago, when our idiot poodle tried to throw up by Curran's chair.

"Conlan?"

A low growling noise answered me.

Oh crap. Crap, crap, crap.

He'd shifted. He'd *turned into a baby lion.*

Oh my God.

I stared at the eyes. Maybe I was imagining it.

"Conlan?"

"Rawwr rawwr rawwroo."

Nope. Not imagining it. He'd shifted.

I reached out and Conlan scooted back deeper under the bed.

Crap.

"Conlan, come out."

"Rawrwr rawr!"

The phone rang. Maybe it was Curran. I grabbed it.

"Kate Lennart."

"Hello," a saccharine male voice chirped. "I'm calling from Sunshine Realty. Are you interested in selling your home?"

"No." I hung up and dropped down again.

"*Rawrrawr!*"

"Conlan Dilmun Lennart, do not growl at me again. Come out from under the bed."

He backed farther into the darkness, squeezing himself against the far wall. The bed weighed a ton. I could probably heave an edge of it up for a few seconds, but that was it. A fat lot of good that would do me.

I could get a broom and poke him with it. It would be long enough. But then that might just panic him more. Maybe if I sat on the floor and waited?

The doorbell rang. If the delivery boy was back, Sarrat and I could give him a piece of my mind.

I jumped to my feet, walked over to the window, and carefully edged the curtain aside, just enough to see. A Pack Jeep sat in the driveway.

"Don't go anywhere," I told Conlan.

The doorbell rang again.

I left the bedroom, shut the door, ran downstairs, and jerked the door open.

Andrea grinned at me. "I finally got away. Lora called me 'Andrea the Merciless' to my face. Can you believe that bitch? Wait until I tell you what she did. I should've given her a month of rock hauling. We can have lun—"

I grabbed her and pulled her inside.

"Okaaay," she said. "Hello to you too, sweet cheeks."

"I need you to help me catch my kid."

"A one-year-old gave you the slip. How the mighty have fallen."

"He's hiding under the bed. I need you to help me get him out."

"Why did you let him crawl under the bed?"

"Shut up and come with me." I dragged her up the stairs.

"Okay, okay."

I unlocked the bedroom door and dropped by the bed. Andrea dropped flat next to me. "What am I looking at?"

Two shining gold eyes stared back at us. *"Arraawrooo rawrrawr."*

She opened her mouth. It stayed open.

Conlan backed into the wall again.

Andrea sat up and pointed under the bed, her blue eyes opened as wide as they could go.

"Yes," I told her.

"When?" she squeaked.

"Just now."

"What does he look like?"

"I don't know. You can see for yourself once we get him out from under the bed."

We both looked under the bed again.

"Okay," Andrea said. "Okay, he shifted, so he should be hungry. Do you have meat?"

"All the meat is frozen."

"What's wrong with you?" she demanded.

"Curran is off on one of his hunting trips. It's just me and Conlan. I've been eating salami sandwiches and ramen for the last three days."

"Why would you do this to yourself?"

"Because it's easy?"

"What do you feed him?" She pointed under the bed.

"Chicken, oatmeal, apples, vegetables . . ."

Andrea stared at me. "Do I even know you? What do you have for a treat?"

"Cookies."

"Your son is a lion."

"I know that!"

"Cookies aren't gonna cut it. Do you know any lion hunters who bait their traps with cookies?"

"I don't know any lion hunters, period. And you know what, apple pie worked for me."

"I've got news for you, it wasn't your apple pie Curran was interested in."

She had me there.

"Do you have any salami left?"

"No."

Andrea growled. "Go get the cookies."

One minute later we sat on the bed, staring at a plate on the floor with two chocolate chip cookies and a small puddle of honey.

"I don't think you understand the whole predatory cat thing," Andrea informed me.

"He likes honey."

We sat in silence.

"This isn't working," I growled.

Her eyes sparkled. "You should try calling, 'Here, kitty, kitty, kitty.'"

"I will kill you and nobody will find your body."

She chuckled.

Another minute. Sounds of muffled chewing came from under the bed.

"He's eating something. What could he be chewing under there?"

Andrea frowned. "Electric cords. Old tissues. Dead bugs."

Kate Lennart, mother of the year. *What do you feed your son? Dead bugs he found under the bed, of course.* I jumped off the bed. "We need to get him out now."

Andrea rolled her eyes. "Have I told you that you're a helicopter parent?"

"I'm going to be the Wrath of Hell parent in a minute." I crouched by the bed. "You lift, I grab."

"Okay." Andrea gripped the edge of the massive bed and jerked it up like it weighed nothing. A black lion cub the size of a small Chow Chow darted toward her. I lunged for him and missed. He snarled and locked his teeth on Andrea's shin.

"Ow!"

"Don't drop the bed on my kid!"

I grabbed Conlan by the scruff of his neck and yanked him back.

"Get him off my leg!" Andrea howled.

I slid my arm under Conlan's furry throat and squeezed, sinking steel into my voice. "Let go. Let go right now."

Andrea snarled and the noise that came from her throat was pure hyena. I squeezed harder, applying a choke hold. Conlan released the bite and gasped. I rolled out of the way, moving my son so I landed on top of him, and Andrea dropped the bed. The floor shuddered.

A red stain spread through her jeans.

"Your son bit me!"

"Sorry."

Conlan bucked under me. I held tight.

"He bit me!" She pointed at her leg.

"He can't help it. You smell like a hyena, and you're scary."

"I'm not scary. I'm nice! I've babysat him like twenty times. I gave him ice cream! Ungrateful brat!"

The brat gave up on trying to throw me off and went flat on the floor. I got up. Conlan shook himself. He looked just like a lion cub. His fur was black and velvety soft, with faint smoky stripes, and his ears were round and fluffy. He blinked at me and twitched his ears. I cracked up.

"He's adorable," Andrea said. "I'm still pissed off, but he is so fluffy. Baby B used to be that fluffy."

"*Rawr rawr*," Conlan told her.

I reached out and popped him on the nose with my fingers. "No."

He recoiled like a chastised kitten and blinked.

"You bit Aunt Andrea. We don't bite our friends."

Conlan noticed the plate and wandered over to it. A pink tongue slid out of his mouth. He licked the honey.

"Now I've seen everything," Andrea said. She hiked her jeans leg up and showed me a red wound on her shin. "I felt his teeth scrape bone. He's got a hell of a bite. That's a lion right there."

"Sorry."

"Oh, you're going to have to do better than 'sorry.' Your son assaulted the alpha of Clan Bouda." She wrinkled her nose at me.

"It's already closing, you big baby."

"It will close better if you buy me a late lunch and some margaritas."

Conlan licked the plate clean, crawled into my lap, and draped himself over me. He had to be at least thirty-five pounds. Probably closer to forty.

"Lunch might have to wait. I'll tell you what, give me a crash course in shapeshifter toddlers, and I'll give you some of our homemade sangria."

The sangria started as an experiment. Before the Five Hundred Acre Wood formed, someone in the area must've grown grapes in their backyard, because we came across a clearing with several old vines. Christopher mentioned that he grew up on a vineyard in California, I asked him to teach me how to make wine, one thing led to another, and now I made forest sangria. I had also planted some of the vines in the backyard, but they were too young to produce fruit.

Andrea's eyes lit up. "Did you make a new batch?"

"I did."

"Deal. Usually they shift at birth and then about once or twice a week, so you get a chance to get used to it. But your boy never turned before, so your mileage may vary."

My mileage always varied. "How long does it last?"

"He'll shift back when there is something he needs hands for or when he gets tired. Same rules as an adult shapeshifter: one shift, maybe two per twenty-four hours, and after that second, he'll need a nap. The babies don't know their limits yet, so be prepared for him to try two shifts in a row and flop right on his face. It's kind of funny. They just go *boop* and fall over."

The last time he fell over and got a knot on his forehead, I drove him to Doolittle like a bat out of hell.

Andrea sat next to me. "Cheer up. Babies are easy. It's the adolescents who make problems. Before you know it, he'll be a teenager and Curran will start teaching him half-form."

"Stop."

"The worst is over. He's well formed, he's proportionate, no weird bones sticking out anywhere . . ."

"I mean it, stop."

"Okay, okay. So what else? Oh, he will have a bit of a learning curve figuring out what he can do in each shape. Some things are instinctive. Like if he is chasing something, he may shift without thinking. But a lot of times, they'll try to bite things while in human form or change shape and want their sippy cup. Baby B carried her spoon around in her mouth when she turned into a hyena. It was the funniest thing. I'd cut up meat for her and she still wanted me to put it on the spoon and feed her. Wait until I tell Raphael."

"I wish you wouldn't."

"What? Why?"

"Because your husband gossips like a church lady."

"Please. Don't insult me. Church ladies line up around the block to take gossip lessons from Raphael." Andrea grinned. "No, seriously, why?"

"Because if you tell Raphael, the entire Pack will run over here to gawk at him, and I can't do this right now. I have shit to deal with."

"Is it Roland?"

"No." I told her about Serenbe.

"Well, fuck," she said.

"Yep."

We sat quietly for a while. Conlan was sprawled on my lap, making a low rumbling noise. It was almost like purring. It felt oddly comforting.

"If you had to shoot a dog in the eye with an arrow from a regular bow, what's the longest distance you could do it from?" I asked.

"Regular bow, I could guarantee a shot at forty-five yards. If it was a highly trained archer who wasn't me, maybe thirty, but an eye is a small target and dogs like to move." Andrea sighed. "It can never just be peaceful, can it?"

"Oh, I don't know. The past eighteen months were pretty quiet."

She snorted. "What about the Cherufe burning down City Hall two months ago?"

"It only scorched City Hall."

"And before that there was the Raijū thing. And before that . . ."

I held up my hand. "Okay, yes. But you know what I mean. All these were normal. This thing in Serenbe isn't normal. This is magic on a massive scale."

Andrea sighed.

As if on cue, a magic wave rolled over us. Conlan raised his head, shook himself, and lay back down on my lap.

"I need Curran to come back," I told her. "He was a baby lion before. It would really help."

"What is up with your lion anyway? This is what, his third one?"

"Fourth."

Curran once explained to me in excruciating detail how he hated to hunt. According to him, he was a lion, he weighed over six hundred pounds, and the last thing he wanted to do was run through the woods chasing after deer. But since Conlan's birth, he and Erra had hatched a plan to extend the Guild's reach past Atlanta for a strategic advantage when my father eventually came calling. Usually this strategic outreach involved hunting some sort of monster on the outskirts of Atlanta. It took Curran three or four days to catch it, and my aunt insisted on going with him.

"He takes Erra with him. That's the most puzzling part."

"Maybe they're bonding."

"My aunt, who continuously reminds me that I married a barbaric animal, and my husband, who thinks she's an insane murderous bitch, are bonding?"

"Stranger things have happened."

Andrea reached out and petted Conlan's head. He sniffed her hand.

"You remember Andrea," I murmured.

"Of course he does. He was just a little scared. Changing is confusing. So, what triggered it?"

I looked at her.

"Baby shapeshifters turn because they get scared. That's why a lot of them shift at birth. Leaving the womb is scary. He didn't turn even when Doolittle terrified him. There had to be some sort of severe threat. What were you doing when he shifted?"

The box. That had to be the thing.

"I was answering the door. Someone left a present for me on my doorstep."

"Was it a nice present?"

"No." I got up. "I'll show you, but I think we'd better leave him here."

We locked Conlan in the bedroom and went downstairs. I got out two bottles of sangria and poured Andrea a glass. She tasted the wine.

"Mmm, I can't understand why you won't drink this stuff."

Because at some point in my life, I was a borderline alcoholic. "Why do you drink it? You can't even get a buzz."

"Because it's delicious." Andrea pulled one of the bottles to her and refilled the glass.

I left her in the kitchen to get the box. It still sat where I'd left it. I picked it up and walked back to the house. The moment I stepped through the kitchen door, Andrea put down her drink. The content smile melted from her face.

Something thumped upstairs, followed by a loud snarl.

"What is it?"

Andrea bared her teeth. "I don't know. It smells bad."

"How bad?"

"I can't explain it. Bad like something really big that could eat you. Like something you should get away from. I'm a former knight of the Order and I really want to go back to my vehicle and take off just so I don't have to smell it. No wonder the little guy flipped out."

Andrea flicked the box open. Her expression grew long. She took the rose out and waved it at me.

"I know," I said. "It may or may not be romantic."

"It's red."

"Yes, and some cultures believe that red roses sprang from spilled blood."

"Aha, keep telling yourself that."

"That's my line."

Andrea whipped toward the door. "A car is coming. Sounds like one of your Jeeps."

Curran. Finally.

Something crashed upstairs. It sounded like splintered wood. Not good. I walked to the stairs. "Conlan, your daddy is home."

A thing perched on the stair rail. It was furry and upright, with over-sized arms and curved black claws. Gold eyes stared at me from a face that was half-human, half-lion.

"Holy shit." I stumbled back.

"What is it?" Andrea reached me and saw the thing. Her eyes flashed red. A shrill hyena laugh broke out of her mouth.

The small fluffy monster with Rottweiler fangs gathered himself for a leap. This should *not* be happening. Toddlers couldn't maintain half-form. That was not a thing.

Calm and soothing. Calm and soothing. Mother-of-the-year voice.

"Conlan." I started toward him one step at a time. "Come here. Come to Mommy."

Andrea moved into the foyer from the kitchen, slick and quiet, ready to cut off any attempt at escape.

Step. Another step. Another foot and I could grab him.

The front door swung open and Julie stepped inside.

"Shut the door!" I barked.

Conlan sailed off the rail, bounced onto Julie, knocking her down, and shot outside.

Damn it!

I ran after him, leaping over Julie, and almost collided with Curran. Grendel bounced around us, barking up a storm, because my life required a giant hyper poodle right this second.

"What the hell was that?" my husband snarled.

"That was your son!"

"What?"

"Which way did he go?"

"Into the woods." Julie rolled to her feet.

My aunt manifested next to the Jeep, a slightly translucent apparition in blood armor. "I told you," she said. "I told you not to marry a shapeshifter. You did it anyway. Now this happened."

"What do you mean, it's our son?" Curran demanded.

"What is going on with this family?" Julie brushed off her jeans.

Derek sprinted into the driveway. "I heard yelling."

"Will everyone shut up!" I snarled.

Sudden silence descended on the driveway.

"There is an eighteen-month-old running around in the woods in half-form. I'm going to get him. Help or get out of the way."

I turned and ran into the woods to find my baby.

≡ CHAPTER ≡

4

"SHAPESHIFTERS HAVE PROBLEMS," Erra said.

I used tongs to grab the meat off the grill and deposit it onto a platter. During his hunting expedition, Curran had caught and butchered a deer, which I found in the cooler in the back of his Jeep, which was a good thing because I was starving, and I was pretty sure he was, too. It had taken him approximately thirty seconds to catch up to and apprehend our son. Once I was sure that everyone was okay, I left them in the woods and went back to the house. They had been gone for about an hour now, and I had a feeling they would be back soon, looking for food.

"The Wild is unpredictable," Erra said.

"I've had a trying couple of days," I told her. "Normally I love listening to a blistering lecture on my failure to choose a proper husband. It's my absolute favorite. But if you don't stop, I will put your dagger into the stables."

Erra fixed me with her stare. "Sometimes I despair at your lack of respect."

"I had the best role model. She once punched the head priest of Nineveh when he told her to bow. Maybe you've heard of her?"

She snorted. "He was an insufferable prick."

"Takes one to know one."

"Your husband loves you," she said. "I suppose you could've done worse."

I stopped what I was doing and did an exaggerated double take.

My aunt rolled her eyes. "Yes, you could've done worse."

"Be still my beating heart. How will I ever deal with such faint praise?"

Andrea snickered. We both looked at her.

"I love the Kate and Erra show," she said. "You should take it on the road."

I picked up my platter of barely seared venison and carried it inside. Andrea held the door open for me.

"As I was saying," Erra continued, "there has never been a child of the Wild within our bloodline. I was hoping that the Wild wouldn't manifest, but it did and now it coexists with our powers inside his body. The might of our magic fuels him. I fear for my grandnephew, for he may be capable of terrible things."

My aunt, the party pooper. "Why should he be any different than the rest of us?"

My aunt opened her mouth and closed it. "Good point."

In the kitchen, Julie pulled three loaves of bread out of the oven. She'd taken over the baking a couple of years ago and always had starter dough on hand. The bread smelled like heaven. Andrea snuck toward it.

"You're not invisible," I told her.

She stopped and gave me an injured look.

I turned to my aunt. "Have you ever heard of someone killing a large number of people and then extracting their bones?"

"How large?" Julie asked.

"About two hundred."

Julie blinked. "That's a lot of people."

Erra mulled it over. "Your grandfather did it once."

"What?"

"The tribes of Hatti had gotten themselves a particularly persistent chief called Astu-Amur. Big on balls, short on brains. He invaded us seven times over a forty-year period. Each time we beat them back, but your grandfather, Shalmaneser, finally had enough, so he ordered the heads of their fallen gathered, cleaned, and piled into a large mound so the next time they came to invade, their army would see what happened to their predecessors."

"Why clean the skulls, though?" Derek asked. "Wouldn't the severed heads be more effective?"

"Because scavengers are less likely to nibble on a clean human skull than on something with flesh still attached. Besides, having a pile of rotting human heads is unhygienic," Erra said.

Of course. When making monuments of human skulls, one must always keep hygiene in mind. "How did he clean the skulls?"

"Dermestid beetles, of course," Erra said. "Fast, thorough, and the flesh is returned to nature."

Scratch dear Dad off the list.

A door swung open. My son stumbled in, still in half-form. Relief washed over me. I hadn't realized I had been that worried.

Grendel got off his pillow, his tail wagging. Conlan shuffled over to the mutant poodle and crawled onto Grendel's pillow. The big black dog flopped next to him. Conlan hugged Grendel and closed his eyes.

Curran followed, still in human form but without shoes. He must've shifted into a lion, then shifted back and put his clothes on.

"Did you have fun?" I asked.

"Yes, we did." Curran grinned. "Our son is a shapeshifter."

He was so happy. I almost laughed.

"Your son is a freak of nature," Andrea offered, munching on a slice of bread. "It's not natural for a toddler to have a half-form."

"He's a prodigy," Curran told her.

The prodigy made a quiet whistling sound. He was snoring. Grendel lay perfectly still, panting, his eyes shining, and generally acting like being hugged by a sleeping monster-child was his highest aspiration in life and now that dream had been fulfilled.

"Freak of nature," Andrea said again.

Curran looked at her.

"Fine, fine." She waved her hands around. "I'm leaving." She grabbed a loaf of bread, snagged a venison steak, and swiped a bottle of sangria off the counter. "I know when I'm not wanted. Kate, you still owe me lunch. I'll let myself out."

She disappeared into the hallway. Our front door clicked closed.

Curran frowned. "Did she just steal our food?"

"You're welcome to take it up with Clan Bouda," I told him. "But since our son bit their alpha today, I don't know how much ground we can gain there."

"He bit Andrea?"

"Mm-hm."

"Ankle?"

"Shin, actually. She said his teeth scraped bone."

"Good bite," Derek said.

Curran grinned wider. It was good that Jim wasn't here. They would probably high-five.

I glanced at Conlan. He was asleep without a care in the world. My life had irreparably changed today. Nothing would ever be the same. I had to figure out how to roll with it by the time Conlan woke up.

Curran wandered over casually and snagged a chunk of Julie's bread. "What set him off?"

I wiped my hands on a kitchen towel. "Do you want to eat first or see the box?"

"What box?" Derek asked.

Curran glanced at my face. His expression hardened. "The box first."

CURRAN LEANED TOWARD the box sitting on the porch table. His nostrils flared. Gold rolled over his gray irises.

Derek's upper lip rose, baring the edge of his teeth. He looked like a wolf now. A sharp, feral wolf.

"What does it smell like to you?" I asked.

"A predator," Derek said. "Never smelled anything like that before."

"Are you sure?" I asked.

"It smells like panic and running for your life," Derek said. "I would remember this."

"Smells like a challenge," Curran said.

Julie frowned at the box.

Curran opened it and took the rose out. His voice took on a quiet measured tone, as if he were talking about the weather. "Interesting."

My aunt focused on the box. "I've seen this before."

Oh goody. "What is it?"

"It's an old way to declare war."

Great.

"It was used to overcome the language barrier. No translation needed. Submit to our demands or . . ." Her translucent fingers brushed the knife. "We'll cut your throats and turn your world to ash."

Better and better. "Would Father . . . ?"

She shook her head. "This was the way of the uru. The outsiders. Barbarians. Your father is a civilized man. If he were to declare war, he would call you first."

Well, at least I could expect a phone call before Roland unleashed Armageddon and murdered everyone I loved.

Julie went inside.

"What about the rose?" Curran asked.

"I don't know," Erra said. "Sometimes they put a bag in the box to symbolize tribute."

"Pay us and we'll go away?" I asked.

"Essentially. I've never seen a blossom like this. The rose is the flower of queens. When your grandmother built the Hanging Gardens, she filled it with roses."

And that was precisely the problem. We knew what a rose meant to us. We had no idea what it meant to whoever sent the box.

Julie came back out with a piece of paper and a pencil.

"How do we know who sent it?" Derek asked. "Why declare war and not identify yourself?"

Erra turned to me. "Did you see the messenger?"

"No."

"If we wait long enough, we'll find out," Curran said, his gaze dark.

"They signed it," Julie said.

Everyone looked at her.

"The box glows blue," she said, drawing. "There is a lighter blue symbol on the lid." She held the paper up. Two circles joined by two horizontal lines. It looked like an old-fashioned barbell.

"The alchemical sign for arsenic?" I frowned. That made no sense.

"Could also be the astrological symbol for opposition," Julie murmured.

I glanced at my aunt. Erra blinked. "Izur?"

"What's Izur?" Julie asked.

Erra stepped down into the yard, where the first stars dotted the darkening sky and pointed in the direction of Ursa Major. "Izur, the twin star."

Julie's eyes lit up.

"Don't do it," I told her.

She held her hands out. "Aliens."

"No."

"Oh, come on, why can't it be aliens? Ooo, maybe your whole family is aliens."

I turned and went back to the house.

"Where are you going?" Derek called after me.

"I need a drink."

I walked into the kitchen. Conlan was still on the pillow. Still in half-form. Julie's mangled body flashed before me, half-human, half-animal, trapped in a hospital bed, sedated to the point of comatose, because the moment Doolittle took her off the sedatives, she would explode into a loup.

Anxiety stabbed me, cold and sharp, in the pit of my stomach.

I opened the bottle of sangria with a jerk, poured a glass, and drank it down.

Curran came through the door. He moved in complete silence. If my peripheral vision were worse, I would've never known he was there. He wrapped his arms around me and pulled me to him. I leaned into him, feeling the warmth of his body. I'd missed this so much. I'd missed him.

He breathed in the scent of my hair. "What's up?" he asked, his voice quiet.

"What if he can't shift back?"

"He'll shift back. It was an exciting day for him. His hormones are high. He'll burn it off in his sleep." He kissed my hair.

"What if he doesn't? My blood is really potent, and the concentration of Lyc-V in his bloodstream is off the charts. What if he goes loup?"

Curran turned me toward our son, hugging me to him. His voice was calm and soothing. "He won't. Look at him. He's proportionate. Look at his jaws. They fit together, they are well formed. The length of his legs and arms is perfect. He did it instinctually. He didn't struggle; he just did it. With loups, there is a stench. He smells clean."

He rubbed my shoulders.

"He bit Andrea. He's known her since he was born."

"He was scared. That's good."

It sank in. "Loups don't get scared."

"No, they don't. They blindly attack. The adults can be cunning, but when children go loup, they turn feral." He kissed me again. "You should've seen him in the woods. He splashed through the creek. He climbed everywhere, sniffed everything, like someone took his leash off. He's our kid. He's got this."

We stood together, wrapped up in each other, watching our son sleep.

"Andrea called me a helicopter parent."

"Andrea needs to shut the hell up sometimes."

"I don't have anyone to measure myself against," I told him. "I didn't know my mother, and Voron wasn't exactly a model father."

"Baby B is a beautiful baby," Curran said. "But she's a bouda. She smells like a werehyena, she acts like a werehyena, and other werehyenas know exactly what she is."

"What's your point?"

"There are no surprises there. He"—Curran pointed at Conlan over his shoulder—"is full of surprises. It will be fun."

"I don't want him to end up with my childhood." Where did that even come from?

A hint of a growl slipped into Curran's voice. "He has me and you. He won't end up like us, and we are not going to end up like our parents. History isn't going to repeat itself. I won't let it."

History had a way of rolling over the best-laid plans like a runaway bulldozer.

"Does he know I'm his mother when he's in his animal shape?"

"Yes. I knew my parents were my parents."

"But does *he* know?"

"He recognized I was his father."

"How do you know?"

"Because I told him to stop and he did."

"Maybe he just thought you were a bigger lion."

"Trust me, he knows us. Our scent, the sound of our voices. He knows we're his parents."

He knew who I was, he knew who Curran was. Okay. I could do this. I'd done harder things before.

The phone rang. I picked it up.

"Yes?"

"Good evening," a familiar voice said. Robert served as Jim's chief of security. Today was a gift that kept on giving. I put him on speaker.

"What can I do for you?"

"I understand you're involved with the Serenbe situation?"

Word traveled fast. "Yes."

"Any chance for a briefing?"

"Why?" Curran asked.

"Karen Iversen's parents owned a house on that street."

I had no idea who Karen Iversen was.

"Clan Jackal," Curran said for my benefit. "Parents are human. She's first generation."

A shapeshifter had attacked Karen Iversen, and she'd survived it and become a shapeshifter. Happened often enough.

"The GBI refuses to let her or us on the scene," Robert said.

It made sense. Karen was a shapeshifter, but her parents were human, which meant the Pack had no jurisdiction. GBI likely didn't want to start a panic before they had at least some idea of what they were dealing with.

"They won't tell us if they are alive or dead."

"They're dead," I told him.

"I surmised that. They're blocking us from viewing the bodies. I need to know what we're dealing with before I file the necessary court documents to force them to release the remains."

I leaned deeper into Curran, letting the warmth of his body anchor me. "Robert, they can't give you their remains."

"If it's the matter of a quarantine, we are immune to most diseases."

"They can't give you their remains because someone forced two hundred people out of their homes and then boiled them."

Curran's hold on me tightened.

"I'm sorry, it sounded like you said 'boiled'?"

I explained the puddle.

Robert didn't say anything. The kitchen was quiet.

"Can we meet tomorrow?" he asked finally.

"Yes. Cutting Edge at nine?"

"I'll be there," Robert said.

I hung up.

"Sorry," Curran said.

"What for?"

"For being gone."

"Did you catch the magic leopard monster?"

"I did," he said.

"Then it's all good."

"I'll make it up to you. What do you need?" he asked.

I glanced at Conlan. "Think he'll be out for the next couple of hours?"

"At least."

"In that case." I put my arms around him and kissed him. It wasn't a tender kiss. I hadn't seen him for three days. The world had turned grim while he was gone, and I wanted him to know just how much I had missed him. His lips seared mine, the familiar taste of him washing over me, harsh and male. Every nerve in my body stood at attention and I shivered.

Then my feet were off the floor, and we were moving up the stairs at an alarming speed.

"Don't want to wait until after dinner?" I murmured into his ear and licked the corner of his jaw, tasting the rough edge of his stubble.

"Fuck dinner."

I laughed, and he closed the bedroom door behind us.

"NATNED! NATNED!"

Curran took his gaze off the road to glance in the rearview mirror for a second. "You okay there, buddy?"

"Natned!"

"No," I told Conlan.

My morning started with Curran kissing me, which was very welcome. At which point we discovered that our son had shifted back into a human in the middle of the night, because he climbed onto our bed in all of his nude glory, slapped his belly, and yelled, "Natned!" Then he grabbed himself, in case we missed his point. After Curran stopped laughing, I handed our child over to him and escaped into the bathroom.

Conlan had been yelling "Natned" since I packed him into his car seat twenty minutes ago. He'd clearly decided that clothes were overrated. At least he'd stayed human.

Usually we had a line of people willing to watch him, but he could decide to go furry at any second, and if he did, both of us wanted to be there, so he was coming with us to meet with Robert.

Outside the Jeep, Atlanta crawled by. Magic drenched the city. I always felt it, a kind of invisible sea, shallower here, deeper there, but ever since I claimed my little chunk of the planet, the invisible currents had gained definition. If I concentrated, I could sense them ebbing and flowing. It freaked me out even after all this time, so I tried not to think about it too hard.

"Natned!" Conlan yelled to be heard over the sound of the engine.

"He needs a deer leg bone to gnaw on," Curran said. "They were my favorite."

"Can it be a cooked leg bone?"

"He is a shapeshifter," Curran said. "You know we don't have to worry about bacteria and diseases."

"What about intestinal parasites?"

"I've been eating raw meat for all of my life and never gotten a parasite."

"I would feel better if it was cooked."

Curran studied me for a moment, reached over, and squeezed my hand. "Still having a hard time with the shapeshifter baby thing?"

"No. I love him whoever or whatever he is. But I spent eighteen months worrying that he would stop breathing at night, or get sick, or become injured, and raw deer femurs don't go along with that."

"Cooked bones splinter. He'll hurt himself."

"It's funny how you use logic in an argument and think it will persuade me."

"He is still teething. He'll need something to gnaw on."

"On one hand, a clean Conlan eating cereal. On the other, Conlan covered in blood gnawing on a deer leg."

"Which one seems more like your kid?" Curran asked.

I gave him the look of death. He laughed.

"Okay," I told him. "But if he gets worms, it's on you."

Curran turned onto Jeremiah Street. "I let him eat a mouse in the forest yesterday."

"Of course you did. Why wouldn't you let your baby eat some filthy rodent in the woods?"

"He caught it himself. I'm not going to take his kill away from him."

Why me?

We parked. Curran shut off the engine and turned to me. His eyes had turned dark. "Don't leave me, Kate."

"Where did that come from?"

"I mean it," he said. "I've got your back."

And I had his. That's why when my father finally showed up to fight us with his army, I would do whatever I had to do to make sure he and Conlan survived. No matter the cost.

"I love you," I told him, and got out of the Jeep.

THE ALPHA OF Clan Rat slipped through the doorway of Cutting Edge as if his joints were liquid. Of average height, Robert Lonesco had a slim build. His hair was coal black, his eyes brown and velvety, and he turned heads whenever he entered the room. He was also happily married to his husband, Thomas, and had no plans to change that any time soon.

Conlan, who'd been running around the tables in a circle, sighted Robert and went into a crouch.

Robert raised his eyebrows and took a step forward.

The shift was instant. One second normal—well, mostly normal— human child, the next an oversized black lion cub.

Robert's jaw hung open. He actually did a double take. I didn't blame him. Conlan made an adorable lion cub. At least he hadn't gone into warrior form again.

"Congratulations," Robert finally managed.

"Thank you," Curran said, his face nonchalant, as if nothing notable were happening.

My son shrugged the shreds of his clothes off himself and showed Robert his lion fangs. *"Rawrrawrrr!"*

"Is he challenging me?" Robert's eyes sparkled.

I put my hand over my face.

"Rawrwrwa!"

"That's the most adorable thing I've ever seen."

"Conlan," Curran said, putting some growl into his voice. "Come here."

"Rawr."

Curran got up and strode toward Conlan. My kid lunged sideways, but Curran was too fast. His hand snapped out, and he lifted Conlan by the scruff of his neck. "No."

Conlan settled into his father's arms, eyeing Robert like he was a cobra. We were currently in waiting mode, gathering strength for the time my father decided to invade us, but if I somehow survived and I got to raise my son, I was in for a hell of a time.

"I want one," Robert declared.

"What's stopping you?" Curran asked.

"We've talked about it." Robert sat in the chair in front of my desk. "We're not sure if we'd go the adoption or surrogate route. In any case, the timing isn't quite right."

"The timing is never quite right," I told him.

"How are you handling this?" Robert asked me.

"Last night my husband let my thirteen-month-old spend an hour in the woods rolling in the creek mud and eating raw mice, and then my son passed out on the dog pillow hugging Grendel."

Robert winced. "I can see how that would be disconcerting. Did you have to sterilize the child after he touched that creature?"

"Ha. Ha." I picked up the file I'd put together last night and handed it to him. "Everything we have. Biohazard did a quick walk-through with a portable m-scanner. The copies of the printouts are in there, together with copies of my notes and Derek's notes. I'm very sorry, Robert."

"Thank you." Robert accepted the file. His expression turned serious. "I have some news to trade."

"It's not nice news, is it?" I asked.

Robert pulled a photo from his pocket and put it on the table. A tall man on top of the roof of a ruined building. His trench coat, sewn together from patches of different leathers and hides, flared as he walked across a steel beam protruding over a sheer drop. The beam had to be less than six inches wide. Wind stirred the man's black hair.

"Razer," I said. I'd recognize that green-skinned bastard anywhere.

When my father felt my aunt waking up, he created a cult of assassins raised to kill her if she became a problem. He called his cult the Order of

Sahanu, after an ancient word that meant "to unsheathe a dagger." He fed them all sorts of bullshit about the divinity of our blood. The sahanu lived for a single purpose: to kill at my father's command, so they could be granted heavenly afterlife. Their highest goal was to murder one of our blood. My aunt, except I killed her first. Me. My son.

My father had skated very close to the invisible line that people in our family didn't cross. Erra reminded me of it at least monthly: whatever you do, don't become a god. Faith had power, and once your followers believed in you, your thoughts and actions were no longer your own. Not to mention that the more people believed in you, the closer to godhood you came, and gods couldn't exist in our reality, not permanently. They required magic for manifestation, and the tech shift would wipe them out. Roland had side-stepped the issue by making the blood divine instead of himself personally, but if the sahanu grew in numbers, he would have a serious problem on his hands. His ability to move freely in our world would be compromised, too dependent on belief and magic.

Sahanu were fanatics, immune to reason, bribery, and pressure. I had managed to break one of them free of Roland's grasp almost two years ago. Adora was still learning to be a person. During her last birthday, she disappeared right before her surprise party. We'd turned the city inside out looking for her. Given that she was one of the most skilled killers I've ever fought, I was sure something bad had happened to her or because of her. She came out of the woods twenty-four hours later, covered in mud. She'd seen some baby otters and followed them around the creek all day.

Adora was ranked fourth in the sahanu ranks. Razer was ranked first.

"Where was this taken?" Curran asked.

"Sandy Springs."

Shit. Razer wouldn't have entered my territory unless he had orders to be here.

"Is Roland moving?" Curran asked.

Robert nodded. "We are receiving reports of increased traffic to Jester Park."

"He's pulling in his troops," Curran said.

"It would appear so," Robert agreed.

"My father is about to restart the war." I leaned back in the chair. Now? He was doing it now, when we had all this other crap to deal with? His timing couldn't be worse.

Conlan gathered himself and jumped off Curran's lap, clear across the table to me. I caught him, but the impact of forty pounds rocked me back. He licked my cheek.

I knew we had been living on borrowed time. The sands had just run out.

"Where does the Pack stand?" Curran asked quietly.

"Jim and I discussed it," Robert said.

Jim's first loyalty was to his people. The Pack lost a great deal in the battle with Roland. Sixty-two shapeshifters never came back to the Keep alive. Nineteen of them were under twenty. I remembered the bodies and the crying, the din of wailing that rose through the Keep when the bodies were retrieved. I still sometimes heard it in my sleep.

Fighting my father without the Pack's help would be very hard.

"I'm here to tell you that the Pack will not stand against Roland unless directly attacked," Robert said.

It hit me like a punch to the stomach. I had suspected this was coming and it still hurt.

"Given that the Atlanta metropolitan area is home to roughly eighteen hundred shapeshifters at last count, we consider any attack on the city to be a direct attack on the Pack," Robert continued.

Wait, what?

"Which is why I'm authorized to bring you an offer of Mutual Aid. In case either your family or the Pack becomes aware of a citywide threat such as Roland's invasion, we agree to assist each other."

Curran had his inscrutable face on.

"Will the Beast Lord put it in writing?" I asked.

"If you insist," Robert said. "But a verbal agreement should be sufficient. It was passed as a resolution by the Pack Council, so it's on record."

"You realized that after he dealt with us, he would come after you, and he would crush you alone," Curran said.

"Pretty much," Robert said. "We need you and you need us."

I looked at Curran. "Are you comfortable with that offer?"

He mulled it over. I petted Conlan's furry head. He yawned. Running around in the office and changing shape really made him tired.

"Is Roland named as the specific threat in the resolution?" Curran asked.

"Yes," Robert confirmed.

"I'm fine with it."

Robert looked at me. "Kate?"

"We agree," I told him.

"Excellent." He took the folder off the table. "Thank you for this."

"Anytime. And, Robert? Could you please not mention that Conlan shifted?"

Robert narrowed his eyes. "Trying to avoid the stampede of excited shapeshifters?"

"Yes."

"My lips are sealed." He walked out.

We stayed silent for several minutes. Shapeshifter hearing was excellent, and Robert's was off the charts.

"That went better than expected," I murmured finally.

"They need us." Curran grimaced. "I wish we had more time."

My heart cracked. "Me, too."

I had things to do. I would need to visit the Witch Oracle and let them know that we had to go ahead with the plan of last resort. My husband and my son would survive this.

The door of Cutting Edge swung open, and Teddy Jo walked in, frowning.

"Knocking, it's a thing," I told him. "You make a fist, lift it, and gently hit the door to let the person inside know you are out there."

Teddy Jo shook his head. "Kate, there is some weirdness happening outside."

Weirdness seemed to be stalking me. I got to my feet and stepped outside, Conlan in my arms.

Sunshine bathed the street, and thirteen people waited there, about thirty yards from our door. Long white robes with deep hoods hid their faces and swept the ground, shifting in the breeze. They stood in two columns, six people on each side, their arms crossed, their hands tucked into their sleeves, with a lone figure in a blue robe waiting between them.

Magic brushed against me. It felt old and deep.

The figures didn't move.

"Is this a present from your father?" Curran asked quietly.

"I don't know." It felt like him, though. Ancient, dark, but oddly beautiful. Maybe this was his version of that phone call Erra was talking about.

Curran put his hand on my arm. His eyes had gone completely gold. The hair on his arm stood on end.

"What is it?"

"Derek's not-loup scent."

The figure in the center raised his arms. The blue robe slid down, revealing a young, dark-haired man, barely older than a boy. He was nude and built like a Greek statue, every muscle perfect. Dark-blue eyes looked at me from a beautiful face. A gash crossed his chest, carved deep into his flesh, and in the depths of the cut golden sparks flashed, as if he smoldered from the inside.

"Daughter of Nimrod," the boy called out, his voice accented. "I await your answer."

He lowered his arms to his sides and smiled. The wound on his chest sparked and ignited from the inside. Fire licked his flesh, spreading from the wound. The stench of burned human meat washed over me.

What the hell . . .

He kept smiling. His skin bubbled and he kept smiling.

I spun to Teddy Jo and thrust Conlan into his arms.

Wings shot out of Teddy Jo's back. Wind fanned me, and then he was on the roof, out of the way, holding my son.

The door to Nicole's Automotive Repair banged open and Mr. Tucker charged out, his placard clutched in his hands.

"Don't!" Curran and I barked in the same voice.

Mr. Tucker grabbed the nearest hooded figure. "Your friend is on fire!"

A furry arm thrust out of the robe. Claws locked on Mr. Tucker's windpipe, squeezed, and Mr. Tucker fell, his eyes shocked, a clump of his bloody flesh clenched in the creature's claws. It happened fast, so fast; it only took a fraction of a second.

Sarrat was already in my hand and I was moving.

The twelve figures dropped their robes. White fabric flew, revealing bodies sheathed in short brown fur. They stood on two legs, hunching forward, their muscled arms dangling, each finger tipped with a claw. Their round heads leaned forward, their mouths wide slashes betraying yellow fangs. Big round eyes stared at me, cold and empty, like the eyes of an owl.

A memory punched me, sharp and vivid, borrowed from my aunt. A room in an ancient palace, shrouded in veils, the body of a child, and an abomination that looked eerily like these chewing on the stump of my uncle's neck.

Curran shot past me and roared. The sound of his fury was like thunder. It punched the beasts. They screeched and cringed back in ragged unison.

The world turned red. Every instinct in my head screamed. They'd killed one of my people. They were an abomination. A corruption. They had to be purged. Rage boiled inside me.

The beasts rushed us.

The first creature swiped at me, raking the air with its talons. I shied away from its claws and slashed at it. Sarrat sliced through flesh like it was butter, cleaving the beast's chest. Blood splattered me, drenching me with foul magic.

The beast screeched and swiped at me. I shied left, ducking, and cut across its outstretched arm, severing the extensors. The hand went limp. I thrust Sarrat into its side, puncturing the stomach and the liver, and freed the sword with a sharp tug. The beast dropped to its knees and surged back up. I buried Sarrat in its chest and kicked it off the blade. Tough bastards.

A second creature tore at my back, the tips of its claws carving straight through reinforced leather into the skin. My back burned.

I spun around, slicing in a frenzy, cut its jugular, spun around again, and severed the first beast's spine as it tried to rise again. The second creature collapsed, blood pouring from its neck, and squirmed on the ground, raking at me with its claws. I beheaded it. Two down.

A body flew, knocked out of my way. Curran tore through the creatures, snapping bones and ripping flesh, his hands clawed, but the rest of him still human.

A third beast lunged at me. I dropped down, cut its femoral artery, and spun out of the way as it fell. It crawled toward me. I stomped on the back of its neck. *Die, you damn bastard.*

The boy was still burning. Ash formed on his chest, but he was still smiling, his eyes tracking me. How the hell was he still alive?

Behind me a sharp lupine snarl cut through the air. Derek lunged at the creature on my right, a short sword in his hand, and chopped through its arm with a brutal swing. To the right, Julie spun, the twin tomahawks in her hands chopping. The kids had arrived.

My shoulders and thighs burned from the scratches, and the gashes in my back simmered as if someone had poured salt into the wounds. Only four creatures left.

A blast of magic rocked me, nearly taking me off my feet. Some massive power had just broken through the boundary of my territory from above.

I spun around. In the northwest, a fireball tore through the clouds.

Teddy Jo swooped over us, his hands empty. Where was Conlan? I spun around and saw Julie holding him.

"Kate!" Teddy Jo pointed toward the fireball.

"I've got this," Curran snarled next to me. "Go!"

He gripped my waist and threw me up. I shot up ten feet into the air. Teddy Jo caught my arms and pulled me up to him, locking his arms around my ribs, and then we streaked through the air toward the column of smoke.

Note to self, once this is over, explain to my husband to never throw me like that again.

The ruined streets slid under me. Wind tore at my face. The column of smoke drew closer. The area above it boiled with magic. Something terrible was happening up there.

"Fly faster!"

"Don't make me drop you."

Seconds ticked by. Roofs rolled under us, followed by ruins, then more roofs, and then we were in the Unnamed Square. The pillar of smoke rose from the middle of the street. Teddy Jo dived. Ten feet above the road he let me go. I dropped down and rolled to my feet.

The street was empty. I spun around, looking for the enemy. *Where the hell are you, bastard?*

Magic punched at me from above. I jerked my head up. Above, in the thick, low-hanging clouds, something flashed with bright red. Magic pealed like a giant bell, vibrations shaking the ground.

"Shit!" Teddy Jo snarled. A sword appeared in his hands and burst into flames.

Something tore through the clouds, glowing red, and plunged to the ground. I dove out of the way. Teddy Jo veered to the side. The object crashed into the pavement like a cannonball, steaming. The asphalt around it softened, melting.

I ran toward the glowing thing, Sarrat ready.

A wall of heat blocked me. I pushed through it, shielding my eyes with my hand.

The red glow was fading. A body sprawled on the pavement. Young, about twenty, male, probably Chinese, his shockingly beautiful face torn and mangled. I knew him. He'd gone to school with Julie. His name was Yu Fong. He'd come to the house to study once or twice with Julie and Ascanio, and he and Ascanio had spent the entire study session glaring at each other.

He had fallen for at least five seconds, maybe more. What the hell was going on?

Magic crackled in the clouds above me. The intensity of it took my breath away. It pressed on me like a massive hand. It wasn't just old; it was ancient the way mountains were ancient. Every hair on the back of my neck rose.

I planted my legs and drew on the currents around me, calling to my land, shaping the magic it breathed into a shield. Phantom wind spun around me. The chunks of fractured pavement shuddered, rising slightly, grasped by the stream of magic surging up.

Above me the clouds churned.

The magic flowed to me, and I built it above the three of us.

A dark shape slid through the clouds, so huge my mind refused to accept that it was real. It was there, and then it vanished into the sky, melting into the mist.

I braced myself inside the maelstrom of magic, my hands raised at my sides, and grinned at the sky. *Come on. I have a score to settle.*

The dark shape hovered above me, hidden by the clouds but emanating magic like a lighthouse emits light.

Bring it. Let's see what you've got.

It hesitated.

Fine. I pushed. The magic shield I built above us split. A geyser of power shot up.

The thing in the clouds streaked away from me, climbing higher with alarming speed. A moment and it vanished.

I waited.

A tense minute crawled by.

Another.

It was gone.

Teddy Jo landed by me. "What in blazes was that?"

"I don't know."

I released the magic, smoothing it back into its natural state, and crouched by Yu Fong. The heat had subsided. I reached over the still-warm asphalt and touched his neck. A pulse.

I couldn't even tell from how high he'd fallen: a thousand feet, two thousand, more? He didn't look completely broken, and he was breathing. I reached out, trying to sense his magic. Nothing but a mere hint. Every drop of his power was directed inward.

Teddy Jo swore.

I turned to him. "He's breathing. Please go back to Curran and tell him we need a vehicle."

"Stay alive!" Teddy Jo spread his wings and soared into the sky.

6

CROUCHED BY Yu Fong's body. The bruises on his face had turned bright red, the gashes closing and smoothing over so fast, I could actually see his flesh moving. The fingers of his right hand jutted at an odd angle. Broken. His clothes hadn't burned off. He'd fallen from a catastrophic height, so hot he melted the asphalt, but his faded jeans and gray T-shirt weren't even singed.

Curran came running around the corner and sprinted to me. Sweat soaked his hair and forehead. He hadn't bothered with the car. I straightened. He almost skidded to a stop and grabbed me, squeezing me to him. My bones groaned.

"Okay?" he asked.

"Okay," I squeaked. "Conlan?"

He let me go, kissed me, and looked me over, as if he didn't believe me. "Teddy Jo has him. He's locked himself in the office."

Oh good. It would take a tank to break into Cutting Edge.

"Look." I pointed to Yu Fong.

Curran's eyes narrowed. "I know this kid."

"Yes. He's been to the house. Used to go to school with Julie."

"What is he?"

"I have no idea," I told him. "But he's something."

Distant water engines roared.

"Are the kids okay?"

"They're fine."

People began to emerge from surrounding office buildings. The morgue at the eastern end of the square glowed pale blue. Its wards must've activated, which wasn't exactly surprising. Anyone with a crumb of magic in a three-mile radius would've felt that explosion. Being directly under it was like standing inside one of those ancient church bells while the priests pulled on the ropes. It had rattled through my skull, and I had better defenses than most of the people in Atlanta. PAD would be here soon, and then we'd have uncomfortable questions we couldn't answer. It would eat a day, maybe more, and we didn't have a day to spare.

We had to move Yu Fong. He'd fallen from the clouds, so jostling him wouldn't exactly make it worse.

Our two Jeeps rolled into the square and stopped. Just in time.

Julie jumped out of the first one, and Derek followed her from the second.

"Honey?" I asked.

Curran reached over, grasped Yu Fong by his T-shirt and jeans, and lifted him out of the warm asphalt. I caught the body for a brief second, and Curran picked him up into his arms, as if Yu Fong were a child, and carried him to the nearest Jeep.

"Yu Fong!" Julie ran over. "Is he okay?"

"He just fell from those clouds," I said. "How is he still alive?"

"He is a Suanni."

I blinked. According to Chinese myths, the dragon had nine sons, each with a female of a different species. A Suanni was the hybrid of a lion and the dragon, a being of fire. That made Yu Fong the closest thing to a dragon to be found in Atlanta.

"Julie. He's been to the house. Why didn't you tell me?"

She waved her hands. "It didn't come up."

"What do you mean, it didn't come up?" Curran growled.

Damn it. "The next time you bring a half-dragon to the house, I want to know about it. That's the kind of essential information I should have."

"He's just a guy I went to school with. We don't make a big deal about it."

Argh. "Can he regenerate?"

"I don't know. I never asked. I think so. Dali would know. They've met before. He calls her White Tiger like it's her name."

"Does he shapeshift?" Curran gently loaded Yu Fong into the backseat.

"Sort of. I've never seen him go all the way. He usually doesn't need to. He makes fire. Fire's usually enough."

"Can he fly?"

"I don't know!" Julie spread her arms.

Argh.

I climbed into the Jeep. Curran got behind the wheel and stepped on the gas. We rolled toward Cutting Edge. Behind us, Derek and Julie jumped into the other vehicle.

I gripped Sarrat. Thin tendrils of smoke stretched from the blade, licking the air.

"Talk to me," Curran said.

"They killed Mr. Tucker."

"They'll pay," Curran said.

"He never did anything to anyone."

"I know," he said. "I know."

The Jeep jumped over a bump in the pavement.

"Have you ever smelled anything like that?" I asked. "Have you seen one of those assholes before?"

"No."

But I had. The memory stabbed me, cold and sharp. Sarrat hissed.

Curran glanced at me. "Tell me."

"Did my aunt ever tell you how my family died?" I asked.

"She mentioned a war."

"An army invaded them. They came from the sea. They had powerful magic unlike anything she had seen before, and they brought a horde of creatures with them. While my father and Erra were gone to a summit with other kings, they were betrayed. When my aunt and my father returned, they found their brothers and sisters murdered and creatures gnawing on their bodies. When I shared my memories with Erra, she shared hers with me."

The vision of a creature clutching the headless body of a child and gnawing on the red stump of his neck flashed before me. "They looked like that. Similar."

"Similar but not the same?" Curran asked.

"Erra's creatures were gray and hairless. These were brown and had fur. But they felt the same. Like corruption. Like something that had to be undone."

"Something that smells like a loup and shouldn't exist."

"Yes."

"We need to save one for her," he said. "I want her to look at it. What else did she tell you about them?"

"They came from the Western Sea, the Mediterranean. Shinar never feared an invasion from the sea before."

"Why?" Curran asked.

"Sidonians," I told him. "Ancient Phoenicians. The way Erra tells it, they called the sea their father and sailed it to raid and to sell their purple dyes. The Sidonians built walled cities inland, farther in the hinterlands, to give invaders a target. When the attacking army disembarked, the Sidonians would melt into the highlands and cut at the enemy as it marched toward the nearest city, slicing a piece there and a piece here, and vanish back into the wilderness."

"They bled them out," Curran said.

"Yep. By the time the army got to the city, their morale was in tatters. If any invaders managed to survive and make it back to the sea, they'd find their ships had new owners. The Sidon had one main port, Tyre, a big merchant city. Huge walls, guarded harbor, with chains across its entrance and sea beasts guarding the waters. A fortress. Impregnable."

I paused. "My aunt told me that she met a man who'd escaped from Tyre. He told her that they had gone to bed with clear seas, and when they woke up, they couldn't see the water because the harbor was filled with sails. The ships rained monsters. The invaders weren't an army; they were a horde. They had magic creatures that stank of corruption, unkillable soldiers, and they burned what they took to the ground. Nothing was left standing. It was all ash."

"Like the box," he said.

"Like the box."

We drove in silence.

"He wants an answer," I ground out.

Gold flashed in Curran's eyes. He bared his teeth. "Oh, we'll answer. It won't be vague, and he won't like it, I promise you that."

Good.

Curran steered the Jeep onto Jeremiah Street. Carnage spread across the asphalt in front of Cutting Edge. Grotesque bodies, torn and mangled, strewn on the pavement wet with blood. Mr. Tucker lay crumpled on the street, small and somehow almost lost in all the gore. In the middle of it all a man-shaped pillar of pale-gray ash rose.

"Did he ever stop smiling?" I asked.

"No. Held it until his eyes cooked in his head."

This was above my pay grade. I had no idea how to deal with this sort of magic. That was okay. I was a quick learner.

BILL HORN CAME out of his tinker shop as we parked. Bill repaired pots, silverware, and anything that was made of metal. He also sharpened knives, and he was carrying a bowie knife large enough to kill a bear. He was short, broad-shouldered, bald, and he looked like he'd be difficult to move if he braced himself.

He walked over to where I crouched by Mr. Tucker's body. It used to be a man. He'd said hi to us. I'd brought him iced tea. Now it was just a corpse. A split second and a life ended.

"Not your fault," Bill said.

"Yeah, it is. I could've yelled at him to not come close when he first stumbled onto the street."

"He wouldn't have listened. The man had no goddamned sense. It's not you. It's this." He indicated the bloody street with a slow sweep of his hand. "It's the Shift."

I didn't say anything.

"He was a nut," Bill told me gently.

"Yes, but he was our nut."

Curran came up and rested his hand on my shoulder. Bill looked at Mr. Tucker's corpse, looked at the slaughter, then looked back at Curran. "You folks need any help?"

"We got it," Curran told him. "Thanks. Sorry about the mess."

Bill nodded again. "I was thinking of visiting my daughter up in Gainesville."

"Good fishing up there," Curran said.

"Yeah," Bill said. "My son-in-law told me he pulled a thirty-pound striped bass out of Lake Lanier. Can't let him beat my record, you know."

"Might be a good time to visit," Curran said.

"You reckon about two weeks ought to do it?"

"Sounds about right."

Bill nodded and went to his shop.

I straightened. "The neighbors are running for the hills."

"In the four years you've had your office here, nobody broke into any of their shops," Curran said. "None of them ever got hurt by any of the magical crap. We protected the street. Now they can give us a break by clearing out while we get this sorted."

"Help me get him off the street?" I asked.

He picked up Mr. Tucker and carried him to the sidewalk in front of Cutting Edge.

I knocked on the door of my office. Teddy Jo swung it open, a very human Conlan in his arms. I took him. My son yawned and groggily smacked my face with his hand. I hugged him to me, went inside the office, and sat in a chair. I just needed thirty seconds to steady myself.

"You want to tell me what that was all about?" Teddy Jo leaned over the table.

"Someone sent me a wooden box full of ash with a rose and a knife in it. Apparently, he wants a response."

Derek walked into the office and went to the supply cage where we kept bleach, gasoline, and other fun things we used for cleanup.

"Who sent it? Why? What does the box mean?" Teddy Jo asked.

"It probably means war."

"Are we getting invaded?"

"Maybe."

"Who's invading us?"

"I don't know."

"But you must have some idea."

"If I did, I would be doing something about it. In your experience, do I typically sit on my hands when someone is threatening the city?"

"Can you at least tell me what kind of magic this is?"

"Why do you think I would know?"

Teddy Jo pointed in the direction of the Unnamed Square. "Because that was an elder power. When someone has a problem with an elder power, they come to you. You're an expert on evil old shit."

"I'm trying to decide if I should be flattered or insulted."

"If they sent you a message, they must think you would understand it. If you don't get it, ask somebody. The city is going to hell. People are getting boiled, people are being burned alive, and you're sitting here. You're the In-Shinar! Do something!"

Curran loomed next to Teddy Jo. His eyes had gone completely gold. I hadn't even heard him come in.

"Uh-oh," Conlan offered.

Teddy Jo realized that now would be a very good time to stop talking and clamped his mouth shut.

Curran stared at him with a singular predatory focus. Teddy Jo straightened and took a step away from the table.

"I am the In-Shinar," I told him. "I'm not omniscient or omnipotent. I'm not a god. If we want to get technical, that's your department."

He didn't say anything.

I took a piece of paper and drew the sign from the box on it. "What does that look like to you?"

"A bra?" Teddy Jo said.

"That's our only clue as to who sent the box. Have at it."

He blinked at the sign for a bit, folded the paper in half, then again, and stuffed it into the pocket of his jeans.

"Do you still have the corpse bus?" I asked. Teddy Jo ran a mortuary. It catered to a specific clientele, most of them Greek neo-pagans, and a lot of his income came through his side business: making and selling human freezers, autopsy tables, and body-transporting cars. He scoured junk-yards, customized his equipment, and rented it out to the city and the sur-rounding counties.

Teddy Jo grimaced. "It's not a corpse bus. It's a Multiple Recently Deceased Efficient Removal vehicle."

"You do realize that spells MURDER?" Derek asked.

Teddy Jo gave him a look. "Yes, I do. That's the point."

Angel of death humor, what would we do without it? "It would really help if you could get the MURDER bus, load these bodies up, and deliver them."

Teddy Jo's eyebrows rose. "Where?"

"Everywhere. Drop a couple at Biohazard, one to the Pack, one to the Casino, one to the Witches. Anyone who should reasonably be made aware that these things exist. Give one to the Order too, what the hell."

"What do you want me to tell them?" Teddy Jo asked.

"Tell them that these things attacked us. There is something wrong with them, and we need to know where they came from. You want to help? Do this, please."

"I'll get the bus," he said.

MIRACULOUSLY THE PHONE worked for Curran and he got through to the Pack on the first try. Dali promised to be right there, and she was bringing Doolittle with her. His next call was to the Guild. He called the medmage and insisted on her coming to Cutting Edge to patch me up. Curran and I had reached an understanding. He didn't protest when I ran headfirst into danger, and I didn't argue when he then unleashed a crew of medmages on my wounds. The medmage arrived half an hour later, chanted my wounds closed, warned me to take it easy, which we both knew I would ignore, and left.

Dali was still in transit, which wasn't surprising. "Right there" in post-Shift Atlanta meant about an hour, maybe two. We used the time to gather the bodies, chain them together in case they rose after death, sweep the ash into an airtight plastic bin, and feed Conlan his second breakfast. I tried to give him cereal. He flipped the bowl and put it on his head. We made the fatal mistake of laughing, and he decided the bowl was an essential accessory and refused to give it up. He also decided that cereal was clearly beneath him and spat it out in various creative ways. Derek ran down the street and came back with a smoked turkey leg from a vendor. Faced with two options, hungry Conlan or Conlan full of turkey meat, I went with the latter.

Teddy Jo returned with the bus. Curran, Derek, and I started loading the bodies, while Julie purified the street. When we were down to three corpses, a Pack van turned around the corner and came to a stop near us. Dali jumped out from the driver's side, swung the rear doors open, took out a folded wheelchair, then picked up Doolittle. For a moment, they made a slightly comical figure, a tiny Indonesian woman with thick glasses carrying a middle-aged black man about twice her size. Then she set him gently into his chair and Doolittle surveyed us.

Curran and Derek were holding two furry bodies. Teddy Jo and I were locking manacles on their feet. Julie had doused the street with gasoline and set it on fire, holding the hose ready in case it got out of control. And Conlan presided over it all from his high chair in the doorway of the office, completely naked, with a half-eaten turkey leg in his hand and a plastic bowl on his head. He saw Doolittle and waved the turkey leg at him.

"Baddadda!"

Why me?

Dali didn't blink an eye. "Where is Yu Fong?"

"He's inside," Julie said. "I'll come with you."

She gave me the hose and they hurried into the office.

"Bada!" Conlan squirmed in his chair.

"Stay," I told him.

"Dadbadaa!"

"Don't talk back to your mother," Curran told him.

After the fire burned itself out, we loaded the last body, except for the one wrapped in chains in our Jeep and the spare I'd stashed, chained into our office body freezer. Teddy Jo drove off, and I went inside.

Yu Fong looked about the same.

"What's the prognosis?" I asked.

Doolittle turned to me. "He's stable. He's in a healing coma."

"How long will it last?"

"I don't know," Doolittle said. "An hour, a day, a century. He might wake up when our grandchildren are old."

Great. "Is there any way to wake him up?"

"Yes," Doolittle said. "We can drown or suffocate him. He might wake up or he might die. If he does wake up, his healing process may be irrevocably interrupted, and he may still die."

"Is there any scenario in which he won't die?" Julie asked.

"Yes," Doolittle said. "Let him sleep."

I rubbed my face. My only witness was doing a version of Sleeping Beauty. Maybe I could scrounge up a Prince Charming to kiss him awake.

"There is something inside him," Doolittle said.

"What do you mean?"

"There is a foreign object inside him. He might have been stabbed with it or perhaps it's something he has put inside his own body for safekeeping."

Shapeshifters occasionally took advantage of their rapid regeneration in weird ways. Before Andrea accepted her true nature, she'd had an amulet that blocked her power embedded in her body. Yu Fong might have done the same.

"Could it be keeping him in a coma?"

"Possibly," Doolittle said.

"Should we get it out?"

"Not unless you want to risk his life."

Argh.

"You're not waking him up," Dali declared. It sounded a lot like an order.

I looked at her. She stared straight at me, her eyes unblinking behind her glasses. A green sheen rolled over her irises. Trying to dominate. Two years as Beast Lady had taken their toll.

I stared back. "Let me know."

"What?"

"When you remember that I'm not a Pack member. You're not my alpha, Dali. Turn the headlights down."

She glared at me. I waited. I lived with a former Beast Lord. My husband hit me with the alpha stare just this morning, after I told him that I was throwing his old T-shirt away. Apparently, as long as it had an intact collar, he considered it a usable garment, no matter how many holes it had.

"You're not waking him up," she repeated, this time softer.

"No, we're not." Although I'd have given a year of my life to figure out what he was fighting in the clouds, risking his life for it wasn't worth it. "Does he have any family? Anyone we should call?"

"His family let him rot in a poacher's cage for years, while they sliced pieces off him to sell on the black market. I doubt they will give a damn. We'll take care of him at the Keep," Dali said.

"No," Julie said.

Dali ignored her. "We're best equipped to handle this."

"I don't think so," I told her.

"I don't need your permission," Dali said.

"You have no grounds to take him. First, he isn't a member of the Pack, Dali. You would be kidnapping a citizen of Atlanta. Second, Yu Fong fell and made that lovely crater because he was fighting something in the clouds. Something ancient and magic that was aware of the boundaries and of my power, because once I showed up and shifted magic to shield us, it took off. It will come back to finish the job. Sheltering Yu Fong will make the Keep a target, and you don't have the power to oppose it. Jim won't let you keep him."

She opened her mouth.

"Third, Doolittle just said that there is nothing he can do for him. Am I right?"

The medmage nodded. "We can only make him comfortable."

"So, there is no pressing need to take him to the Keep."

Dali pushed her glasses back up her nose. "I really hate you sometimes."

"Welcome to the club."

"He is special," she said. "Sacred."

Yes, in the same way she was. "I'm aware of that. That's why I'm taking him home with us."

Where I had wards and friendly homicidal neighbors to back me up.

"You're welcome to visit any time you like, but you're not taking him to the Keep, because you'd call me less than an hour after you got there and ask me to come pick him up. Let's not move him more than necessary. He's under a lot of stress as it is."

She thought about it. "Who's going to be watching him?"

"Adora."

Dali wrinkled her nose. "Is she capable of watching him? You know how she is. What if she sees a butterfly?"

"I'll pay her."

A few months ago, Adora had figured out that when she did a job for the Guild, she earned money, which she could then spend however she pleased. After she'd repeatedly shown the money to me, and I confirmed several times that it was, indeed, her own money, she went out shopping for the first time and we got to find out what $1,200 of candy looked like. She ate candy for three days straight, then spent the remainder of the week on our couch with a stomachache. Now she worked as a merc, with the highest job completion ratio in the Guild. She took her gigs absurdly seriously. Through rain, shine, sleet, and hail, purple corrosive slime bubbling up from the sewers, or mysterious black snow that sparked when it hit metal, Adora would get it done. Dali knew that.

"Okay," Dali said. Her tone told me she didn't like it.

That was okay. I didn't like a great many things, but the universe didn't give a crap, so I didn't see why it should bend on Dali's account.

"You will take the best care of him, right?"

"No, I'll drop him into the nearest sewer and throw dirt on his head."

She sighed. "I've got almost two thousand smart-asses to manage every night. Just tell me you'll take care of him, Kate."

"He went to school with Julie. He's been to our house. He isn't a stranger. Of course I'll take care of him." I would've taken care of him even if he was a stranger, but she seemed like she needed more reassurance.

"I'll hold you to that," she said.

"You should growl a bit to let me know you mean business," I told her. "Just in case you think I might miss the point."

She flipped me off.

"Love you, too." I turned to Doolittle. "Can you please take a look at Conlan?"

Doolittle gave me a look. "I saw him on the way in. He appeared to be in perfect health."

"I know, but—"

Doolittle held up his hand. "Kate, the last time you brought him in was because he fell off his feet."

"He had a bump on his head."

"The time before that you mistook heat rash for chicken pox."

"I understand, but something happened—"

"Something always happens. Your son is a healthy, active toddler. He is supposed to run, fall, climb, and occasionally try to eat things he shouldn't. Your job is to keep him from the worst of it. It would do you and him a great deal of good if you just let him be a child and stop wasting my time." He turned to Dali. "I'm ready to go."

Dali stuck her nose in the air and opened the door. Doolittle wheeled himself out. Curran and Conlan watched them go.

"Thanks for the backup with Doolittle," I told Curran, as the van pulled away.

He grinned at me.

Something crunched. I turned. Conlan spat half a turkey femur out of his mouth.

"Told you," my husband said. "Cooked bones splinter."

Argh.

"THAT KID DRIVES like a maniac," Curran said.

We'd set out from Cutting Edge in two Jeeps at the same time, but Julie and Derek had left us in the dust. I couldn't even see their vehicle. That's what happened when you let a vegetarian, half-blind weretiger with a passion for racing cars give your child driving lessons.

We turned onto the road leading to our street.

"She hasn't wrecked so far," I told him.

An explosion of blood-red fire shot up above the trees on our left.

Curran gunned it.

Please don't be our house, please don't be our house.

We took the turn at a dangerous speed.

The house came into view. A charred metal wreck sat on the curb in front of it, the inside of what used to be the Jeep on fire. Derek stood by it with a fatalistic look on his face. Damn it.

"Three minutes," Curran growled. "They were unsupervised for three minutes."

Apparently, three minutes was plenty of time to blow things up.

Curran steered into the driveway, shut off the water engine, and jumped out of the Jeep. I followed.

The stench of burning flesh and fabric filled the air. Ash floated gently on the breeze.

"What the hell happened?" I asked.

"Your aunt happened," Derek said.

Oh no.

"She freaked out," Derek said. Amber light shone from his eyes. He was not happy. "As soon as Julie and I got out, she made this red fireball and blew up the Jeep."

"Was the creature's body in the Jeep?" Curran asked.

"Yeah. And my gear. And Julie's."

She'd blasted the Jeep. And probably drained herself down to nothing in the process. It would take her several days to recover. Well, I'd wondered if she'd recognize the creature. I guess that answered that question.

"Was anybody hurt?" I asked.

"No," Derek said, his tone flat. "The Jeep was the only casualty."

"I'm sorry."

At least she'd let them get out of the car. "Where is she?"

"In her dagger. She won't come out. Julie's with her."

Derek reached out toward the wreck and pulled back.

"What are you doing?" Curran growled.

"My knives are in there."

"Get the hose," Curran told him.

Derek strode toward the house.

I pulled a sleepy Conlan out of the car seat. "Will you take him? I need to go and give Erra a piece of my mind."

Curran opened his arms and I deposited Conlan into them. Once we were done with this, we'd have to install Yu Fong into the bedroom downstairs and I'd need to track Adora down, so she could babysit him.

The phone rang as I climbed the stairs to the second floor. Curran came in and headed into the kitchen. I heard him pick it up and braced myself. I was getting as bad as Pavlov's dog.

"If you call me again, I'll find this Sunshine Realty and shove your head up your ass."

False alarm.

Erra's room sat in the heart of the house, on the second floor, evenly removed from all the entrances. Daylight streamed through a single window, cut by the silver bars into a lattice. A breeze stirred the long gauzy curtains. In the middle of the room, Erra's dagger rested in a wooden holder on the table, but my aunt wasn't in it. When she withdrew inside the blade, the dagger emitted magic like a warm hearth.

Julie leaned against the wall, her arms crossed.

"Where is she?"

She nodded at the balcony door.

I glanced there and saw Erra on the covered balcony, standing with her hands wrapped around herself. Usually she manifested in blood armor, but lately I'd been seeing her in long dresses, sometimes the color of ruby, sometimes white or deep, rich emerald. She wore the red one now.

I left the room and went out on the balcony with her. The Five Hundred Acre Wood spread before us, verdant and filled with life, the trees rising in a solid wall just past the deer fence. My aunt looked tired, her gaze fixed on something distant on the horizon.

For a while we stood next to each other without saying anything.

"You must call your father," she said.

"No."

She turned to me. "War is coming. Our enemy is coming."

"Roland wants to kill me. He wants to murder my child or kidnap him, I don't think he's decided which yet. I just found out this morning he's mobilizing his forces."

"This is bigger than that."

"Nothing is bigger than that. I saw a photo of Razer today. He was just a few miles north, in the city limits. He's here, because my father wishes him to be. That fae wears a coat made of the skins of creatures and people he's murdered. He isn't going to add a piece of Conlan's skin to his wardrobe—"

She reached out and touched my face. Her translucent fingers brushed my cheek, the magic prickling along my skin. She'd punched me with her power almost every week, but her caresses were so rare, I could count them on my fingers. I shut up.

"Stubborn child," the Queen of Shinar said. "Your world will burn until everything turns to ash. You'll live through unspeakable horrors. You'll see everyone you love fall, and you'll wish you were dead, but you won't die, because you are the Princess of Shinar, the beacon of your people's hope, and if you succumb, that hope will perish with you. Your memories will become your torture. You'll carry that burden with you as you wade through a sea of blood, and when you emerge, you'll become me, your victory a hollow trinket. I cannot watch you suffer through it. You and that boy are everything I have. You are the family I lost and found. Call your father. Show him the creature. Tell him the yeddimur are here. Together we have a chance. Do that for me, In-Shinar. Do that because I'm your aunt and you love me."

I WALKED OUT of the house carrying my backpack. Curran was still holding Conlan. Derek hosed off the Jeep, while Julie watched with a skeptical look on her face. The four of them looked at me.

"Did you talk to Erra?" Curran asked.

"Yep. Come with me," I told Derek. "I need your help."

"With what?"

"With carrying a metric ton of firewood. I'm going to call my father and I need to be out of my territory to do that."

"Gave her a piece of your mind, did you?" Curran asked. "How did that work out for you?"

"I don't want to talk about it."

Julie snickered.

"Your mom got her butt kicked," Curran told Conlan.

"Keep talking, see how that turns out for you."

Curran grinned. "There you go, Conlan. If your mommy is ever mean to you, snitch on her to your great-aunt and she'll fix it."

Conlan giggled.

I growled and got into my Jeep.

. . .

I STOOD ON top of a low hill and surveyed the pile of brushwood and dead branches Derek and I had arranged into a ten-foot-tall cone. At my back, the sunset died slowly as the sun rolled to the west, behind the city. The rays of the setting sun set the world aglow, and against the curtain of light the ruins of Atlanta stood out, dark and shadowy, a mirage of a safer time.

Hi, Dad, it's me. I know you're trying to kill me, my husband, and our son, but guess what, all is forgiven, I need your help. Ugh. I'd rather walk on broken glass.

I was stalling. I came here, I built this damn pyre, I had to get it over with.

"Do we need more wood?" Derek asked.

Ten feet high and about six feet across. Good enough. "No."

I reached into my pocket, withdrew a packet of dried herbs, pushed a couple of branches aside, and sprinkled it into the middle of the pyre. I replaced the branches, struck a match, and lit the newspaper. The fire gobbled up the paper, jumped to the smaller twigs, and began eating its way through the branches.

The sky was cooling off, darkening from near turquoise to a deeper indigo. Hints of the first stars appeared above us.

I concentrated on the fire, funneling my magic into it. The flames caught the herbs and crackled. Blue sparks shot up from the pyre, and thick aromatic smoke drifted through the air.

I pulled a small vial of my blood from the pouch on my belt and poured a few drops into the fire, murmuring the incantation. Bright crimson burst within the blaze, spreading to envelop the whole pyre in unnatural red flame. Magic pulsed. There. It was done.

The ancient words rolled off my tongue. *"Nimrod. Father. I need your help. Please answer."* Well, look at that. I didn't even choke.

Nothing.

Derek drew back. The hair on his arms was standing up.

"Father, speak to me."

Nothing.

I switched to English. "Father, we are facing a terrible threat. The yed-dimur are here. I need to speak to you. It's important. Please."

The flames remained silent.

I sat on the grass.

"Maybe he can't feel it," Derek said.

"My family has used this method to communicate for thousands of years. He can sense the fire. It's like a ringing phone, difficult to ignore. He just decided not to pick up."

Derek sprawled on the grass next to me, looking into the flames. Most of the time when I looked at him, I saw a man, but right now, with the fire dancing in his eyes, he was a wolf.

"Do you miss him?" he asked.

"Yes. No matter how monstrous he is, he's still my father. I miss talking to him. When he lived close, I was angry with him, but there were moments when we just talked."

In those moments, he forgot to be a conqueror and a tyrant. He was just a father, one I never knew during my childhood. And he was proud of me, especially when I managed to stick it to him. I was the child of a monster from a family of monsters. My aunt had burned her way through ancient Mesopotamia. She had committed atrocities and I had learned to love her, too. There was light in Erra. There was also darkness, and when I looked deep into both, I recognized myself.

"Roland loves me as much as he can ever love a child. He just loves himself more."

"I miss my father," Derek said. "Before he turned loup."

After Derek's father turned loup, he'd raped, killed, and eaten his wife and daughters, until teenage Derek finally snapped and killed him. He was the sole survivor of that massacre, and once he was done, he set fire to the house. That was how the Pack found him, mute and unresponsive by the smoldering wreck of his family home. It took Curran months to coax him back to the living.

"What was he like?" I asked.

"Strict. People said he was a good man. He was scared."

"Of what?"

"Of everything." Derek looked into the flames. "The way I grew up, there were Christians and then there was the world. The world was evil and wicked, and only the Christians were good and safe. They talked about it almost as if it were a foreign power out to get them. One time we went to a mountain fair, and a visiting preacher delivered a sermon. He said it was easy to be a Christian when you hold yourself separate from the world, but if you do, there is no temptation, no struggle, and nobody to witness to. That our duty was to go into the world, holding the light of our faith like a torch, and to help others."

"Didn't go over well with your father, did it?" I guessed.

"No. He pulled us out of the crowd and told us the man was a false prophet. Everything of the world was bad: books, toys, school. Anything that conflicted with a clean life."

I didn't know what to say. "Christians aren't the only people who do that. There are shapeshifters in the Keep who never go into the city. They don't want to interact with anyone who isn't a shapeshifter. Some people cling to their tribe, Derek. He took good care of you. He must've loved you."

Derek shrugged. "I got the feeling it was less about love and more like a second job. A man works and takes care of his family, so my dad did that, because he was supposed to do it. We were his responsibility, and it was his job to provide and to make sure we turned out good and Christian. The plan was that I would grow up and turn into my dad. Work at a paper mill or, if I got ambitious, learn to weld or be a plumber. Marry some girl, put a trailer on my parents' land. Have kids. Stay in the mountains with other good Christian folk. Stay safe. I didn't want to be safe. I wanted to be a sailor."

"Why a sailor?"

He grimaced. "So I could sail away from the mountains. I wanted more."

Now he'd gotten more. Way more than he'd bargained for.

"My father never had a lot of patience," Derek said. "Maggie, my older sister, argued with him. She could argue forever. He'd keep it up for a while, until she got to him, and he'd order her to her room. Then he'd go bust wood in the back, ashamed that he lost his temper. But he never laid a hand on us. After he turned, I saw him fucking Maggie's corpse."

My stomach turned. "Loupism drives people insane. You know this."

"Maybe there was always darkness inside him. Loupism just brought it out into the open."

"If there was always darkness inside him, he never let you see it. Doesn't that make him a good man anyway?"

Derek turned to me. His eyes were empty. There was no sadness, no anger, just the watchful emptiness of a predator. I'd seen him do this before. That's how he dealt with it. He went deep into the wolf.

"Voron was the closest thing to a father I had," I told him. "He fed me, he taught me. He cared if I lived or died. The witches told me that the only reason he did any of those things was because my mother fried him with her magic. She cooked him until he loved her above everything else. When my father killed her, Voron couldn't handle it, so he raised me to become a weapon against Roland. Voron wanted to hurt my father. Either I killed my father or he killed me, and either way Voron would be satisfied with the pain he caused."

Derek waited silently.

"I chose to not worry about it," I told him. "I filed it away into the same place I keep things like Earth is a globe and ice floats. I'm aware of it, and when I need it, I'll pull it out and dust it off, but until then I have memories of my childhood when Voron took care of me. They are my memories. I decide how to view them, so I choose to remember him as the man who raised me and taught me to survive. It makes me happier to remember it that way."

"But is it the truth?"

"I don't know. He's dead, so I can't ask him. You can remember your father as a man who hid darkness inside him, or you can remember him as a flawed man who loved his family and died when loupism took him over. You have to decide for yourself what you can live with . . ."

A flash of white light split the ruby flames of the pyre. I stood up. What do you know, Daddy Dearest decided to pick up the phone after all.

The light coalesced into a man. He wore a long robe with a hood. No, not a robe, a cape, lined with wolf fur and fastened with a thick gold chain across his chest. The white fabric draped his wide shoulders, falling down into the flames.

And he was not my father. Not even a little bit.

The man lowered his hood. He was tall, at least six-six, maybe six-seven. Caucasian. Blond hair falling in a long mane on his shoulders. An ornate torque clasped his neck, heavy with gold. Handsome face, broad, with a square jaw, defined cheek bones, straight nose, and sharp eyes under a sweep of thick blond eyebrows. The eyes stared at me with regal arrogance. The pale blue irises glowed slightly. I couldn't tell if it was from the flames or if his magic made them luminescent.

He opened his mouth.

Tech crashed into us. The man and the crimson fire vanished. The flames went out, and the pyre collapsed into a heap of ash.

Okay then.

Derek leaned back and laughed.

I gave him my hard stare.

He didn't even notice. "Does this magic fire come with a warranty, because I think it's defective."

"It's not defective."

He shook with laughter.

"Go ahead, get your giggles."

"We drove an hour and a half out here, spent two hours scrounging for wood and building this fire, and we got the wrong guy. Did you screw up the area code?"

"You should take your show on the road. Make some extra money with all these jokes."

He laughed harder.

"Is this a regular thing? I'm just wondering, did your family usually try to call Attila the Hun and get Genghis Khan instead?"

"I'm not going to dignify that with an answer."

"Maybe you should try calling him on a regular phone," Derek suggested. "I can help you dial the numbers. You know, do the heavy lifting."

"Will you quit?"

He sprawled on the grass on his back, snorting. "No."

"I'll buy you new knives if you shut up."

"I don't want new knives. I want my old knives." He raised his head. "Give me that jerky you hid in the glove compartment and I'll stop."

"Deal."

He rolled to his feet, hauled a drum of water from the back of the Jeep, and dumped it on the ashes. We got into the Jeep and I handed the jerky over. The sounds of a hungry shapeshifter eating filled the vehicle. I steered the Jeep toward Atlanta.

Derek paused his chewing. "That was someone, though. Some god or king or something."

I nodded. There'd been power in those blue eyes. I would have to ask my aunt if the fire call could be intercepted and who would have the magic to do so.

He chuckled.

"What is it now?"

"You can tell he had a whole speech prepared. Now he's probably fuming somewhere."

"That's what worries me."

"I'll always have your back," Derek said. "Even with creepy magic."

"I know. Thank you."

"You're welcome."

We rolled toward Atlanta, where isolated electric lights beckoned, promising the illusion of safety.

"TELL ME AGAIN about the blond guy," Curran said.

"Tall. Muscular. Expensive cloak lined with fur and fastened with a gold chain. Full of himself. Perfectly brushed hair." I drank my tea.

We sat in the kitchen. While I'd been gone, Curran had put our son to bed. He and Julie had already eaten dinner. I grabbed a late bite, too. Julie sat across from me at the table, drinking her own tea. Derek had retrieved his knives from the burnt wreck of the Jeep, had spread a length of canvas on the table, and was painstakingly cleaning them. Most of the blades had made it through the fire, but a couple of synthetic handles had melted.

"Don't forget the dog collar," Derek said.

"Not a collar, a torque," I said. "Collars open at the back. This one opened from the front."

"What kind of a torque?" Julie asked. "Scythian? Thracian?"

"Heavy, ornate, with three stylized gold claws."

"And you're sure it wasn't your dad in disguise?" Curran asked.

"Yes. The eyes were different."

My husband crossed his arms. "How long did you gaze into his eyes, exactly?"

"About three seconds, while I waited for him to speak." I pointed my teaspoon at him. "I know what you're thinking. Stop thinking it."

Julie kept a straight face, but her eyes laughed at me from above the rim of her cup. Derek appeared stoic.

"What am I supposed to think? First, someone sends you a red rose."

"And a knife. And a box full of ash."

"Exactly. Is it a threat? Is it a conditional declaration of war?"

I shrugged. "Maybe it's a gift from a socially awkward horticulturalist."

Julie laughed into her tea. Derek pretended not to hear, but the corners of his mouth curved up.

"Sure it is. Then you call your dad and some golden-haired pretty boy shows up dressed to impress."

I waved my spoon. "I agree with you there. Nobody prances around in a fur-lined cloak in the middle of the Atlanta summer with perfectly brushed hair. It looked like he sensed my fire call, put on all of his regal things, prepared a speech, and only then cut in."

"And then tech hit." Derek flashed a quick smile.

Curran leaned on the table. "So, you tell me how I'm supposed to feel about that. On top of everything else, your aunt blew up the Jeep and over-extended herself."

My aunt had a very difficult time manifesting during tech, and with most of her power spent on that firebomb, she would be sleeping for a while. I'd tried her dagger when we got home and gotten only silence.

I spread my arms. "How is that my fault?"

"I never said it was. I'm expressing my general frustration with this situation."

"I'm frustrated, too. I've got Serenbe. Two hundred people are gone, and their families have no answers. I've got dead Mr. Tucker, Yu Fong in a coma, ancient creatures popping out of my aunt's nightmares and attacking us, my dad mobilizing, and on top of that there is a fae assassin running around in our city likely hoping to kill you, me, or our son, preferably all three. My cup runneth over and I have zero answers. Zilch. Nada."

We stared at each other.

"We should spar," he said. "We will both feel better."

Yes. I needed to punch and kick and do things so badly, my limbs ached. "That's a good idea. No; that's the best idea ever."

Someone knocked on the front door. Derek sniffed the air, picked up a large knife, and hefted it in his hand.

"What?" I asked.

"The pervert," Derek said, and started toward the door.

Oh no, you don't. "I'll get it."

I beat Derek to the door and swung it open. A man stood on our doorstep, wearing gray pants, a light-gray button-down shirt rolled up to the elbows, and tired dark shoes. Bald. Average height, average build, unremarkable features, neither handsome nor ugly. You'd pass him in a crowd and never give him a second glance. Saiman in his neutral form, a clean slate for a polymorph who could impersonate any human on the face of the planet. Behind him a dark van with tinted windows waited in our driveway.

I checked his eyes for the usual sharp intelligence. It was there, together with apprehension.

"What's the emergency?"

"Emergency?" Saiman raised his eyebrows.

"Yes. What bad thing happened to make you show up here? What did you do?"

"Nothing."

I rubbed my forehead. "My husband is generally frustrated and so am I, so it's in everyone's best interests if you tell me why you're here quickly."

Saiman hesitated for a moment. "I don't have a body."

I reached out and touched his shoulder with my index finger. "I've just conducted a field test and it appears you do have a body. Good night."

"I didn't get a body. Biohazard, the Order, and the Pack received a body. I'm the best arcane expert in Atlanta, with a state-of-the-art lab, and you haven't sent me one."

Oh. "I didn't send you a body because you would charge me an arm and a leg for it." There were way too many puns in that sentence for my liking. "I'm not interested in your services. Your price is too high."

Saiman took a deep breath, as if he were about to jump off a cliff. "I'll examine it gratis."

I pinched my arm.

A hint of the old Saiman's arrogance crept into his eyes. "Really, Kate, this is childish."

I turned back to the kitchen and called out, "Saiman is here and he wants to help us for free."

Derek clamped his hand to his chest and dropped to the floor.

"Oh gods!" Julie waved her hands. "Hide the children. The Apocalypse is coming. The werewolves are fainting!"

Saiman spared them a single glance. "They were perfectly reasonable before. This is the result of prolonged exposure and proves my theory."

"And what would that be?"

"You're contagious."

Julie rushed over to Derek. "No, no, that's okay. He hasn't fainted. He just has the vapors! False alarm."

Saiman looked to be in physical pain. "None of this is funny."

"All of that ability to transform and you can't develop a sense of humor. Cheer up, Saiman. The ice of Jotunheim is far away. Your folks won't know if you crack a smile."

Saiman sighed, opened his mouth, and froze, his gaze fixed behind me. I glanced over my shoulder. Curran loomed in the hallway. My husband had a talent for emanating threat simply by standing still, and right now he was exercising this gift to its full extent. If menace were heat, the walls around me would've caught on fire.

"I'm here to help," Saiman said quietly.

Derek rolled to his feet.

"What's the catch?" I asked. "What do you want? I don't want to owe you anything."

"Nothing. No strings attached."

There were few absolute truths in this world, but the fact that Saiman never did anything without expecting a payoff was surely one of them.

"Can you transform during tech?" Curran asked.

Saiman drew himself to his full height. "Yes."

"Good. Come inside."

"Excuse me." Saiman stepped into the hallway and walked past me to the kitchen.

His Furriness was so laser focused on the blond dude, he was willing to work with Saiman. And this wouldn't end badly. Not at all.

"Kate tried to fire call her father tonight," Curran said.

"Fire call?" Saiman asked me.

"Later," I told him.

"Someone cut in. I want to know what he looked like," Curran said. "Can you do this?"

Saiman smiled. "Of course."

"Good. Julie, get the Polaroid camera."

Saiman rubbed his hands together. The skin on his face crawled, as if a pool ball rolled under it. My stomach screeched in alarm and tried to empty itself.

"Really?" Derek raised his eyebrows.

"He's a weird pervert, but he is our weird pervert and he came here to help. Let him help," I said.

Derek frowned.

Curran gave him a hard look. "When you have to, use every resource available."

"Ready when you are," Saiman said.

There was no escaping it. I sighed and started. "Square jaw ..."

Five minutes later, my fire-call visitor stood in front of us. He was still wearing Saiman's clothes, but the face and hair belonged to the man in the fire.

"Yeah," Derek volunteered. "That's him."

Curran examined him, his jaw set. Julie snapped a few pictures. "You didn't say he was handsome."

Thanks, just what I needed. "He was handsome, but there was something wrong with him."

"In what way?" Saiman asked.

"His eyes were ..." I struggled to describe them. "Cold. Not exactly flat, but remote. It was like looking into the eyes of a gator."

"Interesting," Saiman said.

"Does he look like any ancient you know?" Derek asked.

"Nimrod and Astamur are the only ancient humans I've met in person," Saiman said. "They don't exactly wander about like stray cats."

I got up. "I'll be right back. If I come back and our guest is injured, I'll be very put out."

Julie opened her eyes as wide as they would go. "Injure? Us?"

I went upstairs and brought the box down. "I need you to look at this."

Saiman collapsed into his neutral shape and examined the box, lifting the lid with his long slender fingers. "Is this an artifact?"

"It was left on my doorstep." I told him about the boy burning. The more I talked, the deeper his frown grew.

"To burn a body alive but make the human immune to the pain ..." he murmured. "How would you even begin to go about it?"

"I don't know."

"If this is a message, there should be some way to attribute it. Unless this being's arrogance is so great, they believe they would be instantly recognized."

"My aunt indicated the box is a generic way to declare war," I explained.

"And you found nothing in the box or on the knife?"

"Nothing except this shape." I drew the symbol for him.

"Arsenic? Curious," he murmured.

"I have a body for you if you're still interested," I told him. "I took one to show my father." Which was one of the reasons the trip had taken so long. We had to stop by the office and pull the spare out of the freezer.

"I am."

Curran followed us to the Jeep and carried the body bag wrapped in chains to Saiman's dark van. Saiman and I watched him.

"Why are you doing this?" I asked.

"We've had our ups and downs. We are associates. Sometimes business partners. To your father, I'm a bag of magically potent blood. He chained me in a stone cell with a barred, narrow window. Every day at sunrise your father's soldiers would walk into my cell and shatter the bones of my legs with a hammer, so he could take full advantage of my regeneration. I couldn't slow it down. My body would rebuild my bones and make more blood, and every evening the soldiers returned to drain it. I sat in that cell, staring at the sliver of the sky, and I knew nobody was coming for me. I would be there until I died."

We'd had this conversation before, but I didn't want to interrupt to remind him.

"Then Curran came and pulled me out of that cell, because you asked him to." Saiman wouldn't look at me, his gaze fixed on something distant. "I still have nightmares. There are nights when I keep a light on, as if I were a child. *I.*"

I pictured him inside his ultramodern apartment, with his lab, his art, and the trappings of his wealth, on the top floor of an enchanted tower, flicking the lamp on. Oh, Saiman.

Saiman glanced at me and there was sharp green ice in his eyes. He didn't look human. He looked like a creature who had risen from a place where ancient ice never melted.

"I can't leave the city. If I do, your father will find me. This will never end unless you stop him, so I will do whatever I can to help you."

Curran stuffed the body into Saiman's van.

"I'll let you know what I find out," Saiman said.

We watched him pull away.

"What do you think that was all about?" Curran asked.

"I think he's scared of my father. He wants revenge."

"Think he'll sell us out?"

"No. Besides, if you can't trust an ice giant driving a creeper van with a dead body inside, who can you trust?"

Curran chuckled.

"He knows this whole street houses shapeshifters and none of them are his fans. He drove into the mouth of the beast in the middle of the night. Odd. I'm surprised he didn't call ahead."

"He couldn't," Curran said. "I broke the phone."

"How?"

"I crushed it."

I turned and looked at him. Curran prided himself on his control, especially now that he was a father. He didn't punch walls, break furniture, or scream. Even his roar was usually calculated. As much as I pushed and annoyed him, I had only seen him lose control beyond all reason once. Watching him hurl giant boulders off a mountain was a memorable experience. But he had never broken anything of ours before.

"Why did you smash the phone?"

"I was trying to put Conlan to bed and it kept ringing."

"That is not okay."

"I know. It was an impulse."

"You don't give in to impulses. What's going on with you?"

"Who knows."

"Curran?"

"Your dad is getting ready to attack us, that damn fae assassin is running around in Atlanta, people are being boiled, some ass is sending you boxes with flowers and knives and delegations of screwed-up monsters, our son was crying, and that idiot from Sunshine Realty called again asking if we wanted to sell our house. So, I squeezed the phone and it broke. I'll buy us a new one."

"I changed my mind," I said. "Instead of sparring, let's go and take a nice long bath while the kid is asleep."

"Mmm." His expression took on a speculative tint.

"Although with our luck, he'll wake up as we go up the stairs."

"I'll carry you," he told me. "It will be quieter."

"No, it won't."

"You stomp like a rhino."

"I glide like a silent killer."

His eyes shone. "A cute rhino."

"Cute?"

"Mm-hm."

"See, now you've sealed your fate. I'll have to kill you . . ."

He kissed me. It started tender and warm, like wandering through a dark, cold night and finding a warm fire. I sank into it, seduced by the promise of love and warmth, and suddenly it deepened, growing hot, hotter, scorching. His hand slipped into my hair. I leaned against him, eager for the heat . . .

"Get a room!" George called from across the street.

Damn it. We broke apart. Out of the corner of my eye I saw George drop a trash bag into the can. She was grinning.

Golden sparks shone in Curran's eyes, so bright his eyes glowed. Well, how about that?

"We are going upstairs and taking that bath," he said. "I'm not too proud to beg."

Neither was I, and if he kissed me again, he would find that out. "What if our son wakes up and starts banging on the bathroom door while we're busy in the tub?"

"I'll threaten to wash him, and he'll go right back to sleep."

He took my hand, kissed my fingers, and we went upstairs.

≈ CHAPTER ≈

8

THE PROBLEM WITH having a son who'd discovered he was a shape-shifter was twofold. First, Conlan was a hyperactive toddler. Second, lions are cats, and cats like pouncing. They especially like pouncing on their happily sleeping parents and then bouncing up and down on the bed, flexing their claws.

"It's six . . ." *bounce* "in the morning." *Bounce.* "I thought . . ." *bounce* "you hunted . . . in the evening."

"We're . . ." *bounce* "adaptable." *Bounce.* "Lions . . . are . . . crepuscular . . . active in . . . twilight."

"Can we . . . make him . . . less active?"

Curran grabbed Conlan and pinned him down. "Stop annoying your mother."

"*Rawrarawara!*"

"Why is he shifting all the time? Shouldn't he shift once or twice every twenty-four hours and then pass out?"

"He's special," Curran said, holding Conlan down with one hand.

I groaned and put a pillow on my face. We'd had a late night and it was so worth it. But I could've really used another hour of sleep. Or five.

"I can take him to the backyard," Curran offered.

"No, I'm up." I crawled out of bed. "He must've been too tired from all the shape-changing to wake up last night. Now we're paying for it."

"See? There are some benefits to shifting."

"Sure . . ." I dragged myself into the bathroom. I would need a big cup of coffee and at least two aspirins to make it through the morning.

When I came downstairs, Derek and Julie were in our kitchen. The box was still on the table, together with several symbol encyclopedias. I gave Derek a bleary-eyed look of doom. "Why are you up?"

"Curran wants me to come to the Guild."

I grabbed a cup of coffee and sat down next to Julie. "Anything?"

"It might be a symbol for intellect in Islamic mysticism. If you break the symbol into blaze symbols, it spells out Very Good—Doubtful—Very Good. It may or may not be a part of Illuminati cipher. I'm reasonably sure it's not a hobo sign."

I sighed. We had people being murdered and ancient abominations running through the streets, but yay, at least the hobos weren't about to invade.

I looked through the stack of Julie's notes. The symbol looked like something. I just couldn't recall where I'd seen it.

Curran walked into the kitchen, carrying Conlan in human-baby form. The kid changed shapes faster than I could count.

"Roland is preparing for an invasion," Curran said. "We found out yesterday."

Both Julie and Derek paused.

"So, what does that mean?" Julie asked. "War? When?"

"We don't know," I said. "It depends on how he goes about it. He hasn't brought Hugh back from his exile, or we would've heard about it, so at least we're winning there."

"D'Ambray might still prove a problem," Curran said.

"I doubt it. It's been years since he gave any signs of life," I murmured, flipping through the pages. One of Julie's drawings showed a wavy line inside the circles with two dots in the center. I'd definitely seen that before, but where?

"Maybe he's married and living happily in some castle somewhere," Julie said.

I barked a short laugh. "Hugh?"

She didn't answer, so I looked up. Julie had a stubborn look on her face, the line of her jaw firm. Right. Me and my big mouth. Hugh had been bound to my father in the same way Julie was bound to me. He was her only example of what the future held for someone who was bound by our blood. I kept forgetting that every time Hugh was brought up, I needed to take care with what I said.

"I know you want him to find redemption, but that's not who Hugh is. He is a wrecking ball. He destroys. If he hasn't come back to kill me or any of us by now, he's probably dead. Marriage and settling down isn't for him. It doesn't mean it's not for you, but it's not for him."

"Sometimes you can be really closed-minded," she said.

"Sometimes you hero-worship the wrong person, and when they fail you, it hurts."

She gulped the rest of her tea and got up. "I've got to go to the Warren. Somebody is drawing these signs on the walls. I put out some feelers yesterday, so I have to go see if they pay off."

"Wait. What about this?" I showed her the wavy drawing.

Julie grimaced. "When I see magic, sometimes it's clear or radiant and sometimes it's hazy, more like fog. The magic on the box was like fog. It shifted and wavered and kind of curled inside the circles into a pattern. I don't know if it's intended or just magic interference." She turned to the door.

"Be careful," I told her.

"I was planning on blundering straight into danger without any preparation, but now that you told me, I will totally be careful."

"Blunder all you want," I told her. "When you get into trouble, I'm not saving you."

"Ha! You will totally save me." She stuck her tongue out at me and headed out the kitchen door to the stables for her horse.

"The pervert's right," Curran said. "You're contagious."

"Mm-hm." The symbol definitely looked like something now. I stared at the wavy pattern. Where had I seen it before . . . ?

Curran rested his hand on my shoulder. I touched his hand.

"What's the plan for today?" he asked me.

"I'm going to the office and chaining myself to the phone. I've called everyone and their mom about Serenbe, so I'm going to touch base and see if anyone found any similar occurrences. Then I'm going to call about yed-dimur and see if anyone got any insights from our creatures. Then I might drop by the PAD and see if they recognize our blond dude."

"Take the Jeep. I'll ride with Derek and buy us a second car this afternoon."

"Thanks." Score, I got the Jeep. "Adora should be coming back from a gig this morning."

I'd called the Guild last night, and the Clerk told me Adora was on a harpy stakeout and due to return to the Guild this morning.

"I'll tell her to come here to watch Yu Fong. George and Martha will be out today," Curran said. "I can take the boy with me to the Guild."

"Don't you have the budget meeting?"

"I don't mind."

The Guild budget meetings were like intrigues from the Spanish Court: complex, rife with tension, and frequently dramatic. The last thing we needed was Conlan reacting to all that. My imagination painted my son in half-form dashing about as a bunch of mercs chased him with nets.

"I can take him with me to Cutting Edge, and then I'll meet up with you at the Guild. It will buy you some time for the meeting."

"As you wish," Curran said.

WHEN I GOT to Cutting Edge, the light on my answering machine was blinking. When I pushed play, it hissed with static and told me in Luther's voice, "Come see me. I've got something for you." Experience told me that calling Luther would be pointless. Since nobody else left me any enlighten-ing messages, I packed Conlan back into his car seat and we set off for Luther's lair.

Biohazard, or the Center for Magical Containment and Disease Prevention, as it was officially known, occupied a large building constructed of local gray granite. A tall stone wall, topped with razor wire and studded with silver spikes, stretched from the sides to enclose a large area in the back of the center. Several howitzers and sorcerous ballistae topped the roof. The place looked like a fortress. Biohazard took the containment part of their job seriously.

I grabbed Conlan out of his car seat and walked through the big doors into the cavernous lobby. Conlan stuck his hand into his mouth and looked around at the high granite walls, big eyes opened wide. The guard on duty at the desk waved me on without a second glance. I was a frequent visitor.

I carried Conlan up the stone stairs, past people hurrying back and forth, and turned right into a long hallway. Luther's lab lay through the second doorway on the right. Its tall heavy door stood wide open. Music drifted on the breeze, David Bowie singing about putting out fire with gasoline. Conlan squirmed in my hands.

The magic washed over us. The music died, cut off midnote. The black specks of tourmaline embedded in the granite buzzed with energy and glowed as the magic coursed through them. Conlan swiveled his head like a surprised kitten.

"Baddadada . . ."

"Shiny."

"Shaaai."

"That's right. Shiny."

I walked to the wall and let him touch it. He tried to scratch the dark shiny specks out of it, then leaned forward to the wall and licked it.

A woman wearing scrubs passed by us and gave me a weird look.

"That's one good thing," I murmured to Conlan. "We don't need to worry about germs anymore."

Luther packed a lot of magic power, thought for himself, and wasn't afraid to take risks. His work space reflected that. Several fire-retardant lab tables bordered the walls, filled with microscopes, centrifuges, and other bizarre equipment, spawned by the need to perform research through the constant seesaw of magic and tech. A decontamination shower occupied the far corner. The wall on the left supported a shotgun, a fire extinguisher, a flamethrower, and a Viking-style axe. The sign above the odd collection said, PLAN B.

Usually a metal examination table occupied the center of the room. Today it was pushed to the side. A large chalk-and-salt circle marked the sealed concrete floor. Luther stood in the circle, eyes closed, hands raised in front of him. He wore scrubs that had been washed and bleached so many times, nobody could determine their original color without some serious divination.

"This is Luther," I told Conlan. "He's an important wizard. He's also weird. Really weird."

"I can hear you, infidel," Luther said. "It puts its sword into the box or it doesn't enter."

I sighed, pulled Sarrat out of the sheath on my back, and placed it in the wooden box on the metal table by the entrance. This had been a constant ritual ever since I was pregnant. Luther claimed that Sarrat's emissions interfered with his diagnostic equipment.

"And the knife."

"Why the knife? It's not magic."

"You think it's not magic. Everything you handle on a daily basis is stained with your magic. Just because you can't see it doesn't mean it's not there."

I arched my eyebrow at him.

"Box," Luther intoned, as if it were a Buddhist prayer.

I pulled my knife out and dropped it in the box. My shark-teeth throwing blades followed, together with my belt.

"Satisfied?"

"Yes."

"Should I put the baby in the box, too?"

"He wouldn't fit."

I sighed.

"What are you doing?"

"Cleaning my work space. I wish people would stop taking weird crap out of Unicorn Lane and then calling us panicking when it tries to eat the children."

"You're right, they should just let it devour their young."

"Har-har. So funny. As it happens, I had to drop everything and do an emergency analysis of a child-threatening item yesterday, and the tech interrupted me, so I had all sorts of residual mess in this containment field."

He clenched his hands into fists. A pulse of magic burst from him, drenching the circle. "There. Good to go."

He stepped over the magic boundary and froze, his gaze fixed on Conlan. A moment passed. Luther sputtered and pointed.

"Yes, it's a human infant," I told him.

"Give!"

"I'll let you hold him if you swear by Merlin's beard." Because it would be funny.

"By Merlin's beard, whatever, give."

I handed Conlan to him. Luther took him, carefully, as if my son were made of glass. Conlan stared at him with his big gray eyes.

"Hello there," Luther said, his voice barely above a whisper. "Aren't you a wonder?"

The wonder farted.

I laughed.

"When did he awake?" Luther asked.

"Around six this morning."

"That's not what I am asking! When did his magic manifest?"

"A couple of days ago. Something scared him, and he reacted."

Luther gazed at my child in awe. They looked kind of adorable, my baby with his kitten eyes and head of soft dark hair and Luther, a slightly unkempt, eccentric wizard.

"It's like holding a nuclear bomb," Luther said.

"You ruined it."

"He's bursting with magic. Glowing with it. I had no idea this was inside him."

"He doesn't know how to cloak yet."

Luther squinted at me. "Is that what you look like? Show me."

Yes, and for my next trick I'll dance and sing a song. "No."

"I've analyzed your dead varmint for you. Free of charge."

"It was your duty as a public servant. You would've done it anyway."

"Kate! Don't be difficult."

"Fine."

I dropped my magic cloak. Luther blinked. He stepped forward very carefully, deposited Conlan into my hands, and stepped back.

A blond woman wearing scrubs appeared in the doorway. "What is it with all the magic splashing? Damn it, Luther, can't you control your . . ." She saw us and stopped. Her eyes widened.

"Wow," she said softly.

"I know, right?" Luther said quietly.

For a while they just looked at us. Conlan squirmed in my arms.

"Is this what we will be one day?" the woman murmured. "Future us?"

"This is what the past us were." Luther sighed. "Better put it away before Allen runs over here. We'll spend the whole day trying to get him to leave."

I hid my magic.

The woman lingered for a few moments, shook her head, and left. I sat Conlan down on the floor. He ran to the chalk circle, puzzled over the line, and reached out, waving his hand in front of his face.

"He feels the boundary," I told Luther.

"That's sickeningly cute." Luther grabbed a handle on one of the square metal doors on the wall and pulled a body shelf out. On it lay the remnants of my monster.

Conlan hopped in place by the chalk line, achieving about an inch of lift.

"Do you want to jump?" Luther said.

"Don't encourage him."

"It's good for him to try. It's a major developmental milestone. Toddlers learn to take tiny jumps around two years old. It's very exciting for them."

"How do you even know this?"

Luther spared me a look. "I have nieces. There is no harm. All he can do is a hop." He waved to Conlan. "Don't listen to your mom. You can do it. Jump!"

Conlan gathered himself into a tight ball. I'd seen Curran do this a hundred times.

"You can do it!" Luther prompted.

Conlan leaped three feet into the air, cleared a full twelve feet, and landed in the circle. Luther's jaw hung open.

Conlan giggled and jumped out of the circle. Then back in. Then out.

"So," Luther said. "He is a shapeshifter."

"Oh yes. You're slipping, Luther."

"I'm not slipping. He is emitting all sorts of magic, and I don't sniff or lick other people's children, even to diagnose their magic. That would be creepy."

In and out. In and out. When we got home, I would draw a circle for Conlan. It would keep him busy for a couple of minutes.

"He is a shapeshifter," Luther said again.

"We've established this fact."

He faced me. "Kate. He is a shapeshifter with magic."

"Dali is also a shapeshifter with magic."

"Dali is a sacred animal. Completely different. All her magic is divine-based. She curses and purifies. He is a shapeshifter and he has magic. Mountains of magic. Oceans of magic. There has never been anything like it."

Tell me about it. "Any progress with Serenbe?"

"So you're just going to blatantly change the subject."

"Yep. Any progress?"

Luther shook his head. "No."

"Nothing at all?"

"Nothing beyond what I sent you. The GBI is interviewing the surviving relatives. Nobody was courting the dark gods. Nobody was summoning anything. Most of them had little magic. There were a few plant mages and firebugs. The usual. One of them was an ex-merc. You might have known him. He went by Shock."

"Shock Collins?"

"Yes."

"He left the Guild when it almost went bankrupt. I had no idea he moved out there. You know for sure he disappeared?"

"Yes. We found his wallet in his house, with driver's license and Guild ID in it."

This was bad news. Shock Collins had been a careful, skilled merc, who turned nasty when cornered. He'd survived several bad gigs that should've killed him, and he could electrocute an attacker in a pinch. He wouldn't let himself be jumped.

"Signs of struggle in the house?"

"No."

"What the he . . . heck?"

Luther lowered his glasses and looked at me. I pointed to Conlan over my shoulder. Motherhood made you watch your mouth.

"I do have something on your furry monster friend," Luther said. "At first glance, it appeared to be a new species of post-Shift ugly, until we cut this hideous specimen open and played with his innards a little bit."

He pushed a metal table over to the body shelf and flipped the metal door up, revealing a handle. He grabbed the handle, pulled it, and the body neatly slid onto the examination table. Luther rolled the table forward, to a stand with a fey lantern. I followed.

He pulled back the sheet, revealing the neat autopsy scars. With it dead, the impact wasn't quite as strong, but the revulsion squirmed through me all the same.

"What do you feel when you look at it?"

"Hungry," Luther said.

"You need help," I told him.

"I haven't eaten breakfast today, or lunch."

"Seriously, Luther, do you get a sense of wrongness?"

"No."

I sighed.

"Unless you're referring to the corruption miasma so thick you can cut it with a knife and serve it with ketchup. Who do you think you're talking to? Of course I feel the miasma. You would have to be blind, deaf, and anosmic to not react to it, and even then, you would still feel it."

"Why does it do this?"

"Because she might have started as human."

"I figured as much. Julie said they were blue, so they likely had a human ancestor."

"No, not ancestor." Luther grimaced. "She was born human."

I pointed to the furry twisted creature. "That was born human?"

Luther coughed. "Yes. Probably."

"So, what is it, some strange form of loupism?"

"That was the working theory for a bit, but we found no Lyc-V in her system."

"Are you sure? Because they were really hard to kill."

"I'm sure. The body did undergo profound changes. All of the human organs are still there, but everything has been altered. The fascia, which is . . ." Luther coughed again. He sounded choked. ". . . fibrous connective tissue enclosing organs and musculature, has been . . . reinforced . . ." He doubled over, coughing.

Behind him, a cloud of emerald-green dust poured into the room through the doorway. The powder licked the boundary of the circle and recoiled.

Luther straightened. A puff of green powder escaped his mouth. His eyes stared at me, glassy and cold.

There were four feet between me and the circle. I cleared them in a single jump, caught Conlan in midleap, and backed away toward the center of the ward.

The dust filled the room now, shifting like diaphanous emerald veils all around us. Only the surface of the circle remained clear. And Sarrat and all my weapons were conveniently stowed in Luther's stupid box, deep in green dust. Great.

Luther stepped to the circle, rigid, like a marionette pulled by its strings. "Traitor," he hissed in a sibilant voice.

Conlan growled in my arms.

Oh good, it wanted to talk. "Who did I betray?"

"Stupid traitorous bitch. Unworthy."

Was this a box thing? "Of all the insults out there, this is what you come up with? Pathetic."

"He's done everything for you. You're not fit to lick shit off the soles of his boots."

"Shit eating is your job." The more I pissed it off, the more it would talk and the faster I would figure out what the hell was going on. "Try harder."

Luther moved in short jerks. He was fighting whatever it was. He was also a distraction. If you wanted to launch a surprise attack, it helped if your target focused her attention on someone else. Luther was meant to keep me preoccupied. When the attack came, it would be at my back. I was still holding Conlan. I would have to drop him to defend us and trust that he'd stay in the circle. He was only a year old. He had no sense. He licked walls and ate soap, for crying out loud.

"He gave you life."

Not a box thing. A Roland thing.

"He is God. He is life. He is holy. You're an abomination."

Only one group of people thought Roland was holy and their path to heaven. The dust belonged to a sahanu.

I rifled through my mental roster of sahanu Adora had told me about. This didn't match anyone in particular, but she'd said that sahanu kept their powers hidden.

"My father is a liar." The spot between my shoulder blades itched. The sahanu had to be right behind me.

"Blasphemy!"

Religious fanatics. Reasonable and understanding people, easily persuaded by facts and logical arguments.

"There is no heaven waiting for you. He fed you lies and you gobbled it up. My father is too smart to ever become a god. When you accept godhood, your thoughts and your actions are no longer your own. You would know this if you weren't blind and deaf. Thinking for yourself, try it. It will help."

Using power words against my father's assassins was risky. Some of them had the benefit of my father's blood, which made a blowback likely. A lot of them used power words themselves. With Luther infected, there was a good chance that any power word I used would hit him as well.

Luther leaned forward, baring his teeth. "I'll kill you. I'll eat your flesh and then I'll eat your baby. I'll swallow his soft flesh and then I too will be a god."

Cold rage burst through me. The world turned crystal clear. "And what will my father do when he finds out you tried to devour his grandson?"

"He will praise me. He ordered your death. He wants your son brought to him, but I'll eat him instead."

When I finally got through to my father, we would have words.

"I'll suck the marrow out of your baby's bones and consume his magic. Then I will be even more powerful."

No, you won't. I sneered at Luther. I'd had a great role model when it came to sneering. Nobody did put-downs like Eahrratim, the Rose of Tigris.

"You and what army, sirrah? I'm the Princess of Shinar, the Blood Blade of Atlanta. My line stretches thousands of years into the past. My family was building palaces while your ancestors cringed inside their mud huts. You're weak, stupid, and less. What threat could you possibly be? You dream of power I already have. A tiger doesn't notice a worm she crushes under her paw. Slither, little worm. Slither away as fast as you can."

I felt the precise moment she charged out of the fog into the circle. I dropped Conlan and stepped back, twisting out of the way. My brain registered the attack in a fraction-of-a-second burst: lean blond woman, my size, my height, young, a dagger in each hand.

The right dagger stabbed the air an eighth of an inch from my chest. I grabbed her wrist with my right hand, aiming to smash her elbow with my left palm. She dropped into a crouch and slashed across my right bicep with her other dagger. A hot line of pain tore my arm, like a heated rubber band slapping against my skin. I swung into a kick. She raised her arms, covering up at the last moment, and rolled back. My foot barely tapped her. She rolled to her feet and leaped back into the green mist.

I stepped back to Conlan. He'd stayed exactly where I'd dropped him, hugging the floor. *Thank you, whoever you are upstairs, for the miracle. Thank you.*

Conlan sat at my feet. I stood still. My right arm burned with pain. She was damn fast, and her daggers were razor-sharp. The bleeding wasn't heavy. I could seal it, but it wouldn't last. The moment I used the arm, I would bleed. That was fine. I could use the blood.

The fog flowed back and forth, shifting in shimmering patterns. I waited, every sense straining for a hint of movement, a whisper of sound. Something.

Moments crawled by.

Conlan turned his head slightly to the left. I kept my gaze on the mist, watching him with my peripheral vision. He turned more. A little more.

My son was a shapeshifter and a predator. With supernatural hearing.

I kept looking to the right, toward Luther.

A moment.

Another.

Another . . .

She charged out of the mist to my left, leaping. I took a quick step with my right foot to pick up momentum and hammered a sidekick into her. My foot connected with her ribs. Bone crunched. The impact knocked her back into the haze.

I waited. Conlan was turning to the right now. That had to hurt. She'd try to cover up that side now.

A low, animalistic grunt came from Luther. It sounded half-bestial, half-obscene. The grunts kept coming. Noise screen. She was trying to muffle her footsteps.

"I can still hear you, worm." I raised my hand and beckoned, loading every drop of arrogance I had into my voice. "Come to me. Accept your death with grace."

Luther fell silent, but the sahanu stayed hidden. Damn. For some reason the jeering worked for my aunt much better than it did for me. I needed more practice.

Conlan turned right. I had no idea how I knew the strike would come low. I didn't see it or hear it, but something told me he was the target. I dropped into a crouch, clutching him to me, shielding him with my body.

The dagger shot out of the dust and sank into my left shoulder, barely an inch in.

Moron. Throwing only worked in movies.

I jerked the blade out and spun to my feet barely in time to block her slash as she came charging into the circle. She stabbed, and I sliced across her arm. Blood wet my dagger. *Thank you for the knife, asshole.*

The sahanu erupted into a flurry of slashes and stabs. I closed the distance, working her, fast and fluid.

The colors, the noises, her movements, her blue eyes; everything became so clear and sharp, it almost hurt.

When I was eight, Voron took me to a man called Nimuel. His name meant "peace" in his native Tagalog, and that was exactly what his opponents found when they came at him with a knife. As I worked her, blocking her arms with my own, wrapping my fingers around her wrists, using my wrists to channel her strikes, cutting her forearms, I heard his calm voice in my head. *Under the bridge, on top of the bridge, over the bridge, inside, outside . . .*

She would not touch a hair on my son's head.

The sahanu snarled, stabbing and stabbing, and finding only air. I nicked her a dozen times, but she was so fucking fast.

Over the bridge . . . Open the window.

I countered a moment too slow. Her dagger painted a bright red line on my left arm. While she was busy cutting, I drove my dagger into her side.

She tore away from me, taking the dagger with her.

I clamped my arm on my wound and hurled my blood at her, the drops turning into needles midflight. They sank into her face.

She dashed to the mist. I charged after her, but she dove into the green. Shit.

Behind me, magic shifted.

"Not in my house!" Luther roared.

Magic exploded out of him and tore through the room, freezing the green smoke screen. The dust exploded, each emerald dot blooming into a tiny white flower. They floated down in a shockingly beautiful rain, stirred by the slightest draft, and I saw the sahanu ten feet from me, her face stunned, her mouth with sharp inhuman teeth gaping open.

Teeth.

I charged, swiping a heavy microscope off the lab counter.

It's very hard to stop someone charging at you full force, especially when your back is against the wall.

She slashed at me, and I smashed the microscope against her dagger. The blade clattered to the floor. I reversed my swing and drove the microscope at her jaw. Blood flew. The blow knocked her back. She reeled, clawing at me. I hammered the microscope into her face. That one dropped her. I landed on her before she had a chance to roll to her feet and brought the microscope down like a hammer. Blood flew, thick and red.

Eat this, you bitch.

I hit her again and again, with methodical precision, driving the weight in my hand into the strike zone between her eyes. Her face was a mush of bone and blood, but I had to make sure she was really dead.

"Kate!"

Another blow. The red spray of her blood stained the tiny white flowers swirling around us.

"Kate!" Luther barked next to me, his voice sharp. "She's dead."

He was right. She was dead. I hit her again, just to be sure, straightened, and handed him the bloody microscope.

Conlan cried.

Oh no.

I sprinted to him and scooped him up off the floor. "I've got you. I've got you. Mama's got you."

He wailed. I realized my hands were bloody. I got sahanu blood on his clothes.

Conlan cried, his voice spiking, tears wetting his cheeks.

"Shhh." I rocked him. "It's okay. It will be okay. I've got you. Mommy's got you. I won't let anyone eat you. I'll kill every last one of them."

He couldn't possibly understand that she had been about to eat him. What the hell was coming out of my mouth?

I rocked back and forth. Conlan wailed and wailed, tears falling from his gray eyes. Oh dear gods, I'd traumatized my child. I'd beaten a person to death in front of him. He would be scarred for life.

"Do you have any food?"

Luther ran over to the fridge and flung it open. Salad, a pitcher of tea, a jar of honey.

"Honey," I told him.

He brought the jar over. I held Conlan's hand out. "Pour some on him."

Luther got a spoon and scooped a big dollop of honey onto Conlan's hand.

Conlan sniffled and licked his hand. For a moment he wasn't sure it wasn't a dirty trick, and then he stuck his hand into his mouth.

"Babies shouldn't have honey," Luther said, his voice slightly wooden. "It can contain *Clostridium botulinum*. It's a bacterium that causes—"

"Botulism. I know. He's a year old. It's safe. Also he's a shapeshifter and his werebear grandparents have been feeding him honey since he could hold a honey muffin in his hand, no matter what I said, and then lied to my face about it."

"How do you even know about botulism?" Luther asked.

"When I was pregnant, I couldn't do much, so I read all the books. I know all of the bad things that can happen." I hugged Conlan to me. "I know about roseola and RSV and gastroenteritis. His biggest problem isn't catching whooping cough. It's that his delusional megalomaniac grandfather is trying to kill him."

I kissed Conlan's hair. Nobody would touch my son. Not a hair on his head.

Conlan leaned against me and pointed at the body. "Bad."

"Yes," I confirmed. "Bad. Very bad."

He was okay. I'd beaten her to a pulp and he was okay. It would be okay now. I just needed to breathe. The fury was choking me.

He'd ordered a hit on me. He'd put his grandson's life in danger. The prophecy and all the visions of the future I'd received told me my father would try to kill him, but to feed him to his pet assassins, that was beyond even Roland.

Luther pushed a stool to me.

I sat.

He looked at the dead sahanu. "The temerity to attack me with plant magic in my own house."

"Only you would use a word like 'temerity' at a time like this."

He stared at her ruined head. "I've never seen you scared before."

"Well, I've never seen you turn a room full of mind-controlling spores into a flower snowstorm before."

Luther blinked.

"Miasma?" I told him. "You were telling me about the changes in the creature's body."

He stared at me as if I were speaking Chinese, then shook himself. "The creature. Right. Why do you vomit when you see and smell somebody else vomit?"

"I don't know."

"It's a biological survival mechanism. Primitive humans existed in family groups. They slept in the same place and they ate the same things."

Pieces clicked together in my head. "So, if one person vomited, they likely got poisoned, so everyone needed to vomit to not die."

"Yes. It's the same with the miasma. Your body is telling you that whatever made that woman into that furry creature is a critical danger to you. It must be destroyed."

A horrible thought occurred to me. "Do you think it might be contagious?"

"I can't confirm it's not."

Curran and Derek would be immune. Lyc-V would kill the invading pathogen. Julie had my blood. She should be immune as well. But what about other people?

"Did Tucker's corpse turn?"

"No. I checked on him last night in the morgue and again this morning. Whatever this bug is, it must need a living host."

"You're telling me that if these things are contagious, they could infect the whole city?"

"Pretty much. We might have a version of our own zombie apocalypse on our hands."

We looked at each other.

"I need something to drink." Luther jumped off his stool, pulled a flask from the fridge, and held it out to me. I shook my head. He brought it to his lips and took a swig. The lines of his face eased.

"What is that?" I asked.

"Artisanal Dutch cocoa. Fifty percent sugar by volume. Made it this morning just in case of an emergency. You don't know what you're missing." He raised the flask. "To the shiny baby and not getting killed."

The shiny baby. Conlan couldn't cloak. He was emitting magic, like a lighthouse in the middle of a dark night. I hadn't even realized it. It just came on when he had shifted for the first time, and I'd just accepted it without any thought. It felt so natural and normal somehow. If any sahanu could sense magic, they would see him. They could track him. He was enough like me and my father that they would instantly recognize the signature. We were sitting ducks here.

I jumped off the stool and ran to the box.

"What is it?"

"I have to go." I jerked the lid open, set Conlan on the floor, and grabbed my belt. Conlan grabbed at my pants, hugging my leg.

"You're bleeding."

"I have to go, Luther."

"Kate? Kate!"

I thrust my knife into its sheath and slid Sarrat into its sheath on my back. I didn't bother with the shark teeth. They would take too long. I picked up Conlan and took off running down the hallway. People were rushing our way as the rest of Biohazard woke up to the fact that something had gone wrong. I tore past them, took the stairs two at a time, busted out the door, and dashed to the car, scanning the square for danger.

I started chanting twenty feet from the vehicle, thrust Conlan into the car seat, took a precious second to buckle him, and got into the driver's seat, locking my seat belt. Minutes stretched by as the enchanted water engine warmed up. I'd give my left arm to be able to turn the key and get the hell out of here.

Finally, the magic motor turned over. I sped out of the parking lot and almost collided with another vehicle, an armored SUV that had more in common with a tank than a car. I veered right but still caught a glimpse of the driver. Knight-abettor Norwood. I took the corner at a dangerous speed. The last thing I needed now was the knights of the Order asking idiotic questions.

I had to get to a safe place, somewhere where Conlan and I would be protected, somewhere close. I couldn't afford to get stuck in traffic. The Guild was too far. My office was, too. That left only one location. It was safe, secure, and only three miles from me. Three years ago, if someone had told me I would be running there for a safe haven, I would've laughed in their face. They had been the enemy for as long as I could remember. Life was an ironic bitch.

I stepped on the gas.

I WALKED INTO the Casino covered in blood and carrying my son. To the left of me a vast gaming floor offered card tables and slot machines, reconfigured to run during magic. Men and women fed tokens into the machines amid flashing lights; the ball rolled around the roulette wheel; cards fell on purple velvet, all under the watchful eyes of Casino staff, most of them apprenticed to the People, dressed in black pants and purple vests. To the right lay the bar and the patrons drowning their sorrows or celebrating an unexpected win. They might as well have been deaf and blind. Straight ahead was the house counter flanking the stairway leading up and down.

A cacophony of noises hung in the air, a shroud of sound that drowned out voices and footsteps. For a brief moment nobody noticed me. Then the young journeyman at the counter looked up. His name popped into my head—Javier. I'd met him before, during my visits to the Casino. Ghastek had found him in Puerto Rico.

The journeyman's gaze connected with mine. Javier mashed something on his console.

Shutters lowered, shielding the windows. Behind me the massive doors clanged closed. Nobody paid it any attention. A panel in the ceiling slid open, and four vampires dropped through. Gaunt, hairless, little more than skeletons wrapped in dry muscle and tight skin, they surrounded me on four sides, padding in their odd jerky gait in time with my steps. Their minds, each ridden by a navigator, burned in my head like four sharp red points of light. If they wanted to contain me, they'd need a hell of a lot more bloodsuckers.

The vamps moved into formation, one in front of me, its back to me, one behind, and two at my flanks. The light dawned. They weren't there to contain me. They were my bodyguards.

Javier accelerated toward me. "May I escort you to the infirmary, In-Shinar?"

"I don't have time for the infirmary. I need to see Ghastek."

"Please follow me." He headed toward the staircase, murmuring. "Belay medic at the main floor. I need medic at Legatus. In-Shinar and the heir are en route."

A rapid staccato of heels clicking on marble came from the staircase. Rowena burst onto the scene. Her fiery hair fell in a long artful cascade down her back. Her dress, the deep brown of smoky quartz, hugged her perfect figure, staying just a hair on the right side of the line between professional and seductive. Her heels were four inches high. Her skirt was narrow. She was ten years older than me, and she ran down the stairs like a gazelle who'd spotted a lion in the tall savanna grass.

"Thank goodness. I was so worried."

She rushed to me, green eyes opened wide, grabbed Conlan out of my bloody hands, and cooed. "There, there. Aunt Rowena has you now. You are all safe." She turned and hurried down the staircase, carrying my son into the bowels of the Casino.

I looked at my bloody hands for a second, then glanced at Javier. "It's good she was worried about me. We are distant cousins. You can see the family love."

"Yes, ma'am," the journeyman said.

At least he didn't "lady ma'am" me. Thank goodness for small favors.

I hurried to catch up with Rowena. We went down the staircase, through the labyrinth of twisted, branching hallways, and into a cavernous room. Rows and rows of vampire holding cells filled the floor, set in widening sections radiating from the round platform at the center of the room. The bloodsuckers, secured by thick chains, snapped at us as we walked by, their eyes glowing, their foul magic polluting my mind like dirty smears on a window.

Ahead Rowena stopped, holding Conlan. My son sniffed at the vampires and grimaced.

"Daa phhhf!" Conlan declared.

Yep, phhhf *is right.*

We followed Rowena up the staircase to a room raised above the floor. Two-thirds of it was tinted glass. It served as Ghastek's office, and from there he could survey his entire vampire stable. His predecessor had sat on a golden throne in the cupola of the Casino, but Ghastek was a scientist at heart. He never strayed too far from his subjects.

My vampire escort fell away and lined up in a row at the bottom of the stairs, sitting on their haunches like mutant hairless cats. Javier invited me up the stairs with a sweep of his hand. I climbed after Rowena into Ghastek's domain. He stood with his arms crossed, silhouetted against a window, a tall thin man in a black shirt, charcoal pants, and expensive dark shoes. All of the Masters of the Dead dressed as if they anticipated being ambushed with a surprise board meeting, but since he'd become my Legatus, Ghastek had been steadily moving away from suits and corporate-slick toward clean and comfortable clothes, more suitable to a wealthy academic researcher than a captain of industry. As I entered, a vamp scuttled out of the small kitchenette on the side and set a cup of coffee on the polished black granite of Ghastek's desk.

My Legatus peered at me, his eyes sharp on a narrow face. "What happened?"

"Sahanu."

Ghastek pivoted toward the journeyman. "Initiate Counter-Invasion Protocol One, Sierra Delta, Target Group Charlie."

"Yes, sir. The medic team is closing on the office. Should I ask them to wait?"

"Yes," I said.

"No," Ghastek said. "Send them in immediately. Aside from them, I do not want to be disturbed."

"Yes, sir."

"That will be all, Javier."

The journeyman made a shallow bow, or a deep nod, it was hard to tell, and left, closing the door gently behind him. Through the glass I saw him walk down the steps and park himself next to the vampires.

Ghastek faced me. "As I recall, we discussed this possibility thirteen months ago. We both agreed that it wasn't a matter of if Roland would try to obtain your child but when."

"The sahanu who attacked us didn't want to obtain Conlan. She wanted to eat him."

"What?" Rowena drew back. "His own grandson?"

"I'm sure that wasn't part of the plan," Ghastek said. "It makes no sense. Your son is too important to be wasted like that."

"My father kidnapped a bunch of children, imprisoned them in a fortress, and brainwashed them into believing he is a god to mold them into fanatical assassins. Then he turned them loose in the world on a suicide mission without any supervision. You're right, he couldn't possibly anticipate anything going wrong with that plan. I need to call him."

A woman hurried to the door, carrying a bag, two men behind her. Ghastek shook his head. The woman and the men went down the stairs and went to stand by Javier.

"We've been over this," Ghastek said. "One doesn't simply call your father. Especially not now and not from this place."

"We've betrayed him," Rowena said. "All of our contacts are cut off."

"Do I look like an idiot?" I asked.

Ghastek raised his eyebrows.

"I know my father and I know you. He has spies among your people, and you figured out who they are ages ago, and now you're sitting on them."

Rowena smiled. Conlan wiggled out of her arms and padded across the floor to the vampire that sat motionless by Ghastek's desk. My son and the bloodsucker stared at each other, their noses inches apart.

Ghastek grimaced. "I liked you better as a merc."

"Well, too bad, because I spent two years knee-deep in Pack politics, and I know how you operate. Get me a phone number, Ghastek."

Ghastek inhaled. "No."

I spoke slowly, sinking menace into my words so there wouldn't be any misunderstanding. "What do you mean, no?"

Ghastek leaned against his desk, braiding his long fingers into a single fist. "We are aware of three people who report to Roland. Of those three, one is a second-year journeyman and two are apprentices, both of whom are wavering in their devotion to your father since you personally singled them out with your goddess routine."

The goddess routine involved me radiating magic during a tech wave. "You insisted on the goddess routine. You claimed it would boost morale."

"It did. Do you really think that any of these three would have a direct line to your father? They don't. They report to someone and that someone reports up to someone else and so it goes, up a very tall ladder that may reach your father or may terminate with the Legatus of the Golden Legion or any of half a dozen people in Roland's inner circle. These contacts are best used for subterfuge and disinformation. I won't let you throw them away so you can yell at your parent."

"Be very careful with words like 'let,'" I told him.

"If you wanted someone who always said yes, you should've picked someone else."

"I'm reviewing the error of my ways," I told him. "He gave an order that resulted in one of those freaks trying to eat my son. Conlan is probably traumatized for life because he watched me kill a woman in front of him."

"Your kills are usually quick," Rowena pointed out. "Maybe he didn't notice."

"He noticed."

Conlan raised his hand, fingers outstretched, as if they had claws, and slapped the vampire upside the face.

The undead remained unmoved.

"Your son doesn't look traumatized to me," Ghastek observed.

"I'm sure this will surface as a repressed memory fifteen years from now."

Conlan smacked the vampire again.

"Stop," I told him.

"What a shame," Ghastek murmured. "He isn't even trying to pilot."

Conlan raised his hand.

"Har." No. The ancient word rolled off my tongue, suffused with magic. I was too keyed up.

Conlan dropped his hand, backed away from the vampire, and came toward me, his hands raised. "Up."

I swung him onto my hip. My right arm screamed.

"Oh my God," Rowena whispered. "He understood."

Of course he understood. "Erra sings to him in Shinar every night. He speaks it better than English at this point." I petted his hair. "I need to speak to my father, Ghastek. You're my Legatus. Make it happen."

Ghastek leaned over to the window and knocked on the glass. The woman ran up the stairs and opened the door.

"Just you, Eve," Ghastek told her.

She shut the door behind her and crouched by me. "May I treat you, In-Shinar?"

Given that my arms burned like fire, it was probably a good idea. I turned to Rowena, and she took Conlan from me and smiled at him. "There is my little prince."

Conlan petted Rowena's fiery hair and made a cute noise.

I tried to take off my shirt. Pain shot all the way through my shoulder. Nope.

"You'll have to cut it," I said.

Eve opened her bag and took out a pair of scissors.

Conlan cooed, looking like the most adorable child, all innocence and light. The kind of child who would never turn into a monster and eat raw mice in the woods with his father. My son was a con man.

Eve cut my right sleeve. It fell apart. I sent a pulse of magic through the fabric, and black powder rained from it onto the floor. The last thing I wanted was my clotting blood everywhere.

Rowena gasped.

The cut on my bicep was pretty deep. It had turned an odd color of green, too. I'd thought something didn't feel right. The bitch had poisoned me.

"Keep going," I told Eve.

The scissors slid up my arm. My shirt fell away, leaving me in a sports bra. A dozen shallow cuts, blooming with green, covered my arms. My shoulder blade burned where the dagger had embedded itself.

Rowena put her hand over her mouth.

"Why didn't you say something?" Ghastek demanded.

"The medic was on the way."

"You look like you've been through a tornado of knives," Rowena said.

"She had two daggers. I had no weapons, because Biohazard makes me surrender them before I go into their lab. I couldn't use power words because Luther was at risk. I bludgeoned her to death with my bare hands and a microscope."

The two Masters of the Dead stared at me.

"She wasn't going to touch my son," I told them.

Ghastek turned to the medmage. "How bad is it?"

"The cut on the right arm is deep. Slow healing is best in this case. It will take three sessions over the next twenty-four hours if the magic wave holds."

"That won't work for me," I told her. "Fix the arm as much as you can. That's all I need."

She met my gaze. "If I do this all at once, it will be very painful."

"That's fine."

"I'll need to cleanse the wounds. They already closed. The poison is trapped inside."

I pulled on my cuts with my magic, calling on my blood. Red slid from the gashes. Eve shied back as if struck with a live wire.

"Is that enough?" I asked.

She swallowed and held up her hands. "Yes. Please stop."

I stopped the bleeding. A spark of magic and the blood streaking my skin turned to dust.

I held my arm out to her. Eve sat down next to me, touched my arm, her fingers cold on my skin, and began to chant. The burn in my wound exploded into ice, stabbing my muscles with a dozen sharp needles. She was a burst medic. Most medmages poured their magic into the body in a steady current, amplifying the natural regeneration. Burst medmages, who were much rarer, drove their magic into their patients, mending them like they were inanimate objects. They were excellent in emergencies, because they healed even the worst wounds fast, but the pain was excruciating.

Some terrible beast with icicle teeth bit my wound and began gnawing on it.

I unclenched my teeth before I did any damage to my jaw. "I need to speak to my father. The sahanu who attacked us isn't the only one. Razer is in the city, so there will be more."

A muscle jerked in Ghastek's face. "How do you know Razer is in Atlanta?"

"The Pack snapped a candid photo of him prancing on a roof near Sandy Springs some days ago."

The pain was almost unbearable now. I checked to see if my arm was still attached. It was.

Ghastek pushed a key on his phone.

"Yes, sir?" a male voice said.

"Prior to today, were you aware of any sahanu in the city?"

"No, sir."

"Razer was seen near Sandy Springs two days ago by the Pack. Is it our custom now to rely on the Pack for our intelligence?"

"No, sir."

"What's our mission?" Ghastek's voice was almost mild.

"To defend In-Shinar and the heir," the man responded, his voice clipped.

My arm was actually being torn off now. I wished I had something to bite on.

"Can we accomplish this mission without proper intelligence?"

"No, sir."

"Can you tell me why the Pack knows about the sahanu and we do not?"

Silence.

"I'm waiting," Ghastek said, his voice iced over.

"Uh-oh," Conlan assessed the situation.

"Uh-oh!" Rowena smiled at him. "Such a smart boy."

Oh no. Now she was encouraging him.

"Uh-oh!" my son told her.

"Uh-oh!" Rowena said.

"Uh-oh!"

Ghastek gave her a look. She turned away, walking a few steps toward the glass window. "Look there. Look at all the vampires."

The phone still offered only tortured silence.

"Can anyone there tell me why this is the case?" Ghastek ground out.

Silence.

"This is your chance to help me understand why I'm now facing an injured In-Shinar and having to explain our failure. Demonstrate to me that someone in the intelligence division has even the smallest modicum of intellect, or I'll replace the lot of you."

"The sahanu must've identified a pattern to our patrols," said a different voice.

"Who is this?" Ghastek asked.

"Journeyman Wickert, sir."

"Wickert, find the pattern and bring me your results."

Ghastek hung up.

The pain released me. I took a nice, deep breath and checked my arm. I couldn't even see the scar. Eve was a miracle worker.

The ice stabbed into the gouge on my left shoulder. I gritted my teeth. *Here we go again.*

Ghastek knelt next to me, his sharp face serious. "It's my fault. I take full responsibility for this failure. I'm sorry."

He bowed his head. I wished to be anywhere but here. *What do I do now?*

I waved Eve off and she stepped away. "Stop, Ghastek. We agreed. No kneeling, no bowing. I can't do it."

He stayed where he was. "Protecting you and your son is what we do. We exist to fulfill this purpose. We didn't know that girl was here. We didn't know Razer was here. It's a failure of leadership. If my people are incompetent, I didn't realize it. You have given me free rein over my subordinates. I restructured the People, I oversaw personnel assignments, I approved patrols. The ultimate responsibility for this is on me."

I finally understood. Ghastek prized competence above all else. He was deeply ashamed. He didn't want Kate, his friend, right now. Convincing him that he'd done nothing wrong wouldn't work. He needed absolution or punishment. He wanted the In-Shinar.

Something in me died a little. First Raphael, then Teddy Jo, now Ghastek. I would never again be just Kate. *You are the Princess of Shinar, the beacon of your people's hope, and if you succumb, that hope will perish with you.*

Sooner or later, in every relationship I had, I would end up becoming In-Shinar, and once I did, if only for a few moments, it altered that relationship forever. Mercs in the Guild remembered my voice shaking the building when I had spoken in the old tongue to the projection of my father. Shapeshifters who fought in the battle against Roland remembered In-Shinar's rage.

Once I showed my true face, people never forgot it.

I'd fought it so hard for these last three years, but in the end, it didn't matter. I had claimed Atlanta and everyone in it. I accepted responsibility for their safety. I was Sharratum na Shar. The queen who didn't rule, but a queen still the same.

I dropped my cloak and pulled the magic from the depths of my soul. It bubbled up to the surface like a geyser. If it'd had a voice, it would've whispered, *I'm awake. I'm alive.*

Eve knelt by my side.

"Mama!" Conlan said, the same way he'd tried to tell me that the shiny walls of Biohazard were pretty.

I reached for Ghastek and my skin glowed with pale gold. Gently I touched the right side of his jaw and made him look up at me.

"I forgive you."

The reverence in Ghastek's eyes almost broke me. He was a natural skeptic, but in that moment, he would've followed me off a cliff. It was the last thing I wanted.

"I forgive you," I repeated in English. "Keep my son safe. I have faith in you."

Ghastek just nodded quickly several times.

At least I still had Curran. Curran would always want me, Kate. He would be human with me. I was enough.

"Rise," I told him.

Ghastek got up to his feet. As he moved, I saw Javier and the other men staring at me from beyond the glass, awe in their eyes. Oh brother. Just what I needed.

I pulled the magic back, curling it inside myself like the petals of a closing flower. An odd emotion flickered through Ghastek's eyes, almost as if he wanted to stop me. Yep, In-Shinar was addictive, and if I kept showing my inner self to the people around me, soon I would be as bad as my father.

"Thank you for your help," I told Eve.

The medmage startled as if waking up from a trance. "Of course."

She gathered her bag and walked out. I waited until she cleared the stairs.

"She wasn't one of my father's spies, was she?"

"No," Ghastek said.

"Conlan doesn't know how to cloak. He's ridiculously easy to track if you can sense magic."

"Makes sense," Ghastek said, his voice and expression neutral.

"I thought about letting his grandparents watch him at the Keep."

"That might not be a good idea," Rowena said behind me.

"Why not?"

Ghastek walked to the desk, opened a drawer, and brought me a photograph. A shot of a wooded road in twilight. A man in his forties, salt-and-pepper hair, strong profile, walking between two shapeshifters in warrior form, a werejaguar and a bouda. I recognized both. Renders, the deadliest fighters the Pack had at their disposal. Jim wasn't taking any chances.

"This is Avag Barsamian," Ghastek said. "Landon Nez's second-in-command."

Landon Nez was Ghastek's counterpart, my father's right-hand necromancer and the head of his Golden Legion. Any time Nez got involved, things went from bad to worse.

I scrutinized the photograph. Avag was carrying a briefcase. He didn't appear to be in distress. The two shapeshifters flanking him didn't have their claws on him. The lines of their bodies suggested caution, but when guards transported a dangerous prisoner, they watched for outside threats, rescue attempts, and so on, because the person in their charge was properly restrained and unlikely to escape. These two watched Avag instead. He was there of his own free will.

I tapped the photograph. "I recognize this oak. This is the road to the Keep."

"He visited the Keep two nights ago," Rowena said. "I saw him through the eyes of my vampire. He was there for two hours and then he left, except this time he didn't have a briefcase. They escorted him just like that to his car parked on the side of the road."

And the next day Robert came to us with the offer of alliance.

"I was told my father is mobilizing. Is that true?"

"Yes," Ghastek and Rowena answered at the same time.

Wasn't that interesting. "The sixty-four-thousand-dollar question is, what was in the briefcase?"

"We don't know," Rowena said.

The vamp at Ghastek's desk rose, grasped a cord suspended from a roll of fabric above the window, and pulled it down, unrolling a large screen. On it, in painstaking detail, spread a map of Atlanta. In the center of the map sat a small red dot. A ragged ring of city blocks outlined in blue enclosed the dot, followed by another ring in green. Choppy lines crossed the whole thing, looking like some sort of Gordian knot. Colored dots marked other points of interest: the Casino, the Guild, and so on. The whole thing looked disturbingly like some distorted bull's-eye centered on . . .

"Why is there a red dot over my house?"

"I've had two years to prepare," Ghastek said. "The blue is the kill zone, the green is the outer perimeter. About"—he checked the clock on the wall—"twenty-two minutes ago, I doubled our patrols and deployed six strike groups, each member of which has memorized the dossier of the twenty-one sahanu in our database. They know their magic signatures, their movement patterns, and they will recognize them by sight. They will work in shifts around the clock and can be activated at a moment's notice, because they will sleep here in the Casino, next to the OPS room. I know we got off to a less-than-ideal start, but I personally guarantee to you that no sahanu will penetrate our defenses and get through to you."

And if he switched sides, the entirety of the Casino vampire stables could converge on my house and kill my child while I was out, thinking Conlan was safe and protected. He was unlikely to change sides, but then the Pack was equally unlikely to betray us.

Ghastek and Rowena were both looking at me.

"Okay," I said. "We'll do it your way."

"I won't fail you," Ghastek said. It sounded like a vow and I didn't like it.

"Do you still have the body of the creature I sent you?" I asked.

"Yes," Ghastek said.

"The creatures pose an imminent threat. If you encounter them, I want them followed, and if you can't follow them, I want them destroyed. My aunt recognized them and called them yeddimur."

"Understood," Ghastek said.

"It would mean a lot if you could analyze the body. Luther believes these creatures started out as human, and they may be contagious when alive. It would also be a great help if you could study the body or perhaps just display it somewhere where it may be observed by journeymen."

"And possibly apprentices?" Rowena asked.

"Yes. Perhaps someone could be overheard using the word 'yeddimur' when referring to the creature."

Ghastek frowned. "Why?"

"Because I want my father to know about it."

Ghastek thought about it. I could practically see the wheels in his head turning, but he didn't ask. He preferred to discover things on his own, and I gave him just enough to motivate him to continue digging. My hairy abomination would get top billing now at the People's dissection party.

I got up. "Do you have a copy of this photo?"

"We have others," Rowena said.

"Can I take this one?"

"Of course," she said.

I pocketed the photograph of Avag and took my son from her. Conlan yawned and flopped on my shoulder like a rag doll.

"I need an escort to my house."

"It would be our pleasure," Ghastek said.

The phone rang. Ghastek picked it up, listened, and turned to me. "Your husband is on his way to the Casino. He seems to be upset."

"How do you know?"

"He's running. There are two Guild vehicles following him, and they're having difficulty keeping up."

Curran didn't want to wait for the mercs. He ran much faster than an average human, but he was a lion, not a wolf. Long-distance running was never his thing. Either something bad had happened, or he'd found out about the fight at Biohazard and somehow tracked me down. The People worked for me now, but we'd been on opposite sides for so long that even though I'd spent a lot of time with them over the past months, every time I walked into the Casino, I snapped into alert mode. I didn't expect to be attacked, but I wasn't at ease either. Curran had never warmed up to the People. If he'd found out about what had happened at Biohazard and thought that Conlan and I were injured, he wouldn't just arrive at the Casino. He would land like a bomb.

I turned to the door, patting Conlan's back. "Let's go meet your dad outside before he causes an incident."

"I'll never understand what you see in that man," Ghastek said.

"He loves me," I told him, and escaped.

10

I PARKED MYSELF in front of the Shiva fountain. When Curran ran, he took on an odd shape, neither a lion nor a human but a strange beast: compact, powerful, built for speed. Most shapeshifters had two shapes, animal and human. Those with talent could hold a warrior form. I had never met anyone who could turn part of his body into one shape while keeping the rest in another. Except for Curran. He restructured his body for whatever purpose he saw fit.

A sticky warm puddle formed on my shoulder. Conlan drooled in his sleep.

Car horns blared. A man leaped over the vehicles that were stopped at a traffic light. He sailed over them like they were nothing, landed, and kept running, long legs pumping. That couldn't be . . . Yep, my honey-bunny running in human form.

I waited. He saw me. He didn't slow down; he just adjusted course.

A hundred yards. Seventy-five. Fifty. Damn, he was fast. He shouldn't be that fast, not after running for several miles.

Sweat slicked his hairline, darkening his blond hair. His *longer* blond hair. His hair was at least two inches longer than it had been this morning. Maybe more.

What the hell? The only time his hair grew into a mane was during a flare. We weren't due for one for another two years.

Twenty-five yards.

It's hard to look sexy with a drooling child on your shoulder, but I did my best. "Come here often?"

He slowed. For a moment I thought he'd stop, but he moved forward in a slow, sure way, not walking, but stalking, foot over foot. His hair was definitely longer. It framed his hard, handsome face. Gray eyes looked me over, checking for wounds. Our stares connected. A lion looked back at me and my heart sped up. Suddenly I was aware of every inch of distance between us.

He closed that distance, moving with a dangerous, borderline-feral edge. He looked like my husband, *was* my husband, but there was something alarming in the way he held himself. I turned to keep him in view.

He pounced. It was lightning quick, and if I'd wanted to get away, I wasn't sure I could've matched his speed. I didn't want to get away. His arms closed around me and he kissed me. The kiss scorched me, so intense it was almost a bite. I gasped into his mouth.

"Okay?" he asked me.

I had been until he kissed me. "Yes."

"Conlan?"

"Fine. Just tired."

He squeezed me to him. "What happened?"

"Had a run-in with a sahanu at Biohazard. You're crushing me."

He let me go.

"That's twice in two days. We have to stop meeting like this," I told him.

"Are you planning on continuing to run into fights?"

"I didn't run into her. She hunted me down."

Two Toyota Land Cruisers emerged from traffic and roared their way to the parking lot. Each of those carried eight people. Great. First, he dramatically ran over, then he kissed me like the world was ending in public, and now he'd brought a crew of mercs with him, enough for a small siege.

All the navigators piloting vampires on the walls of the Casino had to be loving the show.

"You brought two meat wagons with you? Did you expect to fight an army?"

"They followed me." He grinned at me, baring his teeth. "What happened to the sahanu?"

"She's dead. I'm not. The People patched me up. I need to talk to you. And Barabas."

"Good, because I'm not letting you go anywhere without me." Gently, he took Conlan off my shoulder.

"Letting?"

"You heard me."

The doors of the nearest meat wagon opened, and people waved at us.

"Where did you park?" he asked me.

I pointed at our Jeep on the left.

"I'll get the car," he said, and took off with Conlan.

Okay.

I trotted to the closest meat wagon. Faces looked at me, some dirty, some blood-spattered. Douglas, Ella, Rodrigo . . . Curran's elite team. The roar of the enchanted water engine was deafening, so I had to scream.

"What the hell are you all doing here?!"

"We followed him!" Ella yelled.

"So, what, you just pile into cars whenever he gets a thorn up his ass and chase him around the city?"

"We were on the job," Ramirez told me in his bass voice. "We were finishing up the gig when he said his wife was in trouble and took off."

"We chased him all the way from Panthersville," Ella added.

Curiouser and curiouser.

"Thanks for coming!" I told them.

"Where is the fight?" Douglas demanded.

"I already killed everybody," I said. "You gotta be faster next time."

They jeered at me, and I jogged to the Jeep. Five minutes later we rolled out of the parking lot.

"How did you know where to find me?"

"Just had a feeling," he said.

"That's it? A feeling?"

He nodded.

Odd.

Maybe it was me. Maybe I'd subconsciously called him while fighting. I'd have to ask Erra if that was possible.

"What's happening with your hair?" I asked.

"I don't know. It keeps growing."

"Are we about to have another flare?"

"I don't know. How bad was the fight?"

"It wasn't bad."

"Don't bullshit me," he said quietly. "You went to the Casino."

"I got scared. She said she would kill our son and eat him. I bashed her face in. It was overkill."

He reached over and squeezed my hand.

"Curran, he can't cloak. Ever since he turned, he's been shining like a star. And I was so used to having him with me, it didn't even occur to me that he can be tracked. That's how she found us. I put our kid in danger."

"It's okay." He squeezed my hand again. "You protected him. You will always protect him. You're his mother. They would have to kill both of us to get to him. Think about it."

They would have to go through the two of us. Many had tried before, and all of them had failed. Even my father.

"We've got this," he said. "We'll kill them all."

Our son snored in his car seat without a care in the world. As he should. Curran was right. We would kill them all.

ONCE UPON A time the Guild was housed in an upscale hotel on the edge of Buckhead. Tall buildings didn't weather magic well, and the hotel proved no exception. Its shiny tower had broken off and toppled, leaving a five-story stub. The Guild put a makeshift roof on it, cleaned it up a bit, and called it a day.

A couple of years ago, as the Guild teetered on the edge of bankruptcy, a giant had made some exciting modifications to the roof with his fists, which forced a remodel. About that time Curran and Barabas joined the Guild and eventually took it over. Barabas ran the admin side, Curran served as the Guild Master, and a year and a half ago, the mercs unanimously voted me in as a Steward, which meant whenever the mercs had problems or grievances with either of them, they ran to me and I fixed it. I'd needed the added responsibility like I needed a hole in the head. In fact, I wasn't even at the meeting, because I'd gotten held up getting a boggart out of a local middle school. The mercs conveniently voted in my absence and then presented me with the Steward's scroll when I showed up, dripping slime and picking trash out of my hair.

Bob, of the Four Horsemen, had held the unofficial position of Steward before me and apparently put himself in the running, but after he tried to raid the pension fund, his street cred took a beating. He never did warm up to either my or Curran's presence. His Furriness, never one to waste resources, sent him down to Jacksonville to run the brand-new satellite Guild. Within three months Bob tried to stage a coup and declare independence, and the Jacksonville Guild expelled him. We had no idea where he was or what he was doing.

One of the first things the three of us did was to fix the Guild itself. Curran fortified every place he frequently occupied. I had to talk him out of walling in our subdivision. But with the Guild, Barabas and I gave him free rein. Some battles weren't worth fighting.

The walls had been reinforced, the new masonry seamlessly blending in with the skeletal remains of the hotel. The upper floor sported arrow slits. A brand-new roof, equipped with four howitzers and four sorcerous ballistae, crowned the building. A massive metal door blocked the entrance, and behind it was a second door just in case someone breached the front. It was a wonder he didn't dig a moat around the place.

We parked and went inside. Conlan was still out, so Curran carried him in the car seat. The inside of the Guild matched the outside: clean, functional, professional. I nodded to the Clerk at his counter, and we made a left to the glass walls of Barabas's office.

The former Pack lawyer and current Guild admin sat behind his desk.

Lean, wiry, pale, Barabas brought a single word to mind: sharp. Sharp eyes, sharp teeth, sharp mind. Even his bright red hair, which stood straight up on his head, looking like a forest of needles, gave the impression of sharpness.

Christopher sat in a chair, reading a book. The first time I'd seen him, he'd been locked in a cage. He'd looked fragile and brittle, a ghost of a man, with hair so pale, it seemed colorless. Despite both Barabas and me trying to keep him eating, he had looked like that until about two years ago, when he finally remembered his powers. Christopher was a theophage. My father tried to merge him with Deimos, Greek god of terror. Christopher had resisted, and in a last desperate act of defiance, Christopher had shattered his own mind. As punishment, Roland had delivered what was left of Christopher into the tender care of his warlord, Hugh d'Ambray.

Now he was broad-shouldered and muscular, with a powerful athletic build. Where Barabas was all sharp lines and quick, precise movements, Christopher possessed a kind of quiet calm. Sitting in a chair now with a book, he seemed almost unmovable. Of course, the calm lasted only until Barabas or one of us was threatened, and then Christopher sprouted wings and fangs and went berserk. The human and divine had merged inside Christopher, with the man having the upper hand over the deity. Barabas was forever paranoid that people would start worshipping Christopher and that balance would tip the other way, but so far it hadn't happened.

They were so different. Christopher was in love with Barabas. Barabas loved him back, but since he'd taken care of Christopher while the other man's mind had been fractured, he faced an ethical dilemma. The last time we'd spoken about it, he'd been worried that Christopher's feelings weren't love but misplaced affection for a caretaker. Barabas didn't want to take advantage. They continued to live in the same house. They looked like a couple. They acted like a couple. Neither of them volunteered any information about their relationship. We respected their privacy, and nobody asked.

Both men looked up at us.

"Bad news?" Barabas asked.

"Yes." I shut the door behind us. Curran gently put Conlan on a big pillow on the floor. Shapeshifters had an unholy love of floor pillows, and even though Barabas spent most of his day in his chair, he refused to give his up.

I sat in the other chair.

Barabas sniffed in Conlan's direction. "What's different? Something's different."

"He shifted," Curran said quietly.

Barabas sat up straighter. Christopher's pale eyebrows crept up.

"Is he unusual like you?" Barabas asked Curran.

"He's worse," I said.

"Worse how?" Christopher asked.

"He can hold a warrior form," Curran said.

Barabas choked on empty air. "What do you mean, he can hold a warrior form? For how long?"

"For as long as he wants to," Curran said.

"Also, he's unable to cloak," I said. "So, anyone familiar with my or Roland's specific magic signature can track him down. We were attacked by a sahanu this morning. I killed her, but according to Robert, Razer is in the city. My father must've given a general order to kill my son. So there will be more."

Christopher leaned forward and rested his hand on mine. "Are you all right?" he asked quietly.

"I'm fine," I told him.

Christopher got up, poured a cup of hot tea from the kettle, and brought it to me.

"Thank you." I took the tea and drank.

"The Pack says Roland is mobilizing," Curran said. "What are the scouts saying?"

Scouts? "You have people watching Roland?"

"We," Curran told me. "*We* have people watching Roland."

"He's doing the same thing he did a year ago," Barabas said. "Pulling personnel in from neighboring states. Last time nothing came of it. This time, it's too early to tell."

"How do you know?" I asked.

"He has to move a large number of troops to Atlanta from the Midwest. Last time he sent people to evaluate the ley line route," Curran said.

Made sense. The ley line carried you forward at a high speed, but once it ended, it would spit you out at the ley point into the waiting arms of whoever wanted to ambush you there. There was no avoiding it.

"You didn't tell me?"

"You were in labor," Curran said.

"Doolittle categorically forbade it," Barabas said. "Anyway, nothing came of it. He must've decided the route was too vulnerable. This time he's going with trucks. He's been flirting with the local teamster guilds, and there is a rumor he's hiring mechanics."

"If he starts actively acquiring mechanics and drivers, I want to know about it," Curran said.

Barabas nodded.

"And trucks," I said. "He doesn't have enough trucks sitting around, and he won't be satisfied with just any trucks. He'll get top of the line, probably directly from the manufacturer, so they all match. He might even paint them gold."

"Would he steal them?" Barabas asked.

"No," Christopher said. "It's beneath him. He would take them as spoils of war, but he won't stoop to theft."

"We have two more immediate problems." I brought them up to speed on the box and the burning man parade. Christopher leaned forward, listening intently. When I finished, Barabas glanced at him. Christopher shook his head. "Doesn't ring a bell."

"So, what's the question?" Barabas asked.

"Doesn't matter. They killed Mr. Tucker. The answer is no," I told him.

Barabas glanced at Curran. "What do you want to do about this?"

"There is nothing we can do," Curran said. "We wait until this asshole shows his hand."

"You said there were two problems," Christopher said.

"We have to protect Conlan," I explained. "He's like a lighthouse shining in the night. The sahanu will be drawn to him. Curran and I have to be able to move around the city."

"We can take him to the bear clan house," Curran said.

He wouldn't like this part. I reached into my pocket, took out the folded photograph, and put it on the table. The three of them leaned in to look at it.

"Avag Barsamian," Christopher said, his eyes dark. "Landon's second."

"How dangerous is he?" Curran asked.

Christopher leaned back, one leg over the other, braiding his long fingers into a single fist on his knee. "He's one of the Golden Legion, so he's a formidable navigator. He's skilled in diplomacy in a way very few people are. When Avag negotiates, he crosses from savoir faire into art. He's cunning and cautious, and he has nearly infallible instincts. I used him on several occasions. They send him in when things are complicated."

"He was escorted into the Keep with a briefcase and came out without one," I said.

"How sure are you?" Curran asked.

"Rowena's vampire took the photos. They have others. The next day Robert brought us the offer of alliance from the Pack."

Nobody said anything. Barabas frowned. Curran's face turned inscrutable. Christopher pondered the wall.

"Also, this may or may not be related," I added, "but Raphael asked me to let Ascanio go."

"When?" Curran asked.

"The same day Avag brought them an offer."

"Did you?"

"I did. It's not about me or Clan Bouda. It's what Ascanio wanted."

Silence fell again.

I tapped my fingers on the table. "Something important was in that briefcase."

"It may have been a gift," Barabas said. "They brought a gift, Jim took the trinket, listened to what they had to say, and sent them on their way. I've seen Curran do that a dozen times."

"My father doesn't send trinkets. He poisons the flowers in your garden, and when your child sniffs one and becomes sick, he sends the antidote in a vial carved out of amethyst and corked with a diamond as a gesture of good faith and friendship. Whatever it was, Jim took it."

Barabas frowned. "Robert's timing is obviously suspect."

I nodded. "There are two possibilities: either they said yes to Roland and are going to betray us, or they didn't mean whatever they said to Roland and they are not going to betray us."

"Three," Barabas said. "They may be thinking it over."

"They don't even have to fight against us. They can just not show up and it would weaken us."

"If the Pack abstains from the conflict between us and your father, and Roland wins, the Pack will be next," Barabas said.

Christopher stirred. *"Gallia est omnis divisa in partes tres . . ."*

"The whole of Gaul is divided into three parts?" I asked.

"The opening line to *Gallic Wars* by Julius Caesar," Christopher said. "Caesar conquered Gaul tribe by tribe. Had they unified from the start, Rome's first emperor would've never made it back to Rome. There is a copy of this book in the Pack's library. I've seen Jim reading it. He knows that divided, we will fall."

"Jim isn't an idiot, and he's been Curran's friend for over a decade," Barabas said. "I don't see it."

"Roland has a way of subverting friendships," Christopher said. "It's a policy of isolation. He becomes your family, your friend, your confidant."

A shadow passed over his eyes.

"Then he betrays you," I said. "He did it with you, Erra, Hugh, me. The list goes on."

"Hugh was a special case," Christopher said. "We were adults. Hugh was a child."

"Hugh could've walked away. Instead he committed one atrocity after the next."

"It's not that simple." Christopher shook his head.

There was more there, but now wasn't the time to dig for it. I turned to Curran. His face showed all the varied emotions of a stone wall. He'd gone into his Beast Lord mode.

"Is there any way for us to be sure that Jim won't betray us?" I asked.

"No," Curran said.

That's what I thought. If we confronted him with the pictures, he would deny everything and we wouldn't be able to determine if it was the truth. If he was playing us, he would pretend to be outraged; if he wasn't, he would be outraged that we didn't trust him. Either way told us nothing.

"We have to assume Jim betrays us. It's the only safe way to plan." Barabas rubbed his face.

I looked at Curran. "Does he have any gaps in his armor?"

My husband turned to me, and his face was pure Beast Lord. "Everyone has gaps. Ours is sleeping on the pillow. Thinking of hitting Jim where it hurts?"

"No. But if Roland is pushing on a pressure point, we want to know about it."

Curran leaned back, his voice calm and measured. "Short term, siding with Roland would be to Jim's benefit. They lost a lot of people and an alliance would avoid further bloodshed. There are those within the Pack who would welcome that solution. From that position, not showing up at all is his best option. However, Jim thinks long term. If he fails to support us, he's left with Roland as victor. Your father doesn't do alliances. He wants obedience. Jim will chafe at it and so will most of the others. Besides that, if Jim betrays us, Clan Bear, Clan Bouda, and Clan Wolf would rebel."

"I don't know about Clan Wolf," I said.

"Desandra always votes in your favor," Barabas told me. "She'll often say provocative things to stir shit up, but she always supports you."

Clan Bouda, Clan Bear, and Clan Wolf would comprise close to half of the Pack. Jim would face a civil war.

"Perhaps Jim is thinking longer term," Christopher said.

Curran turned to him. "Explain."

"People always long for the good old days," Christopher said, his light eyes thoughtful. "We look at the past with rose-colored glasses."

"I have no plans to take the Pack back from Jim," Curran said. "He knows this. Jim is paranoid, but he is a more effective Beast Lord."

"But he doesn't have your charm," Barabas said. "He hardly ever roars and makes everyone cringe."

"People as individuals are intelligent," Christopher said. "People as a political body are finicky. They gravitate toward symbols of strength and power. You have a bigger presence than Jim."

"So, you think he hopes Roland will take me out?" Curran asked, his voice almost nonchalant.

"Not you." Christopher looked at Conlan.

No. I could believe that Jim would sit the fight out, but he wouldn't go that far. "He wouldn't," I ground out.

"By now he likely knows that Conlan can shapeshift or suspects he may be able to in the future," Christopher said. "Shapeshifters tell stories about you now. In a couple of decades, they will be legends. If Conlan is allowed to grow up, he'll be the son of the first Beast Lord, the man who created the Pack, the man who knew no equal while he ruled. He will have the physical power and the enhanced shapeshifting of a First. He'll be a natural leader. If you see a weed in your garden, would you pull it out now, while it's small and weak, or would you wait until it grows?"

"This is nuts," I told him.

"In my former life I was the Legatus of the Golden Legion," Christopher reminded me, his voice gentle. "My existence depended on eliminating my rivals before they came into their full power. I would eliminate your son now, in a way that couldn't be traced back to me. Perhaps a raid by Roland's covert team on the grandparents' clan house while your son is there. Everyone would be murdered. A great tragedy, an atrocity. Terrible. It would evoke outrage, of course, but also breed fear. Terrified people cling to familiar leaders. As to the two of you, there are few greater challenges to a marriage than the death of a child."

I hated this. I hated sitting here and imagining people who were our friends plotting to murder my kid. There was something wrong with the world that it was even a possibility.

"What do we do? We have to warn them that this could happen, and we can't tell Mahon," I said. "If he even suspects it, he'll storm the Keep, roaring, and he will get himself or someone else killed."

"We'll tell Martha," Curran told me.

Martha would defend Conlan with her dying breath. My imagination flashed a picture of her mangled, bloody body curled on the floor around my son. It was too much. I got up.

Curran was looking at me, concern in his eyes.

"I need a minute."

I opened the door and stepped onto the Guild's main floor. Mercs moved here and there, some tired and covered in grime or blood coming from a gig; others, clean and bored, waiting for one. A group of Curran's elite team sat on the raised platform stuffing their faces. The food in the Guild mess hall had gone from slop to legendary. Shapeshifters challenged each other to the death for power and had the potential to snap into psychotic spree killers, but give them bad food and they were mortally offended. The first time Curran smelled the old mess hall's food, he'd gagged. He overhauled the mess hall the moment he had the chance.

The mercs were grinning. Ella, petite and pretty, said something. Charlie shot back a reply, his eyes narrowed to mere slits. Douglas King rocked his massive six-foot-five frame back in his chair and laughed, the light reflecting from his bald head and off the mess of glyphs and runes tattooed there. The man was obsessed with "magic runes." The weapon sellers around Atlanta knew this and were always peddling junk to him, because he'd buy anything as long as it had some mysterious inscription on it. The last sword he bought was engraved with a word in Elder Futhark. He'd brought it to me to read. It said DICKHEAD, spelled out phonetically with Norse runes. He barely survived the disappointment.

A few years ago, I would have gone and sat right up there with them. Back then I didn't have a care in the world. My biggest worry was paying my meager bills and trying to earn enough for a new pair of shoes.

Suddenly I felt homesick, not for the house but for a different time and a different me. Not-in-charge-of-anybody me. Not-protecting-the-city me. Not-wife me. Not-mom me. Just me.

That's the way Voron had intended me to be. I'd been his version of a lone gunman. No ties, no roots, no attachment to friends or possessions. Back then I could've picked up at a moment's notice and vanished, and nobody would've worried or cared. I was a no-name merc, minding my own business. But inside I was still the same. Still a killer, still Roland's daughter. Hands still bloody, and no amount of magic could turn that blood to dust.

Back then I'd given Curran a speech. I couldn't remember exactly what I'd said, something about dragging my beat-up carcass to a dark empty house. Nobody cared if I made it home. Nobody waited up, nobody treated my wounds, nobody made me a cup of coffee and asked me about my day. When I thought about it now, my memories of that time seemed gray, as if all the color had been leached out of them.

When I thought of my house now, it was filled with warmth and light. It always smelled of seared meat or a fresh pie or fresh coffee. It was my little piece of the world, welcoming and comfortable, a place I'd built with Curran. A place for Conlan. A place where I belonged.

Christopher was right. We looked at the past with rose-colored glasses.

I'd picked this new life. I built it day by day. I had friends, I had a husband who loved me, I had my son and a city to protect. Standing here wallowing in self-pity and wondering who might betray me next and how I would deal with it accomplished nothing.

I'd made no progress on Serenbe. I still had no idea who'd sent me the box. I had to figure out how to protect Conlan. I would take this moment, get all of my "woe is me" out of my system, and be done, so I could do all of the other things I had to do.

At the table Douglas bared his right arm and flexed, showing off a bicep the size of a baseball. Yes, yes, you are big and mighty. New tattoo, too.

Wait a minute.

I pushed from the wall and made a beeline to Douglas.

"Hey, Daniels." Ella grinned at me.

"It's Lenna-a-a-art," Charlie sang out. "It's been Lennart for two years. Get your shit straight, Elle."

"New ink?" I asked Douglas.

He bared even white teeth. "Yeah." He tapped the skin on his arm, still red from the needle. A serpent in the shape of a sideways S. Between the loops of the serpent, a broken arrow formed a Z, the section with fletching vertical, the rest of the arrow diagonally piercing the loops, and the last bit, with the arrow head, pointing down. Serpent and Z-rod.

I almost heard a click as pieces snapped together in my head.

"It's Scottish," he said.

"Pictish," I told him. "Nice one."

I turned and walked away to my small office.

"What the hell was all that about?" Charlie asked behind my back.

"You cut her some slack," Ella told him. "Someone tried to kill her baby today. She beat her to death with her hands. I was dropping off a package for Biohazard and I got to see the body. The chick had no face left. Just raw hamburger."

I walked into my office, leaving the door open, and went to the book-case filled with my reference books. It was either here or at Cutting Edge. I ran my fingers along the spines. Not that one. No, no, no . . . There. I pulled a green volume off the shelf. V. A. Cumming, *Decoding Pictish Symbols*.

I flipped through it. There. Two circles, joined together, with wavy lines through them, two dots in the center, and a Z-rod, a broken arrow. Double disc and Z-rod. It looked right. The proportion, the thickness of the rect-angular piece connecting the two discs. It felt right.

I landed in my chair, the book in front of me. Nobody knew much about the Picts. Everyone knew about Hadrian's wall, but the Romans had built another one, the Antonine wall, in AD 142. It bisected Scotland. The Romans called the "painted" people on the other side of that wall Picts. Later, they were called Caledonians. Nobody knew for sure who they were or how long they lived in Scotland. Some claimed they were Celts, others argued that they came from Gaul. Pictish myths referenced Scythia and arriving to Scotland a thousand years or so before Anno Domini. Nobody knew for sure.

They left behind metal jewelry and Pictish stones. Dozens of ancient stone steles, covered with mysterious carvings. Most occurred on the east-ern side of Scotland. But the earliest Pictish stones dated back to the sixth century. Way too late for Erra's invaders.

There was no Z-rod on the box, but the knife matched. The knife looked like it came from the British Isles.

Picts didn't wear torques. Some of the archaeological hoards traced to them contained heavy-duty chains, but nobody knew their purpose. However, Celts definitely wore torques, and they had eventually spread through the British Isles.

I needed an expert on Picts. Unfortunately, there was no such thing. The next best bet were the Druids. The Druids didn't like me. They didn't like anybody. The specter of human sacrifice hung over them, and so they did their best to project a benevolent image. They wore white robes, waved tree branches around, and blessed things. But nobody I knew had ever been invited to a druid gathering. They never answered questions about their rituals or ancestry either. Showing up on their doorstep and asking them to help me decipher Pictish symbols would get me a nice pat on the back, followed by a door in my face. I didn't even know where that doorstep could be.

I needed help. Somebody who had an in with the pagans. Somebody familiar with old magic . . . Somebody who wasn't afraid of Druidic history and whom they couldn't bullshit.

Roman. He was a pagan, a black volhv, and his mother was one of the members of the Witch Oracle.

I needed to visit the Covens anyway, now that my father was going on the offensive. We'd made a plan together: the Covens, my aunt, and me. But the witches seemed to be dragging their feet with getting it implemented.

Curran walked through the doorway. He came around the desk and leaned against it.

"I'm thinking of going to see the Witch Oracle," I told him.

He frowned. "It's a bad idea."

It was an awful idea. I avoided the Witch Oracle like I avoided fire. When you consulted an oracle, you rolled the dice. Whatever they said would alter the course you took. It was always accurate; it always applied to the situation but never in the way you thought it would. An oracle could warn you that water would be a problem for your house in the future, so you prepared for a flood, but then your house caught on fire, and you didn't have enough water to put it out. The fact that the oracle was right wouldn't get your house back. Ninety-nine percent of the time you were better off not getting the prophecy in the first place. Unfortunately, I was down to one percent on the scale of desperate. I needed answers about the box, I needed to secure Roman's help, and I had to talk to the Oracle about getting a move on with our final strategy to fight my father.

Besides, we had to prevent a second Serenbe from happening, and if the Oracle could help with that, I'd kiss their feet.

"I need to talk to Roman about the Druids. And I want to ask the Witch Oracle about Serenbe." And a couple of other things. "I can't just sit on my hands and do nothing, Curran. People died. We have to do something about it."

"I'll watch the boy," he said.

"Thank you."

"Will you come home tonight?"

"I will."

"Good," he said. "Because I have plans."

"What kind of plans?"

His gray eyes turned warm. "Come home and I'll demonstrate."

"You're insatiable," I told him.

"Maybe you're just irresistible."

"Sure I am."

He leaned in and kissed me, sending a shiver through me. It was funny how the world stopped when he kissed me. Every single time.

He fixed my gaze with his. "Go do your thing. Nobody will hurt Conlan while you're gone."

I smiled at him and dialed Roman's number. He picked up on the second ring.

"Three months. You don't call, you don't write," Roman's accented voice said into the phone. "I am offended."

"No, you're not."

He laughed. "Fine, I'm not. What do you need?"

"I need to see the Witch Oracle and to talk to you about something."

"Do you need a vision?" he asked.

I took a deep breath. Once I said this, there was no going back, and I would have to live with whatever prophecy they delivered. "Yes."

"WHY DOES IT have to be a tortoise?" I mumbled, moving down a narrow path through the woods that used to be Centennial Park.

"You said you wanted a vision," Roman said.

He was wearing his usual black robe. The Slavic pantheon had two sides, the dark and the light, and volhvs acted as the conduit between the gods and the faithful. They served as priests, enchanters, and, on occasion, therapists. Roman served Chernobog, the God of Death, the Black Serpent, the Lord of Nav, the realm of the dead. On the surface, Chernobog was evil and bad, and his brother, Belobog, was good and light. In reality, things were complicated. Someone had to serve the Dark God, and Roman had ended up being that someone. He once told me it was the family business.

Roman did have the dark priest part down. His robe was black with silver embroidery at the hem. His hair—shaved on the sides and long on top and on the back of his head, so it looked like the mane of some wild horse—was black as well. Even his eyes under black eyebrows were such a deep brown, they appeared almost black.

"I know. I was asking in general."

"Tortoises are ancient. They live for a really long time and grow wise."

"I know what the tortoise symbolizes," I growled. The path turned, and we walked into a clearing where a big stone dome rested on the green grass.

Roman reached out with his staff and tapped the dome.

The dome shuddered once and slowly crept up, rising higher and higher. A dull black snout emerged. Two eyes, as big as dinner plates, looked at me. The colossal reptile opened its mouth.

I climbed into it, stepping on the spongy tongue. "What I meant was, why couldn't the Oracle meet in a building? You know, a nice temple somewhere?"

"Because every Tom, Dick, and Harry would show up wanting a prediction of their next golf game," Roman said, climbing in behind me. "This way, they'd have to risk getting eaten by a giant tortoise to ask for their prophecy. Only two kinds of people would do this: the desperate and idiots."

"If you say I'm both, I'll punch you right in the arm."

"If the shoe fits . . ."

I sighed and made my way through the throat, down the sloping tunnel to the pool of murky water at the bottom. Long strands of algae hung from the walls. The liquid smelled of flowers and pond water. I frowned. Usually it was much deeper. One time Ghastek's vamp came with me and it slipped and went all the way under.

I walked through the nearly dry tunnel. "What happened to all the tortoise spit?"

"I'm wearing my good robe," Roman said.

Having your mother serve as one of the three witches of the Oracle had its perks.

The tunnel turned. I followed it and walked into a large room. A pond spread before me, offering delicate lily blossoms among the wide dark-green pads. A stone bridge, so low that water washed over it, crossed the pond. Above us a vast dome rose, the light of the evening sun shining through its translucent top, setting it aglow with fiery reds and yellows. The walls gradually darkened, first green, then black and emerald.

The bridge ended in a platform where three women sat. The first, ancient and withered, napped quietly in her chair, her hair so light, it looked like fuzz. The first time I'd seen her, she'd been fierce like a predatory bird ready to draw blood. Now Maria mostly slept. She still hated me, though. The first time I visited the Oracle, she locked me into a ring of magic and I broke it. She'd wanted to murder me ever since. Next to her Evdokia, plump, middle-aged, with a brown glossy braid pinned to her head, knitted something in her rocking chair. A small black cat wound its way around her legs. The third girl, blond and slight, smiled at me. I'd saved her from dying, and Sienna always tried to help me in return.

Behind the women a tall mural of Hekatē covered the wall. She stood before a large cauldron, positioned at the intersection of three roads. The crone, the mother, and the maiden, all aspects of their witch-goddess.

"Do you seek a vision?" Sienna asked.

We were going through the whole ceremony, then. "Yes."

"Ask your question."

Evdokia leaned over and nudged Maria with her knitting needle. The old woman startled, blinked, saw me, and rolled her eyes.

I had to phrase this carefully. "The people of Serenbe were murdered for their bones. I want to know who did it and why."

Sienna leaned back. A current of magic pulsed from the other two women into her. She raised her hands, looking like a swan about to take flight. Her eyes glazed over. A smile stretched her lips. Using her magic brought Sienna genuine joy.

She rocked back. The far wall faded.

A battlefield spread before us, people in blue-black armor fighting against people in modern gear. Fire burned long tracks through the field, blazing ten feet high. The scent of charred flesh assaulted my nose. The metallic scent of blood saturated the air. I inhaled it and tasted human blood on my tongue. A moment and I was in it, in the thick of the slaughter. People tore at each other, their faces skewed by rage and terror, emotions so primal, the fighters looked like masked actors in a grotesque play.

Sweat, blood, and tears saturated the space around me, and beyond it was a wall of fire.

Something roared at the other end of the battlefield. I pushed my way toward it. Blades shone in the sun, chopping and slicing. Blood sprayed me. Human bones, free of flesh, splintered in front of me, transforming into powder.

If only I could get to higher ground . . .

The combatants parted. A hill of corpses rose before me. I climbed it, scrambling over the bodies sticky with drying blood. Almost there. Almost.

I climbed to the top. In the distance a golden chariot tore through the fighters. Father . . . Another roar came, low and terrible, like nothing I'd ever heard before. I turned and saw two eyes, brilliant amber and burning, staring at me from the darkness rising over the melee. A dark shape swooped on my right side on two big wings. It looked vaguely familiar, almost as if . . .

Fire drowned everything, its heat scorching me.

The light vanished, and the wall reappeared. Sienna was still.

I waited.

Nobody said anything.

"Is that it?" I asked.

"That's all I could see."

"So, a big battle, blood, flames, human bones, and everyone burning?" She nodded.

"That explains nothing."

Sienna spread her arms.

"Is there a prophecy?"

"Nothing came to me."

Bullshit. There was always a prophecy. "I want my money back," I said.

"You didn't pay us anything, ingrate," Maria told me.

"This is not helpful."

"Sorry," Sienna said. "It's not an exact science. If I get something else, I'll let you know."

I really wanted to bump my head against something hard, but nothing was around.

"My father is mobilizing his forces. He might be moving forward with his invasion plans."

Evdokia stopped knitting. "How sure are you?"

"It's been reported by both Pack scouts and ours. How are you coming along with the White Warlock?"

Sienna scooted in her seat.

Evdokia pursed her lips. "There are complications," she said.

"There can't be complications. You promised me you'd do this ritual. He isn't killing my son or my husband. If he invades, and I have to kill myself, I want to be sure it isn't for nothing. Do I need to go down there and talk to this Warlock myself?"

"No!" Evdokia and Sienna said in the same voice.

"Why not?" They were hiding something.

"This is witch business," Evdokia said. "If you blunder in there waving your sword around, you'll spoil everything. We promised you the ritual and we'll deliver. When have I ever not delivered, Katya?"

The Russian name came out. Oh boy. "I just want to make sure that if worse comes to worst, I don't die for nothing."

"We'll handle it," Sienna told me.

Maria cackled. The other two witches looked at her.

She hacked and spat on the floor. "Evil scum you are. Evil scum you'll always be. I hope you all die in a fire."

Evdokia heaved a sigh.

"Awesome," I said. "Good chat. Thank you for the productive meeting. Looking forward to our next one."

"One other thing," Evdokia said. "Some knights from the Order asked to speak to us."

"Local?"

"No, from out of town."

Knight-abettor Norwood got around. "They're trying to remove Nick Feldman from his position as the head of the chapter. He keeps pointing out that I exist, and they don't like it."

"We'll take care of it," Sienna promised.

I turned and walked back out of the tortoise. Outside, the air tasted fresh and sweet. The trees shimmered in the twilight breeze as the sky cooled after the burn of sunset. Lightning bugs flew here and there, tiny points of light in the indigo air.

Roman thrust himself in front of me. "You're planning to kill yourself?"

Crap. Me and my big mouth. "No."

"Explain."

I sighed. "My father is susceptible to witch magic. It's older even than him, primitive in a way but very powerful. Erra told me that the hardest opponent he ever faced, outside of the war that killed most of our family, was a witch, and that woman almost killed him. The plan is to gather the Covens together on the battlefield and perform a ritual, which would channel their combined power into a single person. I can't be that person. First, I'm not trained enough. Second, the point person in this scenario acts like a prism, concentrating and directing the power outward. I'm a lousy prism. My body just hoards all of the magic."

"Let me guess," he said, his voice dry. "The White Warlock is a good prism?"

"The best they know. The plan is to talk her into it. Except your mom and the other witches have been trying and haven't gotten anywhere."

"You and your father are bound. If they kill him, you'll die, too," Roman said. "This is a stupid plan."

"The witches aren't trying to kill him. They are trying to put him to sleep. If everything works as intended, Roland will fall asleep on the battlefield and hopefully sleep for decades or longer. They did it to Merlin. He is still somewhere out there, sleeping."

Roman thought about it. "Okay. Explain the killing-yourself part."

"The Covens' power might not be enough. My dad is very strong. If he isn't going down, I may have to kill him myself or at least weaken him enough for the spell to take over. There are consequences to that."

Roman shook his staff at me. "I repeat, this is a stupid plan!" The raven at the top of the staff opened its wooden beak and screeched at me.

"Did you know that when you're mad, your Russian accent disappears?"

"This is idiotic. You have a husband and a son. You're not killing your dad and dying because of it. I forbid it."

"Okay, Your Holiness."

"I'm serious. Death is forever. I know. My god is the Lord of Nav."

"There might not be any other way," I said gently. "If I knew with one hundred percent certainty that killing myself would kill my father, I would do it without hesitation. You're right. I have a husband and a son, and I want them both to live long happy lives, even if it's without me. But my dad is a lot older and more powerful than I am. If I just kill myself, he still might survive. With the witches' power upgrade, at least we stand a better chance of taking him down."

"No. I won't stand for it."

I reached out and patted his arm. "Thank you for being my friend."

"Does Curran know?"

"No, and you're not going to tell him. This is the plan of last resort. If you tell him, he'll do something stupid to prevent me from entering that battlefield, and I'm our best chance at counteracting my father. If I'm not fighting, I'll definitely have to kill myself."

He snarled something under his breath. The wooden raven screeched.

"I have an idea. What if instead of being mad and siccing your bird on me, you help me?"

"Help you do what?"

"I need to talk to the Druids about the Picts."

"What do Picts have to do with anything?"

I explained the box and the symbol. He huffed. "Fine. Tomorrow."

"Thank you."

I turned to walk away.

"Kate," he called.

I turned around.

"You're my friend. I don't have a lot of friends because of what I do. Every time my god calls to me, I bargain with him to keep people I don't know alive. 'What if we kill just five people? What if we make it three? If we do it this way, perhaps we won't have to kill anyone.' I fight for their lives. And here you are, not even trying. There has to be another way, you hear me? Find another way."

"I'll try," I told him.

"You do that."

. . .

THE MAGIC CRASHED on my way home. No new vehicles sat in the drive-way and nobody came to the door. Curran usually heard me before I even pulled into the driveway.

I let myself inside. Curran did say he would buy a new car today. He might have gotten held up.

"Hello?" I called. "Anybody home?"

"I'm home!" Adora called from downstairs.

I went down into the basement. Fully finished, it had been converted into a makeshift hospital room, with Yu Fong resting in a hospital bed. An IV stretched from his arm. Next to him, in a large plush chair, Adora curled up with a book. Lean, hard, with her dark hair falling to her shoulders, from the back she looked familiar. My shoulders were broader, my frame larger, and I had a couple of inches of height on her. Other than that, replace her katana with Sarrat, and she might be the younger, teenage me.

"How is he?"

"The same," she said.

Yu Fong showed no signs of life. I leaned close to him and put the back of my hand to his nose. A faint puff of air touched my skin. Still breathing.

"He's pretty," Adora observed.

"That he is." He looked like a beautiful painting. "I wouldn't try kissing him. He isn't Sleeping Beauty."

She wrinkled her nose at me. "Wasn't planning on it."

"Do you want to be paid from Cutting Edge or through the Guild for the gig?"

She tilted her chin. "I'm working pro bono."

"Since when?"

"This is a family matter," she said. "I'll take care of him because you and Curran are family and you need help."

"Who are you and what have you done with Adora?"

She grinned at me. "You're not as funny as you think."

"I'm funny enough. Come and get me if he wakes up."

"You killed one of my sisters today," she said.

News traveled fast. "I did. She wanted to kill Conlan and eat him."

"Did she suffer?"

"Yes."

"Good." Adora winked at me. "I put Curran's sweatpants on the stairs. I'm not going up to your love nest."

"Love nest?"

"Your bedroom where you have sex."

Oh boy.

"I haven't had sex," Adora volunteered. "But I've decided to try it."

"Is there a particular person you want to try it with?"

"No. I'm thinking about it."

"Sex is about trust," I told her. "You'll be at your most vulnerable. Try to choose well."

She wrinkled her nose at me again.

I went up the stairs. A big paper bag sat on the first landing. I looked inside. Gray Pack sweatpants. Curran had grown up in them, and he kept wearing them despite us no longer being part of the Pack. One, two . . . Five pairs? Odd. He had two stacks of sweatpants in the closet.

"Hey," I called down to the basement. "Who brought the sweatpants?"

"Some Pack werewolf."

I walked upstairs and opened the closet doors. All of the old sweatpants were gone. Weird. I emptied the bag on the bathroom floor and sorted through the new sweatpants, checking the waistband and the elastic on the bottom of each pant leg for any hidden items. Nothing.

Okay. I folded the sweatpants and put them back into the bag. Where did his other sweatpants go?

A search of the hamper turned up nothing. Now I was invested in the mystery. I went downstairs and checked the laundry room, the washing machine, and the dryer. Nothing.

That left the trash can outside. I went out and threw the lid open. A large trash bag sat on top, stretched out like someone had folded a blanket and stuffed it inside. I fished it out and pulled the strings open. Sweatpants.

Still clean and folded. Well, and that wasn't weird. Not at all. Why would he throw away all of his sweatpants and get new ones? Did they smell bad? I sniffed the sweatpants. Smelled like cotton to me.

I grabbed a pair of old sweatpants and went down into the basement.

"Do these smell odd to you?"

"You want me to sniff Curran's sweatpants?"

"They're clean. I got them out of the garbage can."

Adora blinked at me and held up one finger. "No."

"Fine." I took the old sweatpants upstairs, pulled the new ones out of the bag, arranged them on the shelf, and laid a lone pair of old clean sweats on the bed next to the empty bag and a clean white T-shirt. Trap baited. Now I just had to wait for the lion to come home.

It took him another twenty minutes. He walked through the door, carrying Conlan. Conlan saw me, scooted out of his arms, and charged up the stairs at breakneck speed. I had a split-second decision: to move or to take the hit. I took the hit. My back slapped the wooden floor. Ouch. He hugged me. "Mama!"

I rolled to my feet. "This sudden love is suspicious."

"He got in trouble for trying to eat scented candles." Curran came up the stairs.

"Where did he get the scented candles?"

"In the Guild's supply closet. Corinna bought a stack of them. She burns them in the locker room. Says it helps her with the wet-dog smell."

Corinna worked for the Guild as a merc, but she was also a werejackal and she was obsessed with her scent.

I carried Conlan to the bedroom. "Did you talk to Martha?"

"Not yet."

"The Pack delivered some sweatpants for you. I put them in the closet. What happened to the old ones?"

"I wore them out."

Bullshit. Coming from the man who resorted to using his alpha stare over keeping an ancient T-shirt, it wasn't just bullshit, it stank to high heaven.

I nodded.

"How did it go with the witches?"

Curran stripped off his T-shirt and I got a view of the world's best chest, all golden and muscled. Mmm.

"Big battle, fire, human bones, blood, more fire."

"That's it?" He put on the white T-shirt and took off his jeans. Mmmm.

"Yep. Not very illuminating. But good news, Maria still hates me."

He pulled the sweatpants on. They ended midway up his shin. What the heck?

"Hold on, baby. Mommy needs to do something." I set Conlan down, turned sideways, raised my leg, bending it at the knee, and extended. I'd done this hundreds of times to tap Curran on the throat when we were sparring. Usually I failed to connect, but the high kick was so automatic, I did it on autopilot. My foot came up short.

"Ooo, foreplay." Curran caught my ankle.

I pulled my leg out of his hand. "Stand straight."

"What is this?" He spread his arms.

I stepped close to him. My nose touched his chest. In his human form, Curran topped me by two and a half inches. I was five-seven and he was close to five-ten. I was looking up at him now.

"You are taller."

"I hate to break it to you, but I'm done growing."

"You're taller and you know you're taller. I found your sweatpants in the garbage." I dropped back and snapped a fast kick, aiming at his head. He leaned back, letting my kick fly by.

"You're at least six-two."

"You measured me with your kick?"

"Yes. And your hair is an inch longer than it was this morning. What's happening?"

"Nothing I understand."

"Why is this happening?"

He raised his arms. "I'm trying to get stronger."

He did work out every chance he got.

"I'm not trying to work on being taller. The hair thing is weird, I agree."

"Is this normal? Is this some sort of First shapeshifter stage of life that you're going through?"

"My father isn't around, so we can't exactly ask him."

"Have you talked to Doolittle about it?"

He smiled at me. "Would you like me to?"

"Yes. I would. What the hell is so funny?"

"You're worrying about my health."

"You scare me." I sat on the bed. I was suddenly very tired.

He crouched on the floor in front of me. "I'm okay."

"I was thinking today about what it was like before."

"Before . . . ?"

"Before the flare."

He grinned. "You mean before I broke into your house and made you coffee for the first time?"

"You didn't break into my house. I left the door unlocked."

"Details."

"Ghastek asked In-Shinar for forgiveness today. He didn't know about the sahanu, and he took it personally. He didn't want the whole me. He wanted the In-Shinar part of me. Raphael told me I was the In-Shinar. Some people will never see me as anything else."

"I want the whole you," he told me. "The merc, the In-Shinar, my wife, all of it. My Kate."

"I know. I have this awful feeling that something screwed up is about to drop on us. I don't want anything to happen to you. I can't roll with that kind of punch, Curran."

"Nothing will happen to me. I've got this." He pulled me off the bed into a hug and kissed me. "Not going anywhere," he whispered into my ear. "All yours. Always."

I believed him, but the sick feeling in my stomach refused to go away.

THE PHONE WOKE me. I slipped from under Curran's arm and dragged myself to it. The clock said 6:20 a.m. Ugh.

"Kate Daniels. I mean Lennart. Kate Lennart."

Curran laughed under his breath.

"Hey, Kate," Sheriff Beau Clayton said into the phone. He sounded dull, like he'd seen something he wanted to forget. I wouldn't like this call.

"You called about Serenbe."

"I did."

"I might have something for you."

"I'll be there as soon as I can."

I hung up. Last night, after we sorted ourselves out, Curran had called Martha and asked her to come watch Conlan today and to bring the book club. She'd asked him if he meant the whole book club, and he said yes. She told him she'd be here at nine.

If I waited until nine, the magic could drop. I needed to go now, while the magic was active.

"I have to go," I told Curran.

"I'll catch up," he said.

THE SMALL SETTLEMENT of Ruby lay deep in the heart of Milton County. Two streets, seventeen houses, a post office, a small store with a gas station, and a Rural Defense Tower. Rural Defense, an extension of the National Guard, was tasked with protecting the small settlements. It was one step up from a militia.

It took Julie and me roughly two hours to get there even with Julie driving, but we'd made it while the magic was still up. Now we stood on the street, the silent houses flanking us. A dead Labrador retriever lay on my left. Someone had built a pyre at the end of the street. It was six feet tall and shaped like a cone.

Behind us, Beau Clayton and two of his deputies waited, all three still on horseback: the deputy on the right with a crossbow and the other with a shotgun. These were cautious people covering all the bases.

Beau, as big as a mountain, had lost all of his usual cheer. His eyes had gone flat and dark. A postal carrier reported the empty village last night, but Beau had been dealing with another matter and didn't get the message until this morning. He and the deputies had swept the village and found abandoned houses, unmade beds, and dead dogs.

"What do you make of the pyre?" Beau asked me.

"I don't know. I got a prophecy from the Witch Oracle yesterday. It had a lot of fire in it. Are you sure the locals didn't build it themselves?"

"There is no way to tell," Beau said. "We don't come this way too often." We waited.

Finally, Julie glanced at me. "Blue."

"Across the board?"

She nodded. "Human magic."

They took the people. Just like Serenbe. It had to stop. It had to stop now.

A man walked into the street, tall, broad-shouldered, and wearing armor tinted with blue. The dark metal scales traced his body, following its contours, wider on his chest and smaller on his waist. The armor flowed, flexible, protecting without impeding his movement, each scale just the right size, almost as if it were custom made. I'd never seen anything like it until yesterday, when I saw that armor in Sienna's vision.

I scrutinized the warrior. One scale on his right shoulder shimmered with gold. His helmet shielded his skull, leaving his face open, a variation of a Chalcidian helm I wasn't familiar with. His face looked oddly blank. He was Caucasian, blue-eyed, and the locks of hair falling from under the helmet were blond. Two sword hilts protruded over his shoulders. He carried a torch in his hand. Fire danced at the end of it.

"I thought you said you did a sweep," I said quietly.

"We did," Beau said.

The warrior dropped the torch onto the pyre. Flames dashed up the branches.

"Did he soak it in gasoline or something?" Julie asked.

"I didn't smell any when I looked at it," one of the deputies told her.

The warrior stepped in front of the pyre, his back to it, and faced us.

"Sheriff's department," Beau called out, his voice harsh. "Get down on the ground."

The warrior reached behind his back and drew the two swords.

Oh good. Apparently, it was cutting time.

The blades looked to be about twenty-one or twenty-two inches long with a swept profile, similar to a modern Filipino espada, a cross between a Spanish sword and a traditional garab blade. Lively and fast, while still delivering a lot of cutting power in either a slash or a thrust.

The fire behind the warrior surged up. Wait, don't tell me.

A figure appeared in the flames, a tall man in golden scale armor. A white cloak, edged with wolf fur, rode on his shoulders, his blond hair falling on it in a combed wave. A golden torque caught his neck.

My box and Serenbe were connected.

That sonovabitch. Anger boiled inside me and solidified into dark ice. All those people, dead. *I'm coming for you. Just wait.*

"What the hell?" the other deputy said.

"We're being invaded," I said. "That's their king and this is his champion."

"Does he do magic?" Beau asked.

"He's leaving a blue trail," Julie said.

"Kenny," Beau said, his voice calculating, "shoot that bastard."

Kenny raised his crossbow. A small blue spark burst at the tip of the bolt. He sighted and fired. The warrior opened his mouth. Fire tore out of it. The scorched remnants of the bolt fell to the ground.

Great. He spat fire. My favorite.

"I think that's my cue." I unsheathed Sarrat.

"There are five of us and one of him," Kenny pointed out.

"This isn't about winning," Beau said. "This is about fear. This asshole has been coming into our villages and stealing our people. He thinks he can do whatever he wants and none of us can stop him. He needs to know that one of ours can beat one of his. Have fun, Dan . . . er, Lennart."

I walked into the middle of the street.

The warrior moved forward one light step. Toe walker. Most people stepped on their heel first. We had the cushy benefits of modern footwear, and we walked mostly paved streets. He stepped on the ball of his foot first, feeling the ground with his toes before putting his full weight on it. You almost never saw this outside cultures that still ran around barefoot.

The warrior rotated his blades, warming up his wrists. I did the same. No gauntlets. Hard to effectively hold a blade with an armored gauntlet. That left his knuckles nice and bare.

I began to circle, slowly. He was six feet tall, at least two hundred pounds, likely more with his armor. The sixty-four-thousand-dollar question was, how thick was that armor?

Let's see how fast you are with your two swords.

He looked at my blade and dropped his left sword to the ground. Smart. Dual swords had their uses. They were effective for cutting yourself out of a crowd or for blocking a much heavier blade. But in one-on-one, the single sword ruled. I was liking this less and less.

I stopped about two feet from him. He watched me. I watched him.

Show me what you've got.

He struck, fast, bringing the blade down from my right. I parried it just enough to let his blade slide off mine and moved back.

Strong. Getting into a hit-for-hit game with him would wear me out.

He reversed the swing. I angled Sarrat to let the blow slide off the flat of my blade and moved back again.

The warrior charged, bringing his sword down in a devastating blow. I lunged to the left, ducking, and thrust Sarrat into his armpit. Like trying to thrust through rock. I jerked the blade back and jumped out of the way. He took a step back, his blue eyes unblinking and cold.

Blood coated the very tip of Sarrat's blade. If it weren't for the armor, he would be bleeding to death. Slashing him was out. The blade wouldn't penetrate. I could power-word him, but that would be against the rules. Beau was right. I needed to beat this guy with my sword, one-on-one. Nothing short of that would give the asshole in the fire pause.

The warrior charged again, raining blows, left, right, left.

Parry, dodge, parry, back away, parry. He was damn strong and he fought like he had gone into battle for his life many times. Nothing showy. No movement wasted. Every blow vicious and calculated.

Strike, strike, nice trick but I saw that, strike.

Parry, parry, parry . . . The tip of his blade carved a path across my right forearm. Shit.

We broke apart.

I had to win this. If he beat me, it would paint us as easy prey.

He lunged. I spun out of the way. He struck from the right again, expecting me to dodge. Instead I stepped into the blow, planting my feet, and caught his wrist. The shock reverberated all the way into my toes, and while it was still moving through me, I drove Sarrat toward his gut. He caught the blade with his hand. I grinned at him and jerked Sarrat back. The blade cut through his hand like it was butter.

He snarled in pain. His eyes flashed amber. The vision from the Witch Oracle flashed before me. Amber eyes and then . . .

I spun away and ran.

Flames burst from his mouth in a cone, roaring after me. Heat bathed me. I dropped to the ground. The scorching heat tore above me.

I rolled to my feet. A curtain of smoke hung between us, flames shining inside it. He broke the rules and went to his magic. Oh goody.

I slid the flat of Sarrat's blade across the cut on my forearm, letting the crimson wet it.

He came through the smoke and fire, his eyes blazing, his sword raised.

I sent a pulse of magic through my blood. A hair-thin red edge crystallized on Sarrat's blade.

He barreled at me, huge, his eyes on fire.

I stabbed him in the stomach. The blade sliced through the armor, flesh, and organs, and scraped his spine, severing the nerves. His legs went out. He dropped to his knees.

The smoke cleared. I slashed at his neck. There was almost no resistance. His head rolled off his shoulders. I picked it up, walked to the pyre, and tossed it at the blond asshole in the flames. It fell through the fire.

There. That's for you. Keep it.

The man in the fire and I stared at each other. His armor matched that of his champion's, but where the warrior's armor was tinted with blue, the scales on his body were a deep reddish gold. A gold chain held his cape in place, its clasp studded with what were probably real rubies. He had so much gold on him, his knees should have been shaking from the weight. If his image was life-sized, he was huge, at least six and a half feet tall. Of course, he could be four feet tall and just made himself look larger.

Heat bathed me from the side. The warrior's body burned from the inside out, his armor melting. *There goes my evidence.*

The man in the fire nodded to me.

Be patient. No ranting. Wait for him to tell you what he wants and who he is, and then tell him you're going to cut his head off. Zen. Diplomacy. I could do it.

"**You murdered my people.**" The language of power rolled off my tongue. Probably shouldn't have started with that.

"*I took from outside your borders.*"

He had a deep resonant voice. The power in it rolled through the village, unimaginably ancient. The tiny hairs on the back of my neck rose on end. Behind me one of the deputies made a choking sound.

"*They are all my people.*"

"*Do you claim dominion over the entire world, then, Daughter of Nimrod?*"

"*I don't claim dominion; I claim kinship. Every time you enter this world and kill, you kill one of my own.*"

He chuckled. "*You're arrogant. Like the rest of your clan.*"

I wished I could reach into the flames. My hands itched. I could almost hear the sound of his windpipe breaking under my fingers.

"*Have you given any consideration to your answer?*"

I raised Sarrat and looked at its edge. White curls of vapor rose from the blade. Sarrat didn't like him.

Diplomacy, Curran's voice said in my head. *Find out what he wants and how big of a threat he is.*

"Let's summarize. You sent me a box of ashes with a knife and a rose in it."

"Yes." He shifted into English too, but it didn't help. His voice filled the space, deep and overpowering.

"What am I supposed to do with it? What does it mean? Is it a gift?"

He paused. "I see. You don't understand."

"I don't. Enlighten me."

"The world is mine. It had a brief reprieve, but now I've returned. Much has changed."

"Go on."

"I will need a queen."

I raised my eyebrow at him.

"I'm offering you a crown. Sit by my side and share in my power. Be my guide in the new age."

"And if I don't?"

Amber flashed in his eyes. "I'll burn your world."

"You need to work on your proposal delivery. First come flowers and gifts, then dating, and only then, offers of marriage."

He fixed me with his stare, a hard, unblinking gaze. "You're mocking me."

"You're a pretty bright boy, aren't you?" I quoted the line from the old story. He wouldn't get it, but I thought it was funny.

"You don't understand what I am offering."

"How exactly did you think this proposal would go? 'Hi, here I am, I murdered a bunch of people in a horrible way, marry me or I'll burn everything down.' Who would agree to it? You're not someone to marry. You're a threat to eliminate."

"Your aunt said the same thing to my brother once," he said.

Oh crap. "How did that go for your brother?"

He smiled. There was something wrong with his teeth. They weren't quite fangs, but they were sharper and more conical than human teeth had a right to be.

"Your aunt and your father killed him. But I am not my brother."

"So your brother got his ass kicked by my family. You can see how that isn't in your favor."

He laughed. "Do you know why my brother sailed to your family's lands? Because he fought me for mine and lost. They faced but a weak imitation of what true power is with their combined strength, and he nearly ended them."

"Let me guess, you're the true power."

"I am. I hold gods prisoner, tormenting them for my pleasure. I bring war and terror. I am Neig, the Undying. I am legend. All who know me bow to me."

The way he said "legend" sent shivers down my spine. I shrugged. "Never heard of you."

"Then I shall have to remedy that."

"Why don't you step out of that fire and I'll cut your legend short."

He laughed. Little streaks of smoke swirled around him. "I will give you a demonstration, Daughter of Nimrod. Then we shall speak again."

The fire went out, like a snuffed-out candle.

I turned to Julie and the lawmen.

"Well," Beau said, his voice calm. "Kenny, climb off Meredith, find a phone, and call down to the station. Tell them we've got another invasion on our hands and to get the evacuation alert out there."

I headed to the gas station.

"Where are we going?" Julie caught up with me.

"We're going to relight that pyre. Are you sure he is human?"

"Yes, I'm sure. Why are we relighting the pyre?"

"Because we've got an ancient fire mage on our hands, and he has a vendetta against my family. I need to talk to my father. Check the phone and if it works, call home and leave a message on the answering machine for Erra with everything you heard. Then call Roman and tell him we had a change of plans. Tell him to swing by the house and pick up the box. Adora should be home and she will let him in. We can't wait till tonight. We need to talk to the Druids now."

"Why?"

"Because Neig promised to give me a demonstration of his power. He doesn't consider anything he's done up to now a proper demonstration. According to him, making two hundred people disappear and sending a human who burned to death to deliver a message doesn't count."

"Crap," Julie said.

"Find the phone. Call Curran after you're done and tell him not to bother coming here. I'm going straight to the Druids once I'm done, and I doubt they'll let him in."

She ran behind the counter. I headed to the pump. Erra had told me that the more I gave of myself to the fire, the louder it would be for my father. This time Roland would answer me. I would scream into that fire and feed it magic until he picked up.

12

"IT WILL BE okay," Roman told me from the passenger seat.

I took the turn too fast. The Jeep jumped over a protruding root. The trees on both sides of the road stood so thick, it was like driving through a green tunnel. The witch forest thrived during magic waves.

"I sat by that damn fire for two hours. I fed enough magic into it to wake the dead. I screamed myself hoarse."

"Parents," Roman said. "Can't live with them. Can't kill them. You call, they don't pick up. You don't call, they get offended. Then they chew a hole in your head because you're a bad son."

"He is a bad father!" I snarled.

"Okay," Roman said, his voice soothing. "Of course he is. Be reasonable. This is the guy who ordered his own grandson killed. Nobody is saying that he is a good father. All I'm saying is that parents don't like being yelled at. He knows you're upset and he doesn't want to take your calls."

"That's family business. This is an outsider attacking us. This is different!"

Roman sighed. "I get it. I really do. Have you tried pleading? Maybe cry a little? That way he would know it was safe to take the call, and he would swoop in like a savior. Parents love to play saviors."

I glared at him.

He raised his hands. "All I'm saying is when I need to talk to my dad, I don't call him and scream at him because he got into a drunken brawl with Perun's volhv, and Perun's idiot kid followers decided to Taser Chernobog's idol in his shrine, because that's the closest they can come to lightning, and now my god wants them all murdered. I call and say, 'Hey, Dad, I know you're busy, but I've got a serious situation on my hands and I need your advice.' Just try my way. I bet it will work."

"Where the hell is this damn camp?"

"Make a right at the next fork."

I took the next turn. The Jeep screeched, protesting the bumpy road. It was just me, the woods, and the black volhv. I'd sent Julie back. I'd wanted to bring her, but Roman had dug his heels in. According to him, he'd had to cash in all his favors, and that would only cover him and me.

"I feel like we're driving in circles."

"We are. They're deciding if they're going to let us in."

I brought the Jeep to a halt and parked.

"What are you doing?"

"I don't have time for druid shenanigans."

I shut the engine off, opened the passenger door, and stepped out.

"This is a mistake," Roman told me.

I looked up into the treetops. "You know me," I called out. "You know who I am and what I do. I brought you a name today. Neig. Neig the Undying. The legend. I spoke to him and he is coming for all of us. I need to know who he is."

The trees didn't respond.

I waited. The forest churned with life. Squirrels fussed at each other. A woodpecker drummed a steady staccato somewhere to the left. Things rustled in the underbrush.

Nothing.

I got back into the Jeep. The witch forest was outside my borders. The land called to me. It needed to be claimed and protected. All that magic, stretching to me. All that life, vulnerable to outside threats. I could claim it and flush the Druids out like foxes out of their flooded burrow.

That was a hell of a thought.

I'd had over two years to deal with having claimed the city. I'd learned to manage the craving for more, but some days the urge to take land, to make it my own, gripped me. My aunt called it the Shar. The need to hold and protect. It was bred into our family to make us better rulers. Most of my now-deceased relatives had been taught how to handle it in childhood. I'd had to deal with it as an adult, and it almost drove me off a cliff. I'd beaten it, but once in a while, when it reared its ugly head, I had to beat it back again.

I wouldn't be claiming anything today. I would chant the engine back into life, and Roman and I would go home.

"Huh," Roman said. "I take back what I said. Your way is faster."

I looked up. A palisade rose in the middle of what a moment ago was dense forest. Huge trees formed its wall, their trunks perfectly straight and touching each other. A gate reinforced with iron and bristling with spikes guarded the entrance. Dark blood stained the tips of the four-foot spikes.

The gate shuddered and slid aside.

"We need to hurry now," Roman said, grabbing a duffel bag, "before they change their mind."

We walked to the gates. A Caucasian man in his forties stood in the center, leaning on a staff. He wore plain trousers, boots, and no shirt. Blue whorls and symbols, painted in blue ink, decorated his muscled torso. His headdress, made of a grizzly's head, gave him another six inches of height. His face fit right between the bear's jaws. If I fought him, I'd come from the side. His peripheral vision had to be shit with all that fur.

The man glared at us, looking like he was about to roar and unleash a Pictish horde. The last time I saw him, he'd worn a snow-white robe and was groomed like he was about to attend a white-tie event. He'd been smiling at some children at the Solstice Festival and handing out candied fruit with the other druids as part of their community outreach.

Hi, we're druids. We wear pretty white clothes, hand out sweets, and teach about honoring trees and forests. Look at us, all gentle and nonthreat-

ening. We'd never strip naked, paint ourselves with battle symbols, and dance around in the woods with savage weapons and fur headdresses. Yeah, right. No wonder they didn't want anyone to come to their masquerades in the woods.

"Is that Grand Druid Drest?"

"Uh-huh," Roman murmured. "Watch what you say."

"I always watch what I say."

"If the words 'I didn't know you were having a fancy dress-up party, pity I wasn't invited' come out of your lips, I'll turn around and go home. And that's a promise."

"Killjoy."

"These are my colleagues from work. I have to have a good relationship with these people."

"Okay, okay."

Next to the Grand Druid stood a woman. She was about two inches shorter than me, with bronze skin and thick wavy brown hair. She wore an outfit of fur and carried a spear. Judging by the definition on her arms, she could use it, too.

"What about her?" I murmured.

"Jennifer Ruidera." He pronounced "Ruidera" like "Rivera," but with a D sound.

"What does she do?"

"You don't want to find out. And call her Jenn."

My luck with women named Jennifer wasn't exactly great, so "Jenn" would work just fine.

Behind the pair stretched a camp. People walked back and forth, some naked, some clothed, most painted. Weapons waited in racks. The magic was so thick that if it were fog, we wouldn't be able to see past three feet. Here was hoping there were no wicker men present, because if they tried to sacrifice someone or something by burning them alive, I wouldn't be able to sit on my hands, professional relationship or not.

Drest met my gaze. "You said Neig."

"Yes."

He looked at Jenn. She shrugged. "Anything is possible."

Two men joined us, one old and stooped, wearing an ankle-length tunic, his white beard stretching down to his waist. The other was in his thirties and looked like he got his exercise by tossing cows into the air for fun.

Roman bowed. I did, too.

Drest held up one finger to us and turned to the old man. "This woman says she spoke with Neig."

"Ah?" the old man asked.

"Neig!" Drest repeated.

"I can't hear you. Stop mumbling."

Drest sucked in a lungful of air. "SHE SAYS SHE SPOKE TO NEIG!"

People stopped what they were doing and stared at us. Drest waved them off.

"Neig?" The old druid peered at him. "Oh, that's not good."

Drest looked like he wanted to slap himself. "Brendan, he has to wear his hearing aid when he comes to the rites."

Brendan raised hands the size of shovels. "What do you want me to do? Sit on him and shove it into his ear? He takes it out. He says he wants to be one with nature."

"Aha!" a male voice called out.

I turned. A man was striding toward us. Thin and painted with blue, he wore a cloak of crow feathers and carried a large black chicken.

Drest's face drooped.

"I told you I had a vision about it," the chicken man announced. "I told you last Thursday. I said Neig is coming. And you said, 'Alpin, stop sacrificing your chickens. Stop putting yourself into a trance, stop looking at the entrails, and stop calling me in the middle of the night.' You said that if I couldn't fall asleep, I needed to drink a beer and suck it up."

"He's right," Jenn said. "You need to leave those chickens alone. It's unnatural."

"For the last time, I don't sacrifice chickens," Alpin declared.

"I saw a dead chicken in your kitchen last week," Brendan told him.

"I was going to cook it for dinner. I bought it at the market! I don't eat my friends. I like to have them, because they help me with astral projection. Their squawking is soothing."

Jenn dragged her hand over her face.

Roman cleared his throat.

Drest looked at him.

Roman unzipped the duffel bag and held it open for me. I took the box out.

The druids took a step back in unison. Only Jenn remained. She reached out, touched the box, and withdrew her hand.

"Open it," Drest said.

I opened the lid.

They peered at the contents. The old druid reached out, ever so slowly, his ancient hand shaking, grasped some ash between his fingers, and let it fall back into the box. His face went slack. He looked like he was about to weep.

"It will be all right, Grandfather," Drest said gently. "It will be all right."

"Everything will burn," the old man said. "He will set the world on fire."

"No, he won't." Drest nodded to Brendan, and the big man gently steered the elderly druid away.

Drest turned to me. "Put it away."

I did.

"Come with me."

He led us deeper into the camp. "What did Neig say when you spoke to him?"

"He told me that he gave the world a break, but now he is back, and he is going to conquer it. We think he has a place outside of time, like Morrighan's mists. We've had people disappear, whole settlements. Serenbe and Ruby in Milton County. He took them, killed them, and boiled them to extract their bones. Any idea why he would be doing that?"

Jenn shook her head. "No. But he is a crafty old bastard. If he's doing that, it isn't for anything good."

Alpin just looked like he would collapse at any moment.

We reached the back of the camp. A big slab of rock protruded from the ground, one side polished and covered in Pictish symbols. Kudzu had climbed it, covering the top. An outline of Ireland and the British Isles was carved in the corner. Drest pointed to Ireland.

"First came the sorceress Cessair and her people. They inhabit the isle for a bit, then die out. Then comes Partholon and his people. They start farming, fishing, building houses. Then in one week they all die of plague."

"Then comes Nemed," I said. I had brushed up on British magic history. Most people thought it was one-tenth history, and the rest was equally myth, wishful thinking, and bullshit, but I'd read it all the same.

Roman threw me a cautious look.

"The correct name is N-e-i-m-h-e-a-d-h," Jenn said. "When you pro-nounce it correctly, it sounds like . . ."

"Neig," Drest finished.

Only Celts would use nine letters to make one sound.

"He called himself that because he wanted people to think he was holy." Jenn sneered. "Neig of the skies. Neig the unkillable. Neig the mighty."

Drest snorted. "He conquers Ireland and moves on to Scotland."

"That's not how the legend goes," I said.

"Legends are often wrong. This isn't legend," Alpin said softly. "It's our history."

"He steals babies and turns them into his army," Drest continued. "The Picts fight him, until he pushes them all the way to the eastern edge of Scotland. There is nowhere to go but the sea and the Scottish cliffs. So, they outsmart him. They build the standing stones. There are many kinds. Some warp the magic around them; they are the curving kind. Others sound an alarm; they are the warning kind. And so on."

He pointed to the carvings on the surface of the stone. "The curving stones hide the villages. Neig's troops can't find the settlements so he can't find the settlements, and if he does, the shielding stones give people protection long enough to escape."

"What do the symbols mean?" I asked.

"Disc and rectangle," Alpin said. "The settlement has a warning stone that will let others know when Neig is coming. The crescent and V-rod means the shield is holding over the settlement. Don't fire arrows at it even if Neig is coming because they won't pierce it. Disc and rectangle means the settlement has the sun disc to signal for help."

They were explanatory signs. Like traffic signals. So bloody simple.

"Double disc and Z-rod?" I asked. "He signed the box with it."

Alpin grimaced. "He picked that symbol for himself. His troops would mark things with it to remind you of what happens when you disobey him."

"What is it?"

"Shackles," Jenn said. "Neig doesn't have servants. Only slaves."

Alpin traced the outline of the symbol on the stone. "When you see it with the broken arrow, it means here Neig can't see you. Here you are free."

"What about this one?" Roman asked, pointing at another symbol, which looked vaguely like a flower.

"Bagpipes," Drest said.

"What do bagpipes have to do with anything?" I asked.

He shrugged. "Bagpipes were battle music."

"He would've killed everyone eventually," Jenn told us. "But then the Fomorians invaded and kept him busy. They killed his wife. His children he either killed himself or ran off."

"He doesn't like competition." Drest grimaced. "His brother tried to fight him, lost, and sailed off with his own portion of the army. They got their asses kicked somewhere in Europe. Only one ship came back."

"What about the Tuatha Dé Danann?" I asked.

"They made a bargain with Neig," Drest said. "Gave him tribute. By that point he'd moved on to Scotland, anyway. Bigger place. More land. He had both islands before he was done."

"How did your ancestors beat him?" Roman asked.

"They didn't." Drest's face was grim. "They outlasted him. Eventually the magic fell, and one day he disappeared. He'd clawed himself a lair outside our world and took his hoard and army with him. Occasionally, he'd raid while the magic held. You never knew when or where he'd pop out. Our people were so scared of him, they kept building curving stones centuries after he went dormant."

"In all that time, nobody managed to get close enough to hurt him?" I asked. "I understand he has fire magic, but I fought Morfran and I met Morrighan. You're telling me nobody could get to this guy?"

"You don't get it," Drest said.

"Show her," Jenn told him.

Drest touched the kudzu. It rolled back, creeping up and over. The stone lay bare. I looked at the carving in the top of it. My insides went cold.

"Neig isn't a man," Alpin said softly.

"He is a dragon," I whispered.

A colossal dragon reared up on the battlefield, the figures of fighters tiny next to him. A cone of churning flame tore out of his mouth, disintegrating the palisade.

That was whom I'd felt in the clouds above me. That was why he'd tried to kill Yu Fong. Goose bumps ran up my arms.

"But his magic is blue," I said. "Like a human."

"All dragon magic is blue," Alpin said.

"Everyone knows that," Jenn said.

"Neig will never find us," Drest told me. "We have curving stones. But you, you're fucked."

ROMAN AND I didn't talk until we reached the city.

"It could be metaphorical," he finally said.

"It's not." I told him about Yu Fong. "Everything we ever read about dragons suggests they are highly territorial. He felt Yu Fong and tried to take out the competition."

"But he was in human shape when you saw him. So, what, he can shapeshift?"

"I don't know."

"Aspid can't shapeshift," Roman said. "It's a blessing too, or he would follow me everywhere, licking me. That would be weird."

Aspid, an enormous black serpent-dragon who belonged to Chernobog, had a deep, all-encompassing puppy love for Roman, which he expressed by wrapping his tongue around the black volhv.

"We need to call an emergency Conclave," I said.

The Conclave had started as a way to avoid conflicts between the Pack and the People, but in an emergency, every magical faction in the city came to it. It would take everyone to fight something like this off.

Roman raised his black eyebrows. "And tell them that we're about to get invaded by a dragon?"

"Yes."

"We don't have any evidence," Roman said.

He was right. Yu Fong was still in a coma, Beau Clayton and his deputies only saw Neig as a human, and the Druids wouldn't back me up in public. They barely even came to the Conclave. I would need evidence. Something more than visions of fire and carved rocks.

At the very least I had to warn the Pack and the People. With those two, my word would be sufficient. I had to call Nick, too.

"Let me out here," Roman said.

I pulled over.

"I'll talk to the volhvs and the witches," Roman said. "But talk is cheap. We need evidence. Witnesses."

"I know. Do you believe me that it's a dragon?"

"Yes," Roman said. "I believe you. But not because of the Picts and rocks. I believe you because you're you. I don't need to see it. It's enough for me that you believe it's a dragon. But it won't be enough for others."

"I know."

"It will be okay."

I doubted that, but nodded anyway.

"Don't kill yourself."

Oh, for the love of . . . "Will you stop with that?"

He shook his finger at me. "Don't do it. I'm watching you."

"Get out of my car."

I drove straight to Cutting Edge. Neig was right about one thing: he was legend. Over the years, legends became warped. They grew and evolved as they were passed from one generation to the next. Everyone "knew" that dragons hoarded treasure, lived in mountain caves, breathed fire, and killed their rivals. But how much of that was true was anybody's guess.

Was there even a point in trying to research? Most of what Drest had told us was considered to be myth. And it was distorted by Christianity. As Christianity had crept across the Middle East and Europe, the priests had realized that fighting old pagan ideas would doom the new religion. They were too deeply ingrained. So instead, Christianity adopted them, incorporating them into their rites, borrowing everything from Christmas and Easter to the idea of the immortal soul that separated from the physical body at death. Christianity tied the timeline of ancient Ireland to Noah's descendants and the flood. None of it would be helpful in figuring out Neig.

I drove into our parking lot and maneuvered the Jeep into the parking space. Mine was the only car. The kids and Curran were gone.

I unlocked the door and stepped inside. Over the years, Cutting Edge had become my fortress. Like my house, it was a place where I could take my sword off my back. I unbuckled the sheath and dropped it on my desk. I opened the fridge, took a pitcher of iced tea out, and poured myself a glass. I'd done this hundreds of times before. There was comfort in the ritual and I needed comfort today, because the dragon had knocked me off my stride.

How the hell do you fight a dragon? How large was he, exactly? If the carving on the stone was to scale, we were in deep shit. I could just imagine the conversation around the Conclave table. *So what evidence do you have of this dragon? Well, there is this overgrown rock in the magic druid camp. You can't see this rock or find this druid camp, but take my word for it.* Ugh.

Someone knocked on my door.

"Come in," I called.

The door swung open. Knight-abettor Norwood stepped through, followed by the two other knights. Just what I needed.

I leaned on my elbow. "The Holy Trinity. Come in, don't be shy. Grab a chair."

"You're disrespectful," the Hispanic woman told me.

"I'm so sorry, I should've used your names. So rude of me. You take the chair on the right, Larry, and Moe and Curly can sit over there."

The Hispanic woman opened her mouth. Knight-abettor Norwood glanced at her and she clamped her jaws shut.

Right. So, there was a script. They weren't sure what I was capable of and they wanted to find out, so they picked her to bait me. Bad idea.

The knights sat.

"Please let me introduce my colleagues. Knight-diviner Younger and Knight-striker Cabrera."

My guardian, Greg Feldman, was a knight-diviner during his life. They didn't always practice divination. They served as a cross between psychiatrists and priests and possessed a unique ability to "read" people. They were the Order's confessors and the advocates for the individual knights. A knight-striker was the Order's equivalent of a bazooka. Nice. Diplomacy and force, the knight-abettor had both sides covered.

"Kate Lennart."

"I think we've gotten off on the wrong foot," Norwood said.

"How?"

"The Order is interested in ascertaining the state of things in Atlanta."

"What does that have to do with me?"

"You are a power in Atlanta."

"The."

He blinked.

"I'm *the* power in Atlanta," I told him. "I claimed the city as my own."

"Wow," Cabrera said. "Humble, aren't you?"

"You came here looking for clarity. I'm clearing things up for you."

"What does that mean?" Norwood leaned forward, focusing on me.

"It means that when something sufficiently large and dangerous threatens the city, like my father trying to invade, I will use Atlanta's magic to protect it."

"So Atlanta has personal magic?" Cabrera snorted.

I ignored her.

"Well, does it? Is Atlanta a person?" she pressed.

"I don't have the time or the inclination to educate you," I told her. "The Mage College is up the street and over the bridge. If you go by there, I'm sure they'll bring you up to speed."

"Do you rule Atlanta?" the blond diviner asked.

"No."

"Why not?" he asked.

"Atlanta is doing fine on its own without my leadership. We have a democratically elected government, and I have no intention of interfering with it."

"If you claimed Atlanta, why don't you stop the crime here?" Cabrera asked. Her eyes were calculating. She was asking leading questions they already knew the answers to. They wanted confirmation that I wasn't omnipotent and omniscient.

"Because it's not my responsibility to stop crime. We have a well-funded police department, GBI headquarters, and local sheriff departments, not including a number of private organizations, like the Guild, the Red Guard, and, of course, the Order."

"But could you stop all crime?" Younger asked.

"Nobody can stop all crime, knight-diviner. You, of all people, should know that."

Norwood studied me. "The Order is interested in forging a relationship of cooperation and mutual understanding."

"I already have a relationship of mutual understanding with the Order."

"Really?" Norwood asked.

"Yes. Nick thinks I'm fruit from the poisoned tree and hates my family, and I tolerate his assholeness because occasionally I need the Order's help. Nick and I understand each other very well."

"We find that people tend to be more productive in a less hostile environment," Norwood said.

I sighed. "Okay, so the Order would like to be friendlier. Great. What do you know about dragons?"

"What?" Cabrera asked.

"Dragons. Weaknesses, habits, how one might possibly go about killing one?"

"That information is classified," Norwood said.

"And here we are. When it comes down to it, there isn't much you can do because you have regulations that bind you. You divide your world into humans and nonhumans, and your definition of human is so circumscribed, your influence is collapsing. I sympathize. It's hard to fight with your arms tied behind your back, but it's not my problem. You are not my problem, unless you make yourself into one."

Cabrera opened her mouth.

I didn't wait for her. "Go back to Wolf Trap. Nick and I have a working relationship. It's not perfect, but it doesn't have to be. I don't need him to be my friend. I need him to put manpower on the field when it counts."

"Nikolas Feldman will be replaced," Norwood said.

"That's the Order I know. Always putting appearances above the welfare of their knights."

"What actions will you take if Feldman is removed?" the knight-diviner asked.

"I will bar the Order from having a chapter in Atlanta."

"You can't do that," Cabrera said.

"I can, and I will. I'm tired of your turnover problems. I prefer to work with Nick. After everything Moynohan put him through, he deserves to have his own chapter. His performance is exemplary. You want to get rid of him because he's politically inconvenient, go ahead. But don't put lipstick on a pig and pretend it's on my account. If you take him out, I promise you, the new chapter of the Order won't be welcome in Atlanta."

"You're a nobody," Cabrera said, biting off words. "You're all talk. I can feel your magic. It's nothing."

The phone rang. I held up my hand and picked it up. "Kate Lennart."

"Conlan escaped," Curran said.

"What?"

"He shifted and ran away from Martha. They are chasing him now, but they're too far behind. He's coming toward you."

Our son was out in the open, with sahanu all around the city.

I focused on the magic around me, stretching through the arcane power drenching the city. *Where are you, baby? Where . . .*

A bright spark moved through the magic. Conlan! He wasn't far.

I grabbed my sword and dashed out the door. The three knights sprinted after me.

I ran like I've never run before in my life. Streets flew by. I turned, guided by magic, focused on the brilliant glowing drop of magic. I was almost on top of him. A deserted street lay in front of me. On the left, the shell of a building waited, its first floor all empty brick arches. The entire building lay exposed, its roof gone long ago, the arches at the far end dark and shadowy.

Conlan was in there.

Someone had cleared most of the debris, pushing it into a large pile at the far end and a smaller one to the right, outside the building. Not a lot of places to hide.

I walked to the building. Behind me the knights rounded the corner.

"Conlan?" I called. "It's Mommy."

A small creature exploded out of the pile and jumped into my arms, shifting in midleap into a human baby. I hugged him to me. My heart was beating so fast, it was about to jump out of my chest.

"Mama!"

"What were you thinking, you little idiot?" I squeezed him to me.

Big gray eyes looked at me, wet with tears. "Bad." He sniffed. "Bad."

Oh no. "Where? Where is the bad thing, Conlan? Show me."

He buried his face in my chest.

Something moved within the building, deep in the shadowy arches on the other side.

The sahanu had stalked my son. They'd found him and scared him, and he ran across the city to me.

They'd scared my son in my domain. Never again.

A splash of magic landed within the arches and died. *I see you.*

A vampire landed next to me, smeared in grape-purple sunblock. "We found the sahanu," it said in Javier's voice. "In-Shinar, do you require assistance?"

A second vamp dropped on my other side.

"Yes." I thrust Conlan into Javier's vamp's arms. "Protect my child."

The vampire took my son.

I grasped the second vamp's mind. The navigator let go.

I unsheathed Sarrat, dropped the sheath on the ground, and marched into the building, the undead at my heels. The sahanu waited for me in the arches. I felt them. The damn building had too many holes.

"I see you." My voice spread through the building. Fury boiled inside me, blotting out everything else. "I see all of you."

I yanked the magic to me. Words of power burst from my lips, the pain barely registering. I'd had a lot of practice.

"Ranar kair." Come to me.

Magic ripped from me like a tidal wave. The arches rained sahanu, my power tearing them out of their hidey-holes and throwing them to the ground. I saw familiar faces in that split second: Gust, pale, green hair, air magic, twin swords; Carolina, seven feet tall, brown-skinned, chain mail, hammer, muscles like a champion weightlifter; Arsenic, bright red hair, wrapped in diaphanous cloth like a mummy, poisonous to the touch. Fourteen sahanu. They had all come for my son. All except Razer.

I sliced the back of my left forearm and slammed the cut against the side of the building. My blood shot out in a hair-thin stream, running along the walls, across the open spaces of the arches, across bricks and holes until it touched itself, completing the circle. A translucent red wall burst into existence and vanished, the blood ward sealing itself.

One of the sahanu, a lean dark-haired man, leaped, aiming to escape through one of the arches, and fell back from the ward. The assassins turned toward me. They finally realized the truth: they were trapped in here with me.

"There is no escape." I crushed the vamp's mind. Its skull exploded. The undead blood surged out of it, obeying my call, mixing with my own.

"Don't let her don the armor!" Carolina screamed.

They charged me.

I vomited a power word. *"Osanda!"*

They crashed to the ground. Carolina tried to crawl to me, but my magic clamped her down.

The mist of undead blood settled over me, flowing, shaped by my will, turning into armor. It coated my arms, my stomach, my back, impenetrable but flexible, the color of a ruby, the color of my blood. The mist congealed on Sarrat, forming a blood edge. I felt all my chains fall away. All the brakes were gone.

The drained vamp fell next to me. I charged.

The first sahanu tried to counter and I cut him in half with one swing. Carolina came at me, swinging her hammer. I sidestepped and cut off her arm at the elbow. She screamed, and I added a second mouth across her navel to put her down. A woman stabbed my back with her spear. A jolt of pain ripped through me as the armor absorbed the impact. I spun and beheaded her.

Gust dropped from above, diving with his blades.

I spat a focused blast of magic at him. *"Hessad." Mine.*

His mind broke under the pressure like a cracked walnut. He landed, mine before his feet touched the ground.

"Amehe," I ordered, sending a sharp arrow of power through him. *Obey.*

In front of me Arsenic spat a power word. I flattened my magic into a shield and it glanced off. *"Kill!"* I told Gust.

The green-haired sahanu sprinted at Arsenic, his twin blades raised for the kill. The other assassin twisted out of the way, sprouting spikes on his arms.

Gust whirled like a dervish. The spikes pierced him in the same moment he buried his left sword in Arsenic's chest. They sank to the ground together, but I was already moving. The world faded to the vivid precision of battle. Every moment mattered. Every step counted. There was no other place like it. This was my calling. This was what I did, and I danced through the battlefield, through the spray of blood and boiling magic, the sword of my grandmother's bones singing a song as it bridged life and death.

I cut them to pieces. I disemboweled and maimed. They would never again scare my son.

The last sahanu collapsed.

The ground at my feet was bloody. Pieces of human bodies littered it.

I turned around.

The knights stood on the street, their faces wearing identical expressions: eyebrows raised, eyes wide open, mouth a tense half-open slash across the face. Fear.

The vampire had frozen, Conlan in its arms. My son was looking straight at me.

Damn it, Javier. That wasn't something Conlan should've seen. I had to mitigate it. I dissolved the ward and walked toward them, killing the magic in my blood armor. It crumpled to dust. I walked to him, my magic swirling around me. I had no cloak and I didn't care.

Cabrera and Norwood took a step back. Younger remained, awe on his face. He raised his hand toward me, fingers trembling, and Norwood yanked him back.

I raised my arms. Conlan reached for me, and I took my baby from the vamp, my magic spilling freely out of me. Conlan hugged my neck and petted my hair. "Shai."

Oh, how I wished I were shiny and not a killer.

A Jeep rocketed onto the street, taking the corner too sharply. Another followed, then an SUV, then a truck.

The first Jeep screeched to a halt, and Martha jumped out of it, moving much faster than a plump woman twice my age should've moved.

Six vampires came scuttling over the roof, in assorted colors of sunblock, like someone spilled a bag of Skittles. Taste the undead rainbow.

"Secure the perimeter," the lead one barked, landing next to Javier's vampire. "Sitrep?"

Beside me Javier's vamp looked to the left, looked to the right, and unhinged its jaws. "The first generation of the sahanu is dead. The second generation of the sahanu is dead. The Order of Sahanu is dead. Everybody is dead." Javier paused. "Praise be to In-Shinar, the Merciful."

"Stop it," I growled at him.

"Right," the team leader said. "Team One Leader to Mother, fourteen bandits down, no pulse, scene hot, the Dove and Chick are secure. Advise?"

The dove? Kate Lennart, the Dove? Just when exactly had I ever done anything remotely dovelike?

The vamps had spread through the street, taking positions on the buildings.

"Roger. Team One, hold position until cleanup complete." The vamp swiveled to me. "Cleanup crew is on the way, ma'am."

Martha reached me, with George at her heels. "I'm so sorry. We thought he was down for a nap. He shouldn't have been able to open the latch on the window bars."

Oh, but he did. I was mother to the smartest boy alive. I hugged him to me. He was still alive. He could've died. He would've died if Curran hadn't called to tell me he was missing.

It hit me like a ton of bricks. My knees almost gave, and I locked them in place.

George wrapped her arm around me. "It's okay," she said. "He's alive and safe. It's okay."

She held on to me for another moment and let me go.

The cars kept coming. The street filled with female shapeshifters. The ones I recognized were from Clan Heavy. Ten, no twelve . . .

"Who are all these people?" I asked George.

"The book club," she told me.

I pulled my magic back into me. "Has anybody heard from Curran?"

"I called him at the Guild when Conlan came up missing," George said.

"Ma'am," Javier said. "I have a report from the patrols. The Guild is under attack. Would you like us to assist?"

"Yes!"

"Team Three, In-Shinar requests assistance at the Guild." Javier's vamp scuttled away.

Martha turned and roared, "Turn around! Everyone back to the cars! My son needs help at the Guild."

Clan Heavy ran back to their cars.

I turned to the knights. "Help or get out of the way."

Norwood stepped aside, and I ran to the nearest car, Conlan in my arms.

≡ CHAPTER ≡

13

DURING THE GUILD'S remodel, the architect decided to mitigate some of the damage to the building by adding a small balcony to the top floor. Framed by bay French doors, the recessed balcony was tucked away in the north wall, facing the Guild parking lot, all but invisible from the ground. The mercs called it Christopher's Roost. Sometimes, at dawn or dusk, he'd come here and stand on the rail, watching the sun, before he sprouted his blood-red wings and soared into the air. I liked to come here during the day. I'd brought some plants—nothing fancy, some ivies, bamboo, and pothos—three chairs, and a big beanbag stuffed with sawdust.

I sat in my chair now, Conlan asleep on the beanbag, and watched the flurry of activity below. Corpses littered the parking lot. Neig had sent a dozen of his creatures to attack the Guild. We pulled into the parking lot in time to see Curran rip the last of them in half. He'd grasped the beast by the neck and the arm and pulled him apart like he was tearing a piece of paper.

Now he was below, supervising the cleanup. Biohazard had been called, but there was no telling when they would get here. Meanwhile, the bodies had to be secured, the parking lot salted and disinfected with fire, and the wounded treated. I'd excused myself from all of it. I'd had my fight.

Someone walked up the stairs behind me. They moved quietly, but all of my senses were still keyed up and I recognized the sound.

"Hi, Martha."

The older woman sat in the chair next to me and handed me a cup of tea. I sipped. It was half honey.

"I'm sorry," she said.

"That's okay. He's full of surprises."

Martha glanced at me and drank her tea. "We put him down in his room for a nap."

George loved her nephew so much, she'd set a room aside for him in her house. Every time I saw it, it always cheered me up.

"There is one window in the room," Martha said.

"I know." It was a small window about five feet off the ground, secured with a grate of silver bars.

"The grate has a latch," Martha said.

I nodded. Most bedrooms had grates that could be unlocked, otherwise the bedroom would become a death trap in a fire.

"A lion cub can't open the latch. It's intricate." She sipped her tea. "It requires human dexterity."

Where was she going with this?

"But a shapeshifter child in human form can't hold on to the bars, because they have silver that will burn their hands."

She paused.

"Aha," I said to say something.

"Conlan opened the latch and escaped. There were claw marks on the wall and claw marks on the latch. He did this very fast. George put him down for a nap, and fifteen minutes later, when I came to check on him, he was gone."

That was how he avoided the silver. He turned into his warrior form, climbed up, and worked the latch with his claws.

"Curran didn't tell me everything." Her voice held a gentle rebuke.

"What did he tell you?"

"That my grandson is a shapeshifter, and assassins are hunting him. What else should I know?"

We would need her to watch Conlan. I had to come clean. "He can hold a warrior form," I said.

Martha startled. "The baby?"

"Yes."

"For how long?"

"For however long he wants." I sighed.

Martha fell silent.

I finished my tea.

"What else can he do?" she asked softly.

"We don't know." I set my cup on the little table between us. "We know he can't control his magic, and it makes him visible to people who can sense it. My father put a price on his head. One of my father's associates was seen bringing a briefcase into the Keep. He was escorted by renders. He left without the briefcase. The next day Robert brought us an offer of friendship and alliance."

Martha leaned back. "Jim will never betray you."

"How can you be sure?"

"Because she'd cut off his balls and feed them to him," Desandra said behind me.

"What are you doing here?"

The alpha of Clan Wolf stalked into the light and leaned against the wall. "I was driving by. Saw the spectacle. Thought I'd stop by. What are those furry foul-smelling dead things in the parking lot?"

"They belong to a guy named Neig. He's ancient, powerful, and he might be a dragon."

"What does this Neig want?"

"To conquer the world. And for me to help him against my father. This was a demonstration of his power."

Desandra sneered at the parking lot. "Not exactly impressive. Oh well, most men have trouble with foreplay."

She had a point. With as much as he'd hyped his demonstration of power, I had expected bigger fireworks.

"Nobody will harm my grandchild," Martha said. "Clan Heavy won't stand for it."

I didn't say anything. Clan Heavy was powerful, but it was only one clan.

"They say a lot of silly things about us wolves."

Desandra studied the polish on her nails. They were long, sharpened to a point, and bright yellow like the mane of blond hair falling on her back.

"They say we mate for life, that we have lupine dignity, that we are all stoic and sour. Rubbish. But one thing is true. We forget nothing. We remember our friends and our enemies. If the Beast Lord were to betray his friends, well, he wouldn't be fit to be a leader. If Martha goes for his balls, someone will have to go for his throat."

Orange light rolled over Desandra's eyes. She smiled. "Poor Beast Lord," she purred. "Why, he wouldn't know where to turn."

A vampire dashed across the parking lot. Grape purple. What now . . .

"Aiming for the Beast Lady seat?" I asked.

"If they begged me to take it on bended knee, I wouldn't." Desandra grinned, baring sharp teeth. "Too much hassle. I'm a single mother. All I want to do is raise my children in peace."

"And rule the largest clan with iron claws," I told her.

"These are plastic." Desandra waved her nails at me.

"Jim knows what he would face," Martha said. "He isn't a fool."

"All the same, I don't want Conlan near the Keep. And I don't want him at your clan house. Too much risk for everyone."

"We will take care of Conlan," Martha said. "We'll do it on your street. Don't worry about it."

"And Mahon?" I asked.

"What the old bear doesn't know won't hurt him," Martha said.

"You do what you need to do," Desandra said. "We'll do our part."

An undead vaulted over the balcony. "In-Shinar!" A desperate note vibrated in Javier's voice.

"What happened?"

"Rowena failed to check in. We can't find her or her vampire."

Damn it.

I got up and closed my eyes. Magic spread before me. I couldn't find someone I didn't know. I could detect when a significant power breached my borders, but the sahanu were invisible to me. They didn't have enough power. I didn't know them well, but Rowena was related to me by blood, a bond strengthened by friendship and a vow of loyalty. It was a tenuous connection, but it would have to be enough.

The sea of magic waited for me. I had to stir it up. I pulled my power in and released it. The pulse of magic rolled through the city like the toll of a giant silent bell. The floor underneath me shuddered.

Pulse.

Another pulse.

Pulse.

There, a faint trail, something weak, something small and insignificant but carrying traces of Rowena's magic. Her vampire.

It was on the very edge of my territory, just inside the border, left for me to find. And there was something else. Ancient and scorching, like someone had raked the fabric of the magic with white-hot claws. Neig.

I opened my eyes. "Get Ghastek," I snarled at Javier. "Get your strike teams. Get the bus. Get everyone."

WHEN TEDDY JO carried me into the air, he did it in a contraption he called "the sling" and I called an old playground swing. When Christopher carried me, he picked me up like I was a child. It wasn't my favorite way to travel, but I needed speed, and he hurtled through the air like a hawk diving for his prey.

We were going southeast, toward Panthersville. The city slid under us, so tiny it seemed unreal. How the hell did people get into planes on a regular basis before the Shift? I did a lot of things well. Heights and flying weren't among them.

"Would you like me to fly lower?" Christopher asked.

"No."

What I would have liked was Rowena, safe and sound. I felt as if I were trying to outrun a giant rolling boulder while more boulders fell on me from every side. Whatever was holding me together was wearing thin, and when it broke, there would be hell to pay.

I just had to find Rowena. I had to find her alive, not in a vat of boiling people . . .

The spark of magic was almost directly under us.

"We're here," I told Christopher.

His great red wings folded. He went into a dive. Wind tore at me. I shut my eyes.

We swooped and miraculously stopped falling. I opened one eye. Christopher stood in a pasture, holding me. A copse of magnolia trees, their thick branches twisting up, waited in front of us, the boundary of my territory just yards away, beyond the tree line.

Christopher set me down, carefully.

The pasture lay quiet. Insects chirped. Birds sang in the branches, some trilling melody. The heat of summer streamed from a sky so beautifully blue, it almost hurt to look at. The weak "glow" of Rowena's magic was right in front of me. I pulled Sarrat out of its sheath and walked forward, under the dense canopy.

The sound of someone's hoarse breathing echoed through the woods, creepy enough to give me nightmares.

A massive tree spread its branches before me. A bloody chain was wrapped around the trunk.

I moved forward, carefully, one foot over the other, circling the tree.

Step. Another step.

The back of the trunk came into view. A dead vampire sagged against the loop of the chain, a massive pike thrust through his heart. Next to it, held in place by the loops of the same chain, a yeddimur sagged against the trunk. Blood stained the fur on its sides where it must've tried to gnaw itself free of the chain. Above them, a single word was clawed into the bark. *Kings.*

"Kings?" Christopher frowned.

I turned in the direction the bloodsucker would've looked if it were still alive. It made sense.

Two vampires tore out of the woods and galloped across the pasture, both so old, no sign of upright locomotion remained. They ran on all fours, grotesque ugly creatures, so warped nobody would've guessed they'd started out as human. Their sunblock, a deep crimson, looked like fresh blood.

"She isn't here," the undead said in unison in Ghastek's voice, his words sharp enough to cut.

"What's Rowena's effective range?"

"Four point six seven miles."

I pushed through the vegetation to the other side.

"Kate!" he snapped.

The underbrush ended. We stood on the apex of a low hill, fields and woods rolling to the horizon. A column of black smoke stabbed at the sky due southeast.

"Kings Row," I told Ghastek.

The distant roar of water engines came from the northwest—Curran and the mercs were catching up.

Ghastek's bloodsuckers streaked down the hill. Christopher took a running start, swept me up, and flew into the sky.

KING'S ROW, POPULATION around a thousand, was born from the remnants of a fracturing Decatur. Most of the people gave up trying to fight nature fueled by magic steroids and pulled into the city proper, but a few neighborhoods remained, turning into small towns: Chapel Hill, Sterling Forest, and Kings Row. They set up their own post offices and water and guard towers and held on to their land.

Christopher circled the settlement. Kings Row was no more. Nothing remained except for a charred ruin. Black ash hid the ground. Smoke billowed from half a dozen places, greasy and acrid, joining together into a single massive cloud above. Here and there remnants of the fire smoldered, red veins in the black crust. With a fire, some structures would've been left standing: fireplaces, brick walls, ruined appliances, burned-out cars . . . There was nothing. Not even the outline of the streets. Only black ash.

He'd taken a thousand people. I didn't know if they'd died in the fire or if he'd kidnapped them, but they were gone and Neig was to blame.

No more. I needed to get my hands on him now.

And what would I do when I did? I didn't even know if a blood ward would hold against *that*.

Christopher took another turn. Something shone through the smoke, a smudged orange glow.

"There!" I pointed, but he had already seen it. We dropped through the smoke and landed on the ash. Heat scoured my face.

A twelve-foot-tall pillar rose in the middle of the ravaged field, a translucent column dusted with ash. Within it, an orange glowing liquid flowed. Glass, I realized. The pillar was glass, its outer crust solid, but inside it was molten.

Christopher made a choking sound.

I looked up.

There was a human being in the pillar.

Oh dear God.

The body was encased in glass up to the shoulders. The head and neck were free, smudged with soot, all the hair burned off, but the body itself floated, submerged in the molten glass. It wasn't burned. The molten glass should've boiled the flesh off the bones, but I could see pale legs dangling in the glowing liquid.

What the bloody fuck?

The head opened its eyes.

Still alive. How?

The dry cracked lips moved. "He . . ."

Ghastek's vampires slid to a stop next to me and froze.

"He . . ." the person in the glass said. "Help."

Rowena.

Every hair on my arms stood on end.

I concentrated on the pillar, pulling magic inside me to shine at it like a light. I couldn't see it the way Julie did, but I felt the veins of glowing power twisting into the pillar in a complicated web. Inside, Rowena was coated in it as if she wore a skintight bodysuit. The web cradled her, winding through every inch of the pillar. The whole thing was bound together. Shit.

Ghastek's left vamp charged to the glass column.

"No!" I yelled.

It turned to me.

"If you break the glass, she'll burn to death."

"Are you sure?" Ghastek asked, his voice clipped.

"Yes."

A Jeep rounded the bend of the road. Julie and Derek jumped out and ran toward us.

"Can we drain it from the bottom?" Christopher asked.

"She's wrapped in a spell. It's clinging to her like a second skin. The skin is connected to the pillar. We break any part of it, she'll die instantly."

The vampire spun around. "Get her out of there." Ghastek's voice vibrated with steel. "Kate!"

"Quiet."

If we broke the pillar, she died. If we tried to lift her out of it, she died. If tech hit, she died.

Vampires dashed out of the woods on the northern edge of the town. The People catching up with Ghastek.

Julie reached me, looked up at the pillar, and clamped her hand over her mouth.

What do I do?

The awful sound of groaning wood rolled through the air. I turned. On the south side, the trees shuddered. Green branches twisted and dropped. Something had snapped the decades-old pines like toothpicks.

Something huge. The druid carving flashed before me. I pulled Sarrat from its sheath.

"Form on In-Shinar!" Ghastek snapped.

The undead lined up into a wedge behind me.

An oak split, spun on its trunk, and plummeted down. A massive snout emerged into the light, six feet across. An enormous head followed, shaggy with brown fur. Two curved tusks big enough to skewer a car flanked the snout, followed by three pairs of shorter tusks. Short spiked horns protruded from the beast's skull.

Well, of course. That's what this party was missing. An enormous, pissed-off pig. Fuck me.

Behind me the Guild Jeeps tore around the bend of the road and sped across the burned ground, raising a cloud of ash.

The colossal boar took a step forward. Ragged gashes crossed its hide, cutting through a network of faded scars. Here and there, spiked balls punctured its hide, half-sunken into its flesh. Someone had tortured this boar.

The beast swung its head toward me. A broken chain dangled around its neck, as thick as a lighting pole. At its end hung a huge metal symbol, Neig's shackles.

"It's a god." Julie took a step back. "Its magic is silver."

I hold gods prisoner, tormenting them for my pleasure.

Neig had captured a god, kept him prisoner for a thousand years, tortured him, and now he'd loosed him on us. There would have been only one boar god on the British Isles for Neig to capture.

"It's Moccus," I said. The Celtic Boar, guardian of hunters and warriors, the Caledonian Monster. A god, or rather its manifestation. Killing it wouldn't kill the deity, but it would banish it from our reality. A tech shift would rip him out of existence instantly. It would also kill Rowena.

"Does it have any weaknesses?" Ghastek asked.

"No."

The boar opened its mouth and roared. The bellow slapped my eardrums, a mad blast of rage. It reverberated through the burned-out town. Ash trembled.

Just what we needed.

Moccus pawed the ground. Another bellow smashed into us.

The bloodsuckers waited, unmoving.

Nothing I had would deliver a punch strong enough to one-shot him. We'd have to bleed Moccus. It would take hours. We didn't have time to fight him.

Out of the corner of my eye, I saw three Guild Jeeps barreling down the road toward us. They went off the pavement and tore through the scarred town, raising clouds of ash.

"We have to kill it fast," I said.

"Fast isn't an option," Christopher answered, his voice detached. "He's too large and he's a god. He will regenerate."

"We have to try. Rowena doesn't have time."

Moccus sighted us. His deep-set eyes ignited with fury. The boar was finally free from confinement. Free to punish. Neig had driven him mad.

"Protocol Giant," Ghastek said, his voice calm. "Prioritize damage over undead casualties."

"You don't owe me anything," Rowena whispered from the pillar. "Go. Leave."

Moccus started forward.

Here we go. I pulled magic to myself.

The leading Jeep slid to a halt. A single man jumped out and sprinted to the boar. I would know that sprint anywhere.

Hi, honey, we're over here, but please ignore us and run at the magic boar all by yourself. It's only a giant enraged animal god. No need to worry. Nothing bad ever happens in situations like this.

"Curran!"

He ran past us at breakneck speed. As if we weren't even there.

"Damn it." I unsheathed Sarrat.

"Idiot," Ghastek volunteered.

Moccus bellowed, giving voice to pain and insane anger, and broke into a full charge. The ground punched my feet and I stumbled to keep my balance.

The boar charged toward Curran like a runaway train.

I broke into a sprint. He'd need backup. The undead followed me.

My husband jumped. His human skin tore. Magic punched me, like the first ray of sunrise coming over the horizon. Fur spilled out, a whole cloud of it, black and huge. A colossal lion smashed into the boar.

I blinked. No, the giant lion was still there.

What the hell? What in the bloody . . . How?

He was as big as Moccus, solid black, a majestic mane floating in the wind, sparking with streaks of magic.

What . . .

The lion opened his jaws, fangs glinting in the sun, and plunged them into Moccus's neck. The boar and the lion rolled. The ground trembled.

"Kate!"

The two colossal creatures snarled and roared, trying to bite and gore each other.

How was this possible?

"Kate!"

I realized I was standing still. My vampire army had come to a halt.

"Rowena!" Ghastek's vamps screamed in my face.

Rowena was my friend. Rowena had held Conlan just yesterday, and today she could burn to death. I couldn't let her die. I knew exactly what I had to do. I just had to do it. It was that or she would be boiled alive.

A clump of dirt the size of a truck flew past me. I ducked and spun back to the pillar. "Get wood. As much as you can. We need a fire. A huge fire."

The vampires spun around. There was nothing to burn except for the distant trees. They would take too long.

"Does it have to be wood?" Ghastek asked through his twin vamps.

"No. As long as it burns. We need a big flame."

The mercs had piled out of the Jeeps and stared at the battle raging only a few feet away. Barabas was on the front line. I caught a glimpse of his face, touched with awe.

I couldn't think about it. I couldn't afford to process it now. There was no time. I turned to Rowena. She stared at me.

"Leave me," she said, her voice breaking.

"Not going to happen."

"You have Conlan . . ."

"Conlan will be fine. I will be fine. You will be fine. Everything will be fine."

I would go to hell for making promises like this.

An armored bus emerged from behind the curve of the road and headed for us. The People's mobile HQ.

It sped to us and came to a stop. The doors swung open and Ghastek stepped out, followed by two Masters of the Dead and a dozen journeymen. I recognized familiar faces: Kim, Sean, Javier . . .

"We'll burn the bus," Ghastek said over the snarls.

The undead attacked the bus, pulling the reserve gasoline containers out of the back and dousing the vehicle with it.

The two giant animals were still fighting. It took everything I had to not run over there and help.

One of Ghastek's undead grabbed him, wrapping its arms around his legs. The second picked up the first and raised Ghastek to the pillar. He raised his hand to her cheek. His fingers stopped just short of touching.

"Let me go," Rowena told him.

"Never," he said.

"Ready," Javier told me.

"Carlos!" I called.

A short merc turned toward me. I pointed to the gutted bus. "Torch it."

Carlos leaned back and flexed, bringing his arms together as if he were squeezing an invisible basketball. A spark burst into existence between his spread fingers and spun, growing, twisting, turning into a flame, first reddish, then orange, then white. His hands shuddered. He grunted and launched the fireball at the bus.

The more of yourself you give to the fire, the louder the call will be.

The armored vehicle exploded.

I reopened the cut on my arm and thrust it into the fire. Heat cooked my skin. My blood boiled into the flames, turning them red. Pain hit me, and I sent it into the blaze with my magic, opening a pathway across thousands of miles. The fire roared, bloody, and I screamed into its depths.

"FATHER!"

The blaze snapped, a glowing silk curtain pulled suddenly taut, and my father appeared within the flames, eyes blazing with power.

"WHAT?"

I pulled my arm out of the fire and cradled it. It hurt. God, it hurt. **"Help me."**

He stared at me. He chose his own age, sometimes young, sometimes older. Today he wore the face I knew, a man in his late fifties, full head of hair, wise handsome face that could've belonged to a teacher, a prophet, or a king. He'd let himself age like this because he wanted to look like a man who could've fathered me. He had still kept it, even two years later.

"Please help me."

"YOU ARE ASKING ME FOR HELP? WHY SHOULD I HELP YOU, SHARRIM?"

My father was proudest of me when I managed to beat him. Weakness and begging wouldn't work. I had to be smart about this.

"Do you remember the ashes of Tyre?"

He looked behind me. His gaze swept over the grave of Kings Row and halted on Rowena inside the pillar. A muscle in his face jerked. Something sparked within his gaze. He buried it before I could pin it down. What I said next would determine if Rowena lived or died.

"He says you killed his brother," I said. **"This is a demonstration of his power. He doesn't think our family can match it."**

The flames went out. The bus lay before me, suddenly cold. My arm hurt.

It hadn't worked. He'd abandoned me. I'd banked on his pride and lost. I turned away.

A draft touched my cheek. Next to me Roland lowered the hood of his plain brown robe and looked at the pillar. The undead scattered. Ghastek stood alone by the pillar, his chin raised, his eyes defiant. The rest of the People huddled in a clump to my right, putting me between themselves and my father.

"Have you thought of a solution?" he asked, as if he'd just given me a complex mathematical problem and was curious if I could solve it.

"I can take control of the pillar, but that will require breaching it, and any breach will break the protective envelope around her. If I attempt to claim the protective envelope around her as my own, it may disintegrate and she'll die."

He nodded, his handsome profile slightly curious. "Continue."

"My best option is to freeze her into stasis with the spell of Kair, while I claim the land. The spell of Kair would hold her separate from our reality."

I wouldn't be able to hold it for longer than an instant either. I didn't have enough practice.

"Claiming would allow me to instantly disintegrate the pillar before it burns her, but claiming is a two-step process: the initial pulse that disperses from me to the boundary and the return pulse that travels from the boundary back to me. In the space between the two pulses, I'm powerless. The spell of Kair requires a constant flow of magic from the mage. It will collapse. The first pulse of claiming will disrupt the magic net that's keeping her alive right now. If she's out of stasis between the two pulses, she'll burn to death."

And I had just told him that Erra was teaching me. I would worry about it later.

My father crouched and picked up a handful of ash. "When their kind scorch the land, they wound it. Are you prepared for what will follow if you claim it?"

I had no idea what would follow. "Yes."

My father nodded. "Three seconds. That is all you have."

Three seconds was an eternity longer than I would've lasted. It had to be enough.

I had only generated a powerful claiming pulse once, and I'd required a tower to do it. Erra had been having me practice claiming small chunks of land, a couple of feet here and there, and then letting them go, and it required a lot of preparation.

All I needed was a twenty-yard circle around the pillar. That would contain any veins of magic stretching from the pillar. I could do this. I just needed an anchor. Claiming required an anchor, whether it was a tower or a nail thrust into the ground. I needed a conduit for my power.

I didn't have anything.

Wait. I had my sword. I grasped Sarrat with my left hand and knelt, holding it straight up.

Slowly, deliberately putting one foot in front of the other, Ghastek walked away from the pillar to the group of People waiting on the side.

My father raised his hands. Light stabbed from them. Words, ancient and beautiful, poured out of his mouth, moving the magic itself. It was beautiful. It was poetry and music wrapped into a song of pure power.

I stabbed Sarrat into the ground and fed every drop of me into it.

A pulse tore out of me, a crimson wave of light rolling through the land. There was a pause, a single heartbeat that lasted for an eternity. Silence met me, and then, in the distance, I heard a noise, like a tornado coming from far away. It grew, deafening, overpowering, and slammed into me, jerking me off my feet. I hovered three feet above Kings Row. My skin turned to ash. Flames burst inside me, incinerating me. My body burned.

Neig had drained the land of its magic to make the pillar. It needed magic to survive and it was taking mine. It was pulling the magic out of my veins.

The agony drowned me. It hurt. It hurt so much. The land would consume me.

Rowena.

Through the bloody haze covering my eyes, I reached toward the smudge of magic burning in my mind and struck the pillar.

My vision cleared for an agonizing moment, suddenly razor-sharp, and I saw Curran lock his huge fangs on the back of Moccus's neck and bite through it. The great boar gasped and went limp, finally at peace.

The pillar shattered, the molten liquid spilling, each drop turning into a perfect globe of glass, suffused with stolen magic.

Don't panic, Erra's cool voice reminded me from my memory.

The glass was mine. I crunched the droplets with my power. They broke as one, then again, and again, raining down in a glittering waterfall, and I crunched them again and again, feeding their magic back into the land while a crystal rain fell onto the soil, slipping into the earth.

The wailing lessened, then grew quiet, then turned to a whimper, a whisper, and finally vanished. I fell on the ground, landing badly on my side, and blinked. My hands weren't charred. Not even my left, which I'd stuck into the fire.

I sat up. A perfect circle spread around the pillar, green with fresh grass. A familiar aroma filled the area. It smelled like spice and honey. Delicate flowers had sprouted all around me, small white stars with black centers. I had made them once before, when I'd cried during a flare, because a man who served Morrighan had died. I cared for him, and I had tried to keep him alive, but in the end, I'd had to let him go.

Rowena lay on the ground next to me, naked but unburned.

She opened her eyes, raised her hand, and struggled to say something. Alive. She'd survived. We'd done it.

I felt oddly numb.

My father sat on the ground next to me and gently touched one of the flowers. Ghastek knelt by Rowena, took her into his arms with infinite care, and carried her away.

The boar's corpse sprawled on the ash, all of its flesh stripped, the great bones rolling gently, as the lion dug into its stomach. The awful chewing sounds of a huge predator eating echoed through Kings Row. A part of me knew this was Curran and he was eating a god, and I should be freaked out by it, but most of me refused to deal with it. I was spent.

"Has the creature spoken to you?" my father asked.

"Yes. He wants to conquer."

"So did his brother. What else did he say?"

"He offered for me to be his queen. He wants me to betray you. He hasn't gotten around to saying it, but he will."

"What did you tell him?"

"I reminded him that my father and my aunt killed his brother and destroyed his army, so he was a losing bet. He told me he wasn't his brother and promised to prove it. This is his proof." I turned to him. "He has the yeddimur."

A muscle jerked in my father's face. "They are an abomination."

So the great and powerful Nimrod had a weakness after all.

"Is he really a dragon? Was his brother a dragon?"

"Yes."

Great. Freaking fantastic.

"He said his brother proposed marriage to Erra."

My father sneered, and I saw his older sister in his face. "We don't marry serpents. We erase them from the flow of history."

"Oh good."

We sat quietly for a long moment.

"Tell me of the dragon," Roland asked.

"His name is Neimheadh. He ruled Ireland and Scotland with his army of human soldiers and corrupted creatures. When the magic weakened, he retreated into the mists with his army. Now he's back. He took people from towns on the edge of Atlanta and boiled them for their bones."

"The tie that binds."

I looked at him.

"His kind make their lairs in pockets of reality, a small fold in the fabric of time and space," Roland said. "They are creatures of immense magic, and they warp the natural order of things to make their homes. This Neig has taken his troops with him into his lair. They existed within it for so long, they themselves became bound to it. The warped magic permeated them and changed them. The magic here isn't ample enough to sustain him or his army, not unless the wave is quite potent. He and his forces must absorb the magic of our reality to reattune themselves. Humans are magic and numerous."

"They eat the human bones, so they can manifest here when the magic is weaker?"

"Drink them, most likely. Grind them into dust with magic and mix them with milk. A barbaric practice."

I rubbed my face. Simple explanations were usually correct ones. Consuming people would be logistically difficult. Too much mass. Bone powder made more sense. *Here is your bone smoothie, great way to start the day.* I wanted to vomit.

Roland reached out and stroked my shoulder. "Most of them never deal with us, but those who choose to mix with humans are a plague on this world. A plague I will one day cure."

"Father . . ."

"Yes, Blossom?"

"If he has to drink this bone powder to manifest during magic, how many people will he have to kill to survive through tech?"

"Hundreds of thousands," my father said.

"Can I enter this pocket realm and kill him?"

"You can't enter without permission."

"What if he gave me permission?"

"You would be very foolish to enter."

"But if I did . . ."

"I forbid it."

Aha, that and a dollar would get him a cup of bad coffee. He wasn't exactly in a position to forbid me anything.

Roland softened his voice. "If somehow you end up within his domain, do not eat or drink. If you consume something, it will anchor you to his realm and you will be subject to his power for a short while. It would wear off unless he continued to feed you. As long as you don't eat anything he presents to you, you can leave at will and nothing within his lair can hurt you. Simply wish to be back here, and the mists will tear, and you will be back in our world. In his realm, you are a ghost. You can't be hurt, but you cannot hurt him in return. But it's not a place you should ever visit, Blossom. Dragons are unpredictable, and their command of magic surpasses ours. They're good at manipulation."

Curran raised his huge head. His mouth was bloody. He staggered from the corpse, a huge nightmarish beast, too big to be real.

"He sent his champion to fight me," I told him.

"Where is the champion now?"

"Dead."

My father smiled.

"You sent assassins to murder your grandson. Your only grandson. They wanted to kill him and eat him. You are despicable, Father. How do you look at yourself in the mirror in the morning?"

"What happened to the assassins?"

"I killed them."

"I know," he said. "I felt them die."

"Your own grandson."

He smiled at me again. "The sahanu were growing troublesome."

I stared at him, speechless. "Wow. Just wow. You used me to clean up your cult."

He shrugged. "You used me to rescue a woman who betrayed me. I'd say we're even. Besides, my grandson was never in danger. You are my daughter, Blossom. One of a kind."

"We are not even. Not even close. Do not come after Conlan again. I swear I will kill you."

A strange contortion gripped the lion's body. He arched his back, then jerked his head to the sky. His great maw gaped open. The sun reflected on his fangs, which were longer than my legs. He roared, his eyes blazing with gold. A nimbus of pale silver twisted around him, crackling with violent energy. Two protrusions burst from his back. He snarled, and the protrusions unfolded into black wings.

That's it. I'm done.

The mercs screamed and howled. The look on Barabas's face could've launched a fleet of spaceships.

"Some are born to godhood," Roland said. "Others attain it. I cautioned you against marrying him."

The lion walked to us.

Wind whispered. My father was gone. The grass where he'd sat was slowly springing back.

The lion stopped in front of me. He folded his wings, lowered his colossal head, and slowly, carefully lay down on the grass, his face to me. He could've taken me whole into his mouth, and there would still be room for ten more people.

"Is he silver?" I asked.

Nobody said anything.

"Is he silver?" I repeated, raising my voice.

"Yes," Julie whispered.

I got up, turned my back, and walked away from him.

"Do you want to talk about it?"

I lay on the edge of the woods, the grass soft under me. The scar of Kings Row lay a few yards away. The sky above me was a beautiful blue, and cute little clouds floated here and there, like fluffy little sheep chasing each other in a vast pasture.

"Baby?"

Curran sat next to me. He'd ripped through his clothes during his dramatic transformation. He'd scrounged up a pair of shorts somewhere, but the rest of him was naked. His hair fell on his shoulders in a blond mane.

I turned my head and looked at him. To say that Curran worked out would be like saying that a marathon runner occasionally jogged. His body was a meld of strength and flexibility that translated into explosive power. He had a raw, feral edge that drew me to him like iron to a magnet. I knew that body intimately. And right now, it was bigger. Taller, with broader shoulders, crisp definition, heartbreaking proportions, corded with steel-hard muscle. He was perfect.

No human was perfect.

He must've been perfect for a while. Funny how I hadn't noticed it before. Probably because I loved him. To me, he'd always been perfect, with all of his flaws. I turned back to look at the sky.

A muscular arm blocked my view of the clouds. He was offering to let me punch him in the arm.

I raised my hand, moved his arm out of the way, and studied the clouds.

"It's not that bad," he said.

"How many animal gods have you eaten besides the tiger in my dad's castle and Moccus back there?"

"Four."

Yep. Exactly what I thought. "Funny how that's the exact number of your hunting expeditions."

He didn't say anything.

And my aunt had encouraged him. Not that surprising, since she'd never liked him. The betrayal stung.

He reached out to touch my shoulder. I slid out of the way.

"Kate . . ."

"You're a god. You're no longer human. Your thoughts and your behavior are no longer your own. With all of the things my screwed-up family has done, they've always steered clear of godhood like it was on fire. And you, you jumped into the flames. You've lost your humanity, Curran. You don't control yourself anymore. You are controlled by the faith of the people who pray to you. What happens when the magic wave ends? What if you disappear?"

He opened his mouth.

I sat up. "I just want to know why. Conlan and I weren't enough for you? What did you want?"

"Power," he said.

"I thought you loved us."

"I love you more than anything."

"I understand if I wasn't enough. It's fucked up, but I get it. But you have a responsibility to your son. How could you?"

I didn't look at him.

"Why the White Warlock?" he asked.

"What?"

"Why do you need the White Warlock?"

Ah. The best defense is a good offense. "The witches and I need her for the ritual to weaken my father and put him into a coma. For it to work, we need someone to channel the collective power of the Covens. I can't be that person. My power is too different, but she can."

"And what happens if the ritual fails?"

"Who snitched?"

He sighed. "Nobody. I saw it in your eyes when we fought your father. How about your responsibility as a wife and mother? What about that?"

"What about it?"

"You'll kill yourself. Or you'll kill him and that will kill you. Either way, you're going to leave me and our son. Do you think Conlan will care that you sacrificed yourself? Is it going to comfort him when he's crying because you're not there?"

"He'll be alive to cry. You'll be alive. That's all I care about. My dad and I are bound. As long as one of us lives, the other does, too. Do you think I want this?" I turned to him. "I would do anything for just a little more time. Ten years. Five. One. Any time at all to be with you both. But he is coming. He already tried to kill Conlan. The only way to keep him safe is to take my father out of the equation."

"Roland won't be the only enemy Conlan will have."

"Yes, but right now he is the worst. I don't want to do it, Curran. I'm not looking forward to it. But if I have to die so our son can live, so my father is stopped, then I'll kill that sonovabitch, even if I die too."

"I gathered," he said, his voice dry.

"If I have to do it, don't try to stop me."

He reached out and took my hand. I let him.

"I won't stop you," he said. "It's your life. It's your choice what you do with it. I've tried to stop you from doing things in the past, and it's never worked. It's pointless. You will do what you will do."

I had expected a fight. This was too easy.

He gave me his Beast Lord stare. "But if I agree to this, you have to accept that I will do everything in my power to make sure things don't go that far."

"Including becoming a god."

"Including that. I needed an upgrade. This was the only way to get it."

"But you're not you, Curran."

He grinned, showing me his teeth. "Still me."

"Bullshit. Have you seen Barabas's face? What happens when shape-shifters start worshipping you?"

"They won't have the chance. It's all coming to a head one way or another." He said it with an awful finality.

There was no way back from godhood. It was terminal. It would eat at him, slowly but surely, gradually changing him until the man I loved disappeared. He knew it, and he went through with it anyway.

He had done it for me. He'd given up his free will so I would survive. *Oh, Curran.*

If we somehow survived, I would stay with him forever, living for the glimpses of my old Curran in the god.

"What happens when the tech hits?"

"Nothing will happen. Erra has been gauging my divinity. There isn't enough to make me a god yet. I'll be fine."

He pulled me to him, wrapping his arms around me, and inhaled my scent. "I'll never let you go."

I put my face into the crook of his neck. "You have to."

"No." He kissed my hair. "You and me, Kate. We're forever. Conlan will grow up and go his own way, and you and I will still be here, squabbling over who is going to save whom."

He held me while I cried quietly into his shoulder and wished with everything I had for a life I wasn't going to get. What good is immortality if the people you love can't be there with you?

For the first time in my life, I wished magic had never come.

Finally, I stopped. The tears had only lasted for a couple of minutes, but it had felt like an eternity.

"We'll have to tell the Conclave," I said.

Curran grimaced. "Yes. They won't like it. They would accept a fire mage, but a dragon isn't something they can cope with."

I knew it. Luther had explained it to me once. We lived in an age of chaos, never knowing if magic or tech would have the upper hand or what they would throw at us. The human mind wasn't built to cope with constant uncertainty. Instead, it sought to find order and consistency, some pattern, some sort of logical equation where a certain consequence always followed a specific event. Water evaporated when heated to a boiling point. The sun rose in the east and set in the west. All magic waves eventually ebbed. We managed to distill rules out of chaos. These core beliefs kept us sane and we protected them at all costs, otherwise the house of logic built on these foundations fell apart and we tumbled into madness.

"An elder being can't manifest unless there is a flare" was a core belief. A dragon was an overwhelming being, a creature of so much power and devastation that nothing in our arsenal could match it. It was like the idea of being hit by a meteorite. Theoretically, we were aware that a burning space rock could fall out of the sky at any moment and kill us, but we refused to dwell on this possibility. The idea that a dragon could manifest at any time and attack the city and there was no defense against it was so frightening that our brains stepped on the brake, rejecting the possibility. And this dragon wasn't just manifesting. He was smart and cunning. He had an army and wanted to invade. We would need ironclad evidence to pull the Conclave's collective heads out of the sand.

"I know the Conclave won't believe us," I said. "We'll have to convince them."

"It will take the entire city." He stroked my arm. "We only have one chance to build this coalition. If we go with a fire mage, and Neig manifests as a dragon, it will come out that we knew and deliberately kept it hidden."

"Then the alliance will fall apart."

He nodded. "And when your father comes, there will be nobody to fight him."

A Jeep drove away. The blond driver took the turn fast. Julie.

"Where is she going?" I wondered.

"Who knows."

As we walked back to the scar, I turned to him. "You should give up and let your mane grow out."

"Mm-hm. And then we can stay up late, and you can braid it, and put ribbons in it . . ."

"Don't you want to show off your pretty hair, Goldilocks?"

"I'll show you hair."

I raised my eyebrow. "Is that supposed to be some kind of threat?"

"Wait and you'll find out."

14

I HUNG UP the phone and gave it an evil stare. It didn't squeak and flee to hide under the kitchen table. A pity.

The light of the morning shone through the windows. The last half of my morning coffee was slowly cooling in my favorite mug. The house was quiet.

Last night we'd gotten in, collected our son from Martha, did the bare minimum necessary to maintain personal hygiene, and passed out, all three of us in our huge bed. I'd had a nightmare that tech hit during the night and ripped Curran apart. I'd woken up in a cold sweat. It took several minutes of Curran holding me for my body to let go of the panicked feeling.

Once we got up, George came and collected Conlan and we split up. Curran went to George's to make Conclave phone calls, and I made mine from our house. I hadn't wanted him to leave. The magic had held through the night. The tech could hit at any minute, yet he acted like nothing was wrong. Nobody knew how much of him was human and how much was god at this point, and my aunt was still out of touch. But spending the entire day clutching at my husband to make sure he didn't disappear wasn't an option. We had to pull the Conclave together, and getting all of the Atlanta bigwigs into one spot was like pulling teeth, only a lot less fun.

The phone rang.

"This is Amy from Sunshine Realty . . ."

"Take me off your calling list, or I will find you and make you regret it." I hung up. Great. I'd graduated to threats now. What kind of sadistic asshole calls the same number twenty damn times in the space of a week pestering strangers to sell their house?

I drank my coffee. This was the first moment I had gotten to myself in days. I remembered I had a great deal of things to sort out, but hadn't gotten the chance to do it while they were happening, and now I just couldn't muster any energy.

Curran was now a theophage, like Christopher, only far more gone. He had eaten six manifestations of various animal gods. Only time would tell if he survived the tech shift. Thinking about it was like having your neck exposed and waiting for the axe to fall.

Julie disappeared after Rowena's rescue. I'd called around to Derek and the Guild, and the last time anyone had seen her, she was driving away from Kings Row at top speed. She would be back. If she went somewhere, she usually had a good reason for it.

A dragon was about to invade the city. A dragon whose brother had slaughtered most of my family. When I finally told Erra, she would go through the roof. She must've suspected a dragon was involved, but I doubt she'd guessed he and our ancient enemy were related. That conversation would go well, I just knew it.

We had to convince the city that a dragon was invading without any evidence.

And my father was still going on the offensive.

I felt like there wasn't enough of me to go around.

At least Rowena was still alive. I'd done something right.

Someone knocked on the door. I walked over and opened it.

Saiman stood on my doorstep, carrying a large Tiffany-style lamp, the kind that would fit on a side table, in one hand and a duffel bag in the other.

"Did you abandon your life of wealth and intellectual brilliance and decide to sell lamps door to door?"

"Hilarious," he said. "I may have a way to communicate with the Suanni."

I stepped aside, let him in, and locked the door behind him.

"Is this more from the David Miller collection?" I asked.

David Miller was a magical version of an idiot savant. A cruel jest of nature or fate, he couldn't use magic at all, but every object he'd handled during his lifetime had acquired some sort of random power. Saiman had spent a fortune acquiring Miller's possessions after the man's death.

"No," Saiman said. "Where is he?"

"In the basement. Let me go first."

I led the way. Adora glanced up from her book, gave Saiman a derisive look, and went back to her reading.

Saiman set the lamp on the side table by Yu Fong and paused, studying him.

"What is it?" I asked.

"Quite a remarkable face," Saiman said.

Somewhere in my future, if I had one, Saiman would show up wearing Yu Fong's face. Ugh.

Saiman knelt, unzipped the duffel, and extracted a roll of fabric, wrapped in plastic. He untied the knot and hauled out a small rug, which he placed on the floor. The old rug must've been vibrant at some point, but now the blues and reds of the blooms twisting across it had faded to near beige. Saiman took a tealight candle from the duffel and put it on the table, next to the lamp. Finally, he produced a small box.

"Hold out your hand."

I offered my palm to him. He opened the box and shook a radiant amethyst into my hand. As big as a walnut, the stone pulsed with brilliant color.

"Don't let go, or you'll break the spell." Saiman pulled a box of matches out. "This lamp came from Cunningham Hospital, a facility in New England that specialized in the treatment of coma patients. Countless people sat by its light and wished with every drop of their being for just one more chance to speak to their loved ones."

All of that energy, all the love, grief, and sadness poured into the light of one lamp. So much desperation wrapped in it.

"Will it hurt him?" I asked.

"The lamp won't wake him from the coma. But if everything goes well, we can communicate with him. The tea light will burn at an accelerated rate. We'll have about five minutes. Ready?"

"Ready."

Saiman lit the candle. The lamp came on with a click. The cord was right there, wrapped around it. It wasn't plugged in, yet it glowed with a familiar electric light.

"Yu Fong?" I asked, the amethyst cold in my hand.

"Yes . . ." a clear male voice answered.

"This is Kate Lennart. You're in a coma in my house. You're safe."

"I'm aware of my surroundings," he said.

Okay then. "Is there anything we can do to help you?"

"The healing I require is beyond the capabilities of a human. Ask your questions. You're wasting time."

The candle was melting before my eyes. He was right. I had to get to the point. "Tell me about the dragon who attacked you."

"He's insane. We are an old species. There are traditions. Rules of conduct. One doesn't just blindly attack another dragon without provocation."

"How large was he?" Saiman asked.

"I've never seen one that large. Even my oldest brother can't match him."

"How can we kill him?" I asked.

"How much do you know about the dragon realms?" Yu Fong asked.

"A dragon realm is a pocket in reality," Saiman said. "A fold in the fabric of space, where time and physical constraints have different meaning. Frequently, it is hidden in a place that one has to enter: a cave, a palace, a gorge, somewhere two separate spaces meet and a boundary exists between the two."

Look at Saiman go. "A place one can't enter except by invitation from the dragon," I added. "As long as a visitor doesn't consume anything, the dragon won't be able to injure them."

"But what makes the pocket?" Yu Fong asked. "What keeps it closed?"

"I don't know," I told him.

"An anchor. Every dragon has one. It is an object of great value to them. It can be a sword, a book, a poem on a scroll, something we treasure beyond everything else. We pour our power into it. We sleep with it, we lick it, we bathe it in our blood and in our magic. We keep it close. True, time doesn't affect us the same way within our lairs, but time still matters. The more time that passes in the outer world, the stronger the anchor. It is the linch- pin on which the entire realm revolves. A dragon as old as that insane asshole would have an anchor of overwhelming power. He can call on it anywhere and it will bring him home."

Shit.

"We can't kill him," Saiman said. "Unless we somehow manage an instant death, he will call to the anchor and retreat to his realm."

"Yes," Yu Fong said.

Crap. Crap, crap, crap. "Can we destroy the anchor?"

"It's an object of great power. If you were somehow to destroy it, the realm would collapse upon you."

That didn't sound good.

"You have a book," Yu Fong said. "About small people. They go to the lair of the dragon and they steal his an—"

The candle went out.

"Small people?" I asked.

Saiman shook his head.

"Can we do another session?" I asked.

"Not now. We'll have to wait at least twenty-four hours."

I sighed.

"At least we have confirmation from an independent source," Saiman offered.

"Fat good it will do us." There were people at the Conclave who would insist the dragon was fake while he roasted them with his breath.

Nothing was ever easy.

"A DRAGON?" NICK peered at me from across the table.

The three knights from Wolf Trap had arranged themselves behind him. Knight-striker Cabrera looked at me like I was a spitting cobra. Her hand kept going to her sword sheath, but weapons were forbidden at the Conclave, so her fingers found only air. I could relate.

"Did I stutter?" I drank my coffee. I had outlined the events in Kings Row and my conversation with Neig.

Around the table, concerned faces frowned.

We had tried our best to get everyone together in the morning, but by the time we managed to wrangle the powers of Atlanta into Rivers Steakhouse, it was eight o'clock at night. Normally we met at Bernard's, on neutral territory, but we needed privacy, and Bernard's had upscale clientele and had declined to close for the night to accommodate us. Rebecka Rivers shut down her restaurant, posted a member of the kitchen staff at the door, and gave us as much coffee as we wanted, which made me want to hug her. The urge was disturbing.

Everyone who was anyone was here. Nick and the Order across from us; Jim, Dali, Robert, and Desandra to the right of them; Ghastek, Rowena, swaddled into a cloak, the hood over her face, and Ryan Kelly, every inch a businessman except for his bright purple Mohawk; the Red Guard; the Mage College; the witches, represented by Evdokia with two younger women, both of whom were probably her daughters; the volhvs, thin, gaunt Grigorii, his brother Vasiliy, who worshipped Belobog, and Roman; Teddy Jo and two others representing the neo-pagans; Saiman, representing himself; and Luther, representing Biohazard. Even the Druids came, Drest in a pristine white robe, solemn and dignified. His gaze caught mine. *Yeah, yeah, no matter how well you clean up, I still saw you running around in animal skins in the woods with your body painted blue.*

"So, let me get this straight," Nick said.

Here we go. "I wish you would."

"You're saying that a dragon is about to invade us from a magical pocket dimension with his army."

"Yes."

"And he wants you to be his queen."

"Yes."

"And, correct me if I'm wrong, but you're technically a princess, are you not?"

Jumping on the table and punching him in the face would be counterproductive to building a coalition.

"Yes."

Next to me, Curran turned slightly, looking at Nick. I didn't have to glance at his face to know his eyes had gone gold.

Nick looked to the rest of the table. "Okay, what we have here, ladies and gentlemen, is a Dungeons and Dragons campaign. The evil dragon wants to steal our princess for nefarious purposes, and she's looking for some knights in shining armor to rescue her."

Nervous laughter ran across the table.

"Are you done?" I asked.

"No, I'm just getting started. Have you actually seen this dragon in his dragon form?"

"No."

"What makes you think it's a dragon?" Phillip from the Mage College asked.

"I've been given information by a pagan faction that states he is."

"Which faction?" Robert asked.

The druids looked perfectly innocent. Nope, no help there.

"A pagan faction that wishes to remain anonymous."

"I can vouch for this," Roman said. "I was there."

"You married them, and you're related to her through her mother," Nick said. "You're not exactly a neutral party."

The volhvs looked like they'd been slapped in the face with a fish.

"Are you questioning my son's word?" Grigorii thundered.

Nick opened his mouth.

"We also have confirmation from Yu Fong," Saiman said. "Obtained through magical means."

Phillip glanced at him. "Let me guess, magical means that only you can replicate that cannot be examined by us at this time because of some technicality?"

"What are you implying?" Saiman asked, his voice icy.

"The dragon," Curran said, his voice cutting others off.

"Yes, the dragon," Nick said. "Has anyone actually seen this dragon?"

"Do you have any evidence of it?" Phillip asked. "Scales, claws . . ."

Rowena lowered her hood. Phillip fell silent.

"Our condolences on your suffering," Robert said. "May I ask some questions?"

"Go ahead."

"Kings Row is outside the People's patrol routes. What were you doing there?"

"I was going to visit a friend. I was there on my own time and had taken one vampire with me for personal security."

"What sort of friend?" Robert pressed.

"Is that really relevant?" Ghastek asked.

Rowena raised her hand. "I'll answer. One of my journeymen died. He left behind a pregnant fiancée. I was fond of him and I occasionally look in on her and her daughter."

"Were you able to visit with them?"

"No. She'd had a family emergency and went to see her family out of state. She'd left a note for me with a neighbor."

At least she and her daughter had survived.

"What happened next?" Robert asked.

"When I stepped out of the neighbor's house, there was an army on the street."

You could hear a pin drop.

"There were warriors," she said. "They wore full armor and they were killing people on the streets. The corrupted creatures served them like dogs. They ran into the houses and pulled the people out."

"What did you do?" Robert asked.

"I am a Master of the Dead." A cold fire flared in her eyes. "I did what I do. I killed as many as I could. Eventually my vampire and I were surrounded. I realized that I wouldn't escape, so I sent my undead into In-Shinar's territory. The warriors then dragged me down the street."

And while they did that, she'd pushed her vampire as far as it could go and made provisions to secure it, so it wouldn't slaughter anyone. And when a yeddimur chased her undead, she used her vampire to trap it. Ghastek's team had recovered it and secured it in the Casino.

"I secured the vampire to avoid further bloodshed," Rowena said.

I'd asked her where the pike in the vampire had come from. She didn't know.

"What happened next?" Robert asked.

"Fire."

We waited.

"Fire?" Jim prompted.

"A torrent of fire from the sky. When I woke up, I was encased in a pillar of molten glass."

"And yet, here you are, unburned," Nick said.

That was just about enough. "We were all there," I said. "We all saw it. I had to call my father to get her out of it."

The knight-protector leaned forward. "And there it is. All this time you've been giving lip service to how you're getting ready to fight your father, and the moment things turned sour, you ran to Daddy."

I would kill him.

"She ran to Daddy because the life of her friend mattered to her," Curran said. "Just as the lives of all of you matter to her. And because she has enough brains to realize that Neig made this elaborate trap to prove to everyone that we couldn't match his magic with ours. Now he knows we can." He raised his hand and counted off on his fingers. "She killed his creatures and rescued Yu Fong. She killed his champion. She neutralized his magic and returned life to Kings Row. Has the Order made any progress in identifying the cause of the transformation in the body we sent you?"

"Don't change the subject," Nick told him.

"It's a yes-or-no question, Feldman," Curran said. "Yes or no?"

Everyone looked at Nick.

"No," he said.

Ha! "Was the Order able to pinpoint the origin of the magic or find any other similar cases?"

"No," Nick said.

"So, you have nothing to bring to this discussion," I said. "You're going to sit there and bitch and moan and push your private vendetta. Here is a thought; if I'm a princess, you're a knight, Nick. It's in your title. Knight-protector. How about you put on your shining armor and do some protecting against this dragon instead of relying on the princess to do your dirty work?"

Nick leaned forward. "You're asking me to accept a mythical creature that nobody has seen for hundreds of years and which requires too much magic to survive invading us with his magical army. There is a simpler explanation."

"I'd love to hear it."

"It's your father."

The People and the Guild representatives collectively groaned.

"Will you stop?" I growled at him. "Just stop, Nick! Stop! It's not Roland."

"How do you know? There are two possibilities: either he is orchestrating this, or you are complicit in his machinations."

"Shut up!" Rowena snapped at him.

"He has a point," Phillip yelled. "There is no evidence of this supposed dragon. It is a magical impossibility. In fact, I wrote a paper—"

"Your paper was hogwash," Luther cut in.

"Precisely," Saiman added.

"I am the Grand Magus. I won't be spoken to like this!"

The table erupted in screams.

"I'll speak to you however I please!" Luther shot back.

"You're a loose cannon, Luther!" Phillip shook his finger at him.

"It's Dr. Loose Cannon to you!"

"Evidence!" Nick raised his voice, trying to out scream the others. "You have no evidence, no armor from these warriors, no scales, no evidence!"

"Tell them!" Grigorii pointed at Drest.

"Tell them what?" Drest asked.

"You know what," Grigorii yelled.

"I have no idea what you're talking about," Drest shouted.

"Coward!" Grigorii spat.

"Senile fool!"

The druids and the volhvs banged their staffs on the floor, glaring at each other.

"We need to wake Yu Fong!" Phillip yelled. "He has actually seen the creature. We can ask him directly."

"Over my dead body!" Dali snapped.

Everyone on the Pack side looked outraged.

On one side, Evdokia sighed and rolled her eyes. At the other end, Desandra clapped her hands over the cacophony, chanting, "Fight, fight, fight..."

I turned to Curran. "Do the roar thing."

He shook his head. "Not yet. Let them scream themselves out."

The front door burst open. Hugh d'Ambray strode inside, huge in a cloak and the black armor of the Iron Dogs. A beautiful woman followed him. She wore a blue dress and her hair was unnaturally white.

I'd left my sword in the parking lot. That was okay. I'd take him apart with my bare hands.

Julie squeezed in behind them.

My mind took a second to process the fact that Julie wasn't trying to stab him in the back. In fact, she looked like she . . . Like they came in together. Like she went and got him.

Why me? Why? I couldn't take much more of this; I really couldn't.

D'Ambray raised a big bag and emptied it over the table. Metal clattered onto the wood: a skull in a helmet, a pair of daggers, amulets, photographs of Pictish symbols tattooed on human skin. I suppose I should be grateful he didn't dump a rotting corpse on us.

The table went completely silent.

"I've come to help you with your dragon problem," he said.

Nick turned the color of an eggplant. Next to me, Curran had gone completely still.

"Well?" Hugh grinned. "Don't all of you thank me at once."

The white-haired woman smiled and gave us a little wave. "Please excuse him. He forgets about manners sometimes. My name is Elara. You may know me as the White Warlock. I've heard so much about you. It's so nice to meet all of you. I'm Hugh's wife."

The world stood on its hands and kicked me in the face.

HUGH D'AMBRAY HAD a wife. He owned a castle. He lived in the middle of Kentucky's wilderness. They'd first encountered Neig's troops over a year ago. They'd fought them and developed some strategies. He was glad to share those strategies with us. He had no doubt that Neig was a dragon. He could field three hundred of his Iron Dogs and personally lead them to assist us with this fight. He regretted he couldn't field more, but he'd had to leave a force to guard the castle. In return, he expected the city of Atlanta to help him with some herb sales.

Herb sales.

I sat and listened to all of it as if I were under water. It didn't seem real. It was so bizarre, my brain refused to digest it.

His wife was the White Warlock. I'd caught Evdokia's glance once or twice. She didn't seem shocked. The witches had known. Julie wouldn't even look at me. They came in together. She went and got him.

Maybe he's married and living happily in some castle somewhere.

She had known where he was, and she didn't tell me.

I realized the room was silent. Everyone was looking at me, including d'Ambray. He must've asked me a question.

I took a stab in the dark. "I need to think about it."

"We should adjourn," Ghastek said.

"Great idea!" Phillip reached toward the pile of armor on the table.

"No!" Luther slapped his hand away.

"Do not touch me."

"This is the best evidence we have so far!" Luther said. "You're not getting your paws on it."

"It's not," Saiman said, turning to Ghastek. "He has a live specimen."

Luther and Phillip swiveled to Ghastek. Luther opened his mouth and struggled to form words, but nothing came out.

"He's had it for twenty-four hours and he didn't notify anyone," Saiman snitched.

"The yeddimur is the property of the People," Ghastek said.

The three experts screeched in unison, like they had suddenly turned into harpies.

"Enough," Curran roared.

Silence claimed the table.

I turned to Luther. "You're the leading expert on infectious magic." I looked at Ghastek. "You're the leading expert on magic virus–induced transformations." I turned to Saiman. "You have a wide variety of expert knowledge across several fields." I glanced at Phillip. "You're a professional skeptic terrified for your reputation. Work together."

Ghastek looked taken aback. "You want me to . . ."

"Share," I said.

He blinked.

"Work together. Publish a joint paper afterward if you want, I don't care. Just get me something we can use."

Curran rose to his feet. I got up and we walked out.

Behind me, Hugh murmured, "That went well."

"Give them time," Elara said.

"Steed," Hugh said.

I stopped. One wrong word to Christopher and I would murder him. Out of the corner of my eye I could see Barabas. His eyes had gone bright red.

"You've survived," Christopher said.

"You know what they say about me. Hard to kill. I have some things to apologize for."

"Come by the house," Christopher said. "303 Forest Lane. We'll talk."

I forced myself to resume walking.

Curran and I got into the Jeep. I chanted at the engine until it turned over, and we drove out of the parking lot. It had rained while we were inside. The city seemed annoyed, like a cat who'd gotten wet.

"Am I crazy?" I asked.

"No," he said.

"That did just happen?"

"It did."

"Julie went and got him after Kings Row."

"It appears so."

The city rolled past us.

"He walks up to Christopher and says 'hi,' and Christopher says, 'Come by my house'?"

Curran didn't answer.

"He put Christopher into a cage and nearly starved him to death, and now it's all forgive and forget?"

"I didn't forget," Curran said, his face grim. "I remember Mishmar."

I'd almost died in Mishmar, because Hugh had teleported me there and tried to starve me into compliance.

"I remember Aunt B," I said.

Curran didn't say anything.

"What the hell did he ask me?" I asked.

"If you would accept his help."

"I feel like I've gone nuts."

"Join the club," he said.

He braked, thrusting his arm in front of me. The vehicle screeched to a stop.

"What is it?"

"Look."

Straight ahead a large post-Shift building sat on the corner of the city block. The lights were on and in the glow, I could see people sitting at the desks, phones to their ears. It had to be almost ten o'clock. Who would be calling anyone at this hour . . .

My brain finally noticed the sign illuminated by the feylanterns: SUN-SHINE REALTY.

I turned to Curran. "Can we? Can we please?"

My husband's eyes flared with gold. "Oh yes."

We left the car running and headed to the door.

"The whole body or just the head?" he asked, cracking his knuckles.

"Just the head." I pulled magic to me. "Freakier that way."

Curran tried the door and swung it open for me. Oh goody. Unlocked. I walked in. My husband followed.

A young blond woman looked up at us from her desk. "Hi, there. My name is Elizabeth. Are you here to sell your house?"

"Elizabeth, is the owner in?"

"He is!" She put an extra spoonful of sugar into her voice.

"Can you get him for us?" I asked.

"Who should I say is here?"

"Tell him it's Kate Lennart." The first pulse of my magic shook the building. "Daughter of Nimrod." A stronger pulse. People looked up from their desks. "Blood Blade of Atlanta and her husband, the God-King Curran Lennart."

The whole building resonated, as if someone had struck a giant gong.

Curran's human face broke and a monstrous lion head appeared on his shoulders. My husband roared.

WHEN WE GOT home, Curran went to Derek's house and I went across the street. George opened the door and held her finger to her lips. I snuck after her upstairs.

"Where have you been?" George whispered. "Derek said the Conclave broke up an hour ago."

"We had to make a stop." We didn't kill anybody. After Curran roared, everyone cleared out and then we had a discussion with the owner about appropriate phone marketing etiquette, calling hours, and the meaning of "take us off your calling list." He walked away on his own power without a scratch on him, but I was confident the unwanted calls would stop.

Conlan was in his room, asleep on the bed. Martha lay next to him, curled up around my son.

"Let Mom have him tonight," George said. "She lost him yesterday. She needs this."

I didn't want to leave him. I wanted to pluck him out of the bed, take him home, and snuggle with him to reassure myself he was okay.

But he was asleep and so was Martha. I escaped the house without waking anyone.

As I crossed the street, I saw wet tire marks leading up Christopher and Barabas's dry driveway. The lights were on.

I should wait. It was late. Even by shapeshifter standards.

No, screw it. I marched to the house and knocked on the front door.

Barabas opened it and stepped aside. "It's for you."

Christopher walked out of the kitchen, a cup of tea in his hands. He was barefoot and wearing sweatpants and a simple dark T-shirt. His eyes were clear—no hint of Deimos—and his pale hair framed his face like a silk curtain. "Come in. Tea?"

"No."

"I'll get you some chamomile," Barabas said. "You look like you need it."

"Right now, I'd have to drown in calming tea for it to do any good."

"I'll fix you a cup." Barabas went into the kitchen.

I slipped my shoes off, walked into the living room, and sat on the sofa. Christopher sat in a big blue chair. There was a quiet elegance about Christopher, even when he slumped barefoot in a chair.

"Go ahead," he said.

"He put you in a cage. He starved you for weeks. You were covered in filth. I don't know of any person, aside from Raphael, who has the right to want to kill him more than you. And you invited him to your house. Help me understand this."

Christopher looked into his cup. "Do you want to kill him?"

I sighed. "No. I don't. I should, because his centurion killed Aunt B, because he broke Curran's legs, and because of Mauro. Curran probably will kill him given a chance. But right now, all I want is to understand you."

"Hugh kidnapped you and starved you nearly to death. Why don't you want to kill him?"

"Because I met my father. I've trained all my life to murder him, and when we met, I put it aside. My father has the impact of a supernova. He had Hugh since he was a small child. He shaped and molded him, and Hugh had no defenses against that. It was never a fair fight. My father bears a lot of responsibility for Hugh d'Ambray. That said, Hugh is a butcher."

"He is," Christopher said.

Barabas came over and handed me a cup of steaming chamomile tea. "Drink."

I took a sip. He landed in a leather chair, pulled a folder from a bag next to it, and began reading the contents, pen in hand.

I drank my tea. We sat in silence for a couple of long minutes. I exhaled. The world settled down.

"Fine," I said finally, setting the cup on the side table. "Tell me about Hugh d'Ambray."

Christopher smiled. It was a small smile, tinged with regret. "The first time I realized something was off, I had just been made Tribunus, second in command after Morgan, who was Legatus of the Golden Legion at the time. We were in Boston: your father, Morgan, Hugh, and I. Roland wanted to meet with a senator about matters of magical policy. The meeting went well. We were planning to leave in the morning. A hospital across the street from the hotel caught on fire. Hundreds of burn victims, mostly children. D'Ambray went down there. He healed for hours. By morning, he could barely stand. Morgan sent me down there to tell him Roland wanted to leave."

Christopher looked into his cup again. "I found him covered in soot, going from child to child, sometimes healing two at a time. D'Ambray told me he wasn't done. Morgan sent me down again, then went himself. We couldn't drag Hugh away from those children. He was manic. By the time we came back, your father was awake, sitting in the hotel restaurant, drinking a cup of coffee and watching the rescue crews. He paid the bill, walked across the street, and told Hugh it was time to go. Hugh told him he wasn't done. He had a boy, maybe twelve, and the child had inhaled hot smoke. It burned him from the inside out. Every time he breathed in, he made this whistling grinding sound. D'Ambray was trying to put him back together. Your father looked at Hugh for a moment and said, 'It will be fine.' Hugh dropped the boy to the ground and followed us out. On the way to the cars, he made a joke about a passing woman's ass."

I knew that Hugh. The one who made jokes and stepped over burning bodies. The healing Hugh . . . He did save Doolittle. He saved Ascanio too, but he blackmailed me to do it. He'd killed Mauro. Mauro was my friend.

"For the next two years, I was busy with Morgan," Christopher said. "After I killed him and became Legatus, I looked further into Hugh. As Legatus, I answered only to Roland. I controlled the entirety of the People. I made a study of any potential rivals rising through the People's ranks, and I studied Hugh. D'Ambray wasn't an immediate threat. We were equal but separate, and he showed no signs of wanting to take my place. Still, one does due diligence."

Christopher drank his tea.

"Other people's pain brings Hugh discomfort."

I almost laughed. "Hugh d'Ambray?"

Christopher met my gaze. "Do I strike you as a man likely to jump to conclusions?"

Barabas chortled in his chair.

"The nature of his magic is such that when he sees an injury, it creates distress. Not pain exactly, but a high degree of anxiety. This mechanism allows him to precisely identify the problem and correct it. He is compelled to heal."

"You're describing someone who is almost an empath, but instead of emotional pain, he feels physical pain. That kind of person wouldn't willingly harm others. Hugh is a killer."

"A paradox," Christopher said. "So I asked myself, how do I reconcile the two? And then I watched your father. What I'm about to tell you is conjecture, but it's conjecture based on careful observation and a lot of thought. I believe your father required a warlord. He wanted someone young and with a great deal of magic. He found Hugh and he tried to mold him into the tool of destruction he needed. However, the position called for a psychopath with a sadistic streak. Hugh was never that. He was perfect in every other way: he was physically and magically gifted, a superior fighter, a talented strategist, charismatic, loyal, happy to serve, but he wasn't a sadist. So your father used the blood bond between them to blunt his emotions. On multiple occasions, I've observed Hugh agitated and arguing his point. Your father would speak to him and suddenly Hugh would come to his point of view and the source of the agitation would no longer matter."

I should've seen it. Suddenly so many things made sense. Mishmar made sense. My father told him to do whatever was necessary to make me comply and numbed him enough to do it, so Hugh did it.

"You have a blood bond with Julie," Christopher said. "Tell me, can it be done?"

I sighed. "Yes. I can impose my will over hers. I can make her not care. It comes with a heavy price tag."

Christopher set down his cup and leaned back, braiding his fingers on his knee. "What are the consequences?"

"If you superimpose yourself on your blood bonded, eventually their mind will break. There will be nothing left except a reflection of you. They will be lobotomized. My aunt gives me a lecture on this at least once every three months, just in case I forget. She's fond of Julie."

"Question." Barabas raised his finger. "Hugh was bound to Roland for decades, and now we know Roland blunted his emotions. Then Roland broke the blood bond."

"Yes," I said.

"Why isn't Hugh dead?"

I raised my hands. "Because he is Hugh. He's unkillable. Curran broke his back and threw him into a magic fire that melted an entire stone castle, and he's still alive. He shouldn't even be able to form coherent thoughts."

The name Iron Dogs fit in more ways than one. A dog is hardwired to please a human. When you got a puppy and raised it to adulthood, you shaped the dog. Take a puppy and give him a loving home, and in most cases, he will be a sweet dog. Take the same puppy and chain him in the yard, and it will be a whole different story. My father had taken a stick to his dog and beaten him senseless every time he strayed out of line. Poor Hugh. But he never turned on his master. He never bit the hand that held the stick.

"Yes, my father imposed his will on him, but that doesn't absolve him of responsibility for having done horrible shit."

"My point precisely," Barabas said. "There is no way to tell how much of what he did was Roland's doing and how much was him. Maybe he is a violent psychopath. He could've rebelled. He didn't."

"Hugh wouldn't rebel," I told him. "He is loyal. The real question is, who are we dealing with now? My father is gone. It's just Hugh. None of us know who Hugh is. He's done so much fucked-up crap. I'm not sure I can deal with it. I don't know if it's in me. I mean, Christopher, he put you in a cage."

"Your father put me in a cage," he said.

"But Hugh kept you there," Barabas said.

"Have you ever wondered how I survived two months in a cage with no food or water?" he asked. "Why I didn't go into organ failure? Why I had no sores, despite sitting in my own filth?"

"Hugh fed you," I guessed.

Christopher nodded. "At night. He talked to me."

I threw my hands up. "He shouldn't have kept you in the cage in the first place."

"He kept me alive."

Barabas sighed.

Christopher's expression sharpened, growing somehow more fragile. "The two of you only remember the man in the cage. Before that I was the Legatus of the Golden Legion. I murdered my way to the top. I committed atrocities. And unlike Hugh, I have nobody to blame but myself. I own everything I've done. I did it because I wanted power. I must live with it. Hugh lives with his memories. It will be his choice to atone for what he has done, or not. But I've forgiven Hugh, because if I don't forgive him, there is no hope for forgiveness for someone like me."

He rose and went upstairs. Barabas went after him, and I let myself out.

I WALKED INTO our house and went down to the basement. Yu Fong was still comatose. Adora was nowhere to be found.

I climbed back up and walked into our kitchen. The light was on, warm and soft. The air smelled of cooked butter and fresh coffee. Curran stood by the stove, toasting bread. A plate of sliced smoked meat sat next to him.

I unbuckled my sheath, Sarrat still in it, and hung it over a chair.

It was so comfortable here, in the kitchen. Just me and him. I loved our son, but sometimes it was nice to take a short break from being responsible for a tiny human.

"Where is Adora?"

"I sent her home to take a break. Shower, sleep, that type of thing. She'll be back in the morning."

I set the table. We would never be ordinary. We would never have sheltered lives. But we could have this, a quiet moment of simple happiness, sandwiched between danger and desperation. I lived for these moments.

"I've decided to give d'Ambray a chance," I said.

"I thought you might."

He slid the last slice of bread onto the plate and turned around to me.

"What gave me away?"

"You tend to give people second chances. And third. And fourth."

"Pot, kettle. Can you work with him?"

He shrugged. "We need him and his wife. I can always kill him later."

His Furriness, the Long-term Planner. "We'll have to sit down with them eventually and have a conversation. Can you be civil?"

I pulled a block of cheese out of the fridge and cut it into paper-thin slices.

"Can you?"

"I'm always civil."

He crossed his arms. The muscles on his forearms stood out. Mmm.

"Really?" Curran asked.

"Sometimes I jump on the table and kick people in the face, but I'm always civil about it."

He moved behind me. His breath touched my skin. I stopped slicing.

"Always civil?" he murmured. His fingers eased my hair from my shoulders. His lips grazed the sensitive spot on the back of my neck. I shivered.

His lips were hot on my skin. I arched my back against him, raised my hand, and slid it into his hair. He hadn't buzzed it down.

"We're childless tonight," he murmured into my ear. "Nobody in the house except us."

"What about Julie?"

"She's sleeping over at Derek's. She thought you might need time."

What I needed was a temper transplant, because if she walked through that door right now, I'd yell at her until sunrise.

"She knew where Hugh was."

"Apparently."

He kissed me again. His arms slid around my waist, pulling me closer to him, the steel cords of muscle warm against me. Yes . . .

"We don't have to be quiet," he promised, and nipped my neck. Tiny sparks of pleasure burst through me.

"We don't?"

"No."

"What makes you think that I wouldn't be quiet anyway?"

"Is that a challenge?" His hand stroked my raised arm. Breath caught in my throat. There shouldn't have been anything erotic about him touching my arm, but my whole body went to attention, tracking the progress of his fingers.

"Would you like it to be, Your Godliness?"

He stopped. "Still mad?"

I turned around and looked at him. Really looked at him.

"Are you still you?"

Gray eyes looked back at me, full of dancing golden sparks. "I've been eating gods for nearly two years. You've been living with me all this time. Eating, sleeping, having sex. You tell me."

"I don't know," I whispered.

"Test the waters and find out. Unless you're chicken."

"I wish you hadn't done it."

"I knew it. Too scared."

"I'm scared *for* you, idiot."

He gave me an appraising look. "Keep telling yourself that. But it would go easier if you just admit it."

"Admit what?"

He pointed at himself. "All this is too much for you."

I rolled my eyes. "You're right. That's totally it. I've beheld your godly manliness and now I'm overcome with womanly trepidation. Get over yourself."

"Don't worry, baby. I'll go easy on you."

Screw it. I wrapped my arms around his neck and kissed him. He tasted of coffee and Curran. I caught his lip between my teeth, nipped, and licked him. He opened his mouth and I slipped my tongue in, teasing him. He picked me up, his hands squeezing my butt, and kissed me back, tasting my mouth. My tongue flicked across his. My breasts ached. My body was aware that I was empty, and I needed to be full of him.

"Playing with fire," he told me, setting me on the kitchen table.

"No, just pulling a lion by his whiskers." I kissed the sensitive skin under the corner of his jaw. He made a deep male noise. We kissed again. The world went hot and focused. I pulled his T-shirt off and ran my hands over the ridges of his stomach, over the hard muscles of his chest, over tight nipples, kissing him, eager and hot and wanting.

He pulled off my T-shirt. His hand slipped into my bra, easing my breast out, his thumb sliding over the sensitive bud of nipple. I gasped and kissed him harder. He was on fire, and if I just kissed him hard enough, I'd coax it out of him.

He worked the bra off me and lifted me up. His mouth found my right breast, sucked, his tongue painting heat and texture across my nipple, and a jolt of pleasure made me moan. I wrapped my legs around him. He carried me to the living room. My feet touched the soft rug. I was hot and wet and in a terrible hurry. He was kissing me, touching me, squeezing, stroking. He couldn't get enough. I worked his jeans open and pulled his shaft out, running my hand up and down the hardness wrapped in silken skin. He groaned and squeezed me to him. His eyes had gone gold. His upper lip rose, baring his teeth.

I tripped him. It was a classic move, simple and effective. He was off balance, because he wanted another go at my breasts. For a moment his weight was on his right leg, and I swept it out from under him. He could've fought me on the way down, but instead he just fell. I pulled off my jeans and my underwear, yanked his off him, and landed on him.

He grinned at me and there was no man more handsome on Earth. "Your move, ass kicker."

He was still him. Still my Curran. Still enough left.

I kissed him and slipped his hard shaft inside me. It felt like heaven. He growled and thrust up. I rode him, matching his thrusts with mine, feeling every inch of him fill me, sliding into my hot slickness. His hands roamed my breasts, slipped over my stomach, and touched the sensitive spot between my legs. I cried out. He snarled in response.

I rode him faster and faster, lost to the rhythm, until the pressure that had built inside me crested and drowned me in ecstasy. And then he was behind me, thrusting hard, and then I was on top again, then we were face-to-face, slowing the pace. Savoring each minute. Every moment was a gift. I loved it all: the taste, the scent, the touch, the way he looked at me, the gold sparks in his eyes, the touch of his hands on my skin, the way his whole body tensed when he thrust into me . . . I came again, and then his body shuddered, and he finished. We collapsed side by side on the rug.

My head was spinning. Sweat cooled slowly on my body. I was so happy. Exhausted and happy. Soft comfortable darkness came.

"Kate," he said. "We can't fall asleep here. Come on, baby."

Somehow we made it upstairs into the bed. He wrapped his arms around me, and I drifted off to sleep.

≋ CHAPTER ≋

15

I KNEW MY aunt had recovered, because she exploded into our bedroom and roared, "The child is missing!"

I sat bolt upright on the bed. Curran groaned. I realized I was naked and pulled a blanket over my chest.

"Knocking," I told her. "Privacy."

She glared at us. "This is no time to have sex! Your son is missing! I can't feel him."

Kill me, somebody. "He isn't missing. He's across the street with his grandmother. You can't feel him because I strengthened the ward on George's house to mask his presence."

She squinted at me. "Are you sure?"

"Yes. I went there to check on him late last night and I saw him sleeping. Grendel is with him. There are enough werebears in that house to hold off an army."

Erra considered it. "Very well. Also, your father's attack dog, what's his name? Hugh. Hugh and some blond woman are in a car in your driveway, talking."

She turned and swept down the hallway, right past the remnants of the door she'd broken.

I turned over and bumped my head on Curran's chest a few times. "Why me?"

"I don't know." He stroked my back. "I suppose we need to get dressed."

"Ugh."

"If I have to murder Hugh, I don't want to do it naked," he said. "It would be weird."

"If you change into warrior form, you will be naked."

"That's different."

I got myself dressed, forced myself to brush my teeth, and then I made myself go downstairs, open the door, and walk down the driveway to a blue SUV and knock on the window.

Elara rolled the window down. Hugh looked at me from the driver's seat.

"Hi," I said.

"We're having a private argument," Hugh said. "Do you mind?"

I pictured myself reaching past Elara and punching him in the jaw. Nope, didn't have the reach.

"In my driveway?"

"Yes."

A little smile tugged at Elara's lips.

"Well, when you're done with your argument, you're welcome to come in for some breakfast."

"Thank you," Elara said.

Hugh reached over her and rolled the window up.

I'd just invited Hugh d'Ambray for breakfast. The world was going crazy. Nothing left to do but hold on and yell "Wheee!" at strategic moments.

I went back to the house. I should've punched him in the face while he was rolling the window up. Shoot.

Curran descended the stairs. "What do they want?"

"They're having a private argument. I invited them to breakfast."

He shrugged in a fatalistic way.

I went in the kitchen and checked the plate with smoked meat. It was still there. It was good that Grendel wasn't here, or he would've cleaned the dishes for us overnight. He was considerate like that.

I took eggs out of the refrigerator.

"What made you change your mind?" Curran asked, setting a pan on the stove.

"About Hugh?"

"Yes."

I cracked some eggs into a bowl, added a spoon of sugar, and whipped them into froth. "Christopher thinks that my father used the blood bond to impose his will on Hugh."

"I agree," Curran said.

"Why?"

"Because your father is a control freak, and he doesn't like leaving things to chance. If it can be done, he would've done it. I still want to kill Hugh."

"I know. Christopher forgave Hugh because he believes that if he can't forgive Hugh, he himself can't be forgiven." I added milk to the mixture, and then flour.

"So you forgave him for Christopher?" Curran lifted the pan to roll a piece of smoked fat all around it.

"No. I haven't forgiven him anything, and if I do, it won't be for Christopher. It will be for me. I don't want to drag the weight around. But for now, I want to know why he is here. There has to be a reason and it's not trade agreements for herb sales."

"Do I have to forgive him?" he asked.

"No."

"Oh good. Because I was worried there for a second."

I rolled my eyes at him.

Someone knocked on the front door.

"It's open!" I called. I'd left it unlocked and opened the ward, too. I knew Hugh was human. Regular wards wouldn't stop him, and he'd broken my blood ward once, which took him out of commission for a few minutes. But Elara was another story. Something about her didn't feel quite right.

Hugh opened the door and held it for his wife. She walked in and entered the kitchen. Another dress, this one a pale lavender. Her hair, braided and pinned on her head, was so light, it almost seemed to glow. There was something slightly regal about Elara. Something magic too, but she kept it hidden deep inside, and if I tried to pry, she'd feel it. What the heck was she?

Hugh leaned against the wall, big, dark, the happy-to-kill-you psychopath I remembered. I handed him a stack of plates. "Make yourself useful."

He winked at me.

I swiped a knife off the island and threw it. It sprouted from the wall an inch from his nose. "You'll need cutlery," I told him. "Second drawer on your right."

"Here, I'll help." Elara pulled the drawer open and began extracting forks and knives.

A few minutes later the four of us sat around the breakfast table, with a plate full of golden round pancakes and a platter of smoked meat between us, and fried eggs divvied up on our plates. We drank coffee. Elara drank tea.

We began eating.

"Anything you want to know?" Hugh asked.

"How good are Neig's human fighters?" Curran asked.

Hugh grimaced. "Good. There is a handful of Iron Dogs who can take them one-on-one, but we've had the most success with a small combat team approach."

"You jump them three or four at a time?" Curran asked.

"Yep. The armor is a problem. It's a strong alloy, and we've had a devil of a time cutting them out of it."

"Is it crushable?"

"You or a werebear, maybe," Hugh said. "For a human, it takes a mace. Unfortunately, they're lively in that armor."

"What about the yeddimur?" Curran asked.

"The beasts?" Elara asked. "Each soldier can control up to five. They're not slaves, they are doglike. Very cruel. They feed on what they kill."

"Are they contagious?" Curran asked.

She frowned. "Not that we've noticed, and we've had very close contact."

A whisper of magic escaped her and fluttered past me, ghostly and cold.

I cut a small piece of my egg and speared it with a fork. She was something, all right.

"What about this army?" Curran asked. "Any idea how large it is?"

Hugh shook his head. "We fought his vanguard, maybe three hundred men and about a thousand beasts. I can tell you that they went through Nez's forces like a knife through butter."

Wait, what?

"Landon Nez?" Curran asked. "The Legatus of the Golden Legion? How did they get involved?"

"They were besieging us at the time," Elara said.

"Did Nez die?" my husband asked.

"No," Hugh said, and his face told me exactly how happy he was about it. "But the Legion had to withdraw."

"We need to figure out what Neig's got." Curran drummed his fingers on the table.

"Unless he invites one of us over, I don't see how that would be possible," Hugh said. "We do know a few things. His people can't be subverted. I have my doubts that they are even people anymore. He attacks small settlements where he knows he will take minimal losses. Dogs hate him and everything that smells of him, which includes his soldiers and the yeddimur. The shapeshifters among my people report having the same urge to kill them as they do with loups."

"There are shapeshifters among your people?" Curran asked.

"I discriminate on the basis of ability, not origin. You know that, Lennart."

"Really?" Curran frowned. "You might need to discriminate harder then, because I don't remember them being that difficult to kill. Didn't you kill one, honey?" He glanced at me. "A centurion, too. Was it hard?"

Elara smiled at me. "The pancakes are delicious."

"Anytime you want a repeat of that rendezvous you and I had on the roof, you let me know," Hugh said.

I set my mug on the table a little too hard, and it made a thud. The two men looked at me. "Honestly, Hugh, why the fuck are you here?"

"I told you," he said. "I have a castle to protect. With a town attached to it. A thousand civilians: bakers, smiths, potion brewers. Kids. Elderly. We are not set up for a long-term siege. If Neig goes through you, he will swing toward us. He has a score to settle."

Elara put down her fork. "My husband has trouble communicating his feelings, so I may have to translate for him. He feels guilt. He remembers everything he has done, the people he killed, and the lives he ruined. It gnaws at him and it's ripping him apart. There are times he doesn't sleep for several days. He works himself to exhaustion trying to protect us, and he blames himself for every death and injury. He left our castle and our people and came here, because you need him. You are in critical danger. He can't change the past, but he can alter the future, and if you let him, he will do everything in his power to help. He isn't trying to win your forgiveness. He is here to atone, because it's the right thing to do. I'm here because I love him. This is very difficult for him and I didn't want him to face it alone."

The table fell quiet.

I looked at Hugh. He looked back at me. There was a sharp pain in his eyes. My father had done his damage, tossed him away like garbage, yet here he was, trying to right lifetimes of wrong, and somehow I was the key to it. I felt it. It was like a live wire connecting us.

"I'm sorry about Mishmar," he said. "I'm sorry about the knights, the castle, all of it."

Sitting here was excruciating. I wanted to fall through the floor.

Silence stretched.

If I slammed the door in his face now, I would be just like my father. Hugh was the closest thing to a brother I had. We were both raised by Voron under Roland's shadow. We were both trained to kill and expected to obey without question. We both would've done anything for our "father's" approval. We were both found wanting by Roland, each of us a disappointment. He had no use for us unless we served him.

If it weren't for my mother's sacrifice, I would be Hugh now, sitting here, waiting for a crumb of kindness from someone I'd hurt.

The silence was unbearable now.

"I have a comatose dragon in my basement," I said. "He fought Neig and he might know something that can help us. We've been trying to bring him back to life, but nothing has worked. Could you please take a look?"

Hugh nodded. "I can."

"Thank you." I got up. "I'll show you where he is."

HUGH PONDERED YU Fong. Adora watched him from her chair as if he were a rabid dog.

"I'll have to cut him open," Hugh said. "There is something lodged inside him."

"Can you keep him alive?" I asked.

"Yes," Hugh said.

"You said the other doctor said it couldn't be done," Adora said.

"The other doctor isn't Hugh," Elara told her. "If my husband says he can heal him, he means it."

Hugh turned to me.

He could be working with Neig against me. He could be working for my father. He could kill Yu Fong and then laugh at me.

Behind Hugh, Curran leaned against the wall, his gray eyes clear and calm. He didn't seem to be worried.

Either I trusted Hugh, or I didn't.

"Go ahead," I said.

He took a knife from his belt. A dense blue light flared around Hugh and spilled onto Yu Fong, binding them together. Hugh leaned forward and split Yu Fong's stomach from chest to groin. A sour stench filled the room. Hugh thrust his hand into the wound and drew something bloody out. He dropped it and I caught it before it hit the floor. My fingers closed around blood-slicked bone. An ivory fragment about the length of my forearm, two inches at its widest point.

"What is that?" Adora leaned forward.

"A tooth," Curran said. "A piece of one anyway."

"Neig's tooth?" I thought out loud.

"It would have to be."

A tremor shook Yu Fong's body. A bead of sweat broke out on Hugh's forehead. The glow around him brightened.

"I think we should go," I murmured.

"I'm staying," Adora declared.

"Don't disturb him," I told her.

We went upstairs single file, first Curran, then Elara, then me. In the kitchen, Elara turned to me. "Thank you for giving him a way to help."

"Oh, he'll do a lot more than that," Curran said. "You're right. We're desperate. We will take him and the Iron Dogs."

"You do know he is a bastard?" I asked Elara.

She tilted her chin up slightly. "I've walked through his mind. He is my bastard."

"Have the witches spoken to you?" I asked.

"Yes. You want to use me as the focus to place your father into eternal sleep. What happens if we fail?"

"We'll go to Plan B," I told her.

"And that would be?"

"I'll kill my father or die trying, which will amount to the same thing."

Elara studied me. "Do you have the resolve?"

"Trust me," Curran said, his eyes dark. "Resolve isn't a problem."

"We have a more pressing issue. Eventually the Pack will track Hugh down to our house, and Raphael will show up howling for blood. Raphael is a bouda. Hugh's centurion killed his mother. I killed the centurion, but Raphael isn't exactly going to bother with the details. He'll see Hugh and then it will be a bloodbath."

"We already settled that," Elara said.

"You did?" Curran asked.

"Yes. Raphael is the dark-haired one in leather?"

"Looks like sex on a stick," I told her.

"Yes. With the eyes." She waved her fingers to imitate fluttering eye-lashes.

"That's him."

Curran looked like he'd just bitten into a lemon.

"He came to see us last fall," Elara said. "He has a short blond wife."

What? "Did you talk to her?"

"I did."

"Excuse me." I got up, walked to the phone, and dialed the Bouda House. A chirpy bouda answered. "Clan Bouda's residence."

"Please tell the alpha that her former best friend is calling."

"She warned us you would call."

There was a click and then Andrea's voice came on the line. "Hey."

"You didn't tell me."

"Nope, I didn't."

"Why?"

"Because you were pregnant at the time and had enough shit to deal with."

I forced the words out. "Why didn't you tell me after?"

"Because I watched Hugh let Raphael cut him to ribbons. If I'd told you, you'd have dropped everything and went there too, and then Hugh would've let you kill him, and then you'd be filled with self-loathing and I'd have to take care of your mopey ass. I have a clan to run, a husband to satisfy, and a daughter to take care of. Call me when you cool off."

She hung up.

Society frowned on killing your best friend. In this case, it would just have to make an exception.

HALF AN HOUR later Hugh staggered out of the basement, his face haggard. He looked like he was about to fall over, but he made it to his chair in the kitchen and drank his cold coffee like it was water. I let him finish.

"He'll live," Hugh said. "He'll sleep for a couple more hours, then he should be fine."

"Do you want to lie down?" Elara asked him.

He shook his head. "I could use more meat."

I brought the whole platter and set it in front of him. He took a pancake, stuffed meat into it, and rolled it up.

Curran got up and moved to the front door. I followed.

"What is it?"

"A Pack vehicle."

Just as predicted. "I'm going to get my sword. If it's Raphael looking for seconds, please don't let him in the house."

"It's not Raphael," Curran said.

The horrible racket of an enchanted water engine cut the silence, growing louder and louder, until the familiar Pack van shot down the street past us. The van screeched to a stop, reversed, and expertly pulled into our driveway. The doors swung open. Dali jumped out, took out a wheelchair, and lowered Doolittle into it. Her glasses sat slightly askew on her nose, and she moved with jerky urgency. She grabbed a wooden box, placed it on Doolittle's lap, and wheeled him to our doors as if she were about to storm a castle.

What the heck was that? Some cure for Yu Fong?

"Where is he?"

"Yu Fong is in the basement. He—"

"Not him." Dali pushed past me, her gaze locked on Hugh's broad back. "Him."

I glanced at Curran. She was always impulsive, but this was taking it to a new level. He shook his head and we followed them into the kitchen.

"Do people just walk into your house like they own the place?" Hugh asked Curran.

"You have no idea," Curran told him.

Dali set the box on the table in front of Hugh. "I need to know what this is."

"I'm eating," he said.

I took my coffee cup off the table and moved out of the way. This should be interesting.

Dali's eyes lit up. "You listen to me—"

"You barged into the house of the closest person I have to a sister and you interrupted my breakfast."

Dali reached to grab him. Elara's fingers brushed her. Dali jerked back, a look of pure horror on her face.

"If you touch my husband again, I'll eat your soul, tiger," Elara said, and drank her cold tea.

"Aww, honey." Hugh smiled at her. "You shouldn't have."

"Nobody is eating anybody's soul," I said.

Curran looked into Dali's eyes and said in a calm, measured voice laced with command, "Sit."

It was his Beast Lord voice. Very difficult to disobey. I still managed, but Dali had grown up in the Pack, and old habits died hard. She dropped into the nearest chair.

"Take a deep breath."

Dali sucked the air in and let it out slowly.

"Why are you in my house?" he asked her.

Dali took another deep breath. Her bottom lip trembled, her composure broke, and she clamped her hands over her face. There was no sound. Just hands over her face and shudders. Poor Dali.

Curran crouched by her and gently pried the glasses from under her fingers. I got a handkerchief and brought it over. Curran took it from me and offered it to Dali. She grabbed it and pressed her face into it. He wrapped his arms around her. Her shoulders shook.

I turned to Doolittle. "What's going on?"

He sighed. "She's been under a great deal of stress."

Dali said something through her hands.

"What is it?" Curran asked gently.

She said it again.

"We can't understand you." I kept my voice warm but firm.

She dropped her hands. Without glasses, she looked ten years younger, her dark eyes wide and tear-drenched. "I'm barren! I can't have children."

I turned to Doolittle.

He nodded.

Dali flipped the box open. Inside was a large crystal vial filled with amber liquid. It shimmered and glowed, as if filled with glitter.

"Roland sent us this. It's a gift." She spat the word out as if it were poison. "We don't even know how he knew we were trying to conceive. The man he sent said it will heal me. Jim refused to take it, but he left it on the ground just outside the gates, and I went and got it. I need to know if it will fix me. He told us to test it to prove that it wasn't poison, but I don't want to be responsible for anyone getting hurt."

Well, now we knew what was in the briefcase.

Hugh kept eating.

Elara looked at him.

He shrugged. "It's not my problem."

"Please answer her," she asked.

"You feel bad, but I don't," he said.

"For me," she asked.

"You know my price," he told her.

Elara leaned back and crossed her arms, her face iced over. "Really?"

"The whole thing. You'll put it in your mouth and you'll swallow."

What?

"The whole thing?"

"I mean it, Elara. You will eat the entire chicken."

"I can't possibly eat the whole chicken. It's too much."

Hugh's voice was merciless. "Do it over the course of the day."

"Do you expect me to eat the bones, too?"

"Now you're being childish."

"I just want to have the terms of this agreement clear," she told him.

"You don't have to eat the bones," he said. "You will consume the meat and skin of the chicken. Possibly some cartilage if you feel like it. All the parts of the chicken normally eaten by human beings."

"You're a bully," she told him.

"You knew I was an asshole when you married me."

"Fine. I will eat the damn chicken. Help her, please."

Hugh stopped eating, placed his fork and knife onto the plate, moved it aside, and nodded at the bottle. "This is ambrosia. Not the actual nectar of the gods, but an all-around curative Roland cooks up. It takes him about a year to make it. It will heal an injury in record time. Personally, I wouldn't take it. His potions come with fun side effects. You might get pregnant, and ten days later you might saw off your husband's head in his sleep."

All the air had gone out of Dali. I stepped closer to her and put my hands on her shoulders. Curran was still holding her. I wished I could make it better.

"So it won't cure me," she said, her voice bitter.

"I doubt it. You didn't suffer an injury that needs to be corrected. Your problem is too much regeneration. Both of your fallopian tubes have fused shut. If you were human, I'd expect to find a severe case of endometriosis. The tissue normally inside your uterus would be growing outside it. But you're a shapeshifter, so Lyc-V is trying to fix the problem by plugging every hole it can find, and it decided your fallopian tubes are a danger zone. Before the Shift, they sidestepped endometriosis infertility with in vitro fertilization. It's not an option for us. I take it you tried surgical options, and the tubes reclose immediately after the operation is completed?"

"Yes," Doolittle said.

Hugh squinted at Dali. "I can fix it, but it will require cutting you open. You'll have to stay awake during the procedure, and it will have to be done without anesthetic, because I'll need you to hold back the Lyc-V, otherwise it will heal you faster than I can regrow your tissue. The moment you go under, you surrender control of your virus and it goes into overdrive, because it thinks you're dying. The surgery won't be fun. Your husband won't like it. Talk it over with him."

"You would do this for me?" Dali asked him. "Why?"

"Because my wife asked me to," he said.

"How are you planning on reopening the tubes?" Doolittle asked.

"I'm not. I will cut them out of her and regrow them."

Doolittle looked at Dali. "Even with his power, that will take hours."

"I said it wouldn't be fun," Hugh said.

"Think very carefully," Doolittle said. "It will be very painful."

She raised her head. "I want a child. My and Jim's child. You have no idea what it's like to not be able to have a baby. All I see are babies. Andrea's baby, Kate's baby, and now George is pregnant."

"George is pregnant?" That was the first I'd heard of it.

"I don't begrudge anyone their babies. I just want to have one of my own."

"Talk to Jim," Curran said.

"It's not Jim's decision," she told him.

"I know that," he said. "But he loves you. He should be allowed to at least tell you how he feels about it."

"I would have to be present during the surgery," Doolittle said to Hugh. "And my assistants."

"I can do it in front of the whole Pack if you want," he said. "Makes no difference to me."

"I just want to be a mom," Dali said softly. "I want to hold the baby that Jim and I made. I want to cuddle him or her. Sing to her. I want a baby."

She glanced at me and a little light of the old Dali sparked in her eyes. "I want to freak out and take my baby to Doolittle in a panic when he sneezes."

Really? "I don't take Conlan in when he sneezes. I have serious concerns."

Curran exploded from his spot by Dali. He leaped over the table and tore out the door. I grabbed Sarrat and ran after him.

We burst onto the street. The window on the top floor of George's house lay shattered, the bars missing. A man landed in the middle of the street with inhuman grace, his patched trench coat flaring around him. Razer.

He was clutching my son to him, pointing the tip of his dagger at Conlan's neck. The dagger gleamed with silver.

Sarrat smoked in my hand. I snapped my magic like a whip, activating the long-distance ward that would lock him in. He'd have to break it to leave the street, and I had a lot more magic than he did.

Curran shifted. An eight-foot nightmare rose next to me, a meld of human and lion distilled into a thing of power and speed, designed to do only one thing: kill. A huge Kodiak, bleeding from a gash on its head, tore out of George's house.

Hugh moved to the right of me, a sword in his hand. Next to him Elara stepped forward. Dali stalked to the left of Curran. Derek and Julie sprinted to us from Derek's house. A trio of vampires burst from the other end of the street, cutting off his exit. More werebears poured out of George's place.

Razer looked up. Christopher swooped over his head, blood-red wings spread wide.

My aunt burst into existence next to me.

"Give us the child," Curran said, his voice a low growl.

Razer clenched Conlan to him and bared his long, sharp teeth. Fae teeth, made to strip flesh off human bones. My son was looking at me, his huge eyes wide and scared.

"Give us the child, and I'll let you live," I told him.

Razer looked left, then right. There was nowhere to go. He was caught in a ring of snarling fangs, glowing eyes, and steel.

"Don't be an idiot," Hugh said. "Give us the kid."

"I hold the cards," Razer rasped. He flicked the dagger and cut Conlan's cheek. Blood swelled, the edge of the wound turning duct-tape gray—the virus dying.

I would kill him.

Everyone snarled.

"Stay back!" Razer barked.

Conlan swiped at the blood, saw it on his hand . . . His lip trembled. He sucked in a lungful of air and screamed.

"Shut up!" Razer snarled into his face.

Conlan's gray eyes went wide and flared with hot, furious gold. His human body tore. A demonic half-lion, half-child burst out. The blood snapped from his wound, forming red blades over his claws. Conlan raked Razer's face, ripping bloody gashes in the flesh. His claws caught Razer's left eye and tore it out of the socket. The fae howled and caught it reflexively into his hand. Conlan kicked free and dashed to me. I caught him in my arms and hugged him.

The whole thing took less than a second.

My son had just made blood claws. He'd made claws out of his own blood.

Blood claws.

The street had gone so silent, you could hear people breathing.

Razer stared at his own eye in his hand.

Curran surged forward.

My aunt softly praised Conlan. "Such a gifted child," she cooed. "Such a talented little prince."

The little nightmare smiled at Erra, showing all of his teeth. He struggled to say something and changed back into a human. "Gama."

"Grandma is so proud," Erra told him.

"That's my boy." I made my voice happy and light.

Conlan hugged my neck. "Bad."

Razer was screaming because Curran had pulled his left arm off.

"Yes, bad. Look at Daddy ripping the bad man to pieces. Go Daddy!"

Conlan clapped his hands.

Curran snapped Razer's spine with a loud crack, then twisted off the fae's head.

"Look, Daddy killed him dead. All dead."

Conlan giggled.

Dali was staring at me with a look of pure horror.

"I don't want him to have nightmares that the bad man is going to get him," I told her. "This way he knows his daddy killed him."

Curran stood over Razer's ruined corpse and roared.

"*Rawrawrawr*," human Conlan said.

"That's right," I said.

"What happened to not wanting to traumatize him?" a vampire asked me in Ghastek's voice.

"I gave up," I told him. "We are a family of monsters and he's our child. People will always try to kill him and we will always protect him. He better get used to it."

16

I SAT ON the back porch in my chair, drinking a glass of iced tea. Curran crouched in the backyard. His gray eyes tracked the faint hint of movement through the raspberry bushes at the edge of the lawn. Elara had walked out into our woods for a bit after the Razer incident. I wasn't sure if she needed to cool off or compose herself, but she was back now, sitting on the lower branch of a large oak and watching Curran.

The door swung open and Hugh shouldered his way out and dropped into a chair next to me.

"Did Dali leave finally?"

"Still on the phone," he said.

Once Razer's corpse was removed and everything went back to normal, Dali decided to have an important conversation with Jim about having Hugh perform the surgery. Unfortunately, she refused to leave because, according to her, I could murder Hugh while she was away. Instead she chose to have this conversation via our kitchen phone. Things weren't going well because Jim, understandably, wasn't enthusiastic about having Hugh d'Ambray cutting his wife open and removing parts of her. She had hung up on Jim twice and he had hung up on her once. Last I heard, they'd gone from wild accusations to cold logic. Given that they were two of the smartest people I knew, they would be at it awhile.

"She's slipping," I said. "I could kill you right now, while you're out on the porch with me."

"If I didn't fight back."

"Would you fight back?"

"I'm thinking about it." He was watching Elara. She sat on the branch, swinging her feet. His expression was still hard, but there was something softer in his eyes. Something warm.

Curran pivoted toward us, away from the bushes.

"You should fight back," I told Hugh. "Nobody likes a quitter."

Conlan exploded out of the bushes and pounced on his father's back. Curran roared dramatically and collapsed in the grass.

"Is this what you wanted?" Hugh asked.

I knew what he meant. He was asking about Curran, and Conlan, about the house with the woods out back, friends, and a house that never stayed quiet for too long.

"Yes."

"You know Nimrod would give you all the power in the world. If you told him that you accepted him, he would turn himself inside out to please you. He would build a palace for your son." A note of bitterness slipped into his voice. He killed it quickly, but I'd still heard it.

I understood. No matter what Hugh did, no matter how hard he tried or how good he was at doing it, my father would never value him as much as he valued me. I was blood and Hugh wasn't. The kicker was, he didn't value me all that much either.

"But all his gifts would come with a collar around my neck."

"True."

"That's not how Roland sees me anyway. He doesn't see me as a daughter whom he can teach. He sees me as a sword he can use. Once in a while he rubs me the wrong way and I cut him, and he's surprised and pleased the sword is sharp, but it never goes past that."

"You have no idea," Hugh said.

"I do. He tried living next to my territory. He would bait me every few days. He couldn't help himself. That's why the castle he started is now a burned-out ruin. You and I have that in common—neither of us will ever get what we want out of a relationship with him. He mostly wants me to be your replacement. He hasn't realized yet that I don't have your training or your mind. If he gave me an army, I would have no idea what to do with it."

"Your aunt did well enough," Hugh said.

"My aunt studied strategy and tactics since she was old enough to read. I'm a lone killer. That's what I do best."

"Whatever you did worked well enough when you fought him, from what I hear."

"He formed his troops in two rectangles and marched them on the Keep. I couldn't believe it."

Hugh grimaced. "Did he ride a chariot?"

"Mm-hm. It was gold."

Hugh shut his eyes for a second.

"It was slow as hell."

"Well, of course it's slow. It's gold. Did you know he wanted to put a figurehead on it?"

I blinked. "What, like on a ship?"

"Yeah." Hugh looked like he'd just bitten a rotten lemon. "Your mother's face with diamond eyes and wings made of electrum. Spread wings." He held his hands up, the tips of his fingers angled back.

"How aerodynamic." I grinned.

"I told him he'd need a damn elephant to draw it forward."

"Did he give up?"

"No," Hugh said. "Last I know of it, he was building a pair of mechanical magic-powered horses to draw the chariot."

"Let me guess, platinum? With gold manes?"

"What do you think?"

We laughed.

"What about you?"

He raised his eyebrows. "What about me?"

"What happens when all is forgiven, and he needs you again?"

Hugh glanced at Elara again. "It already happened."

He'd said no.

Huh. That must've cost him. My father was everything to Hugh: surrogate father, commander, god . . . And Hugh had walked away from it. He could be lying, but it felt like the truth. It was in his eyes, the way they turned a touch sad and resigned.

"All of his children turn on him eventually," I said.

"I was never his child."

I rolled my eyes. "He raised you, he taught you, he encouraged you."

"He fucked with my head."

"He fucks with everyone's head. Yours more than most. For all it matters, you're his son. You're fucked up enough to be."

He barked a short laugh.

"Face it," I told him. "We are damaged siblings."

We watched Curran chase Conlan around.

"What was it like?" I asked.

Hugh's face fell. I didn't need to elaborate. He knew exactly what I was asking.

"It was like having the sun ripped away," he said. "I'd reach for the connection out of habit, and there would be a raw wound there, filled with all the shit I did."

"Sorry," I told him.

"Don't be. I'm me now. Still a bastard, but I'm my own bastard now. Nobody tells me what to do." He glanced at Elara and smiled. "Well, she does once in a while, but it's worth it."

"He would give you the world if you came crawling back," I told him, mimicking his voice.

"I have her. I have our soldiers and our people to protect. I have a castle to run. I don't want the world. I just want that small corner of it to be safe."

"Going to war against a dragon isn't exactly going to keep your Iron Dogs safe."

He looked at me. "No, but it will help you."

"You don't have to pay your old debts, Hugh. Not with me."

"Just accept the help," he growled. "You need it."

"Oh, I'll take it. Three hundred Iron Dogs and Hugh d'Ambray. I'd be crazy to turn it down."

"Smart girl."

"But you and I are fine, Hugh. I mean it."

"Just like that," he said.

"No, I thought about it. I let it go for me more than for you. You're not the only one with corpses in your memories. I killed on command. I didn't ask why. Voron would point and I would murder."

"You were a kid," he said.

"And you had your emotions readjusted. I believe that's what they call extenuating circumstances. Having them doesn't help as much as it should, does it? I can't change what I did. I can only go forward and try to do better. I'll always be a killer. I like it. You'll always be a bastard. There is a part of you that enjoys kicking the door in and throwing a severed head on the table."

"N'importe quoi."

I made a mental note to ask Christopher to translate. He spoke fluent French.

"Some pair we are," Hugh said.

"Mm-hm. Sitting here all sad on the porch, while a dragon is invading and our dad is having a midlife crisis with golden chariots . . ."

Hugh grinned, and then his face turned dark.

"Do one thing for me," he said.

"Mm?"

"Don't do to the girl what was done to me."

"Julie's will is her own. I've never forced her to do anything, and I don't plan on it."

Elara slid off the branch and jumped into the grass.

"It's not all bad." Hugh rose and walked toward her.

I finished my tea.

"Do you trust him?" my aunt asked by my ear.

"I trust the look in his eyes when he speaks about my father. Like he's torn between loving him and wanting to strangle him."

"It may prove foolish."

"If it does, I'll deal with it," I told her.

"Spoken like a queen." My aunt ran her ghostly fingers through my hair. "I finally made you into one."

"Too bad I've run out of time."

"Is that defeat I hear?" Erra raised her eyebrows.

"No, it's reality. We may not have the troops to fight Neig, and we definitely can't face him and my father at the same time. The dragon hates us, but he especially hates him."

"Are you asking me to persuade your father into an alliance?"

"If the opportunity presents itself."

My aunt became still. Facing my father would cost her a great deal.

"You ask much, child."

"Is that defeat I hear?"

She snorted.

"How is it you plan to convince him?" she asked. "Shame? Threats?"

What was it Roman had said? Parents love to play saviors. "No. I'm going to let you use those. If I do it, Dad will just see it as a personal attack and go on the offensive. He wants to be a hero. He wants to come in and save the day and be admired and loved for it. So I plan on being resigned to my fate. Grim, grieving, and in a dark pit of despair."

"So your father can be your lone ray of hope in the darkness?"

"Yep."

She studied me. "You've grown manipulative."

"You disapprove?"

"No. I'm surprised."

"Good. Dad will be surprised, too. I've spent a long time convincing him that I don't do subtle. He doesn't think I have the brains to manipulate him, so he won't expect it."

"You don't do subtle. Your subtle is pulling a kick so you don't kill a man with it, just break his bones."

"I've learned."

She waited, wanting something more from me.

"The word of Sharratum is binding," I murmured. That was what Erra had said to me when she'd demanded I swear to never rule the land I claimed. "I don't rule, but I am a queen. I claimed the city. They all need my protection. They don't even know it, but they need me to survive." My voice sounded dead. "So I'll lie, and cheat, and give up my pride. I'll do whatever I have to do to keep them all safe. I'm not my own person."

Erra stepped to me. Her arms closed around me. I couldn't feel her body, but I felt her magic coursing around me.

"Poor child," she whispered, her voice so soft. **"I tried to keep you from it as long as I could."**

I felt like crying, but it didn't quite come to the surface. I couldn't afford crying. I had things I had to do.

Curran picked Conlan up and tossed him into the air. The sun hit them just right and I saw an aura emanating from him, a faint shimmer of warm glow. My heart flipped in my chest. He was so far gone.

"You encouraged him to become a god," I whispered into her embrace.

"I did."

"I'll never forgive you for that."

"You'll change your mind with time."

No. I won't. I wanted to rage and scream at her, but it was Curran who'd made the final decision. I loved him so much and even now he was slipping away from me.

A dull noise echoed through my mind, a silent sound. Someone had just tested my wards. I stepped away from Erra, got up, picked up Sarrat, and headed for the door.

THE WARRIOR STOOD at the end of the street. He wore dark armor and held his helmet in his left hand and a golden chain in his right. I marched toward him, sword smoking.

I stopped just before my ward. He stood on the other side of it.

He was young, maybe twenty, with clear blue eyes like two chips of winter ice, a line of tattoos running down one side of his pale face, and long blond hair pulled back with a leather cord. The chain in his hand was attached to a locket with a gemstone the size of a walnut that looked like pure red fire caught under glass.

"My lord extends an invitation," he said, his English stilted. "Come with me, and he will show you the might of his realm."

If my father had lied to me and I went into Neig's realm, I could be trapped there forever, or dead.

Behind me Curran walked onto the street. I didn't have to turn to know that by now he was sprinting. If he got here, he would talk me out of it. We needed to know how many troops Neig had. Without it, we were blind.

"Kate!" Curran barked.

My father wouldn't want me to be stuck in Neig's realm, at the dragon's beck and call. He and I had our problems, but he hated Neig. There was too much rage in his eyes when he talked about the dragon. He wouldn't lie to me, not about this.

Curran was almost to me.

"Trust me," I called out. "I've got this."

I would catch hell for this later. I dissolved the ward and held out my left hand. "Lead the way."

The warrior took my fingers in his, pressing the stone against my hand.

Curran was almost to us. He jumped, covering the last twenty feet.

The world turned white and then my stomach tried to go one way while most of me went the other. The white light faded. My body clenched. I spun around and vomited onto the rocky ground. Awesome entrance. So regal and impressive.

I straightened. We stood on a stone bridge spanning a deep gorge. In front of us a castle rose. Built with dark stone, it didn't have the elaborate spires and ornamental work of Victorian English palaces or German gingerbread castles. No, this was an Anglo-Norman square stone keep, with thick walls and a forest of massive towers scratching at the sky. To the left, a mountain ridge curved down and away into the mists. To the right, a deep wide valley stretched, bordered at the horizon by more mountains. Far in the distance, at the foot of that other mountain ridge, a lake caught the sun and glistened. The air smelled like pines. A cold draft slid against my skin and I shivered.

In his realm, you are a ghost . . . Well, this ghost should've brought a sweater.

"This way," the warrior told me.

I sheathed Sarrat. We walked down the stone bridge to the massive gates. I couldn't see the sun, but the sky was light.

"How long have you served Neig?" I asked.

"Forever."

"What about your family? Did you leave anyone behind?"

No answer.

"Do you remember where you used to live? Was it here in Georgia? Was it in Ireland?"

No answer.

We reached the gates.

"Are you sure you don't remember your family? You must've come from somewhere. What was your mother's name?"

No answer.

The gates swung open and we walked into the courtyard. A second pair of gates creaked open at our approach. The soldier halted and pointed at the gateway. I was meant to keep going on my own.

I marched through the doors and into a throne room, lit by glass globes dripping from the walls. The floor glistered. At first glance it looked like glass, but no, it was gold. Melted down and allowed to cool into a perfectly smooth surface that gleamed with a mirror sheen. A man-made stream wound its way through the floor in a gentle curve, only a couple of inches deep. Gems lined the creek bed, gleaming in the water: red rubies, green emeralds, blue sapphires, purple amethysts, light-green peridots . . . A fortune in precious jewels, cast there like sea glass at the bottom of a fish tank.

A throne dominated the far wall, carved from the bones of some enormous creature into the shape of a dragon in profile. A red gem the size of a grapefruit sat in the dragon's eye socket. It felt warm and suffused with magic, as if it were somehow alive. I brushed it with my magic and it sparked off my power. Wow. It was condensed magic, so potent it felt like a tiny sun.

The anchor. The arrogant bastard had his anchor right there, just past his front door.

Neig waited for me on the throne, dressed in full regalia, his fur cape draped over his armor, the golden torque bright. To his left, a long table offered a feast. Roasted meat, golden bread, fruit, wine. The aroma made my mouth water.

"Should've colored the water in your stream red," I told him.

"A river of blood?" he said. His voice enveloped me, deep and vibrating with power.

"It would be more honest."

"But you wouldn't be able to see the beauty of the jewels." He indicated the table with a sweep of his hand. "Please. Sate your hunger."

Nice try. I did my Erra sneer. "Really?"

Neig smiled, betraying a hint of sharp teeth. The table vanished. Okay then.

He stepped off the throne and approached me. I'd clocked him at about six-six, six-seven before. I was off by about half a foot. He towered over me.

"I wish to give you a tour of my domain."

"Oh goody."

We strolled out of the throne room into a hallway of enormous arched windows.

"Are you a man or a dragon?" I asked him.

"I'm both."

"But what were you born as?"

"It was a long time ago. I do not remember. Some of us were born with talons, others with hands, but we are all Dragon."

"What are Dragon?"

"An ancient race. We were here when humans crawled out of the mud. We watched you try to walk upright and bang rocks against each other, trying to make claws and teeth."

Yeah, right. "You're not that old."

He grinned again. Tiny streaks of smoke escaped his mouth. Awesome. If I got too cold, I could ask him to breathe on me.

"Why do you want to conquer?" I asked.

"Why would I not?"

"You brought me here to convince me to join you. So far, you're doing a terrible job of it."

"You're an interesting creature, Daughter of Nimrod."

"The name is Kate Lennart. I'm not defined by being my father's daughter."

"But you're defined by your husband's name."

"I chose that name. I decided I wanted it."

His thick eyebrows came together.

"If you're not going to answer any questions, this will be a very one-sided conversation," I told him.

"Very well. I will answer your question. I want to conquer because it pleases me. I like to rule, I like to own, and I like to be acknowledged as the supreme power."

"Your conquest will cost hundreds of thousands of lives. Millions."

"Human lives."

"Yes."

"There are always more humans," he said. "There is never a shortage."

We passed from the hallway into a massive room. Shelves lined the fifty-foot walls. Books filled the shelves, thousands and thousands of books: some bound in leather, some hidden in scroll tubes, papyrus, clay tablets, Chinese bamboo books, long strips of animal hide sheltered by wooden covers . . . Above it all, a skylight spilled a stream of sunlight into the middle of the room, never touching the precious volumes. My father would kill himself out of jealousy.

"Have you read any of these?"

"Yes."

"Were they written by humans?"

"Most of them."

"Then you saw into their minds. You know that each human is unique. Once you kill one, there will never be another one exactly like it."

Neig stepped to the shelf and pulled out a heavy tome, bound in leather and inlaid with gold. The writing on the cover resembled Ashuri script, but the ancient Hebrews wrote on scrolls, not in bound books. Neig stepped to the window. It swung open in front of him and he tossed the book outside.

"Wait!" I lunged for the window and saw the book plunge down and disappear into mists somewhere far below.

"Fifty humans wrote that book," Neig said, and indicated the library with a sweep of his hand. "Is my collection any less magnificent?"

I sighed.

"Why do you care?" he asked. "You are more powerful than them. You are faster, stronger, better in every way. I watched you kill. You enjoy it."

"I kill to protect myself and others. I don't begin violence, I respond to it."

"Why not kill for pleasure?"

"Because I find pleasure in other ways. When I see people prospering and enjoying their lives, it makes me happy."

He puzzled over me and resumed his walk. I followed him.

"Why?" he asked.

"Because when people prosper, the world is safer. There are pleasures in the world that you have never dreamed of. Why do you read books?"

"To understand those I wish to subjugate."

"Bullshit. You're stuck here, in a place where time has no meaning, with nothing to do. You read because you are bored."

He laughed. Every hair on the back of my neck stood on end. The sharp, cold punch of alarm hit me low in the gut. Note to self: avoid laughing dragons.

"If you conquer everyone, life will be boring and empty of all meaning. There will be no more books to read or fun conversations to be had."

"It will take some time to conquer the world. In the meantime, I will be greatly entertained."

"Have you tried actually walking around among people?"

We passed out of the library into another large room. Heaps of gold leaned against the walls. Coins, nuggets, jewelry. He was showing me his hoard. How predictable.

"I have, when I was young," he said. "I lived with humans for half a century. I've learned that you are weak, stupid, and easily cowed. Given the chance, you would rather fight each other than unite against a threat. I've never seen creatures who hate themselves so much."

"Then you're in for a surprise," I said.

"The twisted furry things you fought and killed," he said. "My slave-hounds."

"The yeddimur."

"Each started its life as a human babe. Each inhaled the fumes of my venom. Now they are beasts, primitive and filthy. They know nothing except rage and hunger. They eat their own. That is the true nature of humanity. I simply brought it to the surface."

Ahead, double doors opened before us.

"Let me show you my power," he said.

We walked through the door onto a balcony. The valley below spread before us, covered in odd blue vegetation. I squinted.

He passed me a spyglass. I looked through it.

Warriors. They stood packed next to each other like sardines. Miles and miles of warriors standing completely still.

Oh God.

"My army," he said. "In my domain, there is no time, no hunger, and no thirst, unless I will it to be. Here I rule uncontested."

They stood in squares, two, four, six, twenty men per row. Twenty by twenty equaled four hundred. How many squares? One, two, three . . .

"They sleep until I call them. They've waited for thousands of your years, but for them it is a blink."

. . . Twenty-one, twenty-two, twenty-three . . .

"Their muscles are trained; their skills are sharp. They live to battle in my name."

. . . Thirty-four . . . I stopped. We didn't have enough people. Even if the Conclave put every fighter they had on the field, we wouldn't have enough.

I swung the spyglass left, toward some dark-brown stains, and saw corrals filled with yeddimur, curled into swarms, piled onto each other. A horde waiting to be unleashed.

"How do I know it's not an illusion?"

"I have no need to lie," he said. "What would be the point? It would be a short-lived deception. Whether you agree to my terms or you don't, I will still field my army. I require sustenance to remain in your world, and I am ready for battle. You will see the size of my force when I unleash it. Nothing would stop you from turning on me if I lied."

Thousands and thousands and thousands of troops. Nausea squirmed through me. Atlanta was doomed. "You cook people and devour their bones."

"Yes. It is faster and more efficient than devouring them whole. Eventually I'll consume enough and will no longer require it."

"How many people will die to reach that eventually?"

"There will be enough left," he said.

He stepped closer to me. His fingers rested on my shoulders.

"You hate your father," he said. "Everyone knows it. People whisper of it."

"I also love my father."

"Families are complicated. I loved my father, but I killed him and took his land. I'm giving you the chance to do the same. I need a guide to your world. You can be my queen. You are brimming with magic. I can taste it."

He leaned down next to me. The smoke from his mouth brushed my cheek. My skin crawled.

"Our children would be powerful beyond measure. They would be kings and queens."

"I'm married, and I already have a child."

"Keep him. Keep your husband as a plaything." His deep voice rolled over my skin. "I will help you kill your father. We will rule the world together."

"And what happens to Atlanta?"

He touched my hair. "The city is yours to do with as you wish. A wedding gift, if you like. I only require the slaves."

"The slaves?"

"The humans. We can bargain, if you want. How many do you wish to keep? I will give you the pretty ones."

"Ugh. You're really inhuman."

"Riches, power, the pleasure of conquest, pleasures of the flesh, pleasures of the mind. What is it you want, Kate Lennart?"

"To cut off your head."

He laughed again. His hands flexed on my shoulders as if his fingers had talons. "I will give you three days to decide. Three days of peace and contemplation. After three days, with the first magic wave that arrives, I come to conquer."

He had enough troops to attack the city from multiple fronts. We had no walls, no fortifications to stop him, and not enough soldiers to respond to simultaneous assaults. We'd be fighting everywhere, and I'd be criss-crossing Atlanta like a chicken with its head cut off, trying to put out the fires. I had to define the rules of this engagement before he tried to do it.

"Meet me in three days on the ruins of my father's castle."

He raised his eyebrows.

"Show me the entirety of your army. Let me behold it. I'll give you my answer then."

"Agreed," he promised, his voice rolling through the vastness of his castle. Smoke escaped his mouth.

"That's my cue to leave."

"Stay with me for a while longer. I'll show you more of my wonders."

"I've seen enough."

"But you haven't seen me."

He stepped aside and slid the fur cape off his shoulders. His armor clattered to the floor. He stood before me naked, big, muscular, and with a champion-sized hard-on.

Really? What was the thinking here? *I know you loathe me, because I'm an inhuman mass murderer, but behold my giant erection. That will make you betray everything you stand for.*

I crossed my arms on my chest. "Is this supposed to convince me?"

"No," he said. "This is."

He ran and took a dive off the balcony. Midway down the catastrophic drop, his body tore. A colossal shape clawed itself free, obsidian black, with a terrifying reptilian head on a long neck and two wings that snapped open. My heart hammered in my chest while every instinct screamed at me to run and hide and hope he wouldn't find me.

He was bigger than Aspid. His wingspan dwarfed the largest airplanes I'd seen.

The dragon swooped, banked, and dived under the balcony. A moment and his head reared above the rail, two fiery eyes staring straight at me. He rose into the air, climbing straight up, his gaze fixed on me. It took every ounce of my will to stay where I was.

His mouth opened, revealing nightmarish fangs.

In his realm, you are a ghost . . .

Fire burst out of his mouth in a blazing torrent and washed over me. The flames blinded me, passing over my body but doing no damage.

I waited until he was done. When the flames fell, I stood exactly where I'd been before, my arms still crossed on my chest.

The dragon's eyes studied me, and for the first time I saw a hint of uncertainty in their depths.

I forced myself to shrug and reached for home in my mind.

The world went white. I landed on the grass, blinked, and saw my father, his face twisted with fury.

"SHARRIM! WHAT WERE YOU THINKING?"

EVERYTHING HURT. THE pain wasn't acute, just thorough. Every cell in my body throbbed.

"ARE YOU HARD OF HEARING, SHARRIM? ANSWER ME! SHARRIM?"

It dawned on me that he expected me to make some sort of sound. "No."

"DO YOU POSSESS THE GIFT OF SPEECH? DO YOU UNDER-STAND THE WORDS I UTTER?"

"Yes." I sat up. I was sitting in the clearing outside our backyard. Curran, Hugh, and Elara were standing only a few yards away. They looked like they were screaming, but for some reason I couldn't hear them.

"REPEAT BACK TO ME WHAT I SAID ABOUT NEIG'S REALM."

"You forbade me to go," I intoned.

"AND WHAT DID YOU DO?"

"I went."

"SO, YOU DELIBERATELY DISOBEYED ME."

"Yes, Mufasa."

"DO I LOOK LIKE I AM IN THE MOOD FOR JOKES?" my father thundered.

When not sure what to say, stall for time. I had a role to play in this drama, and I had to think of exactly how to play it to push my dad over the edge. That is, assuming my aunt didn't chicken out.

"I GAVE YOU A CLEAR SET OF INSTRUCTIONS. MORE, I EXPLAINED WHY CAUTION WAS NECESSARY."

Curran took a running start and jumped. An invisible wall pulsed with bright crimson, and he bounced back.

"Did you set a blood ward around us, so you could scream at me uninterrupted?"

"YES!"

Of course he did. "Carry on then."

I lay flat on the grass. It was nice and soft. *Come on, Rose of Tigris. Don't leave me hanging.* If Erra didn't show up, I'd have to rethink my strategy fast.

He bent over me. "You went into the dragon's den. You could've died."

Ah. That's why the freak-out. "I'm alive. You're still with us, Father. Don't be so dramatic."

"I WAS WORRIED ABOUT YOU, YOU FOOLISH CHILD!"

"You were worried about your own survival."

My father slapped his hand over his face. "Why, gods? Why me? What have I done to deserve this punishment?"

"Conquered, pillaged, manipulated, imposed your will on others . . ."

"Murdered your children," my aunt's icy voice said behind us.

I almost cheered.

My father went completely still. I twisted my neck and saw Erra. She'd strolled through the blood ward like it wasn't there.

"So, it is true," he said, the ancient words lyrical and filled with pain. "You betrayed me."

"You made an order of assassins to murder me." There was so much in my aunt's voice: pain, anger, surprise, grief. It almost broke me.

She could do it. If I had to swallow my pride and deal with a man who wanted to murder my child, she could deal with him, too.

"I never meant for it to be used."

Erra raised her hand. My father fell silent.

"We've destroyed our family, Im," she said. "We ruined it."

"We were fighting a war."

She shook her head. "Death gives you a certain perspective. We broke

Shinar. It wasn't the invaders. It was us. We grieved, and we let rage blind us. We destroyed everything our family had built. Look at us now. Look at our legacy. Mother mourns us."

My father sneered. It was almost as impressive as when my aunt did it. Apparently, it ran in the family. "**Our mother has committed plenty of her own sins.**"

"**This child**"—Erra pointed at me—"**is our best hope for the future. How could you?**"

Roland raised his chin.

"**Yes. I know,**" she said. "**You bound her. Are you really that terrified of death?**"

"**I did it out of love,**" he ground out.

"**You did a thing to a babe in the womb that cannot be undone. Do you wage war on the unborn now, Nimrod? Is this how far you have fallen?**"

I got up to my feet and touched the ward. The magic clutched at my wrist. For a moment the ward became visible, a translucent dome of red glass. It held for half a breath, fractured, and shattered, melting into empty air, and Curran's enraged face greeted me.

Here goes nothing. "It doesn't matter," I said. "I've seen Neig's army. He has thousands of warriors. Enough to overrun the city and murder every single person who lives here. In his lair, a horde of yeddimur is waiting. He takes an offering of newborns and then he poisons them with his venom until they turn into those creatures. He told me that they are primitive and filthy beasts who know only rage and hunger and who eat their own. He says this is the true nature of humanity. He is worse than you are, Father. You seek to rule. He wants to exterminate us."

You could hear a pin drop.

"I have no allies. I'm alone. It's just me and the city. No help is coming. But I'm the In-Shinar and I won't bow to a dragon. I will fight for humanity, even if nobody stands with me. I am Sharratum here. I'm responsible for this city. I won't dishonor my blood and my family."

Curran frowned at me. *Don't you dare ruin my speech.* I pushed every button my dad had.

"Neimheadh is coming for us in three days. Atlanta will fall. We will die. Then you'll follow, Father. Make your peace."

I walked away and didn't look back.

I SAT ON the porch steps and held a glass of iced tea. The ice had melted long ago, so what I had was mostly tea-flavored water. My father and my aunt still argued on our lawn. They put the blood ward back up for privacy, I suppose, which didn't do them a lot of good, because I could still see their faces. All the arm waving and finger pointing was quite entertaining.

Curran sat on my left. Hugh leaned against the porch post on my right. Conlan was inside in the basement, surrounded by werebears and guarded by Adora and Christopher. My father would have to go through me and Curran to get to him, and if it came to that, Christopher would fly him out of there while the werebears held Roland back.

Dali and Doolittle had left once I vanished. It was just us again, family and friends. Well, us and Hugh and Elara.

My father clenched his fists. Light exploded in the dome, hiding him from view. It faded, revealing my aunt, her arms crossed on her chest. She rolled her eyes and said something.

My father spun away, throwing up his arms.

"I stand corrected," my husband said. "There *is* another person who can drive your father as crazy as you."

"This is the most human I've ever seen him," I said.

"You're not alone," Hugh said, his voice flat. "That was some speech. I thought you'd lost your mind for a second."

"We need his army. I primed him for my aunt. If anyone can convince him, she will."

We watched the drama play out in the bubble. My aunt switched to lecturing. My father pinched the bridge of his nose with his hand, looking down.

"Come on, you selfish asshole," Hugh growled under his breath.

At the far edge of the lawn, Julie had parked herself, a determined look on her face. Derek waited with her, his face impassive.

"How many troops does Neig have?" Curran asked.

"I stopped counting at thirteen thousand."

Curran didn't say anything. A thousand wouldn't be a problem. Five thousand would be hard. They were armored, so we'd have to wrench them out of their armor to kill them, while they spat fire at us. Ten thousand was impossible.

Ten thousand troops, that's more soldiers than the National Guard had pre-Shift. And Neig had even more than that.

The bubble of the ward fell. My father turned to us. My aunt walked over to the porch steps.

"Your father has agreed to ally with you to face the dragon."

"Aha." Waiting for the other shoe to drop.

"He wants to see Conlan," Erra said.

"No," Curran said.

"I will hold my grandson," Roland said, "and he will know I am his grandfather. That's my price."

Everything in me rebelled at putting Conlan anywhere within his reach.

We couldn't survive without my father. It wasn't just his army; it was him. We needed my father's power and magic. He'd fought a dragon before and won.

I felt like I was walking down a winding staircase. Every stair was a piece of my life I would fight to the end to keep. My friends. My relationships. Each had a name or some concession I wasn't willing to make. My pride. My dignity. My privacy. Julie. Derek. Ascanio. Ghastek. Rowena. Jim. Dali. Curran . . .

I fought for every one. I clawed onto them, holding on with the edges of my nails, but in the end, I would surrender and step down in the name of the greater good. This was queenship, and if only I could find someone to take it from me, I'd unload it in a fraction of a second.

The name of this step was "Never let my father touch my child."

I let my magic out. It flowed out of me like a mantle. I decided not to bother with hiding it anymore.

The power streamed out of me, branching, stretching, reaching. I became the center of Atlanta, the heart of the land I claimed. I sat on the porch steps, but I might as well have sat on a throne.

My father felt it. His eyes narrowed. He blinked and his whole being seemed to have picked up a faint golden sheen. This was no longer a conversation between Roland and me. This was a conversation between New Shinar and Atlanta. Two rival kingdoms negotiating a brief peace.

"What do you offer, Im-Shinar?" I asked.

My father's eyes narrowed further. "The full power of my army and myself."

"You will fight Neig until he is dead. You will honor our alliance for the duration of this war."

"Yes."

"Kate," Curran said.

"Don't do it," Julie yelled from across the lawn.

This was it. This was the last thing I had to give. I was about to place my son into my father's hands.

"The word of Sharrum is binding," I said. "Swear to me, father, that you will put my son back in my arms after you hold him."

"I swear," he said.

There were lines even my father wouldn't cross. I had to believe that.

"Atlanta accepts your alliance. **Bring my son to me**," I said. My voice carried, slipping through the walls like they were air. I knew Adora heard me.

Julie swore.

There was a scuffle in the house. A moment later Adora opened the door, put Conlan on my lap, and took one step back, her hand on her sword. Blood slid down her left temple, but she ignored it.

Conlan blinked at the light. My baby. My tiny sweet baby. Curran's gray eyes and my brown hair.

I pointed to my father. "This is your other grandfather."

"Gampa?"

"Grandpa. **Grandfather. Great king.**"

My father crouched by me. In these few seconds he somehow became everything a grandfather should be: wise, kind, warm, and filled with love. If I'd met him as a child, I would've trusted him instantly.

Carefully, I passed Conlan to him.

His hands closed around my son.

Everyone on the lawn waited, primed to explode. Curran paused in a half crouch, a hair away from violence. Hugh bared his teeth. Adora focused on my father like nothing else in the world existed. Only my aunt seemed relaxed, standing by Roland's side.

My father straightened and raised Conlan up. My son blinked.

Roland's eyes were full of awe. A smile stretched his lips, a warm, real smile that reached all the way to his eyes.

"You are a wonder . . ." he said softly.

My aunt smiled.

"Do you see the Wild?" Roland asked her.

"I do. You have no idea what he can do with it. Isn't he the most beautiful thing you've ever seen?"

"He is. Well done, my daughter," my father said. "Well done. He is brilliant like a star in the heavens."

Shit.

The same look slapped Hugh's and Julie's faces. They had seen that expression before.

My father liked shiny things and gifted children. It was the potential; it drew him like a magnet. He told me once that Hugh had been a glowing meteor he caught and forged into a sword. If Hugh was a meteor, my son was a supernova. He was like nothing else I had ever seen.

My father wanted my son. He wanted him more than anything in the world. And if he took him, he would raise him like a prince. He would give him everything and it would be terrible.

"Conlan," I called. "Come to Mommy."

My son twisted in his grandfather's hands.

Roland hesitated. Curran leaned forward a quarter of an inch.

My father took three steps forward and deposited Conlan into my arms. I hugged him to me.

"We have three days then," my father said. "Possibly more, since the attack will come with the first magic wave after the three days pass. I shall come to discuss strategy before then."

He vanished in a burst of pale gold light.

Everyone screamed at me at once.

I hugged Conlan to me. "Grandpa is bad," I whispered to him. "I won't let him get you. I won't."

That was one price I wasn't willing to pay.

The magic wave fell, the technology reasserting itself once more.

Curran collapsed.

I CLEARED THE space between us in a fraction of a second. He groaned, blinking. I wrapped my arms around him, squeezing Conlan in, willing with everything I had to keep Curran alive. *Don't disappear. Please, please don't disappear.*

"Curran, look at me. Look at me."

He didn't feel solid. Oh my God. It had happened. The balance within him had shifted. He was more god than man now, and the god part couldn't exist without the magic. I was losing him.

"Curran!" I pulled magic out of myself and sent a burst of it into him.

His gray eyes focused on me.

I hugged him and kissed his lips, desperate. "Stay with me. Stay with me, honey."

The muscles under my fingers gained density.

"I love you. Stay with me."

"I've got it," he said. "I've got it. Just took me by surprise, that's all."

"You shouldn't have eaten the last one," Erra said over me.

"Thanks, that helps." He kissed me back. "You can stop now, honey. I've got it."

I let the magic current die. The pain died with it. I hadn't even realized I was hurting until it stopped.

Curran gripped my hand. I pulled him to his feet. He draped his arm around me. By the time we reached the kitchen, he was moving on his own. He sat in a chair. I kept my hand on his shoulder. I didn't want him to disappear.

"Roland wants the kid," Hugh said.

"Of course he wants the kid," Curran growled. "He'll stab us in the back the first chance he gets."

They both looked at me. "I know," I said. "We don't have a choice. As bad as Roland is, Neig is worse. Neig is death and genocide. Roland wants to rule humans. Neig wants to eat us."

The kitchen was silent.

"We know Roland will turn on us, so we plan for it," Curran said. "We're not going into it blind."

And even if we did get blindsided, there was always the nuclear option. My father couldn't live without me.

"We need to solve the problem of Neig," Hugh said.

"And his many troops," I added.

"Not counting the yeddimur," Curran said. "If I were him, I'd run the yeddimur at us first, and then when we're softened, finish us with troops."

"That seemed to be his strategy when we fought them in Kentucky. Yeddimur are tough to kill. We can fight for hours before we ever touch his army," Hugh said.

"Can we win this?" Elara asked.

Curran's eyes went cold. "We don't have a choice."

"If we can get Roland to follow strategy," Hugh said. "That's a big 'if.'"

"He will follow it," Erra assured him.

"Do we even know where he is coming from?" Derek asked.

"My father's old castle," I said. "I told him I wanted to behold his army. That's the only area around Atlanta large enough for him to field all his troops. I wanted to avoid attack on several fronts."

"With any luck, he'll do what Roland does," Curran said.

"Arrange his troops into rectangles and run them at us?" I asked.

"Mm-hm. He's likely used to relying on numerical advantage."

"And fire," I said. "Don't forget fire."

"He does breathe fire?" Julie asked.

"Like a jet of ignited napalm."

"Can you hold him back if you're in your territory?" Hugh asked.

"Possibly."

Curran leaned back. "We need to call another Conclave."

"The problem is, we can't kill him," I said.

"Who?" Curran asked.

"Neig. If he decides he's near death, he'll just vanish into his lair."

A whisper of movement sounded from the hallway and Yu Fong stepped out into the kitchen, dressed in jeans, a T-shirt, and a light-brown hoodie. He looked no worse for wear. He moved with a slight stiffness, but his color was good.

"I tried to tell you before," he said. "There may be a way."

Everyone looked at me. "Saiman," I told them. "He performed a ritual that let us talk briefly while Yu Fong was comatose. Each dragon lair has an anchor. It is the dragon's most precious possession, his greatest treasure, cherished above all others. They pour their magic into it and it's the foundation of the realm where the dragon makes its lair. But it can't be destroyed."

"As I tried to tell you," Yu Fong said, "we don't need to destroy it. If we can steal it for a time, the realm won't respond to Neig's commands. He will be trapped here and now."

Everyone paused, mulling it over.

"Can you do it?" Hugh asked.

"No. I'm another dragon. Neig will sense the moment I enter his realm. Even if I could, I would not. The anchor is a thing of great magic that can't exist outside its realm for long. It will seek to return. It will take enormous power to restrain it. The temptation for me would be too great. If I touch that anchor, it will pull me into Neig's realm, and I have no intention of leaving this world. My place is here."

"If not you, then who?" Curran asked.

"You have a book," Yu Fong said. "About short people who sneak into a dragon's lair and steal his anchor. Someone small and insignificant."

"I'm small and insignificant," Julie said.

"No," I said.

"Yes," she told me. "Kate, I'm small, sneaky, and quiet. I have a large reserve of magic and I know how to use it."

"The child has a point," Erra said.

"Everyone else is needed," Julie continued. "You are the In-Shinar. Curran has to lead the mercs and inspire the shapeshifters. Hugh has to lead the Iron Dogs, Elara has to absorb witch magic, and Yu Fong can't do it because he is a dragon. I can do it."

"I'll go with her," Derek said.

"It would have to be done during the battle, when the madman is occupied," Yu Fong said. "I know what will occupy him."

I raised an eyebrow at him.

"Me," he said. "The moment he sees me, he will attack. I will buy you some time."

"One flaw in this plan," I said. "How will Julie get to the dragon's realm?"

"Did you keep the shard of his fang?" Yu Fong asked.

"Yes."

"It will act as a key. I will open the way. The timing will have to be perfect." Yu Fong leaned forward, his gaze on me. "I repeat, a removed anchor seeks to reunite with its realm. Neither can exist apart. It will require great power to hold the anchor. And we don't know how vast Neig's realm is. We don't know where he hides the anchor."

The phone rang. Julie picked it up. "Yes?"

She held it out to me. "Ghastek."

I took the phone with one hand, keeping my other one on Curran. "Please tell me you have something."

"I do," Ghastek said.

"I'll be right there." I hung up and turned to Julie. "The anchor is the eye of his dragon throne. It's the ruby the size of a grapefruit located in the first room you enter once you cross the drawbridge. He is an arrogant ass. He doesn't think he has to hide it. No heroics, Julie. Get in, get out, bring me the anchor, and I will restrain it."

. . .

GHASTEK DIDN'T WANT to risk bringing outsiders into the vampire stables. Instead they had moved the yeddimur into one of the side rooms. It sat in a loup cage, staring at us with its owlish eyes. At one point it had been a human baby. Atlanta had a lot of babies.

Ghastek, Luther, Saiman, and Phillip had arranged themselves around a table strewn with notes. Some notes had coffee rings on them.

Curran sniffed the air. His lips stretched, baring the edge of his teeth. The yeddimur stench. I squeezed Curran's hand. He was still here with me. So far, the tech had failed to steal him from me.

Behind me Hugh grimaced at the yeddimur. He had insisted on coming. We had dropped Elara at the Covens. Now we were facing the yeddimur, Luther, Ghastek, Phillip, and Saiman. The four experts looked rather smug.

"We figured out how it was made," Phillip said, excited.

"Venom," Saiman told me.

"Dragon venom," Luther corrected. "Applied very shortly after birth, probably inhaled."

"That remains to be determined," Phillip said.

"Concentrate," I told them, before they launched into another bickering session.

"It's a dog," Ghastek said. "For all intents and purposes, it acts as one. A dog has to be able to discern commands."

"However, according to all of d'Ambray's notes, the warriors never make any gestures," Luther said.

"We theorized that the commands are subvocal," Saiman said. "They have extremely efficient ears, sensitive enough to catch a whisper."

"I could've told you that," Hugh said.

"How does any of this help us?" I asked.

"Wait." Ghastek pushed a key on the phone. "Bring in subject B."

The double doors in the wall opened and two journeymen pushed a second cage in, also containing a yeddimur.

"Where did you get the second one?" Curran asked.

"Beau Clayton," Saiman said. "His deputies caught one."

The journeymen connected the two cages, locking them together. They gripped a steel handle, pushed it to the side, and the gate between the cages fell open. The yeddimur on the left scuttled over and sat on its haunches next to the yeddimur on the right.

"They're us and we are social animals," Luther said.

"They are quite happy sharing the cage," Phillip said. "They sleep together and eat together."

"We had to ask ourselves, if they are controlled by subvocal commands, then what would be the exact opposite of that?" Saiman said.

Ghastek turned to Luther. "If you please."

Luther nodded, reached behind the desk, and produced a set of bag-pipes.

"You play bagpipes?" I asked.

"No, but it was determined via experimentation that of the four of us, I produce the worst sound." Luther stuck a pipe into his mouth and blew on it. A piercing note screamed through the room.

The yeddimur screeched.

Luther blew on the pipes. A cacophony of sounds filled the space. Curran clamped his hands over his ears. The yeddimur snarled and ripped at each other. Fur and blood flew.

Luther stopped.

The yeddimur took a few more swipes at each other and broke apart, each skulking to its own corner of the joined cages.

"We've tried over fifty different sounds," Ghastek said. "Bagpipes are the most efficient. We've attempted them fifteen times and every single time we've gotten the same response."

Suddenly the bagpipes on the druid stone made total sense.

"The sound drives them mad," Luther said.

"It drives *me* mad," Curran said, his eyes shining with gold.

I looked at him and Hugh. "Can we use it?"

"We could," Hugh said.

"If we could make the sound loud enough," Curran said.

Ghastek looked at Phillip. The mage smiled. "The Mage College offers thirty-seven specialties. One of them is sound and light amplification. As long as you find bagpipers, we will amp their sound loud enough to wake the gods."

"That's amazing," I told them, and meant it.

All we had to do now was pull the city together and cobble an army to face Neig. We had three days in which to do it. It had to be enough.

Atlanta would come together. We weren't just one thing. We were many: shapeshifters, necromancers, witches, mages, mercenaries . . . We came in all shapes and sizes, in every age, in every human color, in every variation of magic, and from that we drew our strength. We were surprising and unexpected, and we were united.

Atlanta would hold its own. It always did.

"BABY," CURRAN WHISPERED into my ear.

I opened my eyes. I was so warm and comfortable, wrapped in him. As long as we stayed in bed like this, under the sheets, nothing could go wrong.

The magic was up. It was day five. We'd caught a lucky break, finally, and after a short magic wave on the first day of our three-day timeline, the tech held for three days and four nights. The shift happened while we were awake, and Curran remained solid this time. The tech, like magic, flooded the world with various intensities. A strong tech wave could rip him away from me. I lived these days in a state of constant paranoia.

The rest of it was a whirlwind of negotiating, explaining, demonstrating, pulling the alliance together. Between Curran and me, we'd probably gotten about twelve hours of sleep in the last seventy-two, but last night, after the bulldozers finally rolled off the field and the last of the preparations had been made, we finally went to bed, in a tent, on the outskirts of the battlefield. Martha and Mahon took Conlan, so we could rest. We were alone.

Neig was coming.

I reached for Curran. He kissed me. We shared a breath. I kissed him back, and then again and again, his lips, his stubbled jaw, his face. His hair had grown overnight into a tangled mane, and I threaded my fingers through it.

He pulled me closer to him, our bodies sliding together with ease and practice. He kissed my neck and my lips. For three days, I'd been Sharratum, because I'd had to be. I'd met with the mayor and the governor, as part of the Conclave's delegation. I'd called in favors. I'd promised the sky and the moon for assistance. But right now, I was Kate, and I kissed him with desperate need. He responded as if I'd set him on fire and he couldn't wait to burn.

"This won't be the last time," he said.

"Not if I can help it," I told him.

"I promise you," he said, his voice low, almost a snarl. "This won't be the last time. Do you trust me?"

"With everything."

"It won't be the last time," he swore.

We made love, hot and wild. Then we got up, cleaned up, got dressed, and stepped out of the tent.

In front of us and behind us, tents lined the fields cleared on both sides of the road. A sea of tents. The sun had barely risen above the horizon, and in the young light, the world seemed fresh. I took Sarrat and the other saber I carried and walked east, to the apex of the low hill that stretched north to south. Erra was already there, staring at the battlefield.

It stretched before us, rolling into the distance. My father had cleared it two years back, because he'd planned to build the Water Gardens there, a place of his favorite childhood memories. Normally the vegetation would've reclaimed it by now, but when my father wanted something to stay clear, it did. It was a wide rectangular field, two miles wide and six miles long. The jagged remnants of a stone tower, still black from soot, stuck out in the middle of it, all that remained of my father's castle. We'd left it on the field. According to Andrea, it made a handy marker for her ballistae.

I glanced to the right, where the battery was positioned. She was already there, pointing at something and arguing with MSDU's colonel. The military had joined us. The National Guard came first. The guardsmen weren't full-time soldiers. Most of the time, they were mechanics, teachers, police officers, office workers. As we pulled the city together for battle, a lot of them got swept up in it. On the second day, Lt. General Myers, a fit black woman in her late fifties, walked into our headquarters in the Guild. I was trying to read through the convoluted document the Druids had drawn up, outlining the terms of their cooperation, and I finally threw it into Drest's face and told him that either he fought with us or he could deal with Neig on his own after he burned Atlanta to the ground, but I didn't have time for his machinations. He swore and stormed out, and then she was there. We looked at each other for a long moment, and then she said, "What do you need?"

No conditions. No bargaining. Just "What do you need?" I told her, and she made it happen.

We needed everything. We had everything there was to be had now: the MSDU, the National Guard, the human volunteers, the mercs, the Red Guard, the Pack, the People, the Order, the mages, the Covens, the volhvs, and the other pagans. We even got the Druids, which was why if I squinted hard enough, I could see small white stones sitting on both sides of the field.

We were as ready as we were going to be.

It wouldn't be enough unless my father showed up. He'd come to visit during that short magic wave on the first day to discuss strategy. He sat at our kitchen table while Hugh, Curran, and Erra tried to explain things to him in two languages. At one point he declared that we were making it too complicated, and then Hugh drew stick figures on pieces of paper, trying to explain it. My father had gotten the strategy by the end, but whether he would stick to it was anyone's guess.

"Do you think Father will show up?" I asked her.

"He will," she said.

Martha joined us, followed by George, carrying Conlan. I took him from her and hugged my son. I'd thought about trying to send him out of the city, to hide him somewhere, but it would be no use. My son shone too bright. Either my father or Neig would find him, and if not them, someone else. For Conlan to survive, we had to triumph.

Everything was on the line.

Clan Wolf began to form up in front of the hill, just inside the boundary of my territory. Most of our forces were strategically positioned already, but Clan Wolf was the front and center, backed by Clan Jackal, the Guild's mercs, and the National Guard. I could see Curran's blond mane down there, as he moved among the ranks. The shapeshifters looked at him with awe. He was their god come to life.

The mages were arranging themselves on the hill to the left. A good number of them looked really young. Phillip had brought students.

The witches waited in the rear, flanked by Hugh's Iron Dogs.

Andrea strode up the hill. "Hey, you."

"Hey."

"Are you and I cool? Or are you going to hold this Hugh thing over my head?"

"We're cool." I didn't even care about Hugh anymore. "Knock them dead."

"You still owe me a lunch."

"Oh for the love of . . . Fine. When and where?"

"You know where."

"Fine. Parthenon it is, two weeks from now."

"Deal."

She raised her fist. I bumped it with mine. She went back down to her battery.

My aunt spun to me, baring her teeth in a vicious grin. "He comes."

A line of white light snapped across the horizon, at the other end of the field.

I hugged Conlan to me. "I love you. Mommy loves you so much."

He clung to me, suddenly alarmed.

The light broke and spat a line of armored men onto the field. From this distance, they looked like toy soldiers.

Horns blared on our side. MSDU raised the Red, White, and Blue, the National Guard added Georgia's flag, and then individual standards snapped up at different parts of the field: Pack gray, burgundy for the Red Guard, black for the Guild, and my own green In-Shinar banners among the People.

Another line stepped out of the light. Another. Another. They kept coming.

Javier ran up the hill, followed by two other journeymen, five freshly made undead at his side. Javier bowed his head. "In-Shinar."

"It's time," my aunt said.

I didn't want to let go of my son.

"Kate," Erra said.

I kissed Conlan's forehead and handed him back to his grandmother. Martha kissed him. "You be good for your auntie. Grandma has to go and slap some bad people on their heads."

George took Conlan and smiled at him. "Wave bye to Grandma."

The undead knelt before me. I cut my arm and raised Sarrat. The undead's eyes blazed with red as the navigator bailed, releasing its mind. I swung my sword and opened the undead's throat. My blood mixed with the undead's, and the magic that gave both of us life sparked. I pulled the blood to me, shaping it, sliding it over my body.

The soldiers still kept coming.

To the left Barabas looked at Christopher, then at the lines of soldiers. Christopher's face was calm, but the muscles on his bare arms were bunched up, tense.

"Will you marry me?" Barabas asked, still looking at the army flooding the field.

"Yes," Christopher said.

Barabas turned to him. Christopher leaned in and they kissed.

Julie ran up, out of breath. She wore a reinforced chest plate, painted green and precisely fitted to her small frame. The design looked familiar, even though the color wasn't. I'd seen it before on Iron Dogs. Hugh had had it made for her.

"Where have you been?" I asked her.

"Saying good-byes," she said.

I opened the second vampire, mixed my blood with its blood, and continued. The final drop hardened on my skin. I stretched, testing the blood-red armor. Flexible enough.

"Good." My aunt approved.

I opened the third vampire and let the blood coat Sarrat and the other saber, hardening both to a preternaturally sturdy but razor-sharp edge.

"Sword," I told Julie.

She handed over her blade and her spear. I dipped both into the blood and sealed them with magic. I couldn't make long-lasting weapons like my father. Not yet. But they would last through the entire magic wave, and it would have to be enough.

"You know where to be and what to do?" I asked.

She nodded.

"I love you," I told her. "Be careful."

She hugged me and took off down the hill, back toward the Iron Dogs. Today her place was with the witches and Elara.

Neig's soldiers still kept coming. I couldn't even estimate the numbers. Fifteen thousand? Twenty? Thirty? A dark mass swirled in front of them, streaking through the ranks to the vanguard of the army. The yeddimur.

Curran jumped, clearing the hill in three huge leaps. He kissed me.

"Happy hunting," I told him.

"You, too."

He went back down.

I glanced at the mages. Phillip had rounded up every bagpiper in Atlanta. They crowded behind the line of students. The rest of the mages had moved on farther to the left. Phillip caught my gaze and nodded.

I looked back to the battlefield and waited.

Nick marched up the hill and stopped next to me. "I take it back," he said.

"Which part?"

"You didn't exaggerate the threat."

"Be still my heart. Does that mean you're ready to believe there is a dragon?"

"I'll believe it when I see it."

"You are such an asshole."

"Takes one to know one. Try not to die, Daniels," he said.

"You, too. Who would I fight with if you weren't here?"

The light in the distance blazed bright red. The soldiers parted in two, allowing a chariot to pass between them. It was huge and ornate, and it glowed with pale gold.

"Look, a golden chariot and Dad isn't here," I told Erra.

She ignored me. Well, I thought it was funny.

The chariot came forward, drawn by four white horses. It pulled ahead of the line, past my father's ruined tower. Neig's voice rolled through the battlefield. We shouldn't have heard it from that far away, but suddenly it was everywhere, filling the air, touching us.

"BEHOLD MY ARMY."

The ranks of Atlanta's defenders went still. We looked at lines and lines of soldiers, a sea of armor and weapons.

"WHAT IS YOUR ANSWER, DAUGHTER OF NIMROD?"

I pulled the magic of the land into me and answered, sending my voice down the battlefield.

"YOU WANT ATLANTA? COME AND TAKE IT IF YOU DARE."

NEIG'S ARMY MOVED as one, rolling forward, past him, aiming at our lines. The yeddimur broke into a wild run, swarming like bees. He was running them at us, relying on pure numbers. I almost screamed in relief.

To the left, Phillip's clear voice commanded, "Prepare amplification spheres."

Magic shifted. The line of students raised their arms. A transparent sphere formed above each of them, three feet wide and shimmering like hot air rising from the pavement, and spinning.

The yeddimur loomed before us, screeching excited high-pitched shrieks as they ran.

"Hold it steady," Phillip said.

Eight hundred yards to my boundary.

Six hundred.

I wanted to be down there, on the field, on the front line with the werewolves and Curran.

Four hundred yards.

Yu Fong came up and stood on my right without saying a word.

Andrea's battery fired a volley of sorcerous bolts. Bright green explosions punctured the yeddimur's line, but there were too many. She didn't follow it. The volley was just for show and she wanted to conserve the bolts.

The swarm kept coming. Behind it, Neig's soldiers marched like an unstoppable avalanche of steel.

Three hundred.

"Ladies and gentlemen," Phillip said. "The bagpipes, please."

The shrill howl of bagpipes answered. I'd asked Phillip what they were going to play, and he'd told me "Bloody Fields of Flanders." It was an old bagpipe march, composed in World War I. Later it became another song, "Freedom Come-All-Ye," a story of a nation that loved freedom more than war.

Erra winced next to me. Nick grimaced.

Two hundred yards. The yeddimur were almost on us.

"Engage," Phillip screamed.

The spheres became still. The bagpipes next to us suddenly went almost silent, as the amplification spheres sucked in their sound. A moment later a deafening blast of sound hit the yeddimur.

The swarm halted, collapsing on itself.

"Keep playing," Phillip said, his voice upbeat. "Keep playing. Faculty, continue to project. Everyone is doing spectacularly. I'm truly privileged to be working with such a talented group."

The swarm shattered. Those in the front and middle ripped into each other; those in the back turned around and tore into the front line of Neig's troops. Fighting broke out in the middle of Neig's army.

A ragged cheer came through our ranks.

Neig's troops split, flowing around the lines engaged with yeddimur like a stream split in half by a rock. They hugged the edges of the field and continued their advance, closer and closer to the druids' stones.

Closer.

Closer.

Almost there.

They were a hundred yards from our line when the ground under both columns of soldiers gave. Hundreds of men collapsed into the twin trenches.

We'd dug them with bulldozers and explosives over the last three days. They were ten feet deep and twenty-five yards wide, and they swallowed the advancing columns whole.

Howls of pain went up, almost breaking through the bagpipes. Black shiny tentacles flailed, spilling out of the trenches, yanking the nearby soldiers into them.

"What the hell are those?" Nick asked.

"You don't want to know." Roman had been in charge of the trenches.

Neig's soldiers moved away from the trenches, edging farther to the sides of the field, almost to the tree line on both sides.

The brush on the left burst. Huge shaggy bodies tore into armored men, pushing them toward the trench and the writhing death within. Clan Heavy had arrived. Neig's warriors fought back, but the werebears had mass and momentum on their side.

On the right, vampires dashed out of the woods, slicing at the other column. The tide of Neig's soldiers slowed. We'd cut them in half and bled them. But there were too many. So many.

Minutes crept by. The werebears and the vampires chewed the twin prongs of Neig's vanguard. Blood drenched the grass.

Neig stepped from his chariot. Shit.

I reached out and grabbed Nick's hand. "Look."

Neig strode forward, his furry mantle flowing behind him. His body split open, releasing the darkness within. It billowed, solidifying, growing, expanding, building on itself. A black dragon landed on the field, towering over the battle line, so huge my mind refused to believe it was real.

Nick's mouth hung open.

Neig's soldiers ran to the sides, scrambling away from the dragon, but the front lines, holding back the maddened yeddimur, had nowhere to go.

The colossal reptile opened his mouth. A torrent of fire hit the knot of writhing yeddimur and his soldiers. They vanished in the blaze, dark shadows swallowed by the white inferno.

Neig doused the field like a colossal flamethrower, burning everything in his path. He'd cleared the blockage. It cost him his yeddimur and a good chunk of his soldiers, but now the field was clear and we were screwed.

Nick clicked his mouth shut. "He's going to break through. I've got to get down there."

He took off at a run.

Neig's massive wings opened.

"Retreat!" I yelled at Phillip.

The bagpipes blew a single clear note. Clan Heavy disengaged and broke into a run, galloping toward us. On the other side, the undead streamed for the boundary.

I raised my arms to the sides, gathering the magic to me, molding it into a shield. I had done this before. I held off my father when he tried to rain fire and rocks on the Keep. I couldn't do anything about Neig's soldiers—too few and too insignificant magically on their own—but he was huge and brimming with magic. He presented a very defined target. If Neig thought he was about to fry us, he would be in for a surprise.

Neig's wings beat once, twice, and he took to the air, shooting straight up.

Clan Heavy was running for its life. *Faster*, I willed. *Faster*.

Neig dove from the sky, torching the woods to the left, circled, and set the woods to the right on fire.

The undead were all in, but Clan Heavy was slow. Two werebears lagged behind. The fire caught them twenty yards from the boundary. Their shaggy bodies vanished, instantly burned to a crisp. Neig shot upward, picking up speed.

Here's hoping my magic would be enough.

The dragon swooped down, like a striking hawk, and spat fire. I jerked the shield of magic up. The fire splashed against it. Pressure ground on me. I clenched my teeth and held.

There. How do you like that, you asshole?

Neig climbed higher, turned in midair, and threw himself at my barrier.

Around me people ducked on instinct.

The dragon smashed into my shield. The impact reverberated through my bones. It felt like my whole skeleton snapped. I snarled and held the shield in place. He bounced off it back into the sky, spun around, and hit it again. The shield held.

"Brace yourselves," my aunt roared.

The field was clear. All of the yeddimur were dead. There was nothing between us and Neig's warriors except for smoking corpses.

Neig's army charged.

FIRE.

Claws.

Fire.

Fire.

Ramming at full speed.

Fire.

My nose was bleeding. My breath came in ragged gasps, as if I had run a marathon with a hundred-pound weight on my shoulders.

Below me fighting raged. The trenches funneled Neig's army into a five-hundred-yard killing field, and going around the trenches from the outside wasn't an option. Neig had set the woods on fire. The trees burned like torches. Soot and smoke filled the air, mixing with blood and heat. The sorcerous ballistae whined, sending charged bolts into the mass of troops, followed by the steady booms of explosions. Andrea had tried to hit Neig, but he was too fast.

Neig's troops brought up the engines of war and hurled fiery boulders at us. I held off the first three barrages, so they switched targets and aimed at the front of their own line, just outside my protective boundary. The rocks rolled at our people, and I couldn't stop them and hold off Neig at the same time.

We were trapped together in five hundred yards of hell on earth, and Neig's war machine ground us into mush. Mages hurled their spells and Neig's soldiers spat fire back. Witches summoned horrors, pagans evoked their gods, the military pounded the warriors with advanced magic weaponry, and still Neig's troops kept coming, unstoppable, unending. There were always more.

The bloodbath raged. Screams, howls, and snarls filled the air. The bagpipers had long ago stopped playing. Now only the voice of the battle could be heard. It hung above us like an oppressive din, the song of dying, pain, and fury.

Where the hell was my father?

I didn't know how much time had passed, but it had to have been hours. The sun had reached its apex. My world had shrunk to Neig and magic. I wanted to be down there, in the slaughter, but Neig saw me and Yu Fong next to me, and we were too tempting a target. All I could do was contain him.

He was tiring. So was I. I wasn't sure how much more I could take.

A werewolf swung into my view, covered in blood and someone's guts. She grabbed a bucket of water from next to me and drank, spilling it over her monstrous face. "We can't take much more," she snarled in Desandra's voice.

Neig dove at me, unleashing a torrent of fire. I held it back.

"You have to hold," I told her.

"If you have an ace up your sleeve, now's the time."

An undead ran up to me. "We're taking heavy casualties," it said in Javier's voice. "Lt. General Myers is dead. Ghastek states that in another half hour, we will run out of vampires."

Neig screamed and smashed into my shield. I took a step back, snarled, and shoved the magic back at him.

My father wasn't coming.

We had to retreat. If there was any hope for anyone surviving, we had to retreat.

Another blast of fire. Damn it, didn't that fucking dragon ever get tired?

A clump of Neig's soldiers broke apart below. Curran emerged, bloody, huge in his warrior form, looking like a demon. The shapeshifters rallied around him, but even he was getting worn out.

Roland wasn't coming. He had betrayed us once again.

"Kate," Desandra snarled. "I need a decision."

The vampire hovered by my feet.

To the left, Julie and Derek, both covered in blood, waited.

We'd lost. If we turned back now, at least some people would survive.

I opened my mouth to tell them to retreat.

Magic burst at the far end of the field. The sky above us darkened. Huge rocks plummeted down from the clouds, burning as they fell, and crushed the troops on the field before us.

Oh my God.

The rocks smashed into the ground, cracked open, and glowing swarms of brilliant green bees spilled out, stinging Neig's warriors. The rocks melted, boiling into a glowing slime. The slime snapped out, grabbing at the remaining troops, and they screamed as their bodies melted. A huge hole opened up in the center of Neig's forces, and through it, I saw my father.

I forgot to breathe.

He rode a glowing chariot, drawn by mechanical horses. He was young and beautiful, and full of magic so powerful it hurt to look at him. He shone, brilliant and sharp, like a second sunrise. Behind him, an army rose.

My aunt appeared by my side. "Look! This is your real father! This is the brother I haven't seen for eons. Look, child!"

My father raised his hand. A serpent of pure glowing magic tore out of it, snaking its way through the battlefield, devouring all in its path.

He came. He hadn't abandoned me. *My father had come to fight.*

Neig spun in the air. A terrible screech tore out of the dragon's jaws.

"Your dad is hot!" Desandra said, surprised.

I snapped out of it.

Neig dove at my father.

I spun to Yu Fong. "Do it now."

Yu Fong pulled the shard of a tooth out of his clothes and carved a vertical line, from as high as he could reach down to the ground. A glowing hole opened in the fabric of the world. Derek grinned, a feral baring of teeth. Julie ducked into the gap and he followed. The glow vanished.

Yu Fong tossed the tooth aside. An overpowering heat emanated from his skin, the air streaming from him in transparent currents.

I backed away.

Yu Fong's body burst. A creature spilled out, twenty-five feet long, a muscular leonine body covered in scales. A huge head crowned with a red mane sat on a thick but agile scaled neck, its face a meld of dragon and lion. A serpentine tail snapped.

The beast that used to be Yu Fong charged onto the field. His body burst into flames, red fire coating him like a mantle. Neig's warriors parted like water, letting him pass.

On the other end of the field, Neig spun away from my father.

"I am the Lord of Fire!" the Suanni roared, tearing through the warriors like he was a comet. **"Face me, coward!"**

I grabbed my swords and dashed onto the field, through the gap Yu Fong had made. I had to find Curran.

The ranks of warriors were closing ahead. A moment, and they surrounded me. I spat the power word "**osanda.**" They went down to their knees and I cut my way through them, pushing my way forward, to the center of the battlefield. Blood sprayed. Bodies fell amid hoarse screams. I cut, severing limbs and carving bodies with blades and magic. Fire and lightning streaked above my head, ripped through by a stream of glowing green bullets from a machine gun. Fighters tore at each other, shapeshifters disemboweled their opponents, vampires ripped into bodies. Carnage reigned, the roar, bellows, and moans of the dying blending into a terrible din.

I cleaved a body in two, opened my mouth, and screamed. The word of power burst from me, straight as an arrow, searing Neig's fighters, mangling their bodies. I tore into the gap, cutting like a dervish in a familiar lightning-fast pattern, severing limbs and spraying blood, unstoppable, without mercy.

A yeddimur popped up in front of me, the lone survivor of the fire and bagpipes. I carved him from shoulder to waist and kept going, reaping a harvest of lives, spitting magic and bringing death. On the left a clump of bodies exploded, and Hugh roared, covered in blood, a bloody axe in his hand. We connected, back to back. For a brief moment we stood alone in the carnage, and then we broke apart and charged back into battle.

Suddenly the clump of warriors around me split. They fled, panicked. Wind hit me, nearly taking me off my feet. A huge black lion landed next to me, his wings wide, glowing with silver. Curran had assumed his god form.

I jumped and climbed black fur onto Curran's back. He sprinted and then we were airborne. The battle yawned below us. Ahead, Neig spat fire at Yu Fong in a steady torrent, circling him, great wings beating. Yu Fong limped along the ground, his side torn, sending a torrent of white flames back. My father stood, caught in the middle of it all, a protective bubble of magic glowing around him, reflecting the dueling fires. He held a spear in his hands.

Curran dived at Neig. I jumped, aiming for the dragon's neck, and missed. Damn it.

There was nothing under my feet. I plunged. There was no time to be scared. No time for anything. I was about to die.

The air caught me. I was no longer falling, I was floating down gently. I glanced down. My father shook his head in reproach, as if I'd broken an expensive vase. Above me Curran barreled into the dragon, locking his jaws on Neig's neck. Next to Neig, Curran looked small. The dragon kicked at Curran. His huge claws caught the lion, ripping a gash in Curran's side. Curran snarled and tore a chunk out of Neig's neck. They spun together, clawing and biting.

Hold on, honey. I'm coming.

Fatigue fled. Only fury remained, a hot ravenous beast inside me that had to be fed. I attacked. They fell before me like blades of grass. I cut a clear path around my father's chariot. Blood rained on us, Neig and Curran tearing at each other. Yu Fong sprayed the field with fire so hot it melted the armor of the warriors around us.

My father dropped his protective spell. Neig's warriors tried to rush him from the side. He moved his hand as if swatting a fly and they flew, falling at my feet. I cut them down, still spitting magic and death.

Yu Fong had fallen on his side, a pike glowing with magic thrust between his ribs. Adora burst out of the crowd and stood over him with her katana, holding the soldiers back.

My father raised his spear, a long glowing rope attached to one end.

Curran plummeted to the ground. Neig followed, jaws opened wide, ready for the kill.

My father hurled his spear. It streaked through the air, glowing with violent red, and caught Neig in the throat. The other end of the rope plunged into the ground. My father screamed a command. The rope went taut. Neig flailed on the end of it, like a harpooned fish. Roland gripped the rope. It was absurd, he was so small and Neig was gargantuan, yet my father held him.

"Kate!"

I spun around. Julie limped toward me, her hair caked with blood. Behind her, Derek in warrior form snarled, his left arm hanging from his body at an awkward angle.

"Kate!" Julie reached me and thrust a glowing ruby into my hands. I grabbed it. Magic bit at me with hot jaws. An anchor was right. The damn thing weighed fifty pounds. The weight of it threatened to yank me off my feet. The ruby pulled on me as if it were trying to suck out my soul. It wanted to go back to its realm. It required it, and if I let it, it would pull me right into it.

I thrust it into my armor, over my right hip, where I'd made an enclosure just for it.

"I have it!" I screamed. "Now! We have to do it now!"

Above me Neig let out a horrible screech.

Curran ran up next to me. Half of his body smoked, the fur gone, his skin bubbling from the heat. He rolled and launched himself at Neig. I took a running start, caught his wing, and let it carry me up with him. Neig's scaled back loomed before me.

Second time had to be the charm, because I wouldn't get a shot for a third.

I jumped. The air whistled by me, and then I was on Neig's scaled back. I dashed up it, sliding forward to his head.

Curran had locked his jaws on Neig's neck and was chewing through it. Neig flailed, trying to get his clawed foot up against Curran and rip himself free, but my father held him in place.

Neig rolled his head, trying to shake Curran off. A torrent of flames burst from his mouth. The ground yawned at me. Adora vanished in the fire.

No. No, no, no, no . . .

The flames vanished. A charred body knelt on one knee in the dirt, her katana caught in her hand. A soldier brushed by her, and she fell over on her side.

Dead. Adora was dead. Neig had killed her.

There was so much pain it was ripping me apart. I screamed and scrambled up, over Neig's massive neck, over his horns, up onto his head and face. Two huge eyes, blazing with amber, focused on me for a fraction of a second. I raised my blood swords and plunged them into Neig's eyes. The amber liquid splashed me, hot and magic.

The dragon howled, shaking his head, trying to knock me loose, but I clung to my blades.

"DIE!" I screamed, feeding magic into my swords. **"DIE, DIE, DIE!"**

Neig shrieked and tore free of my father's restraints, shooting up into the sky. Wind tore at me. I held on to my swords, the massive body beneath me trembling and shaking. We climbed up and up and up, higher and higher toward the clouds.

"You have killed me, Daughter of Nimrod," the dragon whispered. "But I'll take you with me."

We plummeted to the ground. The battlefield rushed at us at a dizzying speed.

This is it.

A dark shape surged from the ground and thrust itself under Neig—Curran trying to slow the dragon's fall—but Neig was too heavy.

Hands grabbed my shoulders and jerked me up, ripping me and Sarrat free. Suddenly I was flying and Neig was still plunging down, my other sword still in his left eye socket. Above me Teddy Jo soared on his midnight wings.

Curran twisted clear. Neig's enormous body hit the ground, bouncing once. The mighty dragon's head dropped and lay still. Neig the Legend was dead.

Teddy Jo swooped down. My feet touched the grass. He let go and I rolled clear and up onto my feet.

Curran had collapsed next to the dragon. I couldn't tell if he was dead or alive. Ice-cold fear gripped me. Around us the battle still raged.

"DAUGHTER."

I turned. My father was looking at me from the height of his chariot, and his face was mournful. Behind him his troops stood in a wall, rows and rows of people in tactical armor.

"Don't do it," I told him. "Don't, Father."

His voice rolled through the battlefield. **"Surrender, my daughter."**

He'd betrayed me. I'd known he would. I had expected it, but it hurt so much.

"Don't," I asked him. "Please don't."

"Surrender and I will let your people live."

"How can you do this? You're my father!"

"It's for your own good."

"No. It's only for you."

Hugh burst through the ranks. Behind him, the Iron Dogs parted Neig's troops like they were water, and I saw Elara. She glowed with white: her dress, her skin, her hair all snow-white, one color blazing with power. She didn't feel human.

She opened her arms. I heard a chant floating above the battlefield. The Covens were channeling their power. It hit Elara from the back and burst out of her as a beam of pure white. The beam hit my father. He gasped, spinning toward her. The magic impaled him like a spear.

His troops surged around him and fell on the Iron Dogs.

The beam intensified, so white it was hard to look at. My father staggered. His face relaxed. His eyes glazed over.

We almost had him. Almost. Just a little bit more. *Sleep. Please, Dad, for the sake of all of us. Just go to sleep.*

Magic surged out of him, blocking the beam.

Elara screamed.

Not enough. The witches weren't enough.

Slowly, ever so slowly, my father straightened, his face shaking with effort, and thrust one hand against the beam.

He would win and then there was no hope for Atlanta and Conlan.

Julie sprinted between the fighting bodies, her sword raised above her head.

I felt the magic inside my father snap, blocking Elara's beam. If Julie attacked him now, he would kill her. He would squash her like a gnat.

He would kill my kid.

I saw Julie's arm roll back as if in slow motion, as she prepared for a jump.

If she touched my father, she would die. I had to stop her. I had to . . .

The muscles of her legs tensed, about to send her into the air.

No!

"Stop!" I snarled, sinking magic into the command.

I felt the precise moment my will crushed Julie's. She crumbled in mid-leap and fell to the ground.

Oh no. What have I done?

Blood-red light burst out of my father. Elara stumbled back. The white beam died. He turned to me. **"Did you honestly think that would stop me, foolish child?"**

There were twenty yards between us and a wave of his soldiers behind him. I wouldn't be able to get to him. They would swarm me and then he would hit me with his magic, and it would all be over. He could hold me in stasis until his troops secured me.

The ruby stirred in my armor, as if alive.

The ruby.

It was my only chance.

"SURRENDER, IN-SHINAR. TAKE YOUR PLACE."

I love you, Curran. I love you, my son. I love you both more than any-thing. I love you, Julie. There is no way out.

I raised Sarrat and stabbed myself.

My father screamed.

I felt the blood rush out of me and twisted the blade. There we go. I'd cut the abdominal aorta. Death would be quick.

I dropped to my knees, pulled the ruby out of my armor, cradled it, and fell on my side. My father's face swung into view. He was weeping.

"Why? Why?" He pulled me to him, cradling my head in his arms. **"You had everything, Blossom. Why?"**

His face was turning gray. His fingers shook. He cried out. I felt his magic fighting for his life, hungry, looking for any source to feed itself. I knew that hunger. It was blinding. He would grab at any magic just to keep himself alive, and I had a source of magic handy.

I opened my arms. They were too weak to restrain the anchor anyway. He saw the ruby. He reached for it.

Take it, Father. Take it and use it.

His skin was the color of crumbled concrete. If he'd had a second to think, he would've stopped. But he didn't have a second. We were dying together, and my father wanted to live. It made him careless.

His fingers closed about the glowing gem. The crimson glow melted over him. He fed on the ruby, absorbing every drop, until everything that made the anchor what it was had been fused with my father.

I struggled to say something. Nimrod leaned over me.

"I win, Father."

The anchor couldn't exist without its realm, and it sought to return to it at all costs. My father had absorbed it. They were now one.

A void opened behind him. I only saw the edge of it, but I felt it. It grasped my father and swallowed him whole.

One moment he was there and then he was gone. And all was good.

We'd won. Conlan would live. Curran would live too, if he was still alive. I'd done it.

My blood was all over the ground. I thought it would hurt. It didn't hurt.

My aunt grabbed at me, frantic. "Stay with me. Hugh! Get Hugh!"

"Too late," I told her.

Erra stared at me, her eyes wild, and thrust herself at me. Pain smashed into my body, wrenching a scream from me. She was trying to feed her magic into me to keep me alive.

"No," I whispered. I didn't want her sacrifice, but I didn't have the strength to fight her. She paled and vanished. Magic flooded into me in a cool rush.

It wasn't enough. Julie was crying. Someone was holding me. The light dimmed. Darkness came.

I wish I could hold Conlan one last time.

I wish I could see Curran. To hear his voice. To hold his hand. To not be alone before I go.

I wish I had just a little bit more time. There were so many things I wanted to do. I would give anything for just one more day.

I love all of you.

DEATH WAS A mist.

I walked through it at random, not knowing where to go. It pulled on me, and I let it.

I was fading. The essence of me was fading, unraveling softly into the gray mist around me.

Let go, the mist whispered. *Let it all go . . .*

And then it parted. I stood on a vast plain, green grass under my feet. Golden sunlight streamed from a blue sky. In the distance, herds of wild beasts grazed, big shaggy shapes.

I felt a presence behind me and turned.

A colossal lion walked toward me across the plain. He was black, and his wings were folded over his body. His big golden eyes brimmed with magic. It glowed all around him, coating every hair of his fur. He was a god.

He reached me and lowered his head.

I raised my hand and put it on his nose. He had come to say good-bye. I would get to see him one last time.

The lion opened his mouth, showing me gleaming fangs.

"LIVE," he said.

Silver magic erupted from him and into me.

PAIN.

AGONY TORE MY body into shreds and I screamed, writhing. There was something solid under me.

"I've got her," Hugh's voice said.

He was on top of me. I was alive.

I swung and punched him in the jaw as hard as I could. He toppled over to the side. I rolled to my feet.

Curran lay next to me on the bloody grass, human and unmoving. I crawled on my hands and knees to him and grabbed him. "Curran? Curran?"

He opened his eyes, saw me, and smiled. "Hey, ass kicker."

"Are you hurt?"

"Yes. Very tired, too."

"What did you do?"

"I resurrected you," he said.

The pain blossomed in my stomach and I collapsed on his chest.

"This was the plan the whole time," he said. "My plan and your aunt's. Enough divine power for one miracle."

I curled into a ball, holding on to him. If this was some sort of near-death hallucination, I would resurrect myself just so I could punch fate in the face.

"Sorry it hurt," he said. "It's my first time."

I kissed his chest. He petted my hair.

"Last time, too," he said. "I don't have any divine power left, so let Hugh heal you, because if you die now, there is shit I can do about it and I'll be really pissed off."

I just held him. Slowly it was sinking in.

"I promised you this morning wouldn't be the last time," he told me. "I keep my promises."

Someone else was screaming. I finally realized it wasn't me and turned around. My aunt sprawled on the grass, shaking with seizures, naked, mad as hell, and very much alive.

"Oops," Curran said.

I cried. I lay on his chest and cried.

I SAT ON our porch and watched Conlan play in the grass in the fading light of the evening. He pounced on lightning bugs like a big human kitten. Curran sat next to me, his arm wrapped around my shoulders. One week had passed since the battle.

With both Neig and Roland gone, their troops had scattered. We'd won, but we'd lost so much. We buried Adora's ashes on the small hill behind our house. I'd cried at her funeral. I cried every time I thought about it.

Christopher got caught in the dragon fire, too. He didn't die, but he lost a wing. None of us knew if it would grow back. He mourned his flight the way people mourned the death of a child. Desandra lost her beta couple. They were friends and her grief was still raw. Jim lost his sister. The witches lost Maria. The power drain had proved too much for her. Of Curran's elites, only five remained.

Saiman never came back from the battlefield. He'd always been terrified of physical pain, but for some reason he had assumed his true form and run into the thick of the slaughter. Maybe he'd panicked, maybe he'd become enraged, maybe he'd been trying to protect someone. We would never know. They brought his body to me. He'd been pierced with four spears. I grieved. He'd left a will. He wanted to be buried in Unicorn Lane. We followed it to the letter. It was the least we could do.

Curran the God didn't make it. None of his divine power remained. His hair no longer grew unnaturally fast, although he'd kept his added height, for how long was anybody's guess. He'd lost the mystical awareness of us. His divinity had enabled him to know where Conlan and I were at all times, but he couldn't preternaturally sense us anymore. He said it felt like he'd gone blind. It was a death, of sorts, but I couldn't have been happier about it.

There was another death I didn't mourn. Sharratum also died on that battlefield. When Curran resurrected me, I no longer felt the pull of the land. The claimings hadn't survived my death. I was once again just me. I'd kept my power, but I was now free of Atlanta and the portion of Kings Row.

Ghastek had come to me after the slaughter. He'd seemed lost. He'd told me I would always be the In-Shinar. I told him that he was still my friend, but now he was free.

We buried friends and grieved, but slowly, little by little, Atlanta was waking up from a nightmare. The dragon was dead. Biohazard had claimed its bones, and Ghastek and Phillip had nearly come to blows with Luther over it.

Hugh and Elara both survived and returned to their castle in Kentucky.

Hugh didn't heal Dali. Jim asked her to delay it by six months. From where I stood, that just gave her six more months to work on convincing him, and my gut told me Jim would lose that fight.

Christopher and Barabas set a wedding date. Barabas made a terrible fuss over Christopher's injuries and kept feeding him gallons of chicken soup, hoping his wing would regenerate. The Druids paraded down the streets in their furs and claimed credit for their part of the victory. Martha was seriously injured, and Mahon got to nurse her back to health. He tried to bake her honey muffins, and they were terrible. My aunt wasn't speaking to either of us. She took her resurrection personally. Apparently, she had wanted to stay dead.

Julie wasn't speaking to me either.

I deserved it. I went back on my word. I'd tried to talk to her, but she'd just walked away from me. I had made a promise and I'd broken it. I didn't know if she would thaw with time. I hoped she would, but even so there was no going back from what I had done. Time would help. I hoped.

"I better do it," I told Curran. "It's been a week. He must've cooled off."

"Give him another year," he said.

"If a week won't do it, a year won't." I set my glass of tea down. "I won't be long."

I closed my eyes, and when I opened them, I walked across the drawbridge of Neig's castle. The place lay empty. Nobody greeted me. Nobody tried to kill me. The lack of drama was rather disappointing.

The stones shook under my feet. Oh no. Spoke too soon.

The castle yawned and swallowed me. I hurtled through it, or rather I stood still, and it spun past me until I was face-to-face with my father in the throne room. He was back to his older self. He must've been waiting for me to show up. He was the anchor of the realm. For all intents and purposes, he was the realm. He could never leave. And since we shared a blood bond, I could come and see him whenever I wanted. Conlan, Julie, Hugh, all of us who had the benefit of his blood, could call on it at any time and waltz in and out of his realm as we pleased. It had to be killing him. I did my best not to laugh, but it was really hard.

"You lived," he said.

"My husband resurrected me," I told him. "He gave up his godhood for me. He resurrected Aunt Erra, too. She sacrificed herself to keep me alive, and apparently, we were in the same body just long enough for the two of us to get hit with the same resurrection wallop. She's rather upset about it."

"You banished me," he said. Fury shivered in his voice.

"It's not banishment."

"Then what is it?"

"Retirement, Father. You've had lifetimes. I'm on my first one, and if you had it your way, I wouldn't even get that. It's a very nice castle. The library is to die for. Think of all the things you can do with this place."

"The world needs me. I will save it. I will make it better."

I sighed. "I love you, Father. I'll bring Conlan by when he is older."

"Kate," he said. "I will find a way out."

"Possibly. If anyone can, it's you. But it will take you a long time. Meanwhile, we will have peace. It's what you always wanted, isn't it? Peaceful idyllic existence, free of the ever-present doom?"

"This isn't over," he said.

"Yes, it is, Father. And should you ever find your way back, I'll be waiting."

I closed my eyes and leaned against Curran.

"How did it go?" he asked.

"About as well as could be expected. He's furious. He's also easily bored, and within Neig's realm, he has ultimate power at his disposal. The next time I visit, the place will likely resemble the Water Gardens. I think Conlan will enjoy playing there when he is a little older."

I kissed my husband. We sat together on the porch and watched our son play with fireflies.

"We should have another one," Curran said.

I smiled at him. "Maybe."

"Don't you want a little girl?"

"I do. Once Conlan grows up a little. We have time now, right?"

Curran grinned at me. "All the time in the world."

EPILOGUE

ERRA

THE SUN WAS about to rise. It was already warm. It could've been warmer, really. I was used to hotter summers. I was used to better horses too, although the Friesian was pretty and he stomped down the quiet crumbling road with great enthusiasm.

I could never resist a black horse. Or a black-haired man. Although there'd been a few blonds in my lifetime.

My niece was still asleep. I'd checked on her, her husband, and their son before I left the house. I didn't go in—they kept their door locked—but I sensed them beyond it, warm and safe together. They'd earned it.

I didn't do safe. At least not just yet. A woman had certain expectations after being resurrected, to live life to its fullest. There was no place for me in their world now. I had taught Kate everything she needed to know to survive. My niece had changed me in a way she would never fully understand. Kate had needed a mother, and I had stepped in to fill the spot, never expecting anything in return. Then she'd had her son, and he'd needed a grandmother.

I'd thought Eahrratim was dead. She was a silly girl, the Rose of Tigris, pretty and dumb in the way the very young sometimes are. She played in the water, grew flowers, liked pretty dresses, and made silly little plans for the future. A husband. Children. Nieces and nephews. Family feasts. A life that was happiness and warmth. I had buried her in the ashes of war, so I could pick up a sword. I thought she had melted into the ages of pain and suffering, until only the City Eater remained. But now she was back. She was no longer young or naive, but she was within me.

My mother used to say that family, blood or found, was our salvation. It was the net that caught us when we drowned and gently lifted us up out of the raging waters. She was wise, my mother.

My niece would be sad when she awoke, but then she'd get over it. She had a husband and a son to look after, and the Shar no longer troubled her. It was time to let her breathe. We'd meet again and soon.

The brush on my left side stirred again. The third time now.

"Come out," I said.

A black-and-white horse edged her way out of the woods, carrying a pale-haired rider. Julie.

"Running away from home?" I asked.

She raised her chin. Funny child.

"Yes," she said.

"Is this about your sticking it to your mother?"

She shrugged. "Yes."

"Go back. I don't have time for liars."

The child of the steppes looked me in the eye. "It's about me. She promised to never do the thing she did, and now she's done it. It will eat at her. She will hate herself for it. She will think that for a few seconds she turned into Roland. I don't want her to feel bad about it. She took me in when nobody cared if I lived or died. I don't want to be a walking, talking reminder that she didn't stick to her promise. It will make everything complicated."

Life was complicated. Being dead was a lot easier.

"Either way," she said, "it's time for me to go. I could stay, wait for her to get over it, and go on just like I have been for years. Never changing. Never leaving the city. But I want more. I want . . . my own. I thought about it for a long time, even before everything happened. It's time to go."

"Where are you going?"

"Anywhere but here. I left her a long letter, so she wouldn't think I ran off in a huff."

I sighed. "I suppose you can tag along."

She rode up next to me. She sat like she was born on a horse. Blood always breeds true. I'd told Im this and he didn't believe me. My brother with his crowded mind, so filled with ideas. He often forgot that people weren't simply cogs powering the machine of his ambition. Well, look who was sitting in a dragon lair now.

"What's our first stop?" Julie asked.

"Mishmar. I have a promise to keep to my mother."

"If Kate is my mother, does that make you my grand-aunt?"

"Possibly."

"That's sort of like a grandmother, isn't it?"

"Yes."

"Can I call you Granny?"

"Not if you want to keep your teeth."

She laughed like a little silver bell. The sun rolled above the horizon, shining on us.

Julie looked thoughtful for a moment, then said, "She's his grandmother too. Should we tell him? Can we take him with us to Mishmar to visit her?"

"Maybe," I said.

The boy would need to meet his grandmother at some point. But right now, he had his hands full and I doubted his wife would appreciate us dragging him off on family business.

It wasn't so bad to have a granddaughter, I decided. I'd never had one before, and this one brimmed with magic.

There was so much I could teach her.